BERKLEY UK
MOONSHINE

...urman lives in Indiana, land of rolling hills and cows. Lots and lots
...s. Visit the author at: www.robthurman.net.

Moonshine

ROB THURMAN

BERKLEY UK
an imprint of
PENGUIN BOOKS

BERKLEY UK

Published by the Penguin Group
Penguin Books Ltd, 80 Strand, London WC2R 0RL, England
Penguin Group (USA) Inc., 375 Hudson Street, New York, New York 10014, USA
Penguin Group (Canada), 90 Eglinton Avenue East, Suite 700, Toronto, Ontario, Canada M4P 2Y3
(a division of Pearson Penguin Canada Inc.)
Penguin Ireland, 25 St Stephen's Green, Dublin 2, Ireland (a division of Penguin Books Ltd)
Penguin Group (Australia), 250 Camberwell Road,
Camberwell, Victoria 3124, Australia (a division of Pearson Australia Group Pty Ltd)
Penguin Books India Pvt Ltd, 11 Community Centre, Panchsheel Park,
New Delhi – 110 017, India
Penguin Group (NZ), 67 Apollo Drive, Rosedale, Auckland 0632, New Zealand
(a division of Pearson New Zealand Ltd)
Penguin Books (South Africa) (Pty) Ltd, 24 Sturdee Avenue, Rosebank, Johannesburg 2196, South Africa

Penguin Books Ltd, Registered Offices: 80 Strand, London WC2R 0RL, England

www.penguin.com

First published in the USA by Roc, an imprint of New American Library,
a division of Penguin Group (USA) Inc. 2007
First published in Great Britain by Berkley UK 2012

1

ISBN: 978-0-241-95664-9

www.greenpenguin.co.uk

MIX
Paper from
responsible sources
FSC® C018179

Penguin Books is committed to a sustainable
future for our business, our readers and our
planet. This book is made from paper certified
by the Forest Stewardship Council.

To my kick-ass mom.
She could take on both Cal *and* Niko.
Watch out, guys. There's a new sheriff in town.

ACKNOWLEDGMENTS

I would like to thank several people: as always, my wonderful editor, Anne Sowards; my equally wonderful agent, Jennifer Jackson; the unbelievably talented art and design team of Chris McGrath and Ray Lundgren; sharp-eyed copy editor Michele Alpern; Mara, teller of historical tales; Web queen Beth; second mom (also kick-ass) Lynn; meta River and supergeek Shannon; and finally, Bailey and Mishka . . . elsewhere but never forgotten.

1

I was born a monster.

No big deal, right? Monsters are everywhere in this world. But I'm not talking your sweaty pedophile or your serial killer with a cold and silent harem buried in his crawl space. No, I'm talking about the real deal. Creatures that scuttled across the surface of this world when the air was sulfuric acid and the nighttime moon all but blocked out the sky. Scales and fangs, blood that doubled as venom, minds and bodies twisted in concert, dark legends come to life. These legends had always been a reality, but they were one that refused to register on modern human eyes. Monsters, they existed all right, and they were legion, so what was one more?

Although truthfully, I was only half-monster. My mother was human; my father something . . . else. When we were younger my brother and I had called them Grendels; the rest of the supernatural world called them Auphe. You say tomato; I say murderous death incarnate. It's all good fun. Auphe were the seeds of the elf fantasy, believe it or not, but this seed was poisonous, and it would kill anything it touched. There was no blond hair or limpid blue eyes, no silken voices like a temple bell. There was only skin as palely transparent as that of a salamander, eyes the red of lava, and a mind blackened and putrid as a rotting swamp. Okay, they did have the pointed ears; I'll give you that. Sometimes legends do get the facts right, but that's not much comfort when a thousand metal teeth are buried in your throat.

Half monster or whole, in the end it didn't matter. I had my weaknesses, same as anyone else. And I was facing one of them now.

Clowns.

Yeah, that's what I said. Clowns. I hate clowns. Always have. Point one out to me at the age of three and I would run wailing in the other direction as if the Hounds of Hell had been set on my diapered ass. Even now they still gave me a chill, and wasn't that pretty damn ludicrous? I'd fought creatures more monstrous than the mind could grasp. And I was *related* to things even worse than that, but bottom line, none of it mattered. I just hated clowns. And honestly, what self-respecting person doesn't? Name one, just one person whose flesh didn't crawl at the sight of them. Those puffy, bloated hands. The tiny gleaming eyes buried in pits of black paint. That maniacal grin awash in lurid scarlet, red as blood. Whose blood? you'd wonder uneasily to yourself. Could be yours if you didn't waddle away fast enough on chunky toddler legs. Then there were the people who dressed like cartoon animals, lolling plush tongues, glassy saucer eyes, and thick, unhinged laughs. They were nasty in their own right, but they still had nothing on clowns. Jesus Christ. Don't kids have enough to warp them in this world?

"They're only bodachs, Cal." Niko's voice came with a cool amusement that had me throwing him a black scowl. "You could handle a bodach long before you were potty trained. Granted, that was less than a month ago. . . ."

My brother, his bedside manner was less hand-holding and more a nice brisk thwap to the back of the head. "They're not just bodachs," I gritted. "They're bodachs in clown makeup. And that, Cyrano, makes all the difference in the goddamn world."

The Roman nose made even more generous by Niko's newly shorn hair snorted. "*Still* with the clowns?" Several months ago Niko's dark blond hair, most often in a ponytail or braid, had trailed nearly to the base of his spine. Now it barely touched his ears—or would have if he hadn't ruthlessly skimmed it back. He had cut his hair in mourning, a custom of our Greek ancestors. It was one of the few tales our mother had bothered to share with us. The Gypsy clan she'd grown up in had roamed all of Europe hundreds of years ago. They weren't called Travelers for nothing. Before eventually making their way to the good old USA, they'd settled for a time in Greece, inter-marrying with the natives on occasion, although it was frowned upon by both sides. The result was an odd mixture of Rom and Greek traditions that had lost Niko his hair. I gave him hell about it, but not as much as I could have. After all, he'd done it to grieve my death, to mourn me. Smart-ass comments tended to shrivel in my mouth in the face of that.

And I *had* died, although it had been a temporary thing. First Niko had stabbed me, and then a healer friend had stopped my heart. My death had lasted only seconds, but dead I had been. Not that I held a grudge. It was all done in an effort to stop the creature that had taken control of me—a creature bent on remaking the world. On remaking me. Even a permanent death would've been better than what it had planned.

Yeah, for sheer awe-inspiring terror, that thing had given clowns a run for their money.

"Yes," I snarled. "Still with the clowns."

The carnival was closed for the night, all spiderweb metal and lonely winds rocking the buckets of the rides, especially those of the Ferris wheel. The wheel itself loomed like a petrified skeleton, the slouching beast that had never made Bethlehem. Here its carcass rotted, its bones a darkly encrusted silver hung with the white twinkle of diamonds. The lingering smell of grease and butter had turned rancid, and a cheap and torn stuffed dog, the prize in any number of fixed games, lay at the base of a garbage can. One blank button eye had been torn away, leaving a raveled stuffing socket. Poor bastard, he'd missed his ride to the Island of Misfit Toys. The yellow bulbs strung here and there were either dead or dim as a candle flame. Beneath it all there was the scuttle of rats' claws and the scuttle of something far more lethal. All in all, I could've chosen a better location for our first job. In fact, a mentally challenged plaster garden gnome could've done better.

"I liked working at the bar better." What was that in the shadows? The pale glimmer of greasepaint? "The only clowns in bars are smart-ass drunks who don't tip."

To my right, Niko continued to observe me with brotherly disdain. Dressed in black pants and shirt, he would've blended into the night if not for the lighter gleam of his short hair. He'd recently grown a closely shorn, immaculately maintained goatee—probably to keep the Zen hair ratio happy—which was equally bright against his olive skin. My own hair was indistinguishable from the shadows around us. Normally I pulled it back into a short tail, but tonight I let it fall free to obscure some of the full-moon shade of my skin. Niko could afford to give himself away; he was Bruce Lee with a bleach job. I, on the other hand, didn't mind a little extra help. Don't get me wrong; I could hold my own against most things that go bump in the night. Vampires, werewolves, boggles, ghouls . . . trolls were a little more problematic. Whatever was out there, I could face it, but this time . . .

Strong fingers came over and squeezed an imaginary round red nose that must've hung just before mine. "Honk. Honk," Niko said with the utmost gravity. Picture it if you will. One of the most lethal fighters in the tristate area, a man who in the game of kill-or-be-killed was solidly king of the former category, and he was honking. *Honking.* Jesus.

"You know, since you started getting some, you are really beginning to piss me off." I started into the depths of the carnival, not bothering to check to see if he was following. He was. It wasn't something I had to see or hear to know. Niko watched my back, always. The mountains would fall and the oceans dry to dust before that ever changed.

"One day, little man." A fleeting pat came on my shoulder. "One day."

I didn't respond, only twisted my shoulders slightly and kept moving. That wasn't a subject for discussion, not now and definitely not here. Niko was smart, so damn smart, but when it came to his baby brother he wasn't as calculating or logical as he could've been. Should've been. To me there were things that were clear, so clear, it made me wonder why no one else seemed able to see what I could so effortlessly.

"Cal?" Niko might not see what I saw, but he could see when something wasn't quite right. When you know someone your whole life you can read them quicker than the morning comics, even when they might not want you to.

I ignored the question in the shape of my name and walked on, my eyes searching every inky clot of darkness. "Cal." This time it wasn't a question; it was a demand. And knowing Nik, an undeniable one.

I can honestly say it was the only time in my life I was glad to see a clown. Even one who was doing his level best to disembowel me with seven-inch-long razor-edged nails. It shot out of a mound of trash, the furious motion surrounding it in a shower of stale popcorn, stained napkins . . . and fluttering hanks of children's hair. The silky strands hung like party streamers from jetty claws—the same claws that were flying at me. The old Scottish legend, as methodically stuffed in my head by Niko, said a bodach would slither down a house's chimney much like a satanic Santa Claus to eat whatever children it could find, flesh, skin, bones, and all. Every scrap . . . except the hair. It didn't like the hair.

I felt my stomach twist into a sharp-edged tangle until I recognized the silver locks for what they where. The bodach held a dirty-faced doll in one multijointed hand, a doll with matching blond hair. The fall of hair from its other hand was nothing more than a rain of cheap polyester. It didn't change the fact that it all too easily could have been real. Bodachs aren't known for their willpower in the dieting field. It made the clown costume so chillingly perfect . . . the ideal camouflage to snare the innocent.

Atop the grimy clown suit of blue, green, and curdled cream, under the ridiculous corkscrew wig and white paint, was the face behind the tale. The mummy brown skin was camouflaged by the thick pigment, but the thickly smiling lips did nothing to conceal teeth equally as brown from dried blood. When it grinned you would almost swear its head turned inside out, and it was grinning now like Jack the Ripper on Ladies' Night as it dropped the doll and came for me. I lunged to one side, grabbed the thing's arm with my free hand, and pulled, letting it continue its motion on past me. As the claws and bone white hand cleared my ribs with room to spare, I buried the muzzle of the Glock under a vulpine chin and blew off the top of its curly orange head.

The body fell with limbs twitching in the dance of the electrified. And the smell . . . on their best day bodachs weren't exactly as fresh as daisies. A dying one put off a reek that would take paint off a car. It certainly took the edge off my appetite. Covering my mouth and nose, I felt the distinctive taste of bile creep into my mouth. "Holy shit. That is *rank*." It was a number of things worse than that, but I couldn't get into them without spewing my supper. One of the quirky little side effects of being not exactly human was an excellent sense of smell. I was no wolf, but I'd give a drug-sniffing dog a run for its money. Right now, however, the only running I wanted to do was out of range of this god-awful, hideous stench. Clamping my lips tight, I swallowed several times and blinked watering eyes. It was that pained moisture that had me doubting the sight before me.

The bodach had stopped quivering. Normally that was good, great even. All hail the conquering heroes. Strike up the band, toss us the key to the city, and slap some green across our palms. Unfortunately, normally wasn't the case here. It stopped quivering because it got up. That's right. With the top of its head split open like a rotten egg, it rose to its feet and grinned jack-o'-lantern wide around the blood pouring from its mouth. That was more than disturbing enough, but when it started talking . . . it was a whole new repulsive ball game.

"Little . . . boy . . . blue," it gurgled, each word

fighting to the surface. "Blow your horn." It spit derisively, turning the ground black at its feet, and then pointed a claw at the gun dangling from my hand. "Blow your horn." Then it moved for me, not as fluidly as when it had first attacked, but neither was it coming at a slow stagger.

"You have got to be shitting me," I said in disbelief. As I spoke, the slashing claws came closer. But worse than that, so much worse, was that so did the smell. That, more than the other considerations, had me moving fast. This time I shot it in the kneecaps, assuming it had kneecaps. Whatever peculiar monster parts that allowed its legs to bend, that's what I put a few bullets through. It fell again, yet still it kept coming, dragging itself by jutting knife nails and clown-suit-covered elbows. So I shot those too.

"Blow your horn," it hissed, spraying blood. "Blow your horn." And on it wriggled with the jerky movements of a broken-backed snake.

Looking down at my gun and then back at the bodach, I was giving serious consideration to throwing the useless piece of shit at it when an infinitely patient sigh blew the hair by my ear. Tapping my shoulder lightly with the hilt of his sword, Niko asked calmly, "Are you done playing yet?"

The smug son of a bitch. I waved my gun hand and took a few steps back, hoping for more breathable air. "Yeah, sure. Knock yourself out."

Moving past me with silent grace, he hefted the falchion and then swung it with a speed that was a blur of shimmering silver. Broad and curved, the blade bit through the bodach's neck, decapitating it instantly. The head rolled, bounced off the side of my foot, and promptly tried to bite my ankle. I punted it hard and hissed as the smell clung to my sneaker. "We should've brought a tree shredder," I grunted, rubbing the back of my hand across my nose futilely. All right. Fine. If that was the way this night was going to be, I'd just have to roll with it. Grimly, I toed off my shoes and booted them and the stench far away from me. "Can I borrow a backup since this is next to friggin' useless?" I asked, shoving the gun into my shoulder holster.

I wasn't making an unreasonable assumption to think that Niko would have an extra something sharp on him. What would be far-fetched would be to imagine that his surplus consisted of only one. Niko could set off metal detectors from a hundred feet with all the weapons he carried. His hand disappeared in his long duster, less of a fashion statement and more of a repository of all that was lethal in the world, and reappeared with a small cardboard box. It wasn't quite what I expected and I accepted the box dubiously. "What the hell?"

"Explosive rounds." He continued as I gave a low whistle, "And a Desert Eagle. Amazing what they peddle in some dark alleys."

More happy than amazed actually, but it didn't stop me from immediately loading the gun. While Niko was a worshipper of the blade, I was of a more modern bent. If I could kill from a hundred feet away, hey, it meant fewer dry cleaning bills. What's not to appreciate in that? "Nice. Nothing like an early Christmas present."

"Are you set for any close-up work?" The tone was that of an old-fashioned nun asking if I'd done my homework. Only this nun walked softly and carried a razor-edged ruler. I snorted and pulled my own blade. This one was more a knife than a sword, but it was the type you saw in mail-order magazines . . . the kind that had mercenaries drooling over the ad. Coated with black Teflon, the long thick shank was saw-toothed and capable of treating bone as if it were Jell-O. I might not eat and breathe them like Nik, but I could use blades and was smart enough to know they never jam or run out of ammunition. Guns were preferred; knives were practical. "I sleep with it, Nik. I damn sure carry it when we're facing killer clowns."

"The client said there's at least two more, maybe four. Check back in fifteen." He didn't bother to look at a watch. Niko claimed an innate understanding of the inner workings of time, space, and the universe in general. A result of all that meditation and martial arts training, a natural talent, or simply a desire to show up his little brother—whatever the process behind it, Niko lived as an example to us lesser beings. Pointedly, I checked the watch I'd fished out of last week's cereal box. "If I see one balloon animal, I'm waiting in the car." With that, I turned and jogged farther into the small maze of sagging tents.

I'd never been a fan of carnivals. My brother and I had spent a few years off and on in them throughout our childhood. Sophia, our mother—or, to be more precise, our whiskey-swilling egg donor—had plied her trade in some of the more run-down ones in the business. She was a fortune-teller; I didn't know the Latin term for money-grubbing con artist or if it was in any official medical journal, but Sophia hadn't met the nickel she didn't like or the person she wouldn't gleefully rip off.

Boys living in a carnival—it should've been exciting for us, fun. Carnies' kids got the free rides, the night's leftover hot dogs and cotton candy, the freedom to run wild from morning to midnight, when the place closed down. Heaven for anyone under thirteen, right? Heaven for about two and a half days and then the thrill palled quickly enough. It even put me off hot dogs for a few years, and I loved those damn tubes of mystery meat. But try eating them all day, every day for weeks on end with the only veggie of choice being fries or greasy popcorn, and it won't be long before you're trying to shoplift fresh fruit at the nearest store. Incipient scurvy aside, the summers had been miserable stretches of endless heat and humidity. Niko and I spent most nights outside of our tiny trailer with sweat-soaked pillows and a sheet to sleep on. Just Niko and me under a sweltering soup of stars. Sophia liked her private time. She made money that way too. Infinitely practical, Niko had called her. Nothing like a bunch of fancy words when one of five letters would've done just fine.

Eventually Sophia outstayed her welcome and we moved on. Haven't gone to a carnival since. I also have a love of air-conditioning that will never die. Luckily, it was spring now. The only sweat on me was a cold one, prickling the nape of my neck. Damn clowns. Leaving footprints in the damp dirt, I padded along in socked feet trying to follow the bodach scent. It was so strong now your average human could've picked up on it, no creature-feature DNA needed at all. At the base of the Ferris wheel I circled once, then looked up with pessimistic expectation. Sure enough, the son of a bitch was waving at me. Waving, threatening to eviscerate—it was one of the two. Exhaling, I holstered my gun and checked out the controls. The wiring was torn out in massive chunks, making the ride as dead and petrified as it had appeared from the beginning. Adding insult to injury, my final poke in the innards of the control box had the wheel's white lights flickering and dying.

Wonderful. Goddamn wonderful.

My socks went the way of my shoes and I began to climb. I wasn't afraid of heights. A nice, normal fear like that? Where would be the amusement factor there? But as I pulled myself up by metal handholds covered in soot and grease and felt the slide of oil under my grasping toes all in near-total darkness, I wouldn't have minded saying I'd had better days. Within seconds the ground below disappeared, swallowed up by blackness. If you fell, you would have no idea when you would hit . . . until you did. Some would consider that a blessing. Not me—I liked to see the bad news before it took me down. Continuing upward with a grunted exhalation, I felt a quick bite to the heel of my hand and the warm flow of blood. From the dull twinge it wasn't too bad and I kept on. Far above, one car rocked rhythmically . . . back and forth, back and forth. It was almost hypnotic, the motion.

"Cradle will rock," the voice crooned from above. Barbwire and ice, acid-etched glass, not exactly made for singing. Like an ice pick through the ear, it went on and on. "Rockabye. Baby. Rockabye."

Nursery rhymes and the smiling face of a child's supposed best friend. Bodachs might not be the most powerful of the monsters out there, but they seemed to be smart . . . in their own predatory way. Whether they were smart enough remained to be seen. With four of them in a place like this, it amazed me the place wasn't swarming with cops. They couldn't have been here long or children would've gone missing by now. Lots and lots of children. Up until now I hadn't heard of bodachs. No big surprise. There were lots of boogetys that hadn't pinged on my radar. If it hadn't tried to eat me in the past and wasn't currently gnawing on me in the present, I wasn't going to worry about it. Let Niko memorize the mythology section of the public library; he loved that stuff. Or get the scoop from our new business partner. She had contacts in the after-sundown crowd. If that failed, hit up our friend by default Goodfellow. He'd been around since the dawn of time, our own Avatar of Annoyance; if he didn't know about it, it didn't exist. One way or the other somebody—somebody besides me, that is—could get the info and fill me in. And if Niko wanted to photocopy the picture and blurb about our current baddie and pin it to my jacket, I actually might read it on the ride over. Or I might finish the latest naughty women-in-prison paperback instead. You just never knew.

I kept climbing and the bodach kept serenading. That alone would've been enough for me to kill it. When I had nearly reached the apex of the metal framework, the car continued to rock about two feet above my head. Bracing myself, I balanced as best as I could, then snagged the rising and falling lip of the metal bucket with both hands and surged over it. A red-and-green-clad back was turned to me, the colors appearing as pastel shadows of themselves as the clouds parted overhead to reveal a pale sliver of moon. Wig gone, white paint smeared to show patches of the wrinkled brown skin of its hairless head, the bodach continued to rock, shaking the metal beneath my feet.

"Rockabye, baby," came its singsong. "Rockabye."

It was enough. More than enough. If my ears weren't bleeding already, they soon would be. "Bozo," I growled. "You need to shut the hell up." Reluctantly, I left the gun in its holster. I couldn't be sure of the result of firing an explosive round up here, but catapulting headfirst to the ground was a possibility that would end my bodach-hunting days but quick.

It ignored me. I wasn't offended. My brother did it all the time. No, being ignored didn't offend me, but neither did it stop me from puncturing its spinal column with ten inches of Teflon-coated steel. I didn't give it a second chance to turn around. I wouldn't have given it a first if the caterwauling hadn't driven me to the edge. It was a predator, a child-eating monster. I was going to kill it regardless. Why the hell would I wait for it to turn around? As the knife slid home with a crunch of bone and a spurt of moon-silvered blood, the bodach folded quietly forward. There was no twitching, no thrashing, and no more goddamn singing, just blessed silence. Notch one on the Cal side of the board. Still grasping the handle of the knife, I placed a foot on the bodach's back and gave a hard yank without results. Those suckers didn't come cheap, and I liked this one. I wasn't leaving it. I tried again. Trapped in bone, the blade still wouldn't budge. Swearing, I added my other hand to the grip and gave one last yank. With the harsh sound of metal against stone, the knife finally pulled free. I held it aloft and gave it a flip to free it of excess blood. "Long live the king," I muttered under my breath.

At my feet the body of the bodach had settled back into its crumpled position, its white-painted hands splayed palms up at its sides. It was the contrast I noticed first, dark against pale. In the light of day the color might have been olive tinted or honey brown. Under the come-and-go moon it was gray.

The gray of a corpse.

Lots and lots of children, I'd thought. How lucky that hadn't happened. How amazingly lucky.

Fuck.

The small hand was curled next to the bodach's, a miniature shadow of a hideous counterpart. There was the glitter of sparkle polish on the tiny nails. Pink, I thought. Pink or lavender. It was hard to tell in the dark. I pulled the monster off her in one ragged motion.

"Hush, little baby." There was a heated breath on

the skin of my feet and I looked down to see painted lips writhe in a grin baring bloodstained teeth. "Don't say a word. Not a word."

This time the serrated blade went into an eye, puncturing it like a rotten plum. And it didn't stop there. Neither did I.

By the time Niko found me I was sitting in the car. I'd kept the windows down to hear him on the off chance he called for help. It was a remote possibility at best. Like he'd said, we could handle a few bodachs. I might not be old enough to drink just yet and Niko only a little past that point, but we were adults. Big, grown men with even bigger weapons. We could take a bodach or two.

"Problems?" He leaned in the driver's-side window.

"You get them all?" I countered impassively with my own question. I didn't look up from the dashboard. I'd thought about turning on the radio as I waited. A distraction would've been . . . good. And although it was an old car with an even more ancient sound system and only one working speaker, the radio worked . . . mostly. But the thought of accidentally tuning in to a slow ballad made the silence seem sweet. No more soft, soft singing, not tonight.

The door opened and Niko slid behind the wheel. He wasn't much on letting me drive his elderly baby. Take out one fire hydrant and you're branded an insurance risk, go figure. From the corner of my eye I watched as he turned on the dome light and looked me over. I knew what he saw, a study in black bodach gore. It had splashed me liberally from my neck downward. I'd tried to wipe it off, but it was as sticky and thick as tar. Short of kerosene and a ruthlessly wielded scrub brush, the shit wasn't coming off. "You got them?" I repeated as he continued to study me in silence.

"That's a given," Niko said without an ounce of arrogance. "Although mine weren't quite as . . . mmm . . . permeable as yours." A finger touched an inky swath that coated the back of my hand. The blood clung to his finger and stretched between us, a clot of black spiderwebs, when he pulled away. Niko winced in empathy for the rough night I'd have cleaning off the stuff. "Maybe some sort of lotion mixed with a citrus juice will get it off. We'll experiment, come up with something." Heedless of the further mess on the back of my neck, he laid his hand there and squeezed lightly. "Now, what happened?"

There wasn't much point in putting it off. It wasn't anything I was prepared to share with anyone else, but Niko wasn't anyone. He was everyone, the only true family I'd ever known. And with him I wouldn't have to say the words. Raising my eyes to his, I let him see what lurked in mine.

"Ah, damn. *Damn.*" For a fleeting moment, he rested his forehead against mine. Then he straightened to drop his hand from my neck and ask bleakly, "Where?"

"Top of the Ferris wheel." Along with the bits and pieces of the world's deadest bodach. Little girl lost and not a cop in sight. How could she not have been missed? I rubbed a hand across my mouth and exhaled, "A little girl."

Niko's thoughts were running along the same lines as mine. "It must not have taken her here at the carnival. Perhaps they're too unsure of their new hunting ground, don't have their bolt-holes set up just yet. She was probably taken from town. From her bed. Her parents may not even know that she's gone."

The carnival was upstate, about three and a half hours from our home in the city. On the outskirts of Hudson Falls, it would be simple enough for one or more of the bodachs to slip into town and disappear with a child—a child smelling of soap and toothpaste with her fingernails painted the color of Easter eggs.

"Did you touch her?"

It was a question I expected. Fact was, I almost had. Despite knowing better, I'd reached down to touch the curve of a still cheek, stopping myself only at the last second. "No. But she was there when I killed that son of a bitch. Not a lot of room in one of those cars." And if I stopped to think about it, really examine it, it would be safe to say bodach wasn't the only blood I was wearing. The dirt on my bare feet had a red tinge, one that didn't come from the muddy ground. Leaning my head back against the seat, I closed my eyes and said, "Can we go? I want to take a shower."

"We'll go," he promised. "I'll only be a minute." He climbed back out and I heard the murmur of his voice at the rear of the car.

"He didn't touch her, but there could still be DNA at the scene. I don't believe the police will buy a kidnapping by a literal boogeyman," Niko was saying with a dark irony. "And I'd like to keep my brother from being entered into a criminal database. I need you to clean it up. Thoroughly."

"What about the child?" That was our client's voice, gruff and bass enough to shake the glass in the car windows. He was . . . truthfully, I didn't know what he was. Maybe a giant of some kind, maybe not. He worked in the carnival sideshow as Bartholomew the Bull, World's Tallest Man. He might've been; I don't know. He was about eight feet. Damn big for a man, although not so much for a giant. The second mouth high on his forehead he kept concealed by a long hank of ginger-colored hair. The faint pattern of scales along his oversized jaw he passed off as bad skin, and the heavy gold hoop hanging bull fashion from his nose distracted from the overly liquid brown of his eyes. He did a good job of going stealth among the sheep, but it wouldn't stand up to an intense scrutiny, the kind that would come from a police investigation once kids started disappearing. Having the bodachs on his home turf was bad news for a live-and-let-live kind of monster, but Bart was a little too slow on his feet to catch them. Strong enough to rip them limb from limb, yeah, but just not quick enough.

And that's how we had ended up here. Half a year ago when we'd been on the run from the Auphe, we'd had to take money where we could get it. I'd used a fake ID to work in a bar and Niko had pulled body-guarding gigs for a guy who paid all his employees, including his accountant, under the table. Once we'd defeated my extended and bloodthirsty family, we'd had more options . . . but our talents were still fairly singular. Starting our own agency seemed a natural choice, at least for now. We planned on still doing the usual mundane babysitting of the famous, rich, and attention seeking. But there were other potential clients out there as well. We had more than one foot in the shadow world of the inhuman, and their money spent just the same. And this time we didn't limit ourselves to being bodyguards. If you had the money, we were willing to at least listen. Maybe we would discover if your favorite succubus was seeing you and only you. We might pull a job delivering a shipment of cursed jewelry. Or we could end up as glorified exterminators . . . like now. It sounded humorous, but it didn't feel that way. Not now.

"Put her in the water," came Niko's reluctant reply. "A pond, lake. Make it a place they'll soon find her, but also one that will take care of washing the evidence away or at the very least degrade it."

"And the bodachs?" Bartholomew ground between

overlarge teeth, sounding more disgruntled. It could be he thought cleanup should be included in the price, but those are the breaks. We kill. We don't clean. You have to have some standards. I kept my eyes shut. I'd been swimming in bodach stench so long now I could barely even smell myself anymore. Turning my head to the side, I tried to surrender to the weariness seeping from my overstrained muscles.

"As if I give a damn where you put those bastards," Niko said with icy sharpness. There was the riffle of cash as Barty-boy decided to not push his luck and forked over our fee.

Hardest fifty bucks I'd ever made.

2

It wasn't really just fifty, of course. But after rent, groceries, and Niko's new hobby, fifty bucks was probably close to what was left. Our first official job was a success and not for one second did it feel that way. It was easier when the only asses we worried about were our own. When you're on the run for three years, half a step ahead of certain death or worse, you don't have much time or emotion to spare for anyone else. How much of a bastard did it make me to wish it were still the same? I didn't miss the running, God, no, but the other . . . shit, what could you do?

Take a bath. That's what. Take a goddamn bath.

Put her in the water.

Clenching my teeth, I discarded the fifth washcloth, stained beyond repair, and picked up the next one from the edge of the tub. A shower hadn't touched the bodach blood and now I was sitting in a tepid mix of water, soap, and three gallon jugs of orange juice. It was working . . . slowly. The crap was coming off, more or less, and I counted myself lucky it was taking only a few strips of skin with it. I was scrubbing at one arm with more interest in getting the fetid goop off than keeping my pasty hide in one piece when the bathroom door was opened. Inquisitive green eyes peered around the frame, took in the apparent lack of weapons, and narrowed slyly. "You've the look of a pinto pony," came the amused drawl. "A half-drowned, not particularly well-bred pinto pony."

A perfect ending to a perfect shit of a day. "Boundaries, Loman," I said indifferently. "Personal space. Look into the concept, why don't you?"

Assured that I was armed only with terry cloth, the eyes were soon followed by the rest of the irritating package. Curly brown hair, lithely muscular frame, and a smile so wickedly knowing the Vatican would label it a carnal sin. Robin Goodfellow, the Pan, the Puck, the everything else rumored to be lurking in the forest seducing virgins, conning innocent travelers, and hitting every orgy Rome had ever spawned. We'd met him the previous fall just before the entire Auphe nightmare came to a head. Niko and I had been looking for a car for our getaway and who should be running the lot but salesman extraordinaire Rob Fellows? A better salesman than Willy Loman by far, but the nickname annoyed him so thoroughly that I wouldn't have dreamed of giving it up. Within less than a second of meeting him, or smelling him rather, I'd had him pegged for nonhuman. It took slightly longer to get the whole story out of him. In the end he'd helped us . . . very probably saved us. He was a friend, the best. He was also annoying and vain, never said one word when twenty would do, lied with ease, and could drink Bacchus under the table. And had done so, to hear him tell it.

He was also lonely.

And I don't mean the kind of lonely you read about in great books or see in overwrought award-winning movies. It wasn't the type of loneliness a human could comprehend. Hundreds of thousands of years he'd lived, if not more, and would continue to live. His kind was mostly gone; there weren't more than a handful of pucks left to play Goodfellow these days, and most other monsters shunned him. Robin liked humans . . . for companionship, not a bedtime snack. Doing business with a human might be a necessity at times, but socializing with one? That was just perverse. There was the occasional vampire, as Niko knew from not-quite-intimate experience, who felt the same as Robin did. And there were a few other exceptions that proved the rule, but mostly humans just weren't that popular, and neither were human-lovers. But where vampires might live a thousand years, Robin was pretty much forever . . . excepting a violent end. Everyone he loved died. Everyone he cared for, everyone he hung out with to have a mug of mead or a glass of wine, everyone he *knew*, even in passing . . . they all died. I felt for the guy. God, did I.

It didn't mean I wanted him watching me take a bath.

"Ridiculous human psychological theories." He waved a dismissive hand and took a seat on the edge of the sink, leaning back against the wall. There was no mirror, not there or in the rest of the apartment. Let's just say I didn't much care for mirrors. Not after last year. "Freud, who wore ladies' underwear by the way, didn't have a clue. It was rather sad really, the way he strutted around with that cigar five times bigger than his—"

"Seriously, Loman, I'm not in a good mood right now. What the hell are you doing here?" My arm was raw and slightly weeping, but clean, and I moved on to my chest.

"Not in a good mood now?" he echoed incredulously. "You're *never* in a good mood. If I waited for that momentous occasion to show, you'd never see my suave self."

"And the downside to that is what exactly?"

"Sour as Nero's piss as always." Sighing, he tossed me a plastic bottle filled with milky yellow-green fluid. "Niko called me. Here. This should take off the bodach blood and leave enough of your skin intact that you can walk the streets without scaring children. The orange juice was a good idea, but this will work better."

Shaking the bottle dubiously, I asked reluctantly, "Do I even want to know what this shit is?"

The grin was wide, bright, and utterly evil. "Didn't I just tell you? Nero's piss." The door closed behind him before I could lob the bottle at his head.

Whatever it was, and with Goodfellow there really was no telling, it worked. I had a few spots that were painful and red, but as he'd said . . . I was mostly intact. And some days that is the best you can hope for. Dressed in sweats, I made my way to the kitchen to see Niko sitting at the table with my gun spread before him in pieces. Snorting, I moved to the cabinet that did duty as overflow first aid storage. The fact that the medicine cabinet in the bathroom wasn't big enough for all our supplies told a story, one not suitable for bedtime. "How will I ever learn if you keep that up?"

He picked up a brush and began to clean the Glock's barrel. "Over the years I've learned exactly how long it takes to train you." The smell of cleaner was sharp in the air, but not quite as sharp as the glance he threw me. "My peace of mind doesn't have two more years in it."

Two years added to the two that I'd already been carrying a gun—it was a harsh estimate. Unfortunately, it was also probably true. Sitting down at the table opposite him, I rubbed an antibiotic cream on the only truly bad spot, the long raw abrasion on my arm. "Goodfellow gone?"

"Yes." He watched as I applied the salve, and satisfied with the result, he went on. "Apparently he squeezed us in between an early date and a late-night dinner cruise. Do you want more details? I have them. Quite a few of them."

His vexed tone had the corners of my mouth twitching. Niko liked Robin, and in fact had been friends with him before I had. Being infested with a creature that took control of my mind, body, and scraps that lay between, I'd been too busy with the wreaking havoc and attempted murder to do a whole lot of bonding in the beginning. Still, liking Goodfellow and being able to bear up under the soap opera that was his social life were two different animals altogether. He loved to share every gory detail and he didn't like to spend his nights alone. And considering the fact he was *pan*sexual, as he repeated on more than one occasion with an elbow to the ribs and a gleefully self-amused chuckle, he pretty much didn't have to. It all made for a helluva lot of stories to spin.

"No, thanks," I declined with a faint grin as I pulled the sleeve of my sweatshirt back down to cover my arm. "I'm still reeling over the triplet story."

"Aren't we all?" Within seconds he reassembled my gun with a speed that was straight out of an army training film. Niko might not have a lot of respect for weapons with moving parts, but he was as adept with them as he was with his blades. "He mentioned that you seemed more . . . relaxed."

Careful consideration had gone into that last word, more than enough to let me know it wasn't the one Robin had used. "Less catastrophically paranoid" or something similar had more of a Goodfellow flavor to it. Sprawling back in my chair, I linked my hands across my stomach and admitted ruefully, "It was in the water with me." It was the knife I was referring to. It was a mess of bodach blood, the same as me, and if I couldn't get it clean, it would have to be tossed. It was a nice rational reason and only partly a lie. I didn't go anywhere unarmed anymore. Not to eat my morning cereal, not even to take a leak. I'd been careful before, with the Auphe as ever-present pursuers, but now . . . after their happy little subcontractor had taken me over lock, stock, and every single molecule, I made being constantly prepared my religion. And I embraced it as wholeheartedly as any Southern-fried Bible thumper ever whelped.

Darkling, a nightmare for hire and the last of his kind, had moved into me . . . had *become* me— combining us into one malevolent whole. What I would never have done for the Auphe, he did. We did. This had been no movie possession. There was no lurking in the back of my mind, no wringing my hands over the big bad things Darkling was doing. There was no me to lurk. What he had done, I had done. What he had enjoyed, I had enjoyed. Who he had killed . . . you get the picture. We were one. And if you survive something like that, you're lucky that the least crazy label they slap on you is "catastrophically paranoid."

"Did it come clean?" was Niko's only comment, and I was grateful for the restraint. I knew the malevolent little shit was gone. After all, I'd sliced and diced him myself, but knowing and *knowing* aren't always the same. I, along with my howling subconscious, would eventually figure it out, but it was going to take a little time.

"Yeah, the crap comes off metal a damn sight easier than skin." My eyelids fell to half-mast as I watched him clean away the supplies from the table. I was tired. It had been a long night, a long, god-awful bitch of a night. "Weren't you supposed to see Promise tonight?" Promise, an ex-client of Niko's old agency, was Niko's lady of the moment. Hell, she was his only true lady past, present, and probably future . . . even if neither of them knew it yet. Considering she was a partner in our new agency as well as a vampire, things would be a bit on the delicate side, but I had faith. When you saw them together, both with the same inner stillness and unwavering purpose to them, you knew. They were made for each other and no one else. And if they wanted to call the late dinners they'd been having "financial planning for the agency," who was I to pop their bubble of clueless denial? They would figure it out, sooner or later.

"Not tonight." He laid the gun before me with a sardonic bow and mocking eyes the same gray as mine. "I'm so exhausted from doing your work I think I'll stay in."

As acting went, it was one of Niko's better efforts, but as I couldn't fool him, neither could he fool me. I didn't try to push him on his way, however. That would be the equivalent of my head against his brick wall. After what I'd seen tonight, my brother wasn't going to leave me to spend the night alone. Honestly, although I'd never admit it aloud, I was grateful. "Yeah, yeah. Working your fingers to the bone." I stood and yawned. "I'll fix you a waffle in the morning. That'll make us even." Picking up the gun, I headed back to the bedroom. The bed was soft, the blankets were warm, and the apartment was cool. All good sensations. But when I closed my eyes all I felt was metal and blood. All I heard was twisted rhymes and the laughter of a killer. And all I smelled was death and a little girl's shampoo.

I was up before the sun. As events went, that was pretty spectacular. To mark the occasion I decided to actually keep my word to Niko and make him breakfast. Twenty minutes later I was stirring pancake batter with my nose stuck to the directions on the back of the box. I could slay monsters with the best of them, but cooking usually managed to turn the tables on me in culinary smackdowns that left the kitchen unusable for days. This time I was holding my own . . . barely. I was sliding the last of the pancakes, the uncharred ones, onto a plate when the intercom buzzed. Six a.m., that meant it couldn't be Goodfellow . . . unless he hadn't gone to bed yet. He was as lazy a bastard as I was. Curious, I pressed the button. "Yeah?"

Minutes later Promise was gracing a kitchen chair. The contrast between her and the cheap plastic made my eyes want to cross that early in the morning. Promise had recently changed her look. Her mink brown hair was now exotically tiger striped and rich brown alternated with equally wide chunks of palest blond, worn in a braid that reminded me oddly of Amazons. Her formerly tasteful but sedate clothing had been replaced by a black tank top, matching leather pants, and high-heeled boots. Still tasteful, but damn sure not sedate. The ivory skin and twilight purple eyes were the same, as was the wide curve of her unpainted mouth.

"Your Majesty." I put a plate before her. Catching a whiff of pineapple and coconut, I raised my eyebrows. "Sunblock?"

She tapped a pink-and-white-polished nail on the hooded cape that rested in her lap and gave a dismissive flutter of fingers, indicating it didn't always do the job. "I freckle so terribly," she said gravely. Another popular misconception about vampires . . . they didn't burst into flame in direct sunlight. They would, however, end up with the equivalent of third-degree burns that took quite some time to heal. It wasn't pretty or pleasant, and it was definitely a step or two beyond freckling.

I grinned. I liked Promise. I liked her for herself, but I would've liked her for Niko's sake if nothing else. He'd given up any chance at a normal life to keep me safe. Now that the Auphe were history, ugly, hateful history, I wanted him to have a chance at what he'd missed while we'd been on the run. "Wouldn't want that," I agreed solemnly before ladling two scoops of half-melted chocolate and butterscotch chips on top of her pancakes. "Syrup?"

She regarded the brown and yellow swirl and then me with a gentle uplifting of her lips. "I bow to your expertise, master chef." And well she should. All those fancy restaurants she ate at had nothing on me on the rare occasion I managed to pull off pancakes. As I gave her a generous dollop of syrup, she asked, "Shouldn't you wake Niko? I know he wouldn't want to miss your excellent efforts."

"He's awake." I dumped some liquid chips on top of my own pancakes, then licked the spoon.

"Really?" She cut the smallest possible bite and lifted it on her fork.

"Yeah." I took a real bite and chewed with enthusiasm. It wasn't often I had full-on breakfast food. Along with the martial arts, Niko had picked up the whole body-is-a-temple philosophy. He lived, breathed, and worshipped at its dry, tasteless altar. Soy milk, egg white omelets, organic fruit, no thanks. I'd take my dry Sugar Crunch any day of the week. "He either heard me fixing breakfast or the buzzer. One of the two. The man has the ears of a b—er . . . cat." Hastily, I shoved another bite in my mouth before my size eleven gave me an embarrassing case of athlete's tonsils. After swallowing I finished, "He's just doing his usual morning routine, sitting there staring at the wall like a lobotomy victim."

"It's called meditation, Cal," Niko said from behind me. "It helps me survive the daily trials and tribulations of a lazy, smart-mouthed younger brother."

"He's cleaning up his language for you, Promise." I pushed another plate in front of Niko and loaded him up. "If that's not love, I don't know what is." Ignoring the needle-sharp glare aimed at me, I added, "Breakfast as pledged. Now, eat up."

He didn't want to. Sugar, oil, butter—he probably would've made the sign of the cross if not for the company we were keeping this morning. Still, he recognized the pile of syrup and chocolate for what it was . . . my thanks for his sticking around last night. Sighing, he bowed to the inevitable and dug in, his bite every bit as small as Promise's had been. The whole world seemed to be on the same diet. Well, the hell with them, it just meant more for me. Stacking the last of the pancakes on my plate, I moved over to the living room couch and turned on the TV. It wasn't precisely privacy, but it was the best I could do for Niko and Promise. Our new apartment was actually smaller than our last, but it was a helluva lot nicer with decadent luxuries like heat and hot water. Our last place, sandwiched firmly between a dump and a slum, had been all but destroyed when the Auphe had come for me that last time. Not only had we bitten the deposit on that one; we were probably on a warrant list somewhere. It didn't matter. We hadn't used genuine ID since we'd hit the city. We still didn't. A quirk of Niko's there. The Auphe might be deader than the dodo, but there was no telling when it might prove to our advantage to be invisible to the eye of the authorities.

There was the low murmur of voices as I polished off my pancakes and then Promise raised her voice to include me. "I may have a new client for us."

"Oh joy," I said flatly, dropping my fork with a clatter on the empty plate. At least she'd waited until I had finished before she ruined my appetite. I noticed that she didn't ask how the work for last night's client had gone. Niko must have filled her in on the phone when he'd canceled their plans. "What is it this time? Hansel and Gretel go missing? You find Red's basket by Grandma's partially chewed leg?"

Promise didn't take offense at my irritable snap. She knew well enough where it originated. "No, this is actually somewhat more subtle, some undercover work actually—with werewolves. It may not even come to violence this time, Caliban. At least, I hope not."

Wolves . . . they didn't usually eat kids. Not on a regular basis anyway. I reached for the remote and turned the television down. "I'm all ears," I said, calmer. "And Niko's all nose. In other words, we're a captive audience."

I wasn't sure, but I thought I saw the faintest of pink flushes along Promise's cheekbones as she slid an amused amethyst glance toward Niko. Apparently, she liked his nose just fine. Five dead husbands and she blushed at the sight of my brother. It was enough to make you believe in all that crap they splattered in greeting cards.

"Undercover?" Niko frowned, missing the bigger picture at his side altogether. Or maybe he hadn't, I thought, rather amused myself as he tilted his head expectantly toward Promise. "Among wolves? How exactly are we to accomplish that?"

Sometimes he forgot; he honestly did. That he could amazed me, literally, and it humbled me too. I pushed the plate aside and propped my feet on the coffee table. "Don't worry, Cyrano," I drawled, drawing his attention. "We won't have to tie furry ears and a bushy tail on you. I'll do just fine."

That didn't help the frown much, but he did see the logic in it. I might not be a wolf, but neither was I completely human. A wolf would know that the instant he smelled me coming. "So." Niko stood and began to clear the table. "Who exactly is this client, and what does he want with our services?"

"His name is Cerberus. He's small-time in the Kin, from what I hear, but with aspirations." The slow smile showed just a hint of pearly fang. "And don't we all have aspirations?"

The Kin was basically the Mafia of the nonhuman world. They ran numbers, trafficked in drugs and prostitution . . . you name it. They had a larcenous paw in every till in the city, and while they might subcontract out, werewolves ran the show. They were the power and the glory, and if you forgot that for even a moment, it wouldn't be just kibble they dined on that night. Niko hadn't crossed their path, gambling, snortable wolfsbane, and succubi not being his thing, but I had. Well, not precisely me. While I was under the influence, so to speak, I'd hired two wolves to kill a girl for me. A girl who was quite sure that she was *my* girl. It hadn't worked out too well . . . for the wolves, better for me and mine. I'd moved through their ranks with ease then. There was a good chance I could do it again.

"What kind of aspirations?" Niko asked evenly. "Rising among his own kind or taking over the city?"

"Niko, I wouldn't involve you in anything that might compromise your principles." She touched his arm as he reached down for her glass and plate. "You must know that." That was a pretty broad statement.

As Robin had once said with exasperation, Niko had so very goddamn many principles. I hoped Promise could live up to her pledge. "He simply wants to rise in the ranks and with his . . . differences . . . that will not be easy to do. He suspects one particular 'friendly' rival within the Kin is planning a move on him in the next week, and he wants proof before he makes a preemptive strike. One misstep and all the others will turn on him. They respect his talent and ruthlessness, but as it stands now he lives only by their sufferance."

Wolves didn't have much acceptance for differences. To them difference equaled weakness and a wolf wasn't one to tolerate weakness. That wasn't to say there wasn't a wide range of wolf types. Some were completely human when they wanted to be and utterly wolf when they wanted that as well. Others were stuck somewhere in between, half of one or the other. A human with fur and fangs or a wolf with limpid blue human eyes and hands instead of paws. Bad breeding will tell. But as long as you were strong and could kill with the pack, that made you wolf. As for the moon and the whole werewolf-bite curse, I don't know who started that. It was a good story, mind you, but just a story. Wolves, just like vampires, were born, not made. They could chomp on you all day long; it wasn't going to make you turn furry at the next full moon. And all the Goth-dressing wannabe monsters in the world couldn't change that fact no matter how much they wished it were different.

"What's wrong with him?" I asked with admittedly morbid curiosity. "He missing an arm or something?" That would definitely have him living on sufferance, and a damn uncertain place for a wolf to dwell that would be.

"I have no idea, actually." She shook her head. "I've been dealing with his accountant, a well-mannered if boring creature. Cerberus appears to be far too busy to deal with us on a personal level."

"Or he wishes to keep as much distance between himself and his plot as possible." Niko finished stacking the dishes in the sink, gave me a pointed look to let me know that was my chore for the day, and wiped his hands on a towel. "He's intelligent if nothing else. Cautious as well. Unusual for a wolf." If I'd blinked, I would've missed the almost imperceptible brushing of his fingers over her bare shoulder. "Could you set up a meeting for us?"

"Of course." She gathered the cloak from her lap and stood next to him. Side by side, the vampire whose beauty was mysterious as the morning star and the man whose touch was deadlier than a viper—as couples went, they were cuter than a basket full of puppies. "I have the car waiting downstairs. Would you like a ride to class?"

And that had my humor dissipating into a morose mist. I hadn't had the lecture in a few days; I was about due. It was only brought home by the look Niko flashed me as he accompanied Promise out the door. Education, college, a normal life.

Who needed it?

3

College, he just wouldn't stop with it.

We'd gone on the run just after Niko's freshman year, which had put a decisive end to higher education for my brother. If things had been reversed, it wouldn't have mattered much to me. I might have gone to college, yeah. But I would've been one of the usual students, average, the lowest common denominator. Skipped a lot of classes, drunk a lot of beer. Graduated with a degree in marketing and absolutely no prospects for a job. Don't get me wrong. It would've been fun, college. Hell, yes. But it wasn't something I would have really ached over the loss of.

Niko did. He never said a word to me or indicated it in any way, but he did. So when the whole mess was over and we could lead a life, while not exactly normal, certainly a whole helluva lot more stable, I was glad he decided to go back to school. He was only twenty-two, even if he acted fifty. It wasn't as if life had passed him by or anything. It would've been pretty pointless for him to take sophomore-level classes, though. While we'd fled for our lives he'd kept his studies up while homeschooling me. Imminent death and destruction were no excuse for a wasted mind, he would say. Really, he would actually *say* that.

Can you believe it? Now with the help of a little creative paperwork he was taking grad-student classes at NYU. Robin had presented him with a fake degree from a university in Athens where the puck had an old acquaintance who still got a kick out of teaching, despite hemlock rumors to the contrary. Niko was now well on his way to a master's in history. Considering his love of old weapons and his archaic sense of honor, it was a good fit. Niko was smart as hell; brilliant was probably a better word. He *needed* to learn, to test his mind, to constantly strive. It was exhausting to watch.

I, on the other hand, was happy enough to just lounge on the couch and watch bad TV. I didn't want to take classes or go to college. We had our business up and staggering. It wasn't as if I needed letters behind my name or a piece of paper stuck up on the wall. That made perfect sense to me, but Niko wouldn't let it go.

Yeah, perfect sense . . . and a bit of a lie too, which was how I usually operated when it came to the twisty inner workings of my own mind. True, I didn't see a need for school, but that wasn't the only reason I didn't want to go. I'd come to terms with what . . . no . . . *who* I was. I wasn't a monster, my occasional melodramatic wailings aside. But neither was I human, not completely. Not quite a man and not exactly a monster. College, classes, dating—it all seemed a little like trying to make me into a "real live boy." And that wasn't so much pointless as it was tempting fate. That I'd survived the Auphe was miraculous . . . damn near unbelievable. Now was the time for being grateful and keeping my head down. Poking a stick in the eye of fate wasn't on the agenda.

I'd been swatted enough in my life, thanks so much. I was ready for the easy ride, the coasting. And damned if I wasn't due.

I was also due at a certain soda shop in a few hours. So I might as well take a shower and do a load of laundry to kill some time first. I didn't want to be too early. I was no Goodfellow, not on my best day, but I did have *some* reputation to protect. Okay, realistically, I didn't. But the plan itself was still sound, and I did know how to appreciate a good plan.

Two and a half hours—and three wasted trips downstairs looking for a free washer—later I had dragged a full bag of clean if newly pink clothes back to the apartment. I then grabbed the M15 bus to Pier 17 and the Fulton Fish Market and there I was, hammering futilely on the security gate over the storefront. "Geezer," I called out in exasperation for the second time. "Let me in already."

"Cal." The laughing disapproval came from behind. "How nice is that? Mr. Geever would be hurt if he heard that."

"But he never does, does he?" I grunted with one last rattling bang on the metal. "He's deaf as a post." I'd smelled her coming. Honey and oatmeal soap, the orange and clove shampoo, and underneath it all was the scent of Georgina. Sunlight. Don't ask me how someone can smell like sunlight. I don't know. It was corny and trite and simple truth. Luckily for me she also smelled of shockingly mundane toothpaste, minty and completely ordinary. It let me keep at least one foot on solid ground—at least that's what I stubbornly told myself.

Turning, I looked down at George. Granted it was only by a few inches; I was of average height at best. She stood wearing a white dress that fell to her ankles. Simple cotton and sleeveless, it glowed against the amber of her skin. Most girls her age were wearing jeans that settled precariously below hip bones and tiny tops so skimpy they showed as much skin as a bathing suit. Not that that was a bad thing in my book. I was a twenty-year-old horny guy; tight jeans and lots of skin were a God-given constitutional right as I saw it. But when it came to George, she was more than a girl three weeks past her high school graduation. She was a seer and a prophet.

I'd known her for almost three years now. When Niko and I had first come to the city we'd stumbled into her, a fifteen-year-old miracle, by accident. At least I thought it was accidental. George probably had a different opinion on the matter. The universe moved in ways that were frequently heartbreaking and for the most part unchangeable, but always for a grander purpose. At least it did in her eyes. And she'd kept believing that, although she'd lost her father to AIDS and her uncle to death at the hands of the Auphe. Despite it all she kept the faith that things were as they should be. I wished I had a tiny fraction of her belief in the greater good, no matter how cynically I discounted it.

She had her mass of copper curls pulled up in a ponytail at the crown of her head, an uncontrollable red-gold halo in the morning light. Many races mixed in her dark brown eyes, round face, and full lips. The freckles kept her from being classically beautiful and made her more than beautiful. They made her real . . . touchable.

For some people.

I unconsciously mimicked her posture, folding my arms and tucking my hands out of sight. "So, Freckle Queen, what's the story? I thought Geezer wanted me to watch the place for him today."

She opened a hand and dangled a set of silver keys before my eyes. "He decided to go visit his sister early. I told him I'd meet you and help you open up the shop."

The look on her face was pure innocence and my mental alarm kicked into high gear. Niko and Promise might be lost in a mist of uncertainty, but George knew she was my girl. She knew it though I'd never told her or given her the slightest inclination I thought of her as anything other than a younger sister. In fact I spent the majority of my time keeping her at arm's length. It wasn't a safe distance, but it was the best I could do. As I watched the glitter of the keys reflected in her dark eyes, I had the sudden feeling that the best I could do just wasn't going to cut it.

Silently, I held out a hand for the keys. She dropped them in my hand and I went to work unlocking the security gate. The warmth of her at my back could've been mistaken for the heat of a tropical sun if I hadn't known better. Knowing better . . . it was no goddamn fun. "You holding court today?" I asked, clearing my throat. I already knew the answer to the question; it was just something to say. Something to break what I would swear was a doubling of atmospheric pressure.

"Don't I always?" The touch of her hand resting lightly against my arm had me jumping in spite of myself. "There's a little girl," she said softly, her lashes dropping to screen her eyes. "She's in her pajamas holding a teddy bear. They're red, the both of them. All over red."

I jerked my arm away and said sharply, "Don't."

"I'm sorry," she apologized instantly. "God, I am so sorry. I didn't mean to, Cal. I swear."

George didn't "read" people without permission. It was an invasion of privacy, and no one knew that better than she did. The fact that she had read me unconsciously said very clearly that my oh-so-vaunted arm's-length distance wasn't worth a damn to either of us.

I shoved the gate up, scraping the metal across the

abrasion I'd gained in climbing the Ferris wheel the night before. The momentary sliver of pain grounded me. It was no big deal. As long as that was all she'd seen, it would be okay. I fumbled with the keys and jammed them one by one into the lock of the door. George, no doubt knowing which was the right one, stayed silent behind me until I opened the door and stepped through.

She followed after me. "Honestly, Cal, I would never—" she started.

"It's okay," I cut her off. "I know you wouldn't look without asking." It was the first time George had read me . . . short moment though it was. I was very careful about that. When we needed help or guidance, it was Niko she read. What she had learned about me through him, I didn't know and I didn't ask. What I did know was that I was no goody bag to be rummaging through. There were bad things in me, things no one should have to see. Hell, I didn't even know if George was aware I wasn't fully human. Some days I told myself she had to know. She'd had to have picked up on that while reading Niko. She had known her uncle was destined to die at the hands of the Auphe; how could she not know what that made me? But other days . . . I wasn't so sure.

Moving behind the counter, I checked the temperature on the freezer, fed the slushy machine with ice, and then quickly began to stock the ice-cream bins under the glass counter. The place had once been a drugstore with a soda counter, long before I'd been born. Now it was a soda counter with a lot of empty space and a lonely magazine rack. Mr. Geever kept the place running solely by virtue of George's calling. She sat in the shop for several hours a day and helped those that came. And come in large numbers they did. While she didn't take any money for her services, she always gently urged each person to buy an ice cream from the Geezer. It kept the old guy in false teeth and stool softeners with a little left over for trips to see his equally ancient sister.

"Cal." Funny how a voice of cinnamon velvet could be so utterly implacable.

It was a familiar tone. Horrifyingly familiar. "Niko been giving you lessons?" I grumbled to myself, and then, relenting, I looked up.

An unwavering gaze faced me. "What could I see that would be so bad?" she asked with a shot-to-the-heart honesty.

What a question . . . and one with too many not-so-nice answers. "Dead little girls for one," I said flatly.

Her lips tightened, but she didn't back down. "If you're thinking that's a first for me, you're wrong."

Not much of a surprise. I had one helluva track record with being wrong. "Then why would you want to see any more?" Along with being wrong, I also had a record of digging in my heels. Laying out the last gallon of chocolate, I reached automatically for the spray bottle of disinfectant and the slightly grungy towel beneath the counter and began to wipe off the glass.

"Caliban," she sighed, and bent her head to blow lightly on the surface of the icy glass.

Not so long ago I hadn't been comfortable with my full name. It brought up some conflicted emotions, to say the least. With a dark twist of humor, Sophia had named me for a slouching man-beast of Shakespearean fame. In my snarky and sullen teenage years I'd made a stand and demanded to be called Caliban and nothing else . . . not Cal, not anything that might let me forget what I was. I was certain I was a monster and I was determined to wear the label. Niko ignored me as he always did when he felt it was in my best interest. Even now he called me only Cal.

Lately, though, I'd gotten sort of used to the occasional "Caliban." Promise, George, and Robin, they didn't realize the emotions it carried with it and would use it now and again. And when George called me that . . . hell, the emotions became all new ones. Good ones, if I could let myself admit it.

But they disappeared almost immediately when I saw what her finger was sketching with quick strokes on the frosted glass. She'd drawn on the glass once before like that, but what she'd done then had been much more innocuous than what flowed from her now. Only a few lines, but the face jumped out at me as if it were alive. Pointed ears, streaming hair, a thousand metal teeth. Auphe. How did it go? Say the devil's name and he'll appear? It probably was the same for doodling his driver license's photo. Extinct or not, I didn't want to take the chance. Instantly, I reached over with the rag and wiped it away. She rested her hand on mine before I could pull it back. "That's not you, Cal. It never could be."

I guess that answered my question on how much she knew, I thought numbly. "It is me, George," I countered grimly. "Part of me anyway." The bell tinkled and I looked past her. "Looks like your first disciple is here. Better go show them the light." Carefully I slid my hand from beneath hers and turned my attention to unlocking the cash register.

It was part of me and I could never let myself forget it. Hey, almost destroying the world . . . it's kind of hard to gloss over. And it had been close. Really, really close. That was what the Auphe had wanted me for, from my very birth. I was part of an experiment in breeding, born and bred for destruction. It seemed the Auphe needed a very special type of creature to further their goal. And that goal was nothing short of wiping out this world and replacing it with another. The Auphe traveled via holes ripped in the fabric of space itself. Gates, doors, whatever you called them, they could slice one into the air, step through, and be someplace far away when they arrived on the other side. Now, if only they could form a rip not just through space but through time as well. The few of them that were left could go back to a prehistoric time when they, not the dinosaurs, ruled the earth. Armed with twenty-twenty hindsight, they could wipe out humans before we even got started. And with my involuntary help, they almost had.

Yeah, that kind of thing made it hard to forget just what you were.

"Stubborn." It wasn't said under her breath; it wasn't even a whisper. And it was accompanied by the sharp sound of her heel hitting the floor as she turned on it and whirled away. Georgie in a temper— there was a first, and despite the unsettling turn to the situation I felt my lips twitch. Then the half-born smile faded. She knew. She knew and she didn't seem to care. What that might mean to me I couldn't even begin to wrap my mind around.

Several hours later Mr. Geever returned early from his sister's and I made my escape, giving George a hasty and stiffly casual wave. She was sitting at a small table in the corner with one of a never-ending stream of petitioners, but that didn't slow my pace any. By the time I hit the door I was going at a clip quick enough to have the bells jangling frantically overhead. I'd spent a good period of my life running. Why change my ways now? As defense mechanisms went, I had this one down pat.

The rest of the day was spent very carefully not thinking about what had happened that morning. I did the dishes, put up clothes, even scrubbed the tub . . . things I rarely if ever got off my lazy ass to do. By the time Niko came home, I was so desperate for a distraction that I said something that literally stopped him in his tracks.

"Hey," I said the moment he opened the door. "Good day? Learn a lot? Wanna spar?"

He stood still in the doorway with keys dangling from his hand to regard me with bemusement. "Wrong apartment or pod person. I'm not quite sure where to place my bet."

"Yeah, yeah, smart-ass." I was sitting on the coffee table, and I crossed one ankle over the other. "When you're loaded with natural talent, you don't have to practice. I'm just making an exception to help you out." Never mind that last time he'd wiped the floor with my butt and then for an encore did it again, this time using the ceiling.

"You are quite the philanthropist." Shutting the door behind him, he moved closer and with folded arms looked down at me for a long moment, seeing probably more than I wanted him to. "Bare hands or blades?" he asked finally. "It's the humiliation of your choice."

I chose bare hands. I was many things, but stupid I was not. That's not to say I wouldn't get my ass kicked. If history was any indication, chances were high that I would. But nothing stung quite like the slap of the broad side of a blade, even the wooden ones Niko kept for practice. We could've gone to the gym or Niko's old dojo, but the few times we had we'd attracted too much attention. Crowds at the gym were split between chanting for blood and calling 911, and the dojo was thick with disapproval over our technique. Mine was nonexistent and Niko's was a mixture of many methods. We didn't fight by certain rules; we fought to live. It wasn't always pretty, but it was effective.

Now we fought either in the apartment—and didn't our neighbors love that?—or in more secluded areas of Central Park. Washington Square Park was closer, but there weren't too many private areas there and cops tended to frown on sword waving in public. This time we chose the apartment. Pushing the furniture against the walls, we cleared the center of the room. I gave the couch one last shove and straightened. His back half-turned to me, Niko had lifted his hands automatically to pull back his hair out of the way into a ponytail . . . hair that was no longer there. As his self-exasperated exhalation reached my ears, I was already taking him down. My foot hit the small of his back, knocking him several feet through the air and onto the floor. I would've landed on my stomach and probably promptly barfed up my lunch. Niko, of course, alighted catlike on his hands and knees. Looking over his shoulder, he offered, looking pleased, "Devious and without compunction. Nicely done indeed." The fact that he'd deliberately given me the opening didn't change his appreciation of my performance.

Then he was up and on me as inexorable as the tide. Lashing out, one blow from the heel of his hand hit my chest and knocked me backward. Despite our precautions, I took out a lamp. Hula skirt and generous hips shattered beneath me to gyrate no more. It was my favorite lamp, one I'd picked up at a second-hand store in the Village. "You did that on purpose, you son of a bitch." I glared.

"It's conceivable," Niko admitted mockingly and without remorse. The bastard had never shared my taste for the classier things in life. He didn't wait for me to get back to my feet; he only kept coming. Just like real life.

I aimed a blow at his knee, hoping to crumple his leg beneath him, but he knocked my foot aside before it reached its target. I lunged past him only to receive a roundhouse kick to my hip that had me flying through the air . . . and not with the greatest of ease. The wall broke the first part of my fall and the couch finished up the job. It was a familiar feeling, the give of the cushions under my back. It was where I usually ended up during our practice sessions. And that had given me an idea the last time it had happened. Normally I came up with a groan and mumbled curse. This time I came up with a shotgun. Tucked behind the cushions for a week now, awaiting the perfect moment.

This moment.

Swinging the muzzle his way, I pulled the trigger on the first barrel and then the second. Click. Click. Snarling, I said, "Bang, bang, Professor. Your ass is grass."

He blinked at me and then the corners of his mouth curled slightly, for him a wide smile. Placing a hand to his chest, he then held it up to show imaginary blood. "You got me."

"First time ever." I grinned, dropping the weapon's muzzle toward the floor. "Is there some sort of prize? Weekend in Maui? Year's supply of veggie burgers?"

"I can now let you out without a leash." He sat on the couch. "Trust me, that's prize enough."

I sat beside him and laid the gun on the floor. "Kind of weird . . . pointing a gun at you again." When Darkling had taken me over, I'd done my level best to kill Niko . . . *our* level best, rather. It had gone down in Central Park. I'd been armed with a gun and a boggle, Niko with a sword and a happy little surprise. It wasn't precisely a fair fight, and I'd still lost. Best loss of my life.

"I know." His hand tugged at the dark tail of hair gathered at the nape of my neck. There was a comfortable silence for a few minutes and then he asked quietly, "You want to talk about it?"

Only a brother would know he wasn't referring to the time that the only thing that saved him from a bullet from my gun had been a pricey piece of body armor. No, Niko was all too aware that there was something else on my mind that had prompted my request for a workout. I hesitated, then groaned, "George."

His lips twitched. "My little boy, all grown-up."

"I knew I should've kept my mouth shut," I griped, leaning back into a boneless slouch.

Sobering, he tilted his head toward me. "She's been chasing you for nearly a year now, Cal, and she's as stubborn as you. You know what that means, don't you?"

"What?" I asked with more dread than curiosity.

"That sooner or later she's going to catch you." Gray eyes lit with amusement, he went on. "And would that be so terrible?"

Yeah, it would, but Niko wouldn't be able to see that, no more than George herself could. My brother wanted things to work out for me; he wanted that so damn bad. One of the most aware people in the world teamed with a psychic, and both of them were blind as bats. Utterly. But did I call him on it? No. My day was already ruined; I had no desire to trash his too. I shook my head noncommittally and changed the subject. "We have time for supper before we meet Rover. You want to grab a pizza?"

"The meeting's tonight?"

"Yeah, Promise left a message on the machine. Seven at the accountant's *office*." I gave the word the sarcastic emphasis it deserved. "Apparently Cerberus treats the 'business' like an actual business. Go figure. Are we sure we want to get into the middle of some Kin mess? Whether it's self-defense on his part or not, he is still Kin. He's still a crook. I can live with it, but I know you, Nik. You like things a little more black-and-white."

"I'm that predictable, then?" Not offended, he slapped my shoulder lightly and then got to his feet. "At the very least, we can hear his flunky out. If we find his rival isn't planning anything nefarious, then we prevent a possible war within the Kin. That can only be to the good."

"If you say so," I said skeptically. Leg-humping, crotch-sniffing mutts with a license to steal—it was a strain to see the good there. But as long as we were paid, it didn't make much difference to me what the fleabags did to each other. "Pizza?" I repeated hopefully. "It's the least you could do for breaking the almighty hula lamp."

"The least I can do. Really?" Dark blond eyebrows lifted. "How very wrong you are."

4

With a stomach comfortably stretched with vegetarian Chinese, I shifted impatiently in the overstuffed chair. We'd gone to Niko's favorite place on Sixteenth Street and despite its being meatless they served a nice plate. George had seemed to like it. That's right; she had shown up, had been waiting for us by the door. Trying to avoid a psychic—talk about an exercise in futility. Christ.

She had wielded her chopsticks with aplomb, stolen food from my plate, and said it was a shame Niko had felt the need to tag along on our very first date. That had immediately led to me choking on a piece of broccoli while Niko poured her a fresh cup of green tea and apologized gravely for his intrusion. As her hand patted me helpfully on the back, I had finally managed to swallow. But while I'd been able to dislodge the broccoli, I had less luck dislodging George. She'd stuck around for the whole meal despite my pointed remarks about curfews and pissed-off mothers and then waved a cheerful good-bye as we had walked away to our meeting. I'd looked over my shoulder once to see her give me a smile so bright and warm . . . funny how it felt exactly like a bear trap snapping shut on my leg.

Shifting again, I tried not to think about the logistics of gnawing through a leg made purely of emotion, and checked my watch. "How long is he going to keep us cooling our heels out here?"

"Patience, Grasshopper."

I rolled a jaundiced eye in Niko's direction. He and Promise sat side by side, a matched set in cool composure. "So, you two got a late-night financial-planning session later?"

That shut him up . . . for the moment, anyway. But Promise regarded me with the same amusement with which one would look at a puppy that had piddled on the carpet. I was a bad boy, but I was just so darn cute she couldn't bear to smack me with a rolled-up paper. She had met us outside of the building, her driver dropping her off. It was a business meeting, she had pointed out firmly, and as such all the partners attended. Her hair pulled back into a sleek twist, she wore an outfit in the deepest violet that managed to be both businesslike and subtly provocative. Don't ask me how she pulled that off, because I didn't have a clue.

The three of us were cooling our heels in the waiting area of the accountant's office in the Flatiron District. And it really was an office. I'd been picturing the back of a bar with the stink of alcohol, cigars, and wet dog in the air. I couldn't have been further off the mark. I didn't know what the inside of the sanctum sanctorum looked like, but our tiny bit of it was pretty nice. I was sure Cerberus's would be far more plush, but this was passable. It reminded me of an insurance office, a ritzy one, but nonetheless . . . there were chairs of deep blue and wine, and what looked to be a genuine Persian rug on the wood floor. Sedate prints, walls of pale ivory, and subdued lighting—it was all more than I expected. And it held my attention for an entire minute. I checked my watch again. A quarter of an hour this guy had kept us waiting. Despite what Promise had said earlier, this guy wasn't impressing me much with his manners. He must have missed that day in obedience school. "Fido," I drawled, "are you sure he's actually back there and not out watering a fire hydrant somewhere?"

As Niko raised his eyes upward and Promise pressed fingers to her forehead, the albino wolf guarding the connecting door fixed me with a baleful ruby stare. Apparently, Cerberus was helping out his fellow nonconformists. Yeah, he was all about the civil rights of the differently abled wolf. It didn't make this guy's stare any less rude. Unbroken direct eye contact was a sign of aggression and dominance in both canines and lupines. How did I take it? Pretty much the same way. And this version of it was beginning to piss me off. I leaned forward and watched as the movement caused the wolf's broad nose to wrinkle distastefully. Apparently, the smell of Auphe wasn't exactly sweet as roses to this guy's nose. He was one of the wolves stuck with a paw in both worlds. He had a mostly human face, with the exception of round wolf eyes colored blood-rage red, a wicked wedge of forehead, and very slightly tapered ears. A shock of white hair fell to his shoulders in a wolfish ruff and crept silky fingers onto his transparently pale jaw. That hair he kept trimmed to long pointed sideburns. From a distance, he could pass. From a few feet—no way. Even your average clueless citizen would think him exotic, unusual, oddly beautiful, and nowhere near human. Especially when he opened his mouth to reveal a brace of fangs that would make any orthodontist lose his lunch. They were also bound to make speech difficult. Despite his subtle wolf features he stood upright and with the body of a man. However, the cold intelligence behind those eyes was anything but human.

"No? You don't speak?" I said when he remained silent with a snarl locked onto his pointed face. I patted my pockets. "Maybe I have a nummy-num here somewhere. Lemme check."

A hard swat on the back of my head put an end to my antics. "Stop playing," Niko ordered. "This is business, not pleasure."

"Right now it doesn't seem to be either one," I groused, sliding down in the chair and tapping an impatient foot.

Suddenly, Snowball turned his head toward the door and, hearing something we couldn't, gave a nod before laying a hand on the handle to push it open. The wicked punch of claws painted black weren't exactly human either, but they'd be good for opening the occasional brewski. I noticed he was exceedingly careful not to scratch the finish on the shiny brass. "Go." Fixing those alien eyes on us, he repeated, "Go. In." As I'd thought, the words sounded like chunks of glass vomited forth to shatter in the air. As I started to get to my feet, his throat moved convulsively to produce one more. *"Now."*

"Yeah, right. Now you're in a hurry," I snorted, but picked up the pace as Niko moved up beside me. Snowball I could deal with. I had no such illusions regarding my brother. The doorway was actually large enough for all of us to have walked through side by side—this really was some place—but I hung back and let Niko and Promise pass through before me. We might hold equal partnerships in this new business, but I was aware of my interpersonal-relationship skills. I didn't have any and I couldn't be bothered to pretend. We all have our talents, some darker than others. Niko *was* a leader, through and through. And Promise had obvious string-pulling abilities. Me? I was a loner, who by some miracle of fate wasn't alone. I was also a smart-ass, and oddly enough that didn't seem to pay the bills.

The inside office matched the outside. Expensive, but not especially memorable . . . a lot like the guy behind the desk. Promise hadn't mentioned that he wasn't a wolf and I gave her a sideways look and received a dainty shrug in return. Yeah, I was surprised by Caleb, but then again, with Cerberus's mysterious "difference" making him more receptive to wolves like Snowball, who's to say it wouldn't bleed over onto different races? He was the Albert Schweitzer of monsters, all right, good old Cerberus.

For whatever reason, the accountant wasn't a wolf. In fact, I didn't know *what* he was. He looked human, even smelled human. He was in his late twenties, early thirties. What with his short dark brown hair and amiable blue eyes, lean face, fair complexion, and suit and tie, you would've passed him on the street without a thought. Until he smiled.

Bingo. Membership card in the nonhuman club if ever I'd seen one.

It was the teeth. They weren't anything like Snowball's, not a wolfish array crammed into a small primate mouth. No, numbers boy had the regular amount; they were simply pointed. All of them. He looked like a cheerful piranha, albeit one with an MBA. It was weird, but on the scale that I measured my life against, it barely registered. There were more monsters in the world than could be counted. I had better things to waste my time on and not enough fingers and toes to make the attempt.

"Brothers Leandros, Madame Promise, please, have a seat. I'm Caleb," the piranha said pleasantly, straightening a stack of folders on the desk. "Would you care for coffee? Drinks? Blood? Drugs? No? Very well." He laid his hands flat on the desk and gave us his undivided attention. "Your lovely colleague here has said that you can assist us."

Taking a seat in one of the three chairs facing the desk, I leaned back as Niko seated Promise. "We may," he said noncommittally, settling in the center chair. "However, we'd like to hear more details before we commit."

"Details?" Caleb leaned back as well and picked up a pen to tap it thoughtfully on the desk. "That's certainly fair enough. I thought I'd given all I knew to your ever-gracious partner, but feel free to ask away." He was so goddamn polite and earnest it made my teeth hurt. The Kin were really lowering their standards. Sure, this guy had the teeth and a fast calculator, but where was his homicidal mania? Where was his bloodlust? It was unnatural.

"There can never be enough details, not in a situation such as this," Niko said firmly. "To begin with, we want to know precisely what the result of our actions will be. We certainly won't be involved in setting up an innocent, rival of your employer or no. Our services are for sale, not our souls."

"Innocent" was putting a broad interpretation on any member of the Kin, but Caleb seemed to get Niko's drift. And it amused him; at least I thought that's what caused the curl of lips until he spoke. "Souls," he echoed the word, and fixed his mild blue gaze on me. "How very optimistic of you."

It was a sore point with me; there was no denying it. I wasn't sure what I believed about life, death, and the postparty. Even hanging around George, I didn't know if death was the end and neither did she. Or if she did, in tried-and-true annoying seer fashion she wasn't saying. I suspected this was pretty much it. The whole enchilada. You're born, you live, you get a cheeseburger lodged in your heart, and then you're fertilizer. Anything else would be just too damn easy. You got one chance; blow it and it's over. Don't blow it and it's still over. If I was wrong, that only led to other questions, or one very personal question. I doubted seriously that Auphe had souls, and what did that mean for me? Half soul? No soul? Only James Brown knew for sure.

Niko, a sure bet for being chock-full o' soul, stood the instant the words passed from Caleb's lips. He was pissed at Caleb's disparagement of my spiritual status, and the fact that it showed was an indicator of just how pissed he truly was. "Your business is not our business." The words couldn't have been colder. "We'll see ourselves out."

Instantly, the accountant changed his tune. "I apologize," he said with immediate obsequiousness. Meek and submissive, fawning and scraping. He might not have been a wolf, but he worked with them. He recognized an Alpha when he saw one. Niko was just as capable as Cerberus of fucking him up but good. And if he failed Cerberus in this little task . . . having the crap beaten out of him by my brother would be the very least of his concerns, I knew. Niko might hurt him for the insult; Cerberus would bury him for the result. "I've let internal prejudices get the better of me."

That he had, and, hell, he wasn't the first. I wondered how he'd known about the Auphe in me. First Goodfellow had spotted me, and now this guy. Werewolves and other related monsters smelled me. Robin and this one had simply looked at me and known. How did they do it? Then again, did I even want to know?

Probably not. I did know I didn't want to work for this guy or Cerberus. With his slobbering smiles, "internal prejudices," and rabid lapdog guarding his door, Caleb annoyed me. I'd seen worse. I'd *been* worse . . . easily. But this was a job. We didn't have to take it. There were other scum of the earth out there dying to hire us, I was sure. Maybe we hadn't seen them yet, but they were there. Hopefully they'd show up before the rent was due. Or Nik's tuition.

Goddamn it.

Exhaling, I looked up at Niko and suggested with grim reluctance, "Maybe we should hear him out." Promise remained silent. The insult was mine and so would be the decision, although from the flare of annoyance behind her eyes, she was offended on my behalf. Empathetic even. Maybe vampires had soul questions of their own.

"No," Niko said flatly.

"Nik . . . ," I started.

He didn't glare, only repeated calmly but adamantly, "No. Not for any reason."

Caleb decided to get in on the fun. "Fifty thousand dollars."

"Any," it's a word you really shouldn't throw around. Fifty thousand dollars for what would probably be a night's work. Maybe two. Shit. Still in my chair, I raised my eyebrows at my partners. The "Whatta you think?" might have been unspoken but hung in the air clearly enough. What Promise thought behind her tranquil mask was anyone's guess. But what Niko thought of it was crystal clear—not much. In some ways he was more sensitive about my Auphe heritage than I was, and I was pretty goddamn touchy. Sometimes there were digs. Sometimes fascination, revulsion, or out-and-out terror. I'd seen them all over the years. Auphe had occupied the top rung of the food chain for a long, long time; even other monsters feared and hated them. I understood that; I had feared and hated them myself . . . before their extinction in a warehouse explosion last year. Hell, who was I kidding? I still feared and hated them, historical footnote though they were.

But the bottom line was that this sort of reaction was something I was going to see my entire life. Getting worked up over it was only going to take money out of our pockets. This business meant a lot to Nik . . . and me. Promise didn't need the money or the partnership. She enjoyed it, but she didn't need it. We did. And both it and Niko deserved a fair shake. I gave him a rueful twist of my lips, then an almost imperceptible shrug and nod of my head toward his chair. He frowned and turned toward Promise. She spread her fingers and left this decision up to Niko.

He sat back down. He didn't want to and it was obvious from the stiff line of his back, but he sat. "Fifty thousand is one detail," Niko said flatly. "Now let's hear the more pertinent ones."

It was the usual. I didn't have but the one wolf acquaintance, non-Kin, so how did I know? I watched mob movies, same as any other guy. You have the weak and the strong, the loyal and the sneaky, the constant jockeying for power; it was the same for humans and wolves. Cerberus had a "friendly" rival, Boaz, in the East Side territory who he suspected was less friendly than the guy liked to pretend. They were supposed to be working paw in paw under their Alpha, but Cerberus had suspicions that if he was out of the way, Boaz wouldn't exactly be crying at his funeral and would have a larger section of the territory carved out to boot.

"So Cerberus is wanting to take this guy on a ride,

then?" I asked. "Put the kibosh on him. Have him sleeping with the fishes."

Blue eyes blinked; looking bemused, Caleb said, "No. He wants to kill him."

Apparently Caleb didn't watch a lot of TV.

"And his Alpha wouldn't care for that? I thought that was the general method of advancement among his pungent kind," Promise pointed out.

"Normally. You know the wolves well." The pen continued to tap and the smile continued to beam. Slimy, ass-kissing toad. I was surprised he had the balls to even *think* that soul remark, much less to have let it slip. "However, Cerberus is in a unique position among the Kin. What he does is scrutinized far more thoroughly. A misstep on his part will not be tolerated." And there was the smile again. So polite, so helpful . . . it made the old Tarzan movie flashbacks I was having even more bizarre. A leg falls into the river and is cleaned to bloody bone by teeth precisely like that. Terribly sorry to have eaten you, dear fellow. Mea culpa.

Niko paid little attention to the bowing and scraping as he demanded, "And if we obtain proof that Boaz intends to make the first move, that will put Cerberus in the right with the Alpha."

"He believes so."

There were more details, just as Niko had asked for: where would be the best place to catch Boaz off guard and loose of lip. Who he ran with. How best to introduce Cerberus into the conversation. "He likes to gamble, poker specifically," Caleb said with an accountant's disdain for a waste of good money. "And when he gambles, he drinks. And when he drinks, he talks. Endlessly." There was a roll of blue eyes.

I could see Niko turning it all over in his head,

every fact and nuance. There wasn't much the man would miss in the way of strategy and consequences; I had faith in that. Finally, he folded his arms and slid a glance toward Promise.

Immediately, she stood and said coolly, "We shall discuss it and get back to you."

Caleb was disappointed, very much so, but tried to take it manfully. Or monsterfully, depending on your point of view. Already fair, he paled to a transparent white and his hand shook hard enough that the pen tumbled from his fingers. But he swallowed and said tightly, "I bow to your business protocol, of course. Please, call me when you've made your decision. Day or night. I'll make myself available."

From the looks of it, Cerberus would be even more disappointed, which obviously didn't bode well for our favorite accountant, but color me unsympathetic. When the door was shut behind us and we were making our way out of the building, I said with a grimace, "I'm thinking Cerberus is one big, bad puppy dog. Caleb is all but pissing his pants."

"Disgusting, but accurate," Promise agreed, her full lips twisting slightly. "Obsequious creature. I apologize, Caliban. He was much more socially acceptable at the first meeting. If I had known he would bring up your . . ." She hesitated and then finished, "I would never have considered him as a client."

I shook my head at the words. "Hey, don't worry. It's not the first time it happened and it won't be the last." It never would be the last, so I'd better suck it up and learn to deal. "So, Nik, what do you think?" I added ruefully, "About the job, not our piranha-toothed pal."

His lips thinned in distaste, but he allowed himself to be moved on to the more financially pertinent subject. "I think that the question would be, is Boaz worse than Cerberus?"

"That's what it comes down to, huh?" I snorted. "Bad against worse." I wasn't surprised. Life usually did end up on that particularly nasty seesaw. It was the way of the world. I gave a mental shrug and kept walking down the hall. I passed the bank of metal elevator doors without slowing. Promise, already familiar with my brother's ways, followed along with a gentle sigh.

Niko wasn't one for elevators. He always said if something was trying to kill you, a metal cage isn't the place to be. It made sense . . . assuming my brother wasn't just an ass who enjoyed watching me sweat and swear my way up and down twenty flights. He opened the door to the stairs to wave me ahead with a bow, and then offered Promise his arm. "As our client would be sure to tell you," he said dryly, "every dog has his day. We simply have to make sure it's the correct dog." I had a feeling that would be easier said than done.

And for once I wasn't wrong.

5

The next night, the stack of Niko's books was tumbling to the floor as I bumped the kitchen table in passing. I dodged the dusty avalanche and said in exasperation, "Cyrano, you have got to get out more often. Seriously. I mean it." Stepping over the pile, I promptly stuck my head in the refrigerator. "If financial planning's not your thing . . . ," I continued slyly as I sniffed the colorful contents of a casserole dish. It was an attractive color; I just wasn't sure if that was the *original* color. ". . . then check out a bar. Go see a movie. Read something noneducational for once, like the *Post*."

"I happen to like financial planning," he said, more amused by my sniping than anything else. Obviously, the Promise situation had been good for one cheap shot and no more. Pity. I did live to annoy. "Actually I have a session scheduled in a few more hours." He moved up behind me and peered over my shoulder into the depths of the icebox. "Over candlelight, wine, and dinner." Uh-oh. I slid a slightly panicked look his way. Don't say it, I thought. Do *not* say it. "Why don't you and Georgina participate in the brainstorming?" he finished, his mocking gray eyes fixed on mine.

Too late, I thought to myself morosely. It's out

there now. The infamous double date. Determined to do what damage control I could, I carried the casserole to the microwave. "No, thanks," I declined casually. "All that restrained passion and lust in the air is bad for my sinuses. And George is just a kid. You'd scar her for life." I popped the glass container in and twisted the dial, relying on good old cancer-causing waves to zap the food fungus free. "Hey, here's a thought. Call me crazy, but why don't you tell Promise it's a date—a real live date for grown-up boys and girls who are so horny they can't stand it?" The microwave pinged and I finished with a shrug and a wave of my hand. "Like I said, just a thought." The fungus was still there, only now brown and singed. Joy.

"Georgina is two years younger than you, Cal. That hardly makes her a little girl in pigtails." He handed me a fork with a challenging quirk of his lips. "As for passion and lust, what makes you so sure it's that restrained?"

He had me there. I dumped the fork and the dish in the sink and then gave him a good once-over. I'd said at the carnival that he'd become unbearable since he'd been getting some, but I hadn't really believed it. Well, the unbearable part I believed, in spades. But the other? Furrowing my brow, I tilted my head, then shook it. "Nope. I stand by my original assessment. Restrained lust, all the way." I held my thumb and forefinger about half an inch apart. "You're almost there, which is why you're so goddamn happy all the time." I looked at him again, *tsk*ed under my breath, and moved my fingers a little bit farther apart. "Almost, but just not quite. Maybe Goodfellow could give you some lessons."

Now he was annoyed, which meant my work was done for the day. "Do you really wish to go there, little brother?"

I had a thousand and one sensitive spots, some reasonable . . . some not so much. Nik, however, had only a few. Robin's past jones for him being an extremely humorous one. Humorous for me at any rate. "Nah, that's okay." I returned to the fridge. "I'm too hungry to get my ass kicked right now. When you see Promise, bring her up to speed." A thought hitting me, I stood and draped myself over the top of the refrigerator door. "Oh, and tell her I suck at poker. So she better draw up some subcontractor fees, because Goodfellow isn't going to come cheap." I waggled my eyebrows. "Although you could maybe bargain him down. You know, with your studly body."

Hungry or not, I ended up with an ass kicking to my name anyway. It was all in good fun. Good black-and-blue fun, but more important, Niko had forgotten the entire George issue. At least I was hoping he had.

As a further diversion, I told him I'd put a call in to Robin and see if he was up for a little undercover work in case we decided to take the assignment. And as there were three or four reasons we shouldn't as opposed to fifty thousand why we should, I had a feeling how the decision was going to go. Cerberus might not be who I'd want carrying my slippers and bringing me the paper, but was he worse than any of the other Kin? There was only one way to find out. Take his money and check out this Boaz. The worst we would be out was a little time, and that we'd be well compensated for.

"How do you know that Goodfellow even plays poker?"

I commented in disbelief, "You're shitting me, right?"

"In retrospect, not the most astute question, I admit," Niko sighed. "Well, he is an excellent fighter . . . when he wants to be. Since you seem to be under the impression Georgina is still in diapers, why don't you and Robin meet Promise and I for dinner? We can discuss all of this then."

"And after?" I grinned.

"You and Robin go home, before dessert, politely minding your own business." And from the iron in his voice, I knew that was probably exactly the way it would be.

"Do I play poker? He really asked if I played poker? Hermes save me." Robin was on his seventh glass of wine and was still sober as a judge, the non-Southern variety. After thousands of years of good living, his tolerance was legendary, though the waiters at the dim sum place we'd stopped at in Chinatown were clearly taking bets on when he'd pass out. Of course everything about Goodfellow was legendary, as he would tell anyone who cared to listen. Repeatedly. "I *invented* poker. It was about two thousand B.C., and naturally it wasn't called poker then. What a crass name. I called it . . ."

I let the words wash over me, the background noise of the never-ceasing surf, and gave Niko a grin. He seemed less entertained by the situation, which naturally made me enjoy it all the more. What Promise thought I wasn't sure. She sat to Niko's right, a serene presence in a sleek sheath of dark violet silk. Black pearls with a peacock sheen looped around her ivory neck and her striped hair was swept up into an intricate coil. She looked like a queen, but the glitter in her eyes was anything but queenly. It was sharply annoyed, down and dirty. She and Goodfellow had crossed paths only rarely, and their interactions were prickly at best, Niko being the juicy bone of contention between them. A front-row seat to the sniping was better than cable any day of the week. Still, if nothing else, Robin and Promise had a mutual respect . . . of sorts, at least enough of one to keep them from killing each other. For now.

I crossed my fingers under the table, then reached for my own glass of wine. It was still my first. Dear old Mom had been an alcoholic, along with her other even less pleasant vices. Niko didn't drink at all and I drank only in moderation. Tempting fate had never been much of a hobby for either of us. Still, a little something for jangled nerves was called for. I kept looking over my shoulder, expecting George to show up again. My defenses were getting less and less effective all the time, and, damn it, I thought that she was more than well aware of the fact.

"So, up for it, Loman?" I asked after one more suspicious glance around the room. "Wanna pull the tail of this mutt?"

"No tail pulling," Niko corrected instantly. "This is reconnaissance work, not a stick-poking exercise for your personal entertainment."

"Spoilsport," I grumbled, and shoved my untouched salad to one side. Rabbit food, no, thanks. "Robin?"

"It sounds diverting." He finished his glass and waved a peremptory hand at the waiter, who promptly scampered for another bottle, bowing and scraping the entire way. I didn't know if it was the cut of Goodfellow's suit or the fact that he seemed to ooze dollar signs, but the waitstaff hung on his every gesture. Promise received the same attention. Niko and me, they tended to study with cautious curiosity. We didn't quite belong. In many ways a puck and a vampire fit into the mundane world better than we did. Maybe it was the clothes, I thought ruefully as I took a look at the tie I'd borrowed from the maître d'.

"Gambling, drinking, furry women," Robin continued with an arched and sly eyebrow. "Furry men.

What's not to like? Count me in. We'll play your little game and come out a few thousand to the good on top of the fee. And, by the way, *my* fee is fifty percent."

"Fifty?" Promise repeated with an outrage that was all the more evident for the simmering restraint in her smooth voice. "Twenty-five thousand and for what, pray? For you to drink, flirt, and steal money from the unwary?"

"It's nice to meet someone with an identical life philosophy, isn't it?" Robin raised his newly filled glass to her in salute.

I quickly reached for a roll and took a large bite. It wouldn't be the smartest thing to give myself away with a shit-eating grin. I had no idea how Promise's five husbands had shuffled off this mortal coil, but I did know I wasn't looking to find out. Niko was making his serene way through his salad. It was impossible for him to be oblivious to the conversation, but that didn't stop him from pretending.

Chewing and swallowing the bread, I said softly, *"Bwok, bwok."*

The precisely placed sharp kick to the side of my knee had the nerve there tingling as Niko calmly took another bite of his salad. His movement hadn't even rippled the water in the glittering crystal glasses on the table. As I hissed in pain and rubbed my knee, I noticed Promise's and Robin's attention had turned from each other to me. Not the happiest turn of events for yours truly. "Surely it wouldn't be such an injustice to slide a portion of his split my way," Goodfellow drawled.

On that, Promise agreed with Robin, not the disputed fifty percent, but one hundred. "No injustice at all," she murmured as she rang a painted nail on the rim of her wineglass.

I gave my knee one last massage and scowled. "As

always, everyone's against me." Deciding a change of subject was my only hope, I demanded, "Where the hell's the real food?" A long time coming, apparently, as the waiter ignored me as thoroughly as he'd slobbered to do Goodfellow's bidding. I might be a dark and brooding figure of mystery, albeit in a bad tie, but apparently the dark and brooding don't have a history of tipping well.

After putting me in my place, Robin and Promise eventually came to a figure that they were both satisfied with. Not that it stopped the squabbling between them. Only a well-placed sword and stake were likely to do that. Aside from Niko, the two of them had little in common . . . beyond the supernatural thing. Goodfellow was vainer than hell and showy as a peacock, bragged to infinity, and talked even beyond that. He was a walking, talking, screwing party and he was coming to a town near you. Promise was in all those things the exact opposite. She was calm tranquillity, an enigma in silk. She rarely spoke, and when she did it was never about herself. Everything I knew of her was from direct observation and the grapevine. I had the feeling, though, she might be a little more forthcoming with my brother. There was something in their shared glances. . . . You only had to see it to know.

Robin saw it too. He didn't want to, but he did. And when we left Niko and Promise, before dessert as commanded, I caught him looking back wistfully. Affection toward someone other than Niko didn't come easily to me. Still, I raised a hand and awkwardly gave Goodfellow's shoulder a squeeze. Envy shifted from melancholy to rueful resignation and he shrugged. "They're a good match. Dull and duller."

I knew all about sour grapes myself. "Too dull to live," I agreed. "Besides, only the undead could deal with Nik's snoring."

We'd reached the street and he exhaled, then looked up at nonexistent stars. "I was to be married once, did you know?"

Surprisingly enough, no, I didn't know. That was a story he hadn't told me before, a miracle in and of itself. Add the combination of Robin and marriage to it and my mind reeled. "Really? You? No shit?"

"Really." The corners of his mouth tugged upwards. "Me. I shitteth you not. It was in Pompeii. Cyrilla." There was a thread in his voice, one of softness and reverence I wouldn't have guessed he had in him. Or maybe I simply thought he wouldn't let anyone *see* it in him. "She had a way of tolerating my gloriousness that brings you and your brother to mind."

"Gloriousness?" I grinned.

"Gloriousness . . . eccentricities." He rocked back on his heels. "One and the same."

"You and monogamy. There's a helluva concept. So, why didn't it happen?" Sometimes your mouth is faster than your common sense by barely a second. It's a nasty sensation. The mind does flip-flops, flailing mentally to recapture the words, but it's too late. They hit the air as garish as neon and then there's no taking them back. There's only mumbled apologies. "Sorry. I didn't think." Pompeii. Even a lazy student of history like me knew about Pompeii.

"Don't worry. It was a long time ago." From the tight set of his jaw, long was a relative term at best. He began to walk, and I followed along beside him. "Sometimes I lie in bed and try to recall her face . . . the feel of her skin against mine." He paused, eyes distant, before shaking his head slightly. "I can't. I remember she had black hair that fell in long curls over her breasts. I remember that her eyes were brown and her skin pale gold. I remember the color of the paints . . . but I can't see the picture." Matter-of-fact, he added, "Someday Niko will be that to me as well, a beautiful shadow long passed from this world." He shook his head briskly, did a Goodfellow lightning change of mood, and asked cheerfully, "How goes it with your girl? Georgie Porgie pudding and pie? Discovered what flavor she is yet?"

Cinnamon ice cream, I thought instantly before I could rein in my traitorous imagination. I hadn't kissed George. I might never kiss her, but I knew without a doubt what that kiss would taste like. "How about we don't go there?" I countered grimly.

"Oh, I beg to differ. How about we do?" His grin was simultaneously wicked and cajoling. "I'm in pain, mortally wounded. Distract me from my grief that I shall never know the size of Niko's most infamous sword."

"Jesus, Loman. I just ate. Cut it out, will you?" Still walking, I watched as his hand, featherlight and hummingbird swift, drifted out to one side and returned with a plump wallet that had belonged to a heavy-jowled businessman. Robin liked to keep up his skill in petty larceny. The original trickster, he said it paid to stay in practice . . . for the good of his magpie soul if nothing else. I would've checked the silverware every time he came to the apartment except for the fact we had nothing in that department worth stealing.

He thumbed through the wallet and gave a self-satisfied smile at the wad of cash that peeked free. Tucking it away, he clucked his tongue. "Come on. Tell Uncle Robin." There was a bit of a bounce to his step now, my troubles being more interesting than his own. "Of course, they do say abstinence is the best policy . . . 'they' being people who aren't getting any and want to spread the woe. You, on the other hand, are already all about the woe. Lighten up, kid. Do the deed already. We'll hit a place on the way home, stock up on every prophylactic known to man."

"It isn't disease that concerns me, Hef," I snapped darkly, stopping in midtrek. "It's a helluva lot worse than that. So lay off already, all right?" What I had so far managed to keep out of the limelight with Nik, Robin had managed to provoke out of me with very little effort. He was gifted in that respect.

"Well, it should concern you. Crimson creeping crud on your privates is nothing to sneeze at." An appraising gaze took me in as the people jostled past us. "So then what—ah," he said with quick comprehension. You could say many things about the puck, but one thing you couldn't say was that he was slow on the uptake. "Another potential consequence, but with a twist."

Yeah. A twist of Auphe thrown in for kick and flavor. What fun. What fucking fun. I walked on and zipped up my leather jacket to have something to do with my hands. It was a warm spring night and the leather only made it warmer, but the jacket hid my gun and my newly cleansed-of-bodach knife. Trailing after me, Robin folded his arms and offered lightly, "A potential consequence isn't a certainty. If you're careful—"

"There isn't going to be a certainty. There isn't even going to be a potential." I cut him off without emotion. Down went the jacket zipper, then up again. It was better than impotently clenching my fist. "I was lucky." Yeah . . . if you could call it that. "Next time it might not happen that way. You really want to try to find day care for a flesh-eating baby? I think they charge extra when your kid goes cannibal during nap time."

"I see your point," he admitted with a wince. "Re-gardless, I think the chances are low. *If* the precautions failed and *if* there was a baby, who's to say it wouldn't be like you? Melodramatic and sullen, yes, but obviously no Auphe."

I shook my head and walked into the side street–cum-alley that cut between Canal and Walker. It was a shortcut, if one didn't mind the small workout that went along with it now and again. "I'm not like you, Loman. I'm not a gambler, not even with the little things, and this is no little thing. The Auphe line dies with me."

He considered for a moment, the streetlights bright on his curly head. "Well then, I see two options left to you. First, find your healer friend Rafferty, and . . ." He scissored two fingers together with a *snip-snip* sound.

I had the feeling that Auphe DNA wouldn't let a minor thing like a vasectomy stop it, but it was a thought. "The second?"

"George. She *is* a psychic," he pointed out with a patience that wasn't usually part of his kinetic personality. "Why don't you ask her what would happen?"

Another thought, one I'd come up with on my own long before. "Maybe," I said noncommittally. The trouble was I didn't know if George would tell the truth. She wouldn't lie, but that didn't mean she would tell me what I wanted to know. George had an outlook on life that was completely at odds with my own. What should be, will be, and vice versa. There were no good moments without bad ones. No joy without sorrow. No pleasure without pain. No light without darkness. Yeah, it was all very Zen, I'm sure. She was so *reconciled* . . . so at peace with the world. That is to say, so not like me. If a bouncing baby killing machine was the result of us being together, she would accept it. She would know . . . without a shred of doubt . . . that was the way things were meant to be. *Must* be.

I didn't know any such goddamn thing.

"Until you decide what to do, I can think of one thing that might help tide you over." Goodfellow had stopped in the middle of the alley to remove a silk tie every bit as fashionable as mine had been cheap and ugly. He put it in his pocket and then removed his suit jacket.

"And what's that?" I asked with a healthy measure of skepticism.

"There's only one surefire substitute cure for a rabid case of horniness. . . ." My glare had him choosing his words with more care. "Ah . . . lovesickness. One cure for lovesickness." He rubbed a dusting hand over the nearest garbage can lid, then laid the jacket over it and went to work rolling up his sleeves.

"Yeah? What?"

His predatory grin bared white, even teeth. "A good fight."

The guy slithered out of the shadows behind us. Not much illumination from the streetlights penetrated this narrow bottleneck of brick and concrete.

I rolled my eyes at Goodfellow, who naturally stood smack-dab in what little light there was as if it were his own personal spotlight. "They say don't swim right after you eat. I'm sure the same goes for kicking ass." I'd known someone was in the alley. Someone usually was. It was the price of a good shortcut.

"You came." The man was still only a hulking shadow, big from his outline, with a voice weaned on brutality and alcohol. "He said and you came."

I frowned. Either this guy was nuts, a good possibility, or someone was keeping a close eye on either Robin or me. I'd take nut job any day of the week over that second choice. "Yeah, we came. What the hell is it to you?"

"Your repartee is scathing, as always," Goodfellow snorted. "Who needs a blade when you can simply run him through with your razor-sharp wit?" Needed or not, a blade appeared in his hand. It was short but sturdy, a modern version of a Roman short sword. "Why don't you and your overly stuffed stomach take a seat and allow me the pleasure?"

"Knock yourself out," I grunted. There was no place to sit that wouldn't result in a wet or garbage-stained ass, so I leaned against the alley wall to watch the show. Goodfellow had issues of his own. I didn't begrudge him the first psycho mugger to take them out on. I could always grab the next one. "But make it quick, would you? This place reeks worse than that cologne you bathe in."

"It's two hundred an ounce and an olfactory work of art, you philistine." He gave an idle swing of the sword, the metal an arc of glittering silver. "And take that from someone who knew quite a few of the bastards. Now let me work."

Our new pal still hung in the shadows' darkest depths. I couldn't see if he was armed or not, although I imagined he was. I did know chances were good he didn't have a gun. If he had, it would've already been out and pointed between Robin's eyes.

Goodfellow tilted his head lazily, casual and curious as a cat. "So, friend, what is it you want? Money? Perversities? An interview with New York's most eligible bachelor? Speak up."

"He said and you came." The hulking figure moved closer, one slow methodical step at a time. "He said. He said." I could now see more of him. A gleaming bald head was dwarfed by the stretch of his muscle-bound shoulders. A black T-shirt that was ripped and

worn was stretched tight across the barrel of his chest,
and jeans stiff with dirt encased legs like tree trunks.
"He said and you came. He said. You came."

Crazy or bad steroids, only his pusher knew for
sure. Either way I felt better about it. It meant no
one was keeping tabs on Goodfellow or myself. "He's
big, Loman," I drawled. "But not too bright. I don't
think you're going to get much of a workout here."

When I'm wrong, which I've already freely admitted
is pretty frequently, I'm usually spectacularly wrong.
This time wasn't much of an exception. The nut job
didn't have a gun, no, but he did have a shiny new
crossbow. In fact, if I wasn't mistaken, there was a
price tag still dangling from the trigger guard. A meaty
fist swept from behind his back to reveal the weapon,
which was reduced to a delicate toy by the size of the
hand that held it. Delicate it or not, it nailed Goodfellow where he stood.

The titanium quarrel punctured his upper leg, ruining what I was sure was a shockingly expensive pair
of pants. Robin had already been in midlunge for
cover when he was hit. The momentum took him on
to tumble behind a metal Dumpster. He hit the asphalt hard but with sword still in hand. In the dark,
combined with the charcoal gray of his pants, I
couldn't see the blood, but I could smell it. It was an
oddly sunny tang in the air, much less coppery than
human blood. "You alopecic, bedlamite son of a
bitch," he gritted. "Do you know how much these
cost?" Yeah, Robin was nothing if not predictable.

I'd sought cover myself from the sudden hail of
metal, sliding in beside Goodfellow. He was banging
his sword against the side of the Dumpster, each blow
a punctuation. "I bought these in Rome." Bang.
"Rome." Bang. "The finest tailor slaved for days."
Bang. *"Days."*

I fished in my jacket pocket and pulled out the linen napkin I'd swiped from the restaurant. We were running low on washcloths at home, and I'd picked up more sticky-fingered habits from Robin than was good for me. "Here. Wrap your leg up before the next suit that tailor makes is for your funeral."

He grumbled and cursed but obeyed. While he worked I took my Glock in hand and peered over the top of the Dumpster. Mr. Clean was still coming, step by plodding step. And with every one of those steps he reloaded and fired and there was the ping of metal against metal. Step. Ping. Step. Ping. The intensity of it was creepy as hell, but when it came down to it, it was a situation that could be easily resolved. There was a hiss of breath as Goodfellow cinched the makeshift bandage around his leg. Then he snapped, "What are you waiting for? Shoot the *malaka* already.

"Gee, what will your next two wishes be, Master?" I asked dryly. I couldn't say I'd never shot a human before. I couldn't even say I hadn't killed one, but circumstances had been different. This guy was dangerous, but not to the point of a bullet in the brain. My conscience was as underweight and scrawny as they came, but even it would suffer a twinge at putting down a loony.

On the other hand, it wasn't as if I could leave him running around. Not unless I planned on setting up house behind this Dumpster. I aimed, then popped off two shots. The slugs in his right shoulder and left thigh were the best compromise I could manage at the moment, especially with Goodfellow griping in my ear. Mr. Clean fell in near silence, the only sound a soft grunt as his back hit the concrete. He was alive, albeit with a good deal of his blood pumping free. I discovered that my conscience had no problem with that whatsoever. "Come on, Goodfellow. We better get out of here before the cops show up."

With a hand gripping the top edge of the Dumpster, Robin pulled himself up to balance on one leg. "A little assistance here, if you please." The gesture he made was remarkably similar to the one he'd given the waiter. Demandingly autocratic. If it weren't for the scent of his blood mingling with the stranger's in the air, I might've let him fall right back on that arrogant ass. Putting the gun away, I slid an arm under his and growled, "Grab your jacket. I don't want to hear the Rome speech all the way back to your place."

Not waiting for the reply that was bound to come, I grabbed a quick look at our attacker. He was still down, the crossbow lying inches from his fingers. Blank eyes stared upward as he mumbled his peculiar mantra over and over, "He said. He said. He said."

Deciding to get out of there before the guys with butterfly nets showed up, I swung Goodfellow out into the street and took off at a good clip. I ignored his outraged yelp of pain, but I was less successful with what followed. "Shouldn't you take the crossbow?" Hopping on one leg, he held the other bent at the knee between us. "You and your cannibal-baby genes may find this world too much to bear, but I personally don't relish a bolt to the back."

It never ended. It honestly never did. "I got him in the right shoulder," I replied impatiently. "He was shooting with his right hand. Unless he's ambidextrous I think we'll survive." Despite my logical words, I took another look over my shoulder. Yep, he was still down and still nuttier than an all-squirrel buffet.

"Why wouldn't he be ambidextrous?" Goodfellow muttered under his breath. "I am, a master with both hands in the art of war."

"I don't think being able to jack off with either hand makes you an expert in anything." I craned my head to scan the alley, what I could see of it. There was something . . . something besides the guy with the crossbow, but what? I couldn't have said what told me, but I felt it all the same. And then I saw it from the corner of my eye, a pale glimmer at the rooftop. "What the hell is that?" I started to say. I managed to get about half of it out when a titanium bolt furrowed a raw path across my jaw. It was a rude wake-up call to my complacency, and Robin's snapped "I told you so" didn't improve matters either. Scattering garbage like runners in the surf, we careened around the corner to safety. I started to stick my head back around for a last look when another quarrel came flying by.

"Is he coming?"

I wiped a hand across my jaw. It came away wet and red. "I don't know, Loman. Why don't you lean over and take a look? A nice *long* look. I'll wait right here for you."

"Never mind, then." Struggling into his suit coat, he leaned on me and made pretty respectable time through the crowd for a man with one good leg. You didn't get to be as long-lived as Goodfellow without a healthy survival instinct. "What did you see on the roof of that building?"

I frowned. I didn't know what I'd seen. It had been too fleeting a glance and the distance too far. There was something indefinable . . . something I couldn't quite put my finger on that made me think it wasn't human. But, hey, in this city that wasn't so unusual. You think a human invented the falafel stand? Yeah, right. "It was the Easter Bunny, Loman, come to plant an egg up your ass if you don't get moving." He grumbled and complained but hopped a little faster. And that suited me just fine. The more distance between us and the thing on the roof, the better. I had a feeling, one of those goddamn feelings, that whatever it was up there was far from bunny territory.

Unless the Easter Bunny was one nasty son of a bitch.

6

Two days later I was experiencing the drawbacks of a mirror-free life. I didn't much mind. After nearly a year, fumbling around had become second nature. With short careful strokes, I applied the liquid bandage to the three-inch cut on my jaw. It was long and ugly, but not particularly deep. Other than cleaning and disinfecting it I'd left it alone. But tonight was poker night. Walking into a building full of wolves when I smelled of raw flesh wouldn't be conducive to anything but becoming a doggy treat. The clear liquid would dry in seconds and seal off the wound and the scent.

"Do you need help with that?"

Niko stood in the bathroom doorway already dressed and ready for the game. It would be hard to guess that this grim figure, all in black with an expression nearly as dark, didn't own a mirror either, out of respect for my twisted little phobia. A doorway was a doorway, whether it was mounted over a bathroom sink or tucked away in a purse. And Darkling had come through just such a doorway to fuck me up but good.

"I think I've got it." By feel I applied one last

stroke, sealed the bottle, and gave my brother my full attention. "Jesus, Cyrano." I grimaced at the set look on his face. "Who pissed in your wheat germ?"

"You did," he said calmly. "You and Goodfellow and Promise. You've taken what was an iffy situation to begin with and actually managed to make it, if possible, more hazardous."

"All three of us, huh? That's a lot of piss." He was right, though. Between my shortcut, Robin's leg, and Promise's stubborn will, we had managed to screw things up more than a bit. "Hey, I was willing to go in by myself." Unfortunately, being lousy at poker ruled that out. I knew what a pair was . . . barely. With that in mind, getting in a game with Boaz would be a neat trick. And being on point on this one wasn't an option for Goodfellow now. He could hobble at a fair speed, but when you're running from wolves, fair isn't good enough. Promise had offered to step into his place. Actually, "offered" wasn't quite the word. Promise had laid down the law. She was a full partner too and she was determined to carry her load.

Robin had sat the two of us down and played a hand with us. Before that hand was over, there had been a knocking at the door. George didn't need to be buzzed in on the rare occasion the front-door lock worked. Anyone who saw her would just open the door. It was impressive, uncanny, and, at that moment, a pain in the ass. George had given us all a smile, stood at my side, and said she would just watch. Anything else wouldn't be fair, she'd added cheekily. And Robin, who could say no to anyone and everyone, couldn't say no to her. She had pulled up a chair next to mine, and as we'd played, brown eyes peeked at my cards, warm fingers meandered up and down my arm, and explosive red hair lurked in the periphery of my vision like a field of poppies. Probably the same field of poppies that had taken Dorothy down on her way to see the Wizard.

Needless to say, I hadn't done so hot. At the end of twenty games Robin had decided that when it came to gambling I was unsalvageable, unteachable, and borderline mentally challenged. Promise was a competent player and he'd decided to concentrate his efforts there. Truth was, she'd never be half the player Goodfellow was, but she would pass. More importantly, she was nonhuman. She could walk into that bar at my side and raise fewer eyebrows than I would.

I stood and said seriously, "Don't worry, Nik. I'll take care of your girl. Nothing will happen to her."

"Strange. She said the same of you." From behind his back, he revealed a thick roll of white tape and stretched out a long piece with a ripping sound. "What portion of skin do you mind losing the least?"

I eyed him with suspicion. "This isn't revenge, is it?"

"Vengeance is a petty endeavor." With quick and efficient motions he taped the tiny microphone just below my chest. "Petty," he repeated, slapping on several more completely unnecessary pieces of the adhesive stuff, "but enjoyable. In any event, Promise is perfectly capable of taking care of herself. And she can fly. Can you?"

"She can . . . ," I started, then finished up with a scowl, "You're shitting me, aren't you?"

He put the tape aside and studied his handiwork. Satisfied, he passed me my shirt. "You watch too many movies, little brother."

The shirt was courtesy of Goodfellow. Black silk, it was worlds away from my more casual style, but the scent would match that of the silk tape on my chest.

It should fool curious wolf noses. I buttoned it, lifting my upper lip. "Who said disco was dead?"

"Actually I thought it more of the gigolo genre, but whatever lets you retain your self-respect." He looked me up and down, his own lip twitching slightly. "Such as it is."

Robin's silk shirt was the only exception to my normal look. I was still in my ever-present jeans with my hair pulled back. Hardly charging-for-it wear. "I'm beautiful and you know it." I grinned.

"You have been spending too much time with Goodfellow. Far too much time."

I ended up spending even more time with the puck. We all did. An hour later the four of us sat in a van from Robin's car lot, the same lot where he let us park Niko's ancient car, and went over last-minute details. Niko tested, retested, then tested again the reception of the microphone taped to my chest, while Goodfellow, wrinkling his noble brow in manfully concealed pain, propped his leg on a crate and pillow. I'd already fetched him two aspirin and then a bottle of water. I drew the line at the requested leg massage. "The wolves are looking better and better all the time," I commented to Promise.

"The growling and snapping will certainly be less," she said solemnly, her gaze candidly aimed at Niko.

"I do not growl or snap." Niko didn't need to look up to register her glance. How telling was that? "I am centered and at peace." Deciding there was too much tape muffling the sound quality, he jerked off a piece with no consideration for my pained yelp. "Perfectly at peace."

I rubbed my chest gingerly and let the shirt fall down into place. Maybe it would keep my peaceful brother's hands to himself. "I think we're more than

ready here, guys. How about we get the show on the
road while I still have some skin left?"

The place was out in Jersey . . . Newark. And while
that made living with yourself harder, it did make
parking somewhat easier. The van was parked about
two blocks away, close enough for Niko to come to
our aid if needed, and far enough not to arouse
wolfish suspicions. Humans didn't tend to frequent this
type of establishment; when the bouncer at the door
has raw-meat breath, rabid eyes, and the personal hygiene of Sasquatch on a low-deodorant day, you tend
to move on. It was called a social club, a private one.
What that actually meant was a gambling "den" for
the unnatural, den being a remarkably apt word, all
things considered. Wolves loved to gamble. A chance
to throw their money away had tails wagging like
nothing else but a good juicy massacre, and this place
promised to give them just what they wanted.

Moonshine did look to be your typical wolf hangout.
I hadn't been to but the one; still, the pups seemed
to have a theme going. Seedy, smelly, and probably
wall-to-wall fleas. Absently I scratched my arm in anticipation. A split second later a can of flea and tick
spray was slapped in my hand. Always prepared—it
wasn't a personal mantra for my brother; it was pro-
grammed into his genetic code. Slipping the small can-
ister into the pocket of my jeans, I reined in my usual
sarcasm. "Thanks, Cyrano. Last time I was scratching
for days." Before Goodfellow could open his mouth, I
aimed a warning glare at him. "No smart-ass cracks."

His mouth, already open, snapped shut and he returned the glare with an added helping of wounded
hurt that I wasn't buying for a second. Ignoring him,
I turned my attention to the shirt. Normally I would've
left it hanging loose. I wasn't a tucked-in kind of guy,
but for extra security for the microphone, I shoved

the silk under the waistband. The shirt wasn't skintight or gigolo tight, but it was snug enough that you couldn't have fitted a weapon beneath it, and I didn't even try. Instead I wore my holster outside the shirt. One side held my Glock, and the other side was modified for my knife. The leather was black, but that hardly had the whole setup blending in with my shirt. It didn't matter. The bouncer would've been more suspicious if I *hadn't* been carrying. There wasn't a creature alive who would walk into that place unarmed.

Holding out my arm, I said formally, "Is milady ready?"

Amused, Promise tucked a hand into the crook of my elbow. "How gallant you are, sir."

"When you're dressed like you charge five dollars an hour, you have to be," Robin observed caustically, the moratorium on sarcastic comments apparently having passed almost instantaneously.

Never mind, it was his shirt. I gifted him with the finger, then stepped down to the street after Niko slid back the cargo door. Promise followed. Her hair floated loose to her hips, a stained-glass banner in the red and green of the neon lights. Looking over my shoulder at Niko, I taunted lightly, "If we come back engaged, you have no one to blame but yourself."

Pale brows pulling together in an annoyed V, he shut the door firmly and silently in my face. "Cranky, cranky," I murmured, and started walking.

"He's worried," Promise said after a long moment of contemplation. She rarely said anything without considering it from all angles, and this was no exception.

"He's the only grandma I have." I grinned. "Now the same goes for you."

Surprisingly, the bouncer at the door was female and petite. That only meant she was more dangerous, a buck five of ass-kicking fury. Inky black hair pulled back in a long tail was paired with arresting yellow green eyes. To your casual human eye the split upper lip could've easily been mistaken for a cleft lip and not the beginnings of a muzzle. It kept her from being classically beautiful, but that didn't mean she still wasn't gorgeous. Exotic and strange, but gorgeous nonetheless. As we approached the door, she looked us up and down, sniffed, and then wrinkled that bifurcated upper lip in disgust. It was the same reaction I'd gotten from the albino wolf at Cerberus's office. The wolves I'd come into contact with last year, when I was possessed by Darkling, had been fascinated with my scent. The combination of human, Auphe, and Darkling had been a canine potpourri, a feast for the senses. Apparently plain old half-human, half-Auphe wasn't nearly as pleasing.

Tainted or not, we were allowed to pass. And lucky us, there was no cover charge. The club was smaller than I would've guessed from the outside. That indicated either a helluva lot of walk-in closets or a few back rooms set aside for more interesting activities. Taking a look around, I didn't see too many fashion plates in the immediate area. All right, then . . . back room it was. No doubt that was where the poker game went on. The rest of the place was typical for what it was. Roulette and blackjack tables, occasional slot machine, tables and chairs, suspiciously wet floor, empty makeshift stage, poor lighting. Except for the regulars, it looked like every bar I'd ever slung a brew in. "Drink?" I asked Promise.

Raising her eyebrows, she declined. "That adventurous I am not. But, please, help yourself."

At the bar I ordered a beer, less for drinking and more for blending in. Not having had my rabies shot, I made sure it came in a bottle. The bartender was a surprise. A big one. Bored green eyes, wavy brown hair, and a foxlike face that was all too familiar. I couldn't help but stare. It didn't go unnoticed.

"You seem to have a problem, freak." It was Goodfellow's voice, only arctic and empty. Goodfellow's face, although set with a supercilious sneer. His eyes, lacking even a sliver of a soul. "Shall I cure you of it?" The blade he laid on the counter beside the beer was a Spanish poniard, more ice pick than dagger.

"No problem," I said evenly. Now was not the time or place for a fight. Not if we hoped to get in a game with Boaz. Pissing off the bartender—and, if I knew pucks, the owner of the club—wasn't the way to go about that. "It's just been a while since I've seen a puck," I continued on, lying smoothly. "Hard to believe this city is worthy of your presence." Complete sincerity over unadulterated bullshit.

The toxic ennui in his eyes was eddied momentarily by conceit and self-satisfaction. "None is worthy. What can one do?" He tossed a towel over his shoulder and said dismissively, "Take your drink and go, freak. That shirt is an assault to my eyes." Freak. He was even quicker to pick up on the Auphe in me than Robin had been. Maybe like called to like. I'd never thought of Goodfellow as a monster. Annoying, vain, arrogant, glib, unscrupulous . . . and, yeah, an out-and-out crook, but never a monster. This guy was. It came off of him in waves. A rapacious predator, an utterly amoral sociopath . . . this particular Pan would gut you in a heartbeat for a penny. He did have better taste in shirts than Goodfellow, though. I had to give him that.

Picking up my beer, I left as ordered. I, better known as the freak, would've preferred to take the poniard and pin his hand to the bar or at the least plant a fist in his face. But neither was an option, not right now. Undercover work, let me count the ways in which it sucked. Promise tilted her head as I approached. "Peculiar, is it not?" she said as her eyes rested on the puck across the room. "How identical they all are . . . what few that are left."

"Trust me," I responded soberly. "They're not identical."

We chose a table close to the back of the room. We sat side by side, both of our backs to the wall. Niko would've been proud. The place was half-empty; it was still fairly early. Within the next hour that began to change. Moonshine might've been a predominantly wolf hangout, but it attracted all kinds. Sprinkled among the lupines were an afreet, a few ghouls, succubi plying their dangerous trade, and three lamias on what looked like a girls' night out. There were others, creatures I didn't recognize. Promise probably did, but quite frankly my curiosity just wasn't high enough to ask her. I was more concerned with Boaz. When Niko had called Caleb to accept the assignment, he'd gotten a description of our mark, but so far I hadn't spotted him. Around us the wolves, some in human form and some not, drank, laughed, howled, cursed, and fought. It brought back memories, not particularly good ones. The last time I'd been in a bar like this had been to hire a pair of assassins. And although I hadn't been behind the wheel of my own body at the time, it was hard to forget that except for Niko and Robin, George would be dead now.

"Niko is a fabulous lover."

It was a good thing the beer was only for decoration. Otherwise I would've choked on it, or at the very least spewed it a few feet. As it was, I felt my face take on a hunted expression. As subjects go, this was not one any brother wanted to discuss. "Jesus, Promise," I said with not a little desperation, "that's the kind of information that could scar a man for life."

A dimple appeared in an ivory smooth cheek. "I'm sorry, Caliban. I was only testing you. Your attention seemed far from here."

"Yeah, it was. Sorry." Rolling the now-warm bottle between my hands, I scanned the crowd again.

She gave a gracious nod before speaking again. "Actually, Niko and I have not yet—" I groaned out loud, cutting her off. Amused, she relented and changed the subject . . . sort of. "Tell me, what was Niko like as a child?"

What had my brother been like as a child. It seemed like a simple question. But like most things that seem simple on the surface, what lurked beneath was a different story. Niko was two years older than I was, although when we were children he'd been four ahead. Neat trick, eh? When the Auphe had kidnapped me at the age of fourteen, they'd taken me to a place where time ran differently than it did here. For Niko it seemed as if I were gone only a day, but I had come back approximately two years older. I'd also come back a raving lunatic, but that was beside the point. Niko dealt with it, just as he always had.

One of my earliest memories as a kid was around the time I was four. I'd been sick. Who knows with what? It was mostly fuzzy, but I did remember vomiting miserably all over myself. And I remembered it had been Niko cleaning me up while Sophia drank whiskey in the next room. He would've been eight. And when I was well enough to eat again, it was Niko who fed me soup and crackers. It was Niko who walked me to school and picked me up afterward. Niko who bought me birthday presents, complete with a grocery store cupcake and candle. Promise wanted to know what he was like as a child?

"He never was one," I said soberly.

That was when Boaz walked through the door. I didn't need his description to know who he was. He strolled in like he owned the place . . . owned the world. He, like the higher wolves, was able to convert completely to human form. Whippet lean, he had his pale brown hair shaved close to his skull and a face carved from cold white marble. With eyes so black that they swallowed the light, he looked over the crowd with a curl of thin lips. Then motioning to the four wolves flanking him, he moved toward the back and disappeared through the only door. So much for ingratiating our way into a game.

"Well, shit," I growled succinctly.

"That does seem to sum it up." Promise rose and discarded her cape over her chair. "Give me a moment." With that, she then moved toward the one wolf left guarding the door.

It was something to see, Promise at work. It brought home how much she truly cared for Niko. I had never seen her use on him what she laid on that poor goddamn wolf. It wasn't sex or even the hint of it, although it was erotic as hell. I'd compared her to royalty before and that was part of it. She was a goddess come to earth; at least she made you believe that. She didn't walk; she flowed. And when she smiled, she put the Mona Lisa to shame. Promise was a promise of more than you could ever imagine.

Five rich husbands . . . it was a wonder she hadn't had a hundred.

I whistled low under my breath. "Nik, she's going to eat you alive." That was all right. He was going to enjoy every minute of it.

In less than five minutes she was back. Scooping up the pile of violet silk, she said lightly, "Come along,

Caliban. We have an invitation to a very private and exclusive game."

"Lucky us," I offered blandly. Carrying my beer, I followed in her wake.

The room was the same as a thousand others like it. Spare, smoky, and marginally clean. The owner wasn't wasting any overhead prettying the place up—that was clear to see. Although the painting of dogs playing poker that hung crookedly on the wall was a weirdly appropriate touch. Maybe that sociopathic puck had a little of Goodfellow in him after all.

As we stepped through the door, all eyes locked on Promise. The circle of black, brown, yellow, and pumpkin orange eyes held an identical emotion: awed lust. Then those eyes moved to me, but the looks I received were a helluva lot less complimentary. It was the same reaction I received from most nonhumans. There was the incredulous sniff, followed by expressions of sheer disgust and revulsion. This time, however, as the cherry on top, one of the wolves actually peed himself. Now, there was someone who'd obviously actually crossed paths with an Auphe at some point.

To most, the Auphe were a legend. Real and true, but with such a dwindled population that chances were good you might luck out and never see one in your lifetime. It was the kind of luck to pray for. But Auphe had always been the top of the food chain, and wolves, full-blown egotistic predators that they were, didn't like being reminded that once in a while they too were prey. And I wasn't about to tell them that a new spot had opened up for King of the Mountain.

The wolf in urine-stained jeans moved out of his chair and slithered past us through the door, giving me the widest berth he could. I lifted an arm and gave my pit an experimental whiff. "What? Do I offend?" In reality I didn't blame him. There had been times that the Auphe had me wanting to piss my own pants.

Boaz ignored me for a more pleasant subject. "We have a new player, I see," he said, unreadable icy eyes resting on Promise.

"May I take a seat?" She gave him a slow smile. "Preferably a clean one."

Nodding at the wolf across the table from him, Boaz ordered flatly, "Leave." The guy scrambled to obey, scattering cards before him like leaves. As I held the chair for her, Promise took a seat and I took up position behind. With arms folded and eyelids drooping, I did my best to look sleepy and harmless. Niko would've said that was essentially my natural state. There might have been some truth in that, but pulling it off in a room full of werewolves wasn't as easy as all that.

"Why is *that* with you?" The repulsed sneer on Boaz's face as he bared teeth in my direction needed no faking at all.

Promise reached back and gave my arm a proprietary pat. "He's here to carry my winnings."

At least she hadn't said to carry her purse. It was nice having a shred of masculinity left to my name. As she gathered the cards before her, Boaz grunted, "A dangerous pet to keep."

"Where is the pleasure without the peril?" With a fathomless gaze from beneath sable brown lashes, she handed the cards to the hulking figure to her right and asked, "Shall we play, then?"

The game started and I was witness to some of the most subtle flirting I'd seen in my life. Granted, with my social agenda, that wasn't saying much. Still, I recognized excellence in the field when I saw it. Surrounded by creatures both lethal and of questionable hygiene, Promise was as at ease as she was at a charity event or dinner party. Soft conversation, pale polished nails touched to ivory skin. The hair of a jungle cat. Those pooches didn't have a chance. Grinning to myself, I watched the players and tried to keep my eyes from settling on Boaz too often. It didn't stop the doubts. Caleb had said that Cerberus's rival was a drinker and a talker. From what I'd seen so far he didn't seem the type. Cold, controlled, he was a wolf of ice and steel. But after an hour passed, my skepticism was proved wrong. Boaz started tossing them back. It started slowly, but by the end of hour two his drinking hand was in near-constant motion.

Despite a discipline that I would've guessed ruled his business as well as his personal life . . . kinky . . . he was really putting the booze away. It was a fact that everyone had a weakness, and the more common ones were common for a reason. He stuck with the hard stuff as the game wore on, and finally, just as my legs started falling asleep, he began to talk.

It wasn't exactly a river of information, more of a vodka-flavored trickle, but it was what we were there to hear. "That two-headed son of a bitch."

The human wolf to his left hunched slightly, ears twitching with an unlikely flexibility. Apparently this was a familiar and potentially explosive refrain. "He's a shit all right, boss. We all seen it," he offered in a placating tone.

Boaz was in no mood to be soothed. "Misshapen thing, he's no good for the pack. No good for the hunt. He should've been culled." He drained his glass. "Culled a long time ago."

"Culled." It was whispered around the circle. Heads nodded, some human, some shaggy.

"He's deformed, weak, *wrong*." Knuckles blanched white around the cheap glass tumbler.

The heads nodded again. "Deformed." "Wrong." None repeated the word "weak." They seemed sure that while Cerberus was many, many things . . . disturbing things . . . weak wasn't one of them. As much as Boaz didn't want to admit it, that telling omission said that Cerberus was strong, cunning, and a power to be reckoned with. And wasn't that really what got Boaz's goat?

"He's an aberration." The glass shattered in his hand, blood-coated shards falling to the table, and a homicidal grin of suddenly lengthening teeth was aimed in our direction. "An aberration who sends his spies among us. Did you like the show, spies? Were you entertained?" Growing nails speared through the table as if it were cheap cardboard and his gaze focused on me. "You smell like Auphe, but I think you'll taste of human."

Spies. It was either a paranoid and freakishly good guess or someone under Cerberus had loose lips. And I wasn't a big believer in good guesses. It was a safe bet that someone had given us up, but I didn't wait around to ponder the subject. Neither did Promise. She performed a flip over my head that was a quicksilver study in deadly grace. I heard her land behind me and I wasted no time in pulling my Glock. I was going to get off only a few shots in these closed quarters; I had to make them count. Boaz was my choice for deadliest flavor of the month and I popped off my first shot in his direction. He was already half-changed as he catapulted across the table toward me, twisting to avoid my bullet. It was a lost cause. It took him high in the chest. Then his lost cause became mine; he kept coming. Silver bullets, like so many other things, were a myth. Your average lead worked just fine . . . eventually. But right now his jaws, about the size of a Kodiak bear's, were headed inexorably for my throat. I blocked him with my left forearm, ramming my arm far enough into his mouth that I could've tickled Boaz's tonsils. Less than that and my bone would've snapped like a twig. But back where the leverage was weaker, it held . . . barely. Granted, there was a white-hot pain from my fingertips to my shoulder that had black spots clouding the edges of my vision, but that was the absolute least of my concerns. I still held the gun in my right hand and I pulled the trigger again and again. With his chest against mine I couldn't aim for his heart, but there was someplace else open and vulnerable. Every one of my bullets found a home in Boaz's center torso, about diaphragm level. If that didn't stop him, nothing would. He might be the biggest baddest son of a werebitch to walk the earth, but he had to breathe.

Or so went the theory.

In reality, Boaz was doing his damnedest to rip my arm from my body. With the last shot in the magazine, I blew off a good hunk of the lower part of his jaw. Pulling my arm free, I wedged a knee between us and flung him off. The brown wolf, half again bigger than a Shetland pony, tumbled onto the table, which promptly shattered beneath his weight. Dropping the gun, I staggered to my feet, unsheathed my knife, and whirled to slash at the throat of the next wolf in line. Vision clearing, I kept Promise in sight out of the corner of my eye. I'd made a pledge to my brother; I wasn't about to break it. Lucky for me, being a little occupied at the moment, she was more than holding her own. In a pirouette as flowing as that of any dancer, she spun her cape of purple silk around one wolf's head, blinding him, and then tossed him headfirst into the nearest wall. I heard something crack . . . wall or skull, I couldn't say for sure. Then she leaped backward and up, clinging high to the wall and facing the fight with calculating eyes. Now that was something I hadn't seen out of her before. It was kind of . . . well, spooky as shit just about covered it.

"Okay, Princess," I called out, "you are seriously freaking me out." I didn't mention her real name. Wouldn't do to put any of us on the radar of Cerberus's enemies. Life was complicated enough. She didn't acknowledge the comment, instead descending again into the milling pack with the grace of a diving falcon. Wolves scattered beneath her. Yeah, she was holding her own all right. Now time for me to do the same.

Gushing blood from his carotid artery, my wolf went down and two more rose in his place. These were a little more wary. From the panicked flaring of wolfish nostrils and the rolling of white-ringed eyes, they were far more impressed with my Auphe heritage than Boaz was. What had been a bald guy and a black one had turned into a sadly mangy wolf and a rangy, long-legged obsidian one. Growling and snapping at each other to bolster their courage, they finally managed to get up the furry cojones to make their move. Patches went down with a blade in the eye. I felt queasy on that one. He was a Were determined to rip me into Snausage-sized pieces, but that moth-eaten coat gave him the last-dog-in-the-pound look. Albeit a rabid dog with a thirst for blood and pain. As I pulled the blade free, his pal hit me from the side, and down I went again. This guy had nothing on his boss. He growled like an entire pack of wolves and lunged at my face with snapping jaws, but hesitated for one critical moment when I snarled back.

I took advantage and broke Bowser's top teeth out with the blade of my knife. Pointed fangs half the length of my hand went flying accompanied by a pained howling. If a wolf had vanity, it lay in his pearly whites. Snatching a glance over my shoulder, I

saw the spike heel of Promise's elaborately strappy
shoes take one wolf directly between the eyes. He
somersaulted head over paws backward with a glazed
sheen across his yellow eyes. We had six wolves down
for the count, or so I thought. That left three more . . .
three until Boaz resurfaced from the wreckage of the
table. Goddamn, what did it take to keep that hairy
bastard down? Even in wolf form, oddly enough, his
eyes were still black, and they held the same pitiless
and implacable chill of death.

It had been barely two and a half minutes since the
fight had begun. Still, it didn't surprise me in the
slightest when Niko came through the door, a dark-
clad missile of destruction. I was wearing a wire for a
reason, and my brother wasn't one to let the grass
grow under his feet. The wood of the door was sturdy
enough; it didn't matter. It disintegrated under Niko's
kick. Boaz didn't turn; he didn't have a chance. The
gape-jawed wolf was the recipient of Niko's sword
through his broad brown chest. "Let's go," Niko ordered tersely. "This isn't what we're here for." Gee,
a little death and dismemberment wasn't on the schedule? What a pity. I dodged a big gray wolf—all of
them by now had turned—and booted it in the ass
hard enough to send it flying into a still-thrashing
Boaz. Goddamn, that was one tough wolf.

Promise flowed past me with, if you could believe
it, her cloak retrieved and folded neatly over her arm.
She paused for the briefest of moments to murmur in
Niko's ear and then passed through the door to the
outer room. Niko turned his attention to the convuls-
ing Boaz with calculating consideration. I saw his hand
tighten slightly on the hilt of his sword before he came
to a decision. Killing Boaz wasn't the job we'd taken.
It wasn't one we *would've* taken. Boaz was Cerberus's
problem, not that that changed the fact there were

three more wolves rushing forward to take us out. Niko looked at me sharply and repeated, *"Go."*

It was a tone I'd learned not to argue with when I was in diapers. With one arm virtually out of commission I had to leave the Glock. It was stolen and untraceable, with the numbers destroyed by acid, though no one in this crowd was going to be calling the police. It didn't change the fact I was going to miss the hunk of plastic and metal. It had gotten me out of a jam or two in its day. Knife still in hand, I made to follow Promise. "They're going to smell your blood," he added grimly. "So use some speed, little brother."

That Promise, what a tattletale. Cradling my arm against my chest, I went with one parting shot. "Nothing but my dust, Grandpa." Ignoring his snort, I headed out. Speed was a relative term, but I liked to think I set a land-speed record for an injured man in gigolo wear. Throughout the club heads were turning in my direction, some lupine, but not all. I saluted them with my knife hand and drawled, "Good game, great company. Thanks for the hospitality."

Some wanted those thanks personally. Two lamias drifted up and away from their table. The round and blazing gold eyes of owls peered through strands of floor-length inky black hair. Flashes of their pale skin could be seen through the black veils as they moved toward me, their lipless mouths showing round rings of transparent baby teeth in hungry smiles. There was a flutter of silk at my elbow and Promise said firmly, "No. Go back to your muck, leeches. This one is mine." They hesitated for a moment, and taking my good arm, she goaded me into a faster pace. As the relatively fresh night air hit my nose I heard the scrape of more chairs and tables behind me. Everyone smelled the blood all right, and there was plenty of it. The cold sweat of adrenaline and pain was probably a savory olfactory side dish. I wasn't too worried, though. They might be behind me, but Niko was behind them. And that wasn't a fair fight in anyone's book.

Outside, the van was only inches from the door, pulled up on the curb with reckless disregard for the life and limb of your average pedestrian. Robin waved an impatient hand from behind the wheel. "The meter's running, kid. Get your disco ass in here."

Hissing as the movement jostled my arm, I climbed into the back of the van after Promise. "Your evil twin in there isn't nearly the pain you are, but damn if his carbon-copy ass isn't dead-on you."

Dark brows winged upward. "There's another puck in there?" There was definite ambivalence in his voice. "Which one?"

Yeah, that wasn't an unrealistic expectation to dump on me. I doubted they could tell one another apart, supernatural clones that they were. I knew I sure as hell couldn't. "The annoying, smart-ass one," I growled. The van was made for deliveries, and there were no seats in the back. Instead, I took one on the floor and wedged myself into the corner in preparation for a fast getaway. "That narrow it down for you any?" Ignoring his caustic humph, I told Promise, who crouched gracefully by the door, "Better get back. Nik is going to be moving."

That was an understatement if ever I made one. Niko came through the opening so fast I was halfway expecting a sonic boom to follow him. He slid the door into place with a metal-rattling slam a split second before something hit it hard enough to dent the metal. "Drive," he rapped. "Now."

Goodfellow obeyed with alacrity. The wheels of the van squealed as we bumped over the curb's edge, and the smell of burning rubber followed us down the street. I'd already shoved my knife back in its sheath and used my hand to grab on to the driver's seat. Leaning my head back, I closed my eyes. "Well, that was fun."

"Anyone for a late supper?" came Promise's voice. "My treat. I came out nearly five hundred ahead in the game."

"Two hundred and fifty of that is mine," Goodfellow reminded over the struggling engine. "And I'm not treating anyone."

"Of course not. Your next perm should cost at least that much. I wouldn't dream of depriving your fashion budget."

The squabbling went on and I let it wash over me like a fractious lullaby. Job number two and it hadn't turned out any better than the first. Mission accomplished, if you call fucked-up and blown out of the water an accomplishment. Bad luck or bad karma, things just weren't working out for us lately. A touch on my shoulder had me opening my eyes. "You're dripping," Niko said quietly.

In the dark it was difficult to see the color of the puddle that was forming on the floor beside me. But there wasn't much chance of it being purple, now, was there? "The true tragedy is I'm ruining Loman's shirt," I said with a halfhearted grin. My arm was propped carefully on my knees and the blood was briskly wending its way to the tips of my fingers, then trickling to the floor. It didn't make a difference. I could be gushing a river; a hospital wasn't a choice for me. Or Goodfellow or Promise for that matter. Of the four of us, only Niko had that option. If my arm were broken, maybe I could've risked it. But with a very obvious dog bite, there would be rabies shots and blood tests. I had no idea what a blood test would say about me, but I doubted it would be anything normal.

We had had a local healer, the one who had once knit together the Niko-inflicted hole in my stomach and then later had stopped my heart to drive out Darkling, but Rafferty had left several months ago. I couldn't much blame him. He was on a hunt for something, *anything,* that would cure his twin of a particularly nasty and wolfish illness. Luck to the poor bastard, but with him gone, this healing was going to be a do-it-yourself job.

Joy.

7

"Tylenol or something stronger?"

The voice was muffled by the pillow over my head. That same pillow was soaked with sweat and the victim of one or two vicious bite marks. Hey, I had a bite of my own and I didn't mind sharing the wealth. Blindly, I raised my good hand into the air and held up four fingers.

"Something stronger it is." In less than a minute Niko was pulling the pillow away and depositing two bright pink pills into my hand. Illegal prescription drugs we had, numbing lidocaine for the stitches . . . nope. We'd run out a few months back and with Rafferty missing in action, we hadn't been able to replace the anesthetic solution. It wasn't exactly in high demand on the street. Sitting up, I chased the pills down with the bottle of water Niko brought me. If my hand shook a little, he didn't comment. I imagined that after cleaning the multiple slashes, checking the bone to see if it was broken, then putting in over fifty stitches, he'd had better days himself. Inflicting true pain—and a helluva lot of it, thanks for asking—on his only family was not in his nature. After another swallow I said tiredly, "I hope Caleb's boss appreciates the loss of life and limb." Their lives, my limb.

"I hope he does as well, considering someone in his organization sold him out." He placed the pillow at the top of the bed with precise, economical motions that revealed exactly how pissed he was. "Sold us out."

"Not very professional for crooks . . . are they? Naughty, naughty." The bottle slid from my fingers to bounce off the carpet. The pills hadn't gotten to me that fast. It was more a combination of weariness and the last jangle of adrenaline running its course.

"Naughty indeed." Niko's face was expressionless, but the thread of steel in his voice was anything but. He pulled the blankets back, then bent down to pick up the bottle before my fumbling fingers reached it. "Go to bed, Cal. You've lost blood; your arm was nearly broken. You've perhaps even ingested a hair ball or two. You need the rest."

When it came to that particular command, you didn't have to tell me twice. Usually not even once. Guarding my arm, I lay down. Yanking the blanket up, I said, "Humor, Cyrano, doesn't cure all ills. Don't believe the fortune cookies."

The light was switched off and he added blandly, "By the way, Promise apologizes for not babysitting you better."

Oh, I liked that. If I could stick to a wall like human flypaper, maybe I would've come out better off myself. "Asshole," I muttered, rolling over onto my side.

"Good night to you too," Niko said dryly, and then there was the click of the door being pulled shut. When the drowsiness came I welcomed it. My arm had been gnawed on by a garbage disposal on legs, and not only that, Goodfellow was charging me for his ruined shirt. Right now sleep was my last refuge and I plunged into it wholeheartedly. It didn't last. Damned if the good things ever do. It was all right.

What woke me up was a good thing too. As good as they came.

It was a soft touch on the back of my hand that woke me. Even mired in a haze of heavy sleep, painkillers, and morning grumpiness, I instantly recognized her presence. Sliding my hand slowly but not as casually as I would've liked from beneath hers, I opened my eyes. "George, you shouldn't be here."

She overlooked my rudeness. George spent a lot of time doing that. With a muted smile, she said, "I brought you ice cream. Cherry chocolate, your favorite."

I was pretty sure ice cream was for tonsillectomies, not wolf bites, but I accepted the small pint container and spoon nonetheless. It probably wasn't the smartest thing to do, but, hell, it was cherry chocolate. Feeling the iciness of the cardboard beneath my hand, I tried not to notice George was a vision in cherry chocolate herself. The flowing dress that draped her slim form was a swirling pattern of deep browns and warm reds, the copper of her bracelets the same color as her hair. The same damn color exactly. Sitting up, I pried the lid off the ice cream, winced at the movement, and wedged the container between my sheet-covered legs to scoop out a small spoonful. "So, why the ice cream? The mystical friggin' universe tell you I was chomped last night?"

"Actually it was Promise, and her cellphone, but who's to say her call wasn't the work of the infinite universe? It does work in mysterious ways." Her legs were tucked beneath her and I noticed that her brown feet were bare. The toenails were painted the same deep red as the dress. Funny how such a minor detail could make me glad that I had the next best thing to an ice pack cradled near my crotch.

"Yeah, mysterious," I snorted. "A gossipy vampire

and cellular technology. The universe at work, that's not, George. Sorry."

"You'd be surprised." She tilted her head and said with mock innocence, "I wonder what Promise would think of being called gossipy."

"Threats, Georgie Porgie? Is that any way for a beloved prophet to behave?" My arm throbbed, the ice cream was cold and silky against my tongue, and the scent of George was in the air, nutmeg and warm sugar. It was a lot of sensations to take in all at once. I concentrated on just the one . . . the ice cream. It was comfortable, painless, and safe. And safe was good for me, good for us both, although I was feeling more and more like a wounded gazelle being cut out of the herd. Worse yet, I didn't want to run.

"Beloved of whom?" she asked with a wistful curve to her wide mouth. A spiral ringlet hung to her collarbone, fallen from the casual upswept mass of her hair. Just one strand, one curl perfect in its wildness and exuberance.

Everyone whose path she crossed. Shrugging, I silently licked the spoon clean and replaced the lid on the container. "All the ones you help with what you see. That cranky old ice-cream pusher who lives off you. Little old ladies you help across the street. You know, people." And at that moment you didn't have to be a psychic to know that I was lying.

She studied me, then sighed and took the ice cream from my hand. "To have faced the monsters you have, you are the biggest coward." Standing, she shook the smooth fall of her dress out, slid her feet into sandals, and said without pity, "We're going to talk, Caliban, you and I. If I have to lock the door and have Niko tie you to a chair, we're going to talk. So get prepared." Before I could move, she bent and brushed a kiss on the corner of my mouth. "It's going to be a very long conversation, cherry chocolate boy." And then in a swirl of sheer cotton and copper hair she was gone. Gone from the room. Gone from the apartment.

Gone from my life.

"Gone?" I said hollowly, the numbness spreading through me with firestorm speed. I didn't ask if he was sure. Niko was always sure. "How?"

"I don't know. I don't know much of anything." He pushed me toward the kitchen chair and put a cup of tea in front of me. Niko . . . he'd come away from martial arts training with the unshakable belief that there was a tea for every occasion. If the herbs didn't help, then the warmth of the liquid and the very act of drinking would give you something to focus on . . . other than the shit that was bringing down your world as efficiently as Samson at the Temple. I didn't know what kind this was; it smelled like licorice. I'd never liked licorice, even as a kid. I wasn't in the mood, to say the least. I pushed the cup away.

"Tell me," I demanded with frozen lips.

He exhaled and sat opposite me at the table. Taking the tea for himself, he turned it one way and then the other with his long fingers. "She didn't make it to the ice-cream shop. As far as I've managed to piece together, she left here and simply vanished. She didn't show up at the shop and Mr. Geever became concerned and called her mother. That was seven hours ago and no one has seen her. Her mother just now became desperate enough to call us."

George's mother had never been our number one fan. Her daughter hadn't told her I was behind the wolf assassins sent to her apartment to kill George. I was possessed at the time, but still. And although she was grateful, if confused, that Niko and Robin had saved the family from some peculiarly hairy burglars, she still had questions as to the lucky coincidence of their lurking in the vicinity, armed and ready. She knew George was a friend . . . goddamn it, a *friend* . . . of ours, but for her to break down and call us, she must be terrified.

She wasn't alone.

Friend. The plastic of the table bit into my palm as I gripped the edge with locked, aching fingers. It was amazing the catastrophes that had to occur to get you to stop lying to yourself. Yeah, fucking amazing. Pushing my chair back with a violent motion, I stood. Niko didn't need to ask where I was going. He only stood with me. "We'll find her, Cal," he said firmly. "Don't doubt it."

We'd find her all right. We'd find George, and then we'd make someone very, very sorry. The kind of sorry that involved spilled blood and a suddenly silent heart. As for the search . . . I knew George. She would've headed straight for the soda shop. Duty, responsibility, she took all that as seriously as my brother did. People would've been waiting for her, just as they did every day. We followed the path she would've taken. It was something of a walk to the shop, thirty to forty minutes, but George didn't like to take the bus or the subway if she could avoid it. Too many people in too confined a space, that sort of thing was rough on a psychic, even one with the power and control that she possessed. So she walked.

But not a single soul had seen her.

In this city I didn't expect any differently. But what was telling was that not even the hot dog guy on the corner had seen her go. Both George and I were on a first-name basis with him. God forbid I should bring mystery meat into the sanctity of Nik's kitchen. It might taint his karma, his tofu aura, his whatever. When the urge for a chili cheese dog hit me, I went to the corner and saved myself a lecture. Body. Temple. Yeah, you know the rest. Marvin the hot dog guy knew me all right and he especially knew George. He had a thing for her. It wasn't sexual, not in sixty-six-year-old Marvin's case, but it was a definite thing regardless. Her hot dogs always came with a free soda or bag of chips, and she wouldn't have walked by his wagon without stopping to say hello. But she hadn't.

That meant she hadn't even made it a block. Between our building and the corner she'd vanished. Bright and warm in her cherry chocolate dress, she'd melted away as quickly as the ice cream she had carried to me.

"Cal."

We were going to talk, she'd said. No way out of it for me. No way at all. I guess I'd proved her wrong there.

"Cal," more insistent this time.

The taste of supper, chicken burrito, lingered in the back of my throat. The salty tomato salsa was so similar to another darker flavor that I wanted to gag. George was strong-willed, independent, quick-witted, and fierce, but she wasn't like us. Not like me or Niko or Robin or Promise. She wasn't a killer. And sometimes . . . sometimes you had to be.

To survive.

"*Cal.*" The hand pinched a nerve in my shoulder, generating an electric tingle.

On autopilot my hand rubbed at the spot. It hurt, but it hurt in a place that wasn't here . . . wasn't now. Or maybe it was me that wasn't here, wasn't now. "We're screwed, aren't we?" I asked colorlessly.

"No," Niko said instantly. "We're not. You were gone much longer and I found you."

"Actually, I found you." Then I'd fired a bullet right at his heart. And I was a good shot. Helluva one, really. I hadn't missed. Closing my eyes, I felt a slow acid burn pass through to the back of my brain. "Not the best example you could've come up with."

"Perhaps not." His hand pushed mine aside and efficiently rubbed out the ache of the twisted-nerve attention getter. "But it doesn't change the fact that we'll find her. And then we'll clean our swords." The promise, deadly and gray as a hurricane sea, wasn't for me. "But for now you'll stay with me, and I'll call Caleb."

By staying with him he wasn't referring to being glued at the hip holster. He was talking mentally, not physically. Big order. Making with the superglue would've been easier, proved by the fact it took a few moments before I caught on to the mention of Caleb's name. "What the hell are you calling him for?"

"Goodfellow and Promise are already contacting everyone they know. But Caleb works for Cerberus and is in a unique position for gathering information."

It was true. Not only were the Kin involved in 99.9 percent of supernatural crime, but they also kept a greedy eye on that tiny fraction that they *didn't* own. All well and good except for two things. "Why would Caleb or Cerberus help us?"

"We waive our fee for last night's job."

We hadn't exactly found out the info Cerberus had wanted, but we had discovered there was a spy in his organization. We also might have sent Boaz to the pet cemetery. I know I was keeping my fingers crossed. As for earning Cerberus's goodwill, it might be enough. That and a fifty-thousand freebie. It was a hope, not much of one, but something. That left only the second problem.

"What if . . ." I grimaced in self-disgust as the words stuck in my throat. Yeah, this was the way to get her back. This was the way to be her salvation. Being afraid to look at the entire picture, being too cowardly to even say the words. "What if it's just a guy?" I said bleakly.

"Just . . . what do you mean?" It wasn't often Niko was puzzled. And it was far more rare that my mind moved faster than his razor-sharp one. We'd lived this life so long, even he had trouble seeing beyond it.

"What if it's just a nut? Your average human psycho," I said bluntly. A rapist, a murderer, a monster of strictly human origin. What the hell would Cerberus know about your average Gein or Dahmer holed up in Mommy's basement? "What do we do then?"

"A demon is a demon, Cal. If he's human, he'll simply be easier to kill. Finding him won't be any more difficult," he said with absolute conviction.

As lies went, I wasn't sure if it was solely for me or if he was lying to himself too. The really good lies are flexible that way. Two days later we made a deal with the devil and all lies went out the window. And so did the comfort that went with them.

8

Caleb's message was stained with blood, fresh and red.

It wasn't George's blood. No, the warm liquid flowed freely from another source, the message itself. That would be Flay, or, as he was better known, our old pal Snowball. A message, he wasn't bright enough to be a messenger. Inert piece of shit was the best he could hope for.

He had come to our door only minutes ago. After two days . . . two days of no sleep as we scoured the city. Endlessly falling. Two days of hating myself for not telling her what she wanted to hear, not telling her the truth of what I felt for her. I could've been honest with her for once. I could've made her happy. Could've made myself happy, but no. Why the fuck would I want to do that?

And then Caleb had called this morning. He'd accepted our deal when Niko called days ago, accepted it promptly. We would waive our fee for the Boaz job and the Kin would help search for George. He told us that Cerberus would be sure to go along. Not a problem. The Alpha knew a good business deal when he saw it. We should've been suspicious, but we weren't. It *was* a good deal for them. Yeah, we just didn't know how good. At least, for Caleb.

He'd said he'd send Flay, his wolf, with information on what they'd found so far in their search. He lied. That wasn't the information Flay had come bearing at all, and what he had brought was now causing the living shit to be beaten out of good old Snowball. We'd thought Cerberus had a spy in his organization. He did and he didn't. The spy was Caleb, but he wasn't in the organization. Wasn't Cerberus's accountant. Didn't work for Cerberus at all, although he coveted something of his pretty fiercely, it seemed. He *was* the one, however, who had leaked the information to Boaz that we were coming. He'd wanted to know if we could "handle" ourselves. Lucky us, we proved that we could. And when we did, he had taken George. Now he wanted to make a trade. He wanted us to do the dirty work, and it was Flay's bad luck he got to pass along this little tidbit of joy. Get me what I want or your little psychic dies. "Dies"—that wasn't the word Flay had dutifully parroted in his shattered-glass voice. It was something far worse than that.

My hands circled the wolf's throat and slammed his head one more time against the floor. Crimson bloomed brilliantly against the blank canvas of his white hair and trailed from the corner of his mouth across transparently pale skin. And with the next thudding blow our floor turned red as well. The contrast wasn't as striking as it could be, but it still made me happy. Very, very happy. Goddamn ecstatic, in fact.

"If he kills him, it could make things worse." Goodfellow's voice came faintly through the haze, sounding indifferently musing and not particularly sympathetic to a certain albino wolf. "Of course, could isn't *necessarily* would."

While Robin didn't have strong feelings either way about Flay living or dying, Niko did. A hand fisted itself in the back of my shirt and lifted me off the wolf. "Cal, stop it."

With the sound of tearing cloth, I pulled away from his grip. The rage was a white-hot noise in my brain that blocked any other emotion from penetrating. But that was fine by me. I loved rage. It was better than fear or pain or agony. Better than despair, guilt, and desperation. Yeah, rage was my friend right now, and I wasn't ready to turn loose of it yet.

But before my hands could regain their grip I was yanked backward again, this time with an unyielding arm around my throat. "Don't make me choke you out, little brother," Niko warned quietly at my ear, "because I will."

Sucking in a breath that did little to tame the bubbling acid rising through my stomach and lungs, I rested my chin on Niko's arm. I stared down at the blood on my hand that made the fist I formed slippery and warm. The stitches that wreathed my other arm from elbow to hand were torn in spots and leaking my own blood to mix with Flay's. "Okay." It came out strangled and hoarse and that had nothing to do with the arm pressed against my neck. "I'll be"—the grin that twisted my face was carved with the darkest of knives—"good."

"Good is a relative term. As long as you don't kill him." The arm fell away as Niko amended grimly, "At least not quite yet."

Not yet. I could live with not yet . . . just barely.

Niko crouched beside the fallen Flay. He took in the blood, the lips locked in a rictus of pain, the ruby quartz eyes full of seething fury. "Not a good day for you," Niko observed icily. "Quite a shame."

"Oh, I don't know." Still leaning against the kitchen

counter, Robin examined his latest manicure. "Caleb seems like a progressive creature. Perhaps our hairy friend here has a nice worker's comp package. This may be a dream come true for him." The smile he flashed was vulpine. "Then again, funeral benefits might be even better."

"Now . . . I'm certain Caleb has long deserted his office, but why don't you verify that for me." Niko straightened the collar of the wolf's black jacket with exquisite care, then wrapped his hand lightly around his already bruised throat. His fingers rested on the carotid pulse. "If you lie, I'll know it, and then . . . well, then I'll have to hurt you. Perhaps even maim you for life. And I don't want that. I don't enjoy setting a bad example for my impressionable younger brother. So, please, do cooperate."

It was a long speech for Nik, and he meant every word of it. Standing behind him, I watched as white lashes blinked with an uneasiness the automatic snarl couldn't hide. Working his mouth, Flay turned his head cautiously in Niko's grip and spit blood onto our floor. Oversized pointed yellowed teeth showed as his lips peeled back and he gave a strangled hiss. "Gone. Caleb . . . gone."

Big surprise.

"Do you know where he is?" The long fingers tightened on the pale throat until they almost sank from sight. "And, Flay, do think carefully before you answer. An albino wolf might not ever be Alpha in the pack, but a *paralyzed* wolf is five steps below a lame sheep."

Flay didn't have to think. His options were extremely limited at the moment and he knew it. With hatred warping the lines of his face into a violent mask, he told the truth. "No. Don't. Don't . . . know. Gone."

Caleb was gone and damn unlucky Flay was left in his place. Murderous, stupid, and too loyal for his own good—it wasn't a combination tailor-made for survival. Now ask me if I give a shit. Braced on one knee, my brother continued to study the increasingly blue wolf under his hand. When the blue shaded to a delicate lilac and Flay's heels began to drum against the floor, Niko released him. "Annoying." Standing, he repeated, "Very annoying." Insinuating a toe under the wheezing, coughing wolf's side, he expertly flipped him over onto his stomach and pulled his hands behind him. "Handcuffs," he said tersely.

Despite being in the midst of emotions as malignant as any cancer, I felt my eyebrows rise. We didn't have handcuffs. It wasn't as if we were going to drag a howling, jaywalking ghoul down to the local jail. If any eventuality could be prepared for, Niko would be standing at the front of the line. But this? But before I could ask what the hell he was talking about, Goodfellow dangled a pair from a finger. "I could show you something in a velvet-lined manacle," he offered matter-of-factly, "but I doubt you would be interested."

With a sideways glance, I took them and handed them to Niko, murmuring into his ear, "I know you two bonded while I was off trying to destroy the world, but exactly *how* did you go about it?"

The provoked indignation narrowing Nik's eyes was faked, but it helped. It did. As much as it could. "Needlepoint, mainly," he said with a quirk of his lips. "Backgammon on occasion." Cinching the cuffs tight enough to draw a protesting groan, he yanked the panting wolf to his feet. Pointing at the couch, he ordered, "Sit." Foam on his lips, both from near strangulation and fury, Flay staggered, then obeyed. "Good boy. Behave and I won't kill you. Misbehave . . . and

I still won't kill you." Niko didn't smile often, and this tiny, lethal curve of the lips was no exception. "But, Flay, my fluoride-challenged friend, this not killing of you? It will last a week . . . minimum."

Flay wasn't at the top of his puppy class by any stretch of the imagination, but he got the drift. Ducking his head, bone ivory and scarlet, he stared sullenly downward. White lips writhed. "Behave."

"That is *so* what Daddy likes to hear." Robin moved over to Niko, then leaned past, and with a motion so fast that I barely caught the blur of it, he rammed a butcher knife from the kitchen into the millimeters-thick space separating Flay's legs. George was cherished, and by more than just me. With the handle resting snugly against his goody bag, the wolf went instantly green. It wasn't as if he could get much paler. "Simply because I'm third in line for your company, you parasite-ridden cur, I don't want you thinking I'll miss my turn," the puck said silkily. Straightening, Goodfellow tilted his head in Nik's direction. "Sorry. I know you chop your tofu with that." Then his eyes cut to me and he gave a disparaging sniff. "Or trim your toenails."

More desperate humor that fell flat, but I appreciated the effort. I appreciated anything that for a split second kept me from picturing George in Caleb's keeping. His not-so-gentle keeping. He'd fooled me, the son of a bitch. I should've known teeth like that are never purely decorative.

"Snowball." I wiped Flay's blood from my hands onto my jeans. "Snowball, Snowball." Resting my foot against the coffee table, I rammed it hard enough against his knees that the wood splintered and he howled in pain. Oddly enough, that fell squarely in the category of things I just didn't give a shit about. When he was done moaning, and it was fairly quick—

Caleb had hired a tough bastard—I asked in a voice empty and sterile, "So, what does the son of a bitch want?"

Flay's voice droned. On and on. A broken chunk of word here, a bit of twisted-metal phrase there—he coughed up Caleb's instructions . . . along with the occasional spray of blood. Yeah, wasn't that a shame? Not too surprisingly, it wasn't going to be simple. That didn't mean we couldn't do it. We could. To get George back we could do anything. And afterward, Caleb wouldn't live long enough to enjoy his little trinket.

"A crown?" Robin echoed disparagingly. "Really? That look went out long before toupees and polyester did, but if Caleb is so determined, I'm sure any rhinestone-loving street vendor can help him out."

"It . . . special. Special," Flay pushed out doggedly. He'd already said that. Trouble was, he didn't know what type of special it was. He had a description; hell, he had a full-color sketch in his pocket, but why Caleb lusted after the damn thing . . . on that, he couldn't guess. That was making the generous assumption Flay had the brain cells to even wonder at his boss's motivation.

On the paper, Caleb's desire was depicted as a simple circlet of metal, an oddly rosy gold. It didn't look like much, but that didn't change the fact that to get it was going to take some doing. Cerberus had it. The Cerberus we'd thought we were dealing with all along. Caleb didn't work for him, but Flay did. Snowball, double agent. It was laughable and even Flay knew it. Niko had asked him why he couldn't sniff around and find the thing himself since he was one of Cerberus's own. "Stupid." Bloody lips twisted. "Stupid. Caleb say. Cerb . . . erus say." The eyes flared in dull outrage, but there was also acceptance. Flay recognized his limitations, no matter how he might resent them. Since both his bosses derided him, Caleb must've been paying the most. Betraying someone like Cerberus couldn't come cheap.

Flay might not have been smarter than your average toilet fungus, but Caleb was. He'd planned this all perfectly. We'd proved we could take on a wolf as powerful as Boaz. In the same stroke we'd also been given an in with Cerberus. We'd kicked Boaz's ass, maybe killed him. Cerberus couldn't help but have at least a mild interest in someone who had taken down his rival. It would get us an audience with His Furry Majesty if nothing else.

There was more from Flay, but it was all repetition. Useless bullshit. I walked away as Flay mumbled on. Just . . . walked away. Down the hallway, into Niko's room, and out of the window. The metal of the fire escape clattered under my weight as I sat. The evening air was thick and humid, unwilling to cool, and the snarled traffic moved sluggishly like a turbulent river of overheated metal. I rested folded arms on raised knees and let my eyes unfocus. I kept my eyes on the river, traveling with it as the light disappeared from the sky and hundreds of lights blossomed below. Yellow, white, and eye-searing blue, a river full of stars.

"Is there room?"

Wordlessly, I moved over and Niko settled beside me, shoulder to shoulder. "Goodfellow left to see if he can trace Caleb with his much vaunted 'connections,' " he said quietly after a moment. "He's also taking care of Flay."

I didn't ask what he meant by that. I'd like to have hoped it was shorthand for Robin shoving the wolf headfirst down the garbage disposal, but unfortunately I had my doubts. My brother was too smart for that. Whether we liked it or not, Flay was our only real connection to Caleb *and* Cerberus. Keeping him alive was the only choice we had, as much as I hated it. Maybe Robin would board him at the nearest kennel and have him neutered while he was at it. Hell, I could dream, couldn't I?

"We have a starting point, Cal. It's something."

I gave a distant nod. Sure. It was something. And the river flowed on.

With olive-skinned hands clasped loosely over a knee, Niko waited. He patiently sat with me in silence, and it was what I needed; it was all I was capable of right then. I didn't try to guess how many hours I was out there or how many Niko sat at my side, but when I finally spoke my voice was rusty with disuse. "What's one more undercover gig, right?"

His eyes moved from the flowing lights to me. "After what you've been through, I never thought there would be a time that I would wish I weren't human. Yet lately it seems to happen more and more."

Niko couldn't go with me. A half Auphe might be reviled, but a human was less than nothing. You don't fraternize with your food. And you definitely don't hire it. "Promise would never let you around all those foxy were-babes anyway." I tried for a grin but my mouth wouldn't cooperate. I closed my eyes and leaned my head back against the window frame. "You'll still be there, Cyrano, in all the ways that count. Every ass I kick will be thanks to you."

"It should be enough for a teacher." There was the faintest whisper of cloth against cloth. "It's not."

It was a bitch of position for Niko to be in, worse than the poker game. This time there would be no wire, no bailout if I got into trouble. No way to even *know* if I was in trouble. While a wire could go undetected for the few hours a poker game would take, it wouldn't do for deep cover, the kind where you lived and breathed your role every minute of the day. But I'd be all right. Hell, I'd only be faking what I'd been in reality the year before.

"You don't have to go in alone."

But I did. Robin couldn't go. Most of the monsters considered pucks inveterate liars and thieves, capable of bleeding you dry between one breath and the next. Greedy, rapacious, and incurably light-fingered. Good-fellow wasn't like that. Well, okay, maybe he was, but he was also a friend. But even if the wolves thought Robin was pure as the driven snow and worthy of a friendly butt sniffing or two, I didn't want him in the direct line of fire. Promise either. Look what had happened to George. Just goddamn look.

"Yeah, Nik, I do," I said solidly, opening my eyes and turning to him.

"No." He exhaled and forged on without visible emotion. "I can't go, but you're forgetting Flay. Robin's turning him loose in the morning."

"Rover? You've got to be kidding," I said incredulously. "He's a crotch-sniffing moron."

"Yes, but he's Cerberus's crotch-sniffing moron. Caleb gave him to us for a reason. We would be stupid not to use him." A pigeon, silver and white, flashed overhead in the twilight. "And right now we can't afford to be stupid, for Georgina's sake."

Truth. I shoved fingers in my hair and tried to clear the thickness in my throat. "What do you think this thing is for?" I asked abruptly. "What Caleb wants." I doubted seriously that he was into it for the fashion aspect only. There was a purpose to it, had to be.

"That's a good question and Promise is working on that as we speak. She said it will keep her scarce for a day or two."

"So much for romance, huh?" The dating life of

vampire and do-it-yourself ninja once again took a backseat to my train wreck of a life. "Sorry," I said briefly.

"Don't be an ass, Cal," he said sharply. "None of this has anything to do with you. With both of us, yes, but not just you. Caleb wanted us as a team. I may not be on the inside with you, but that doesn't mean I'll be idle." No, Niko could never be that. If something happened, he would have to find another way to save George.

"Any guilt on this we share fifty-fifty," he continued. "You understand that, don't you?" No one had a way of turning a question into a threat quite like my brother.

"Gotcha." I climbed to my feet and gave Niko the faintest of smiles. "You're the king of tough love, Cyrano. All hail the king."

The long nose snorted. "You on bended knee. Why can I not picture that?" He nudged me toward the window. "Go to bed, Cal. You need the sleep or you won't be any good to anyone tomorrow. Not to me. Not to Georgina," he finished seriously.

He was right. But it didn't stop the sound of her name from hitting me like a punch to the gut. Still, I'd made a promise. No more angsting, no more wailing and beating of the breast. It wasn't helping me, and it wasn't helping George.

Right now, nothing was.

9

Cerberus.

Let's talk about Cerberus. Days ago, when this shit had begun, Promise had said she didn't know what his "difference" was, why he was considered damaged and unfit by most of his fellow Kin. And I hadn't thought any more about it. In the beginning, I didn't care. And in the end . . . I didn't care, although for different reasons. Apathy versus berserk rage, yet the results were the same.

But back to my new boss, Cerberus. There were a lot of things to be said about Cerberus, but let's focus on the primary one.

Cerberus was freaky as shit.

I wasn't saying that I hadn't seen some weirdness in my day. Nothing could be further from the truth. So while Cerberus wasn't the most bizarre thing I'd ever come across, he was damn close. And would it have killed Flay to just throw out the word "twins"? Granted, Snowball was as incoherent as your typical pot-smoking fast-food worker, but one simple word was all I was asking for. Okay, I might have wondered why twins went by one name, but I might have been a little more prepared. Because, honestly . . . I took a closer look . . . *damn.*

"Flay says that—" one began.

"You wish to join us," the other finished.

I hoped that they didn't do that a lot. It was disturbing . . . like a cutesy gum commercial gone horrifically wrong. There was no pleasure here to be doubled, that was for damn sure. Taking a seat in one of the two chairs facing the desk, I leaned back in the opulent leather and tried to give the impression that I was unruffled by what stared at me from behind the desk. "What better place for someone like me? I've heard you look past differences, past"—I didn't have to fake the bitter twist of my lips—"bad breeding."

Look at me. Cool and calm. Hell on wheels and the biggest balls around. That was on the outside. On the inside I had to wonder if I was more than a little nuts to be pitting my woefully amateur undercover skills against *that*. I definitely saw why that son of a bitch Caleb wanted someone else to do his dirty work. To give my own eyes a rest, I snatched a fleeting look around the office. The place was a palace. All that was missing was the harem. Although, to give credit where credit was due, Cerberus did have a good start. A succubus was filing her three-inch pointed nails while draped liquidly over a couch against the far wall. With hair of midnight blue and storm-cloud silver cascading on her shoulders, she gave me a quick pout that had her finely scaled mother-of-pearl breasts heaving. A flutter of sapphire-colored eyelashes over liquid black eyes ended the flirtation, and she went back to ignoring me.

Cerberus, on the other hand, studied me unblinkingly from behind a desk the size of a small car. At least, one of them did. One head stared at me with slanted brown eyes that flared molten gold as the other turned to address the guard at the door. "Find Orrin. He's overdue and I want a report." The voice was cold and utterly emotionless, just like the eyes. It was unusual for a wolf. Whether it was raging anger, murderous glee, or overwhelming horniness, the lupines usually wore their tiny hearts and even tinier minds on their sleeve for everyone to see. The difference in Cerberus was startling and a little troubling.

Both of the heads had zeroed in on me now, and I made a mental note to kick myself later on for not wondering how Cerberus had gotten his name. The three-headed dog guarding the gates of hell . . . this Cerberus had only the two heads, but, hey, who was I to bitch? Humans produced conjoined twins on occasion and so did the animal kingdom, but I'd never heard of the wolf community producing any. As I'd thought to myself earlier, weakness was not tolerated in lycanthropic society, and as a rule a wolf like Cerberus should've been promptly killed at birth with one swipe of its mother's jaws. How these two had survived was a mystery, a damn unnerving one. There had to be a name for that type of conjoining. Niko would know it . . . if he were here. One heavily built body, two sleek heads with identical vulpine faces, short black hair slicked back into an impenetrable pelt over well-shaped skulls—that was the human form of Cerberus. I wasn't looking forward to seeing the wolfen version. Unlike Snowball, Cerberus was of the old breeding; he could choose to be either wolf or human.

The twins wore a suit in charcoal gray, expensive even to my untrained eye, and, beneath that, an ebony-colored shirt with two mandarin-style collars. It must have been a bitch to accommodate the unnaturally broad shoulders and bifurcated spinal column, but the unknown tailor had risen to the challenge. Thick but immaculately manicured nails tapped the desktop in a vaguely familiar rhythm. Then it hit me.

Peter and the Wolf. Jesus, this guy was something else. "Bad breeding indeed." Identical broad noses flared to gather my scent. "A foul, disgusting joining."

The one to the right had spoken first and then the one on the left. I realized I was going to have to either designate them as Cerberus One and Cerberus Two in my head or simply go with the flow and think of them as one creature, as Cerberus seemed to think of himself.

"Foul and disgusting," I drawled, slouching down farther and crossing my ankles. "That's me. But I'm also loyal, if the money's right. I can take care of myself, not to mention pretty much anything else that crosses my path." The grin I flashed this time wasn't bitter, but it was still dark . . . dark and gleeful. And then I gave him the cherry on top. "And I'm mean."

In wolf terms that meant one thing. I played with my food. It was a trait with which any of the Kin would find favor—because, after all, killing is business. But torture? That's *art.*

"Ah, is that so?" The nails stopped tapping, fingers stilled. The eyes took in the stitches that showed on my wrist, peeking from beneath the sleeve of my jacket. "Boaz."

"A bad poker player," I snorted. "And a worse loser." He was bound to have heard of the Boaz incident and not just from Flay. I only hoped the fight had been wild enough to make the details less than clear. Promise, as she wasn't here to kick my ass, I could pass off as a lover or an employer. Niko, however . . .

"He plays less now that he rots in a Jersey pet cemetery." There were identical cold grins, and then a less-than-casual "I hear there was a human there who did damage as well. Blond, with a sword." The head on the right was still with me. The one on the left had let his grin disappear and his eyelids fall to a brooding half-mast, but still kept his gaze fixed on me. Fixed on me hard.

"Yeah." I gave a light sneer. "I figured he was a bouncer." Cerberus had only to check to know that wasn't true, but even if he did, I hadn't said Niko was the bouncer . . . only that I thought he was. Facing my prospective new employer, I'd take uninformed and not particularly bright over the label of liar any day. "A puck will hire anything. But to give credit where it's due, he was tough." My sneer deepened. "For a human."

"For a sheep," came the correction. The massive body shifted, only slightly, but it still displaced the air like an avalanche. There was an innate sense of power about Cerberus, more natural than supernatural. A force of nature—tornado, hurricane, earthquake—it could be more destructive than any monster. I could see Flay's motivation to betray him. With this holding your leash, how could you fail to be chronically pissed? No doubt Cerberus didn't react to failure well. Hell, a bad hair day probably resulted in bodies far and wide. Flay wasn't the quickest, wasn't the smartest. He had to screw up on occasion. And he was bound to pay the price. Maybe it wasn't money he wanted for his betrayal—maybe it was simply revenge. But whatever Flay's reasoning, he had gotten me an audience with Cerberus. Now it was my job to make it work.

"For a sheep," I agreed lazily.

"You're half-sheep as well." A knuckle, thick and large, rapped the satin surface of his desk once. Immediately the succubus abandoned her couch and nail file to slink over. And a very definite slink it was. It wasn't all sexual (although certainly that was a big portion of it). It was partly the snake genes. Succubi couldn't walk without a wiggle even if they wanted to. She moved behind Cerberus and began a slow massage, paying equal attention to both necks. Not stopping there, she used a forked black tongue to caress the curve of each ear. Considering my own genetic makeup, I didn't have a lot of room to talk, but that didn't stop an inner "*gah*" and shudder.

I tried to ignore the *Wild Kingdom* mating bleeps and blunders before my eyes and tilted my head slightly. "Yeah, Mom. What a woman. There wasn't a dick that wasn't her friend, demonic or not." Of course that wasn't precisely true. Sophia had done it for the money, but now was not the time to be splitting hairs.

"Human or Auphe. Hard to determine which is more objectionable." Both heads exhaled and then said together with distaste, "Human."

To them it was probably true. Auphe had been feared and loathed, but they were still reluctantly respected. Humans, though . . . what was there to respect about them? From a Kin point of view, absolutely nothing. "And what happened to your slut of a sheep mother—"

"Who fornicated above her station?"

I smiled. It was a happy smile. Pure, honest, and satisfied.

"I ate her."

Of course, I hadn't actually eaten Sophia, but I couldn't help thinking she would've fit in here better than I did. Flay was introducing me to creatures with no conscience and a leg-humping rampant sexuality, and that was Sophia all over. The process of introduction wasn't exactly painless, but I wasn't sure who was more put out by it: my new co-workers or me.

Needless to say, I wasn't enjoying it. But I had to

pretend that I was. The story went that Flay had known someone who had known someone who was the cousin of someone who'd been at the bar when the poker game went down. Or the equivalent of it. And that's how he'd come to make my unparalleled acquaintance. It was weak, but it made more sense than that he had tracked down the presumed Boaz slayer on his own initiative. Anyone who'd met Snowball would know that was damn unlikely. So, for now, Flay and I were buds, pals . . . probably borrowed each other's flea collar on a regular basis. Until I could kill him, that's the way it would have to be.

Cerberus had his office in a converted warehouse on Watts Street. I didn't know why he needed all that space, but at least it wasn't quite as clichéd as setting up shop in a bar or strip club. While his office was an oasis of all that was rich and decadent, the rest of the place was typical. Concrete floor, high unfinished ceiling, the smell of sawdust and mold, puddles of suspicious fluids . . . I glared at Flay and shook my foot. Droplets flew through the air and I gave an annoyed hiss at the ammonia stench. "You walk upright, most of the time, and you fur balls aren't even house-trained? Jesus."

Flay bared his teeth at me. It could've been a grin, could've been a threat; it was hard to say. It was also hard to care either way. "Fenrik. Jaffer. Lijah. Mishka."

It seemed that Snowball, brain cell diminished or not, was as good at ignoring me as vice versa. He coughed up the names as if I hadn't just shaken stale piss on his leg. The four wolves they belonged to stared at me as if I'd fallen from the sky. White-eyed, lips stretched to nothing, and claws shredding the cardboard cards they held . . . they had me amending the thought. They stared at me as though I'd fallen from the sky to rape their women, turn their children into beer cozies, and try to sell them life insurance.

I grinned with faithless and malevolent cheer, then sketched a casual wave. "Hey, fellas, I'm the new guy. Bet you didn't smell *that* coming."

In the silence, a string of saliva dripped from one foreshortened muzzle to pool on the crate that doubled as a makeshift table.

"What? No fruit basket?" I leaned down and picked up a card, bending it back and forth between my fingers. "Poker again. You pups really have a thing for the game, don't you?"

"Auphe." It was the one that Flay had designated as Lijah that spoke. Jaffer, of the unhappily wet muzzle, simply continued to stare and drool.

"Really? Where?" I looked over my shoulder. Turning back, I rocked on my heels and folded my arms. "Oh, you mean *me*? Hardly. Half-Auphe at best. Maybe a hint in my profile." I tilted my head to give them the full effect. "Or in my sparkling personality."

"Definitely the humor of an Auphe," grunted Fenrik, a short but impressively squat wolf. "Funny as an infected anal gland." He took a handful of Jaffer's shaggy hair and shook the head without mercy. Clumps of fur flew. "You're a wolf, you neutered bastard. Act like one."

Jaffer cowered under the treatment and hastily wiped his mouth with a hairy arm. Fire engine red, the pelt sprang up in tufts from his arms and beneath the collar of his Yankees sweatshirt. The hair on his head he kept cut to about an inch in length, but it stood straight up. It looked like a brush fire was racing across his skull. His eyes were round and yellow and his face a furred expanse of muzzle and wet nose. Jaffer didn't go out much, I was guessing. For all intents and purposes he was an upright wolf with a buzz cut. There was no way he could pass. Not at night, not among the drunkest of humans. I felt an unwilling tug of sympathy for him. The rest of us monsters in the room could. I could fool any human. And Flay, Fenrik, Lijah, and Mishka, while not completely normal, could walk the streets with no more than a few curious glances. Actually Fenrik appeared nearly as human as I did except for his eyes. Almost white, the silver blue was the same color as a husky's eyes. His hair nearly matched. Despite that, he wasn't old, late thirties maybe. When he looked at me, I thought I saw a glitter of interest behind the repugnance. He might not love the Auphe, but he was curious to see one close-up . . . even the bastardized shadow of one. Fenrik would bear watching. He was smarter than the others.

Mishka had to be related to Jaffer. His hair was a lesser red, more of a dull copper, and his muzzle was really just a pronounced overbite, the nose human. His eyes were a green-and-gold hazel. Lijah was more greyhound than wolf. Whipcord lean, he had a sleek fall of brindled hair. Black flecked with gold and brown, it fell loose past his shoulders. It did a good job of concealing a pair of pointed ears and a jawline far too narrow for any distant relative of a primate.

All in all, a motley crew, and except for Jaffer, they all had an air of ruthless competence. They possessed a tautness, an invisible twitch under the skin that spoke of readiness and an aggressiveness stronger than a starving shark's. Some wolves loved the chase. Loved the taste of blood on the run. These guys definitely fell in the kill-to-run, run-to-kill category. Whatever the Kin might think of Cerberus, he wasn't a fool when it came to his boys. Even Flay. Snowball might be a betrayer and unlikely to follow in Einstein's footsteps, but he was tough. Resilient.

At the continuing silence, I moved over to shove Jaffer out of his chair. Fenrik was the obvious Alpha of this little group and Jaffer just as obviously low wolf on the totem pole. I wasn't about to take his place. The red wolf showed his teeth, oddly enough utterly human, but ducked and scuttled his way to one side. "Since I'm not much on butt sniffing as an introduction, why don't we play a hand?" I scooped up the cards and gave them a casual shuffle. "I guarantee you'll get next month's dip-and-groom money off of me. I suck."

Fenrik's pale eyes dilated and he changed. One second a man, the next a wolf. There was only a blur before my eyes, so quick that if I'd blinked, I would've missed it. Boaz had been fast, a trait of the old breeding, but this guy . . . he was quicker. I felt like applauding, so what the hell. I did. Three short claps. "Goddamn," I said. "I didn't even have to buy a ticket for the magic show. Is there popcorn? Can I buy a T-shirt when it's over?"

Two massive paws rested on the crate and black lips peeled back silently. It was shaping up to be Boaz all over again, except this time I was without Promise at my back or Niko busting down the door. And those were not good things to be without, trust me. Reaching under my jacket, I pulled out my shiny new gun. Flay had given it back to me after Cerberus had agreed to take me under his motherly wing. A thing of beauty, it was, and only slightly smaller than an anti-aircraft gun. I'd learned my lesson with Boaz and his boys, and I wanted stopping power this time. With stainless steel, a black rubber grip, and a futuristic barrel over ten inches long, the .50 Magnum was most often being used in big-game hunting. If these guys didn't count as big game, then I didn't know what did. It weighed more than your average five-year-old kid and I plunked it down with force on the crate between Fenrik and me. "You're making me cranky, Lassie," I said amiably. "Timmy might put up with your shit, but I won't."

The silent snarl turned into a buzz-saw rumble that ripped the air to shreds. Apparently Lassie wasn't particularly appreciative of *my* shit either. Then an unlikely peacemaker stepped in. Red eyes annoyed, Flay moved up to the crate, took a handful of silver fur and another of my jacket collar, and then shook us both—much as Fenrik had shaken Jaffer. "Work for Cerberus." He gave us another shake. "*All* work for Cerberus." Letting go, he took my gun and shoved it back against my chest and then pushed Fenrik's furry ass back down on his chair. "Stupid. Cerberus eat both. Stupid." He folded his arms and shook his head with disgust. "Shitheads."

I stood corrected. There was an Alpha, but it wasn't Fenrik after all. It was Flay. Flay of the sloping forehead, garbled speech, and self-proclaimed low IQ. I didn't know what the hell I thought about that. I reholstered my gun and reconsidered the situation at hand. "What the hell. Getting eaten on my first day isn't really a sound career plan anyway. Truce, Lassie?"

A naked Fenrik materialized out of the mass of wolf and stared at me with narrowed eyes. He might be interested in me, but it didn't mean he liked me. Who knew? Maybe that interest was more oriented on how a half Auphe would taste as opposed to simply seeing one in living color. As for his not liking me, that I was used to. If the situation were reversed, I probably wouldn't like me either.

"Truce." Fenrik ground out the reluctant word and started to dress. "I don't question the judgment of Cerberus. Not even in this."

"That's big of you." Smart as well. Cerberus didn't strike me as the kind to tolerate dissent in his ranks. At the ruby gleam aimed my way, I sighed and shifted my shoulders. "How about lunch on the new guy? Pizza. Steak. You guys name it. I'm buying."

I'd been working since I was sixteen, when we'd first gone on the run. Mostly in hole-in-the-wall bars, places that didn't care if you disappeared one day. Places that paid you under the table and didn't give a shit if you had ID or not. If I'd learned one thing there, it was that the way to coworker harmony was through food. And alcohol. Lots and lots of alcohol. I might not drink much of it, but I could fork over the money for it. "And I'll buy the first pitcher," I added. "Anyone got a bag to put over Jaffer's head?"

Steak it was—naturally. About four cows' worth. Below Fourteenth Street, the restaurant was medium-sized, dark as a cave, and fairly cheap. Of course, fairly cheap multiplied by five wolves was sure to empty the deepest wallet. There were porterhouse steaks all around, potatoes smothered in butter, sour cream, and cheese, and a pitcher of beer per wolf. Just breathing the air around us would harden your arteries, an exercise in secondhand cholesterol at its best. I chewed my own steak, rare—it wouldn't do to look like a predator puny enough to like his meat well-done. Who would buy that? The mouthful, harsh with the tang of blood, stuck in the back of my throat as I caught a glimpse of red in the gloom. A slim figure and copper hair, but the skin was creamy pale and the hair a short, straight cap. Not George. The pretty waitress saw me watching her and smiled a bit hesitantly. Considering the friends I was keeping, I didn't blame her.

I ducked my head, breaking the contact, and grimly continued with my meal. I was Auphe. The Auphe were ravenous in their appetites . . . all of their appetites. If I hoped to stay under Cerberus long enough to find what I was looking for, I would have to keep up with the boys. And right now the boys were making their way through slabs of meat with the speed and finesse of tree shredders. I stabbed another barely browned chunk with my fork, chewed, and chased it down with a swallow of beer. That was the one thing I held back on. As much as I needed to blend in, I couldn't afford to get drunk. I doubted I'd get loose of lip and jump up on the table to do a happy jig while singing the joys of being a spy. But it would slow my reflexes, not to mention any pretension at wits I might have. So I stuffed myself with steak and occasionally took a small sip of the beer.

It should've been noticed. Would've been, in fact, if Flay hadn't been helping himself to my glass on the sly. His tolerance was fine. The table was good-sized, but there were six of us with enough food for five buffets. It made for an impossible jumble of dishware. Since Flay was sitting beside me he could drain my glass without suspicion. And he did so, frequently. I slanted a sideways glance at him. No one had much faith in his intellectual skills . . . Caleb, Cerberus, even Flay himself, but I wondered. Did he maximize the minimal amount he had to work with? Or was it low self-esteem because of his wolf-scorned albinism?

Let daytime TV sort it out. My concern was George and only George. To get her back, I would take any help Flay would give me and be grateful for it. Right up until George was safe and Flay a badly skinned rug on my bedroom floor. As he noticed my attention and met my gaze, I tapped my fork against the edge of my plate and gave him a smile cold enough to burn my lips. White eyebrows lowered and a lip lifted just enough to reveal one jagged tooth. Genius or idiot, either one would know what I was picturing doing with that fork. Niko was more than capable of killing someone with the most innocent of kitchen utensils. I don't know if I could or not, but I was perfectly willing to throw myself into the spirit of experimentation and find out.

"More beer!"

Jaffer's slurred voice shifted my attention. He was wearing a sweatshirt with the hood pulled so far over his face that I could see only the faint glitter of his eyes and the wet shine of his nose, which seemed to be getting progressively more damp. I shook my head and hoped I wasn't going to end up washing dishes before this was over. The alcohol tab alone was going to be staggering. "More beer it is." I held up five fingers for the waitress, then pointed at an empty pitcher. "Cerberus doesn't mind the liquid lunches?"

"Not so much," Fenrik grunted. "Most of our work is done at night. During the day we just make ourselves available in case anything comes up. Consider us on call."

"Like doctors," Jaffer said with a happy slurp of tongue. The spray of saliva hit me all the way across the table and I reached for a napkin to blot my face.

Yeah, just like doctors. All they were missing were the stethoscopes. Dropping the napkin, I looked to my right, where Lijah had finished his third steak while I was still working on my first. Thin as a rail, but damn if he couldn't pack it away. "You guys been with Cerberus long?"

There was a shrug of the lean shoulders. "Long enough. He's a good Alpha, as long as you do what you're told." He said it with a confidence tinged faintly with uneasiness.

"And do it well," Mishka added glumly, raising a hand to reveal three missing fingers. Doing what you're told was easy enough . . . if that's what you wanted. Doing it well was sometimes a little harder.

"Looks like you screwed up at least once there, Mish." I pushed my plate away, my stomach tight with food. "Or Cerberus is seriously into the finger foods."

"Cerberus is a good Alpha," Fenrik repeated stone-faced. "He gives many a chance that no other Kin would touch." He pointed his own fork at me. "Many like you."

The thing was . . . it was true. Well, not that there were many quite like me, but I got his point. There were all sorts of monsters, layers upon layers and always one worse than the next. Monsters being monsters, there was also prejudice, blatant and severe. If you were different, in any way, someone would be happy to eat you for it. The nonhuman were completely honest in their hatred, no government mandate required. Cerberus was a change from the norm. Overcoming his own difference—by sheer force and a river of blood, I was guessing—he'd gathered other outsiders around him. And he'd made it work. He'd made the Kin accept him and his pack. That was one helluva feat, even for a cold-blooded Kin murderer.

"You're right," I admitted as I reached for my wallet and turned it inside out over the table. "No one likes the Auphe. No one respects a human. And no one, but no one, wants to work with either one. Cerberus is *the* Alpha in my book." I thumbed through the pile of cash. There was enough, barely, and I wedged it under an empty pitcher. "You guys finish up the beer. I've got some business to take care of."

"What kind of business?" Fenrik asked with immediate suspicion.

I aimed a leer at the gaggle of waitresses by the bar. "Guess."

"Back . . . eight." Flay scowled. "Business . . . too. Cerberus business."

"Eight. Gotcha."

"Human?" Mishka looked at the waitresses and made a hissing sound of disgust. "They're soft. No fire."

"Hey, unlike your gals, humans are in heat *all* the time." I tried for a Goodfellow tone, salacious and carnal. I'd heard it so often I could probably do a reasonable imitation in my sleep. "And they make a nice snack afterward." Slapping the table, I headed out . . . just your average cannibalistic ladies' man. Nothing to see here. Outside, lunchtime had faded into late afternoon. The sky was blue tinged with yellow, the air heavy and thick. It glued my jacket to me with a wallpaper paste of my own sweat. It would've been a relief to sink into the dubious air-conditioning of a taxi, but in this instance comfort would have to be sacrificed for caution. Wiping at the back of my neck, I trudged into the crowd and hopefully disappeared.

The hostel room was several layers below disgusting. Or it had been. Now, thanks to my visitor, it was immaculately neat and as sterile as an operating room. Nik, only Nik. He couldn't do anything about the bedspread and carpet of hideous, clashing colors that only a clown on acid could love or the junkyard-cheap furniture, but the dirt was a different matter. He'd apparently scrubbed the place down with ruthless efficiency and an entire vat of bleach. I closed the door behind me and gave a low whistle. "Dr. Obsessive-compulsive, I presume."

"You stink of beer and red meat." He sat cross-legged on the bed, a serene statue repeatedly tossing and catching his knife so quickly that it was a silver pinwheel spinning in the air before him.

"Bonding with the boys." I grabbed the desk chair and straddled it. "They ravaged my liver and then my wallet."

The long nose wrinkled fastidiously, but he let it go. "You weren't followed?"

"No." Which was why I'd walked, taken the subway . . . doubled back at several stops, then walked some more. Rubbing at my eyes, I asked, "Promise or Robin get any information on Caleb or his crown?"

"Not so far." Catching his knife, he uncoiled and moved to the edge of the bed. Tapping my knee with the point of his throwing blade, he asked quietly, "Are you all right?"

"Yeah," I said, dismissive. "So far I've just eaten steak and been hit with about a gallon of drool. Nothing to write home about."

There was one more tap, oddly reassuring; then the knife vanished. "And Cerberus?"

I grimaced, caught in the lie. "I didn't need a change of shorts, but it was a close thing. He's a cold son of a bitch. Or they are. Hell, I don't know."

"Ah." His mouth twitched, Niko's equivalent of a smug grin. "We may have come up empty on Caleb's location or the history behind the crown, but getting a background on Cerberus was easily enough accomplished. He has no secrets he wishes to keep hidden—on the surface, anyway. And the word you've no doubt been searching for is 'dicephalus.' One body, two heads."

"Smart-ass." The air of industrial-strength cleaner

clung to the plastic and imitation wood of my chair and I swallowed a sneeze. At least it smelled clean . . . for the first time. I'd been staying at the hostel on the Bowery for two days now. I needed to be well and truly separated from the others if Cerberus did some cursory checking of his own. I could've stayed someplace a little more upscale, but I also wanted to give the impression I was in this for the money. Just your average working stiff willing to kill, mutilate, and wreak havoc for the Kin's version of minimum wage.

"How is Flay living up to his felonious end?" he asked, his austere features tightened with minute distaste. A traitor and a kidnapper's accomplice—neither would appeal to my brother's code of conduct, and Flay was both.

"Believe it or not, pretty well." I frowned, then straightened to shrug off my jacket and holster. A gun that size was good for one thing and one thing only, and carrying it under your armpit wasn't that one thing. Massaging the chafed area through my shirt, I continued. "Either he's smarter than we thought or he's hell on wheels in the instinct department."

"It could be both. Either way, don't be tempted to turn your back on him."

"Grandma, please," I snorted. "Who are you talking to here?"

"You've been under too long already. You're speaking like a thug." He reconsidered dryly, "Then again, you've always spoken like a thug. That's one thing we can't lay at Caleb's door." Standing, he held out his hand. The throwing blade had reappeared to lie flat across his palm. "It's balanced for you."

I took it and hefted it. Nik's were normally featherlight, but this one was significantly heavier. Myself, I'd never owned one. I had my talents, but knife throwing wasn't one of them. "How do you know?" I said skeptically. "I don't use the toothpicks."

"It's weighted for a beginner—a rank amateur. I believe that would cover you." With a resigned exhalation, he patiently manipulated my hand into the correct position. "Not that it matters. This one isn't designed to do much damage. All you have to do is hit something . . . *anything* with the tip. It's silver-painted glass. Under that is a bit of electronic elegance that will let us know you need help." Satisfied with my grip, he let go. "That you're in trouble."

"Ye of little faith," I said absently, tucking the altered blade away. He was right, though. There was little chance that I would find the crown, steal it, and make it out without running into some sort of trouble. We both knew it, and Niko had to know it from a powerless distance. "Thanks, Cyrano. Worse comes to worst, I'll break it over my own head."

"It would be gratifying to see you use it for something," he retorted, leaving no doubts to what he was referring.

"Yeah, yeah." Pushing the chair away, I headed to the bed and flopped onto my stomach. I was still chronically short on sleep. There were dreams. Dreams of red hair soaked with redder blood. I was tired. So goddamn tired. I pillowed my head on my arms, closed my eyes, and delivered the bad news, "There's a job tonight. Eight. No idea what."

"Not unexpected." His tone said "not unexpected, but certainly unwanted." There was the light squeeze of fingers on my shoulder. "I'll be there." Niko already had the address of the warehouse from Flay. He would be able to follow us on whatever little job Cerberus had in mind. George wouldn't thank me if I hurt someone innocent while trying to save her. And she would know. Hell, *I* would know. I rolled over and grimaced at the sight of a cockroach trundling happily across the wall.

"Why didn't she see it coming?" I asked abruptly.

The change in subject didn't throw him. Knowing Niko . . . or better yet, knowing Niko *knowing* me, I realized he had to have been aware the question was lurking in my mind somewhere. There was a moment of silence as he considered the question. "Difficult to say," he said thoughtfully. "I would say that perhaps Georgina can't 'see' herself. At the center of her own psychic nexus, there could be a natural blind spot that surrounds her. But . . ."

"But what?" I prompted, when he paused.

There was the warmth of affection underlying the next words. "But knowing Georgina, she most likely simply didn't look."

Hadn't looked. And the thing was, I knew that was exactly what had happened. I'd known it all along, but I didn't want to admit it to myself. If I admitted it, then I also had to admit that it could've been avoided. It meant that if George had managed to overcome that whole "what's meant to be is meant to be" crap, even for just a minute, she might be safe now. If she had for once recognized like the rest of us that life was brutally short and mercilessly chaotic, she might have used a little goddamn common sense. She might be safe.

Blaming George for her own kidnapping—how much of a bastard did that make me? Maybe I deserved those dreams. From the exhaustion creeping in, I wasn't going to be able to avoid them much longer anyway. I rolled back over, subject closed. "Nap time. See you tonight, Nik."

"Doubtful." The mock disdain was a shade less convincing than usual. "I'm the wind, invisible. Untouchable. Unknowable." Then he made a subject change of his own. "How's your arm?"

"Fine," I murmured, voice and thoughts equally thick. "What arm?"

"That's what I thought."

He might have said something further, but I was out.

10

I woke up to the near-simultaneous sounds of a quietly closing door and the less subdued beeping of the alarm clock. Spitting out a mouthful of bedspread, I silenced the squealing box on the bedside table with a slap. I rolled out of bed and trudged to the door to check the hall, but Niko was already gone. As he'd said . . . the wind. He'd stayed to watch over me while I slept, and I vaguely remembered the occasional touch to my shoulder that had brought me out of nightmares into blissfully empty sleep. He'd also left a present for me on the table beside the clock. Hydrogen peroxide, antibiotic ointment, and a happily informative note telling me to clean my gangrenous arm before he was forced to chop it off. Brotherly love, the original sweet-and-sour dish.

I did as I was told. Contrary I might be, but truthfully the wounds were reddened and puffy. And the last thing I needed was for an infection to slow me down while I was in the midst of the dog pound. First I showered and took care of my arm, and then I made my way back to the warehouse for my first day on the job. I couldn't say that I was exactly showered with camaraderie when I stepped through the doors, but a beery burp and perfunctory growl instead of sincere

ones let me know I was one of the gang. A handful
of murderous lupines, and I had their acceptance. I
didn't want it, but I needed it. I needed it badly.

What I didn't need, however, was the foul and stinking breath ruffling the hair at my nape, but it was
there all the same.

"Do ya mind?" I snapped. "I'm half-human, and I
need the oxygen, okay? Your funky stench isn't quite
satisfying the lungs." It was a revenant. If you could
say one thing about Cerberus, it was that he was down
and dirty committed to the equal-opportunity concept.
A revenant . . . Jesus. Forget their pleasing and well-
rounded personalities for the moment; their stink
alone could clear a city block. Eat the dead, smell like
the dead; it was a logic that couldn't be escaped. Not
that they were above a warm meal once in a while.
Dead was just a preference.

There was a hiss like an angrily deflating balloon,
but the heat retreated from the back of my neck. I
felt the iron stiffness of my spine relax slightly. The
situation was tense enough; it didn't need poisonous
gas emanating from this shithead's filthy pores to
make it worse. Cerberus had personally given us our
marching orders for the night. It had been in the office
again, but this time he was alone . . . except for his
meal. The succubus was nowhere to be seen, which
was too bad. Whether she would know any deep, dark
secrets such as where Cerberus kept his jewelry box
was questionable. The head honchos didn't strike me
as the types to spill the post-coital beans, but who
knew? One thing I did know was that Goodfellow
would be better qualified to find out. At the end of
that exchange, if anyone were sucked dry of their life
force, I'd bet my first Kin paycheck that it wouldn't
be Robin. A dirty job, he'd say, is the very best kind.

My dirty job, a much less enjoyable one, was watching Cerberus eat. Wolves liked to eat, big surprise, almost as much as they liked mating and killing. They gave a new twist to the old adage: If you can't eat it or screw it, you may as well kill it. Fine as far as it went, but wolves were of a mind to do at least two at once . . . if not all three. The whole species wasn't psychotically bloodthirsty, not entirely. But as I watched a liver ripped from a gaping wound and shredded under bloodstained fangs, I found that truth hard to hold on to.

Cerberus hadn't completely changed to wolf form, which was too bad. That might not have been as disturbing. The hands had thickened and gnarled, sprouting claws and a fine downy coat of black hair. Teeth had elongated to fangs as thick as my thumb and half again as long. The two skulls had flattened into wicked wedges with overgrown jaws, low foreheads, and moist flaring nostrils. Otherwise, the mostly hairless faces and ferociously intelligent eyes still looked human. The body itself was nude and faintly sheened with the same misting of black hair found on the hands. The nudity was a combination of a wolf's natural lack of shame and a convenient way to avoid ruining the expensive suit folded off to one side. Cerberus wasn't what you'd consider a tidy eater. As the body crouched over its dinner, blood splattered onto its broad chest. Still, if it weren't for the hands and faces, it would be possible to take them for men . . . hairy men, but just men. Yeah, let's revisit disturbing. Disturbing just wasn't doing the job in the description department. It was a night-and-day contrast to my morning meeting with the wolves. Cerberus had been all business then . . . coldly powerful and deadly, yes, but restrained. Now . . . now the savagery was so matter-of-fact, so casual, that you knew ripping apart a still-warm body was nothing more than supper, mundane as a tuna fish sandwich was to me.

"I have business for you," the head on the right spoke, the words dropping like stones from blood-stained lips.

That wasn't news. It was why we'd been called into the principal's office, to get the details. But when the one on the left gave us those details, I wished I'd stayed in the hostel and played count-the-cockroach. I'd known it might be bad. Hell, I was the last one to wallow in delusions of optimism, but I hadn't realized how grisly it could be. Would be. Swallowing the bile that burned bonfire hot in my throat, I exited the office with my partners in crime. Behind me the sounds of feeding resumed. There was one poor son of a bitch who should never have signed his donor card.

And that's how I ended up outside a homeless shelter picking out people to die.

I was also wondering fairly frantically what Niko was going to do about it. A hard, painful grip on my injured arm ended my wondering for the moment. "Choose. Lazy," Flay hissed in my ear. "Lazy . . . *work*." If he was overheard, and with the wolf ears around us he would be, it would look as if Flay was only giving a slacker a boot in the ass. A slacker was better than a spy any day of the week. I jerked my arm out of his grip and did as ordered. I chose. Randomly. I couldn't look at the people and I didn't . . . only pointed at them and then the bus. The others, on the other hand, were selecting by size, wanting the plumpest of prize pigs. We'd brought a bus for the livestock; it was dingy white, beat-up, and old, but scrupulously clean. The story was that we were a charitable medical organization busing a lucky group of the homeless to a new free clinic in Brooklyn where they would be given a physical. The ones that were sick would be promptly treated, also at no charge, and all provided with a nutritious box dinner. Yeah, it was a load of crap, but it would work. It *was* working.

Where this busload of people would end up, I wasn't precisely sure. It was in Brooklyn, Snowball had said, but it sure as hell wasn't at a clinic. Being sold for food was probably what lay in their future. To whom? Anyone. Everyone. Offhand, I couldn't think of too many monsters that *didn't* eat humans. Cerberus had driven that home earlier. Usually monsters caught their own, but you had to hand it to the Kin and my new boss. Sometimes you liked a full-on, dress-for-it dinner and sometimes you liked to pop something in the microwave, quick and easy. And now, for a price, they had your quick and easy right here. Don't feel like leaving the house to bag supper? Why should you? You've got a homeless Popsicle neatly folded in your freezer.

Despite myself, I did a quick scan of the general area, looking over the street and ugly, run-down buildings. Nothing. Niko had been right; I didn't see him. Although I knew he was there and knew it without a doubt, I still wished I could see him, calm and confident. Planwise, I was coming up empty. I couldn't make a move without giving myself away, and if I gave up myself, I gave up George.

Feeling eyes on me, I turned to see the milky orbs of the revenant staring at me from behind dark glasses. He was lucky it was twilight. With perpetually moist, salamander flesh, multiple joints, and the teeth of a demonic ferret, he'd have a harder time passing than Jaffer did. Some quarters said revenants were people returned from the dead. Nah. From a distance, a *long* distance, they did have the appearance of a corpse in the first stages of decomposition . . . a corpse with the speed and appetite of a trapdoor spider. But that aside, revenants had never been human.

I ignored him. Easy enough to do since he was downwind. It was less easy to watch as shambling men and women with ragged clothes and thousand-yard stares climbed onto the bus to be transported to their deaths. And fucking clever guy that I was, I couldn't think of a damn thing to do about it. Hands in pockets, acid burning the back of my throat, I counted twenty condemned souls filing past. Some had gray strands straggling from knit caps; others had black or brown hair. A few mumbled to themselves, several talked quietly with one another, and some remained stoically silent. One or two met my eyes with streetwise suspicion and wretched gratitude. The hot breath of the revenant was back on my neck, and his fingers felt like bare bone when they gripped my arm above the elbow as I nodded at the last of them, an old lady with one filmy-cataract-covered eye. She grinned with toothless cheer at me and went through the folding doors as I gave her a hand up.

Being torn to pieces would've been less painful.

"Aren't you a good little boy? A good little human." The revenant had a hard time twisting his thick tongue around the words, giving them a glottal grunt. The same slab of meat slathered the skin below my ponytail. "A tasty human."

It was worth the painful bite I received when I ripped half his tongue out. The wolves only snickered as the revenant drooled and spit blood onto the asphalt, his eyes lurid with pain. I was expected to be loyal to Cerberus. I was not expected to roll over and offer my throat to some stinking lump of wet flesh wrapped in a concealing raincoat and baseball hat. Being seen as weak would get me killed only slightly slower than if I yelled at those people on the bus to run for their lives. "Here's your souvenir, bucko." I slapped the tongue against his chest. "Maybe you should've tasted my Auphe half instead of my human one." With that, I took my place on the bus and settled into the front seat as Fenrik slid behind the wheel. Wiping brownish black blood on my jeans, I then spread my hands and shrugged as pale blue eyes gave me a disapproving glare. I knew Fenrik couldn't have cared less about the revenant. I could've popped off the head and used it for a bowling ball and the wolf wouldn't have blinked. What he did care about was the homeless catching a glimpse of the moment and panicking. Of course, thanks to my infallible lack of luck, none of them had.

As my newly detongued pal climbed on after me, I opened my jacket to flash him a peek of my shiny new gun and raised an eyebrow. He bared rodent incisors at me, but kept trudging toward the back with bowed shoulders. He'd gotten off lightly and he knew it. The tongue would eventually regenerate; revenants could regrow almost any body part given the opportunity. He'd be running his mouth again in no time, and if that wasn't proof there was no justice in this world, I didn't know what was. I closed my jacket as the doors shut and the bus lurched into gear. As I stared blindly out of the fogged window, my mind raced in tight circles. I could all but feel the bruises as it bounced off the inner confines of my thick skull. Thick and useless. Come on, Nik, I thought grimly. If you're going to get these people out of this, there's no time like the present. And if you can't, I'll have to try, because George would never want this, could never be a part of it. And possible lack of soul aside, I couldn't be a part of it either. The fact that I'd probably die futilely without saving a one of them was just my misfortune, because I'd have to *try*.

The gears shifted again, diesel fumes belched into the air, and we rumbled our way down to hell, hitching a ride on the back of my good intentions. The buildings crawled by and I closed my eyes to them, leaning my forehead against the cool glass. I won't let it come to that, I promised George . . . and myself. This can't happen. It just can't.

And then suddenly, the tortured scream of metal came as the bus shuddered and yawed sideways like a drunken elephant. My head smacked against the window frame, giving me an instant headache, but I ignored it and jumped to my feet. Hanging on to the back of the seat, I managed to stay up as the floor rocked beneath me. There were cries of shock and surprise around me, and one worse-for-wear set of dentures went flying through the air to clip Fenrik behind one ear. He snarled but kept fighting with the large steering wheel, attempting to keep the white whale from tipping over. He was successful, just barely, until we careened to a jolting halt up against the curb.

For a moment it seemed like we would stay upright; then we went over. All the windows on the downside of the bus shattered at the impact, spraying glass upward. It was tempered and the one piece that grazed my jaw barely scratched the skin. There was no way to keep my feet as the bus tumbled over, but my natural grace, such as it was, kept me from falling face-first. Ass first was a different story. I looped an arm around the metal pole by the door and swung around, landing on my back as the bus hit and teetered on its side before stabilizing there. I blinked, feeling the grit of pulverized glass through my jacket. Inhaling an experimental breath, I took inventory and discovered I was in one piece, more or less. Turning my head carefully, I looked through the cracked windshield and saw what had caused the wreck.

We'd been rammed . . . by a garbage truck. The front of it was barely in view, but the shape was unmistakable. The engines of the hulking green metal monster growled, although the driver's seat was empty. Abandoned, a hit-and-run, but I did see something. It was gone so fast I might have imagined it, if I hadn't known better. A flicker of dark blond hair disappearing fast through clogged traffic and around a corner, was all the clue I needed. Within minutes there would be the telltale sounds of sirens, police and ambulance, and getting these people back to Cerberus would be a hopeless cause. Just like Niko had planned, and one helluva plan it was, considering he'd come up with it on the spur of the moment. Sitting up gingerly, I reached over and shook Fenrik's shoulder. He hadn't been wearing his seat belt—naughty, naughty—and was crumpled and bleeding against the door beside me. "Fen, on your paws. It's time to cut our losses."

Blue eyes rolling toward me, the bloody face twitched as he threw off the shock of the collision. Growling low in his throat from either pain or confusion, he pushed up to his knees and started crawling back toward the emergency exit. Flay, who'd been several seats behind me, was already kicking the rear door open with both feet. I followed in Fenrik's wake as the men and women in the bus started to come to their senses. Some began to shout for help, while others simply moaned. None, however, seemed fatally injured, and that put them heads and shoulders above where they'd been five minutes ago. I kept crawling and within seconds tumbled out onto the street, shortly followed by Jaffer, Mishka, Lijah, and that nameless, tongueless decomposing piece of shit.

A crowd was beginning to form in the deadlocked traffic and I winnowed my way through it with several well-placed elbows. Leaving the scene of the accident—in any other city it might have raised some protests. Leaving the scene with the overly hairy, the white-eyed, and the disturbingly slimy of skin—you'd think that would trigger *something*. At least one "Holy shit." But there was nothing but murmurs and the occasional whistle at the sight of the overturned bus. I wasn't all that surprised. Over the years I'd learned that people saw what they wanted to see. And what they didn't want to see, they absolutely refused to. I'd be wishing for a little of that blissful ignorance when we faced Cerberus with this news. The displeasure was bound to be nice and visual, painted in bloody scarlet strokes. Yeah, the shit was sure to hit the fan, but like those people on the bus I was still in much better shape than I had been. But unlike them I knew it, and I knew something else they didn't.

I knew who to thank.

"Where have you been? I was beginning to worry."

Same ugly room, same hideous bedspread, same bossy and demanding Niko. Okay, that wasn't strictly true. Niko looked less demanding and more concerned than anything. It would've been touching, if he hadn't had dinner set up on the small table by the bed. Vegetable lasagna, garlic bread, and a salad, it obviously hadn't come from the soup kitchen next door. "Darn, hope I didn't spoil your appetite," I sniped as I leaned wearily against one wall.

"It's for you, thankless brat." He pulled out the chair and planted me in it with a heavy hand on my shoulder.

"Thankless is right." Goodfellow's peevish voice came from the bathroom. "I'm starving and neo-ninja here wouldn't allow me even a bite." Moving into the room with a roll of duct tape under his arm, he toweled off his hands.

I looked at the tape, then him. "I knew it had a mind of its own, but you're taping it down now? Jesus."

"As if mere duct tape would hold it," he snorted, and tossed the roll onto the bed. "I fastened a little surprise to the back of the toilet tank. If you don't have a weapon hidden in every room, then your decoration skills are sorely lacking."

There was no denying the truth of that statement. I picked up a fork and took a bite of the lasagna; it was cold, but good. It was past midnight and the last time I'd eaten had been the orgy of steak and beer around noon. "Not bad, Cyrano. Thanks."

"I'm glad you're in the condition to appreciate it. I know Cerberus couldn't have been exactly pleased over what happened."

" 'Not exactly' is one way to put it." If not exactly pleased could also mean eating Fenrik alive. Someone had to take the blame for the accident and the loss of the livestock. Since he'd been driving, Fenrik had been the one to take the fall. I'd escaped relatively blameless, along with the others. We were still on Cerberus's shit list, but far enough down that we'd survived for now. If we didn't screw up in the near future, we might even live out the week. I took a bite of the garlic bread and chewed mechanically. I hadn't liked Fenrik . . . Hell, he was a cold-blooded Kin killer. A cold-blooded Kin killer who, in turn, hadn't much liked me either. He'd been driving those people to their deaths without a second thought. It was business to him and nothing more. Yeah, a killer, but . . . I dropped the bread onto the plate and pushed it all away. Within the savage circle of his life, Fenrik had been honorable. Loyal to his own. Loyal to his Alpha. It had been hard to watch him die. I'd shared only one meal with the guy and nothing that could be considered an actual conversation, but watching his entrails spill steaming onto the floor wasn't the highlight of my day. It had, in a word, sucked.

"Here, Loman," I offered with a sudden lack of appetite. "Eat up."

Robin accepted the plate with alacrity and settled onto the bed, pausing only to waggle his eyebrows at Niko in invitation. It was proof positive Promise wasn't going to join our little party or Goodfellow would've had nothing left to waggle. Niko, as always, ignored him and looked me up and down. "I'm guessing Cerberus didn't take his displeasure out on you or you would've signaled us for assistance."

Guessing, hoping. Niko had known when he'd rammed that garbage truck into the bus that he'd been taking a chance. He'd made the right choice, but it had also been the hard choice, and he deserved credit for both. "No, he saved the displeasure for someone else." I pushed the ugly mental picture from my brain and let my lips quirk upward. "How long did you wait outside the warehouse?"

The gray eyes narrowed with haughty question. "Did you *see* me by the warehouse?"

"No," I admitted ruefully. "Big surprise."

"Then how do you know I was there?"

"The same way I know Goodfellow's staring at your ass. It's a law of nature. Can't be changed."

Niko glanced over his shoulder, eyes narrowing further. Not bothering to look innocent, Robin shrugged and gave an unrepentant and utterly wicked grin as he continued to work his way through the lasagna. Turning back to me, Nik said, "I waited as long as was necessary."

Until he had seen me . . . undamaged and in one piece. And if he'd seen me, he would've seen Cerberus. They'd come out of the office this time into the warehouse proper. The office was good-sized, but for true bodily destruction you really needed room to work. "You saw them, then," I said quietly.

"Only glimpses through one poorly boarded-up window, but . . . yes, I saw Cerebus." As a rule, Niko took most things in stride. As far as I could tell, Niko had been born unflappable. Very little impressed him: the Auphe trying to destroy the world, Abbagor . . . a creature almost beyond description, and a homicidally possessed brother—it was a short list. Short, but I think Cerberus had just made it.

As impressions went, he'd definitely made one on me. To take Fenrik down he'd gone completely wolf. Only Cerberus's wolf was nothing like any other wolf I'd seen. I could see why the Kin had given him a chance; they hadn't had much choice.

"So?" A green gaze flickered between my brother and me. "You saw a wolf. Cerberus is simply another bad-tempered Kin bastard, or bastards as the case may be. Why the long faces?" The garlic bread was waved in casual punctuation. "A swat of the muzzle with a newspaper and you go your merry way."

"Yeahhh. I'll let you do the swatting, Loman." Fenrik hadn't bowed to certain death. Like any good wolf he'd gone down fighting. Fangs, jaws like a bear trap, incredible speed, and still he'd been nothing to Cerberus. Less than nothing. It could have been over in seconds, but where would be the lesson for the rest of us there? Cerberus in human form was impressive; Cerberus as wolf was . . . dread. Pure and simple. And having had my fill of dread for the night, I changed the subject. "Where's Promise?" I asked curiously. It wasn't like her to sit on the sidelines for very long.

"Still researching the crown with little luck. You're to meet her tomorrow for breakfast and she'll tell you what she's discovered."

"Make her pay," Goodfellow added with pointed annoyance. "I have yet to see my split from the poker game." Leaving the now-empty plate behind, he slid off the bed smoothly until he was forced to put weight on his injured leg. Straightening his charcoal pin-striped jacket and running a hand over the short brown waves of his hair, he limped toward the door. "I have another appointment," he said in farewell. "Watch the first flush, Caliban. I would hate for you to blow off anything of importance."

I made a mental note to check what exactly the puck had taped to the back of the toilet before I went to sleep. It sounded . . . interesting. As the door shut behind him, I tilted back in the chair. "Where's he going?"

"To watch over George's family. We've been doing our best to keep an eye on them when we can."

"Oh." I let the chair's front legs hit the floor and rubbed the back of my neck. "How are they doing?"

"Much the same as us," Niko said gravely.

"That good, huh?" I murmured to myself.

A hand gave me a light shove out of the chair and pushed the dirty discarded plate into my hand. "Make yourself useful. I don't think you want to see what this will attract in the middle of the night." As I scrubbed over the bathroom sink, we discussed what my next move should be. Niko agreed with me that it wasn't likely that the succubus would know any more than Flay did, but he pointed out we couldn't afford to overlook any potential source of information.

"I should've asked Goodfellow for pointers before he left," I said glumly.

"Talk with Promise instead," Niko suggested. "She

may know a way to interrogate your new friend that won't involve a jealous Cerberus castrating you."

"Always a plus." I grimaced. The alarm clock flickered red in the corner of my eye, reminding me that time was ticking away. It had been almost a week since George had disappeared. Six days. In the real world, it was barely a week. In our world, it was more than long enough to *pass* from the world.

11

The next morning I was waiting in the diner, resting my head facedown on a Formica table. It was a good position for me and I was embracing it thoroughly when a hand skimmed lightly over my hair. I knew who it was. I'd smelled her unique scent the moment she'd opened the door to the diner. Promise.

"I thought I was the night dweller." There was the whisper of a kiss against my jaw. "Not sleeping well, little brother?"

Apparently I was being adopted. More family who could kick my ass; love does take some curious forms. "Little?" I yawned hoarsely, straightening and rubbing the bristle I hadn't bothered to shave. "Bigger than you."

"Certainly you are," she said solemnly, patting the back of my hand lightly. "Big and strong and ever so brave."

"Yeah, that's me all over. I got here a little early and decided to put my head down. It wasn't as if I were napping or anything." Yet. Belatedly I remembered to stand. She gave me a gracious smile that ignored my defensiveness, and sat in the cheap plastic chair. The diner was practically a fishbowl, the front all glass, and Promise kept on her cloak. She seemed to have an endless supply of them; I guessed all vampires did. At least all the ones that didn't want to end up in a burn unit. This one was the same deep brown as the glossy streaks in her hair. The hood shadowed her ivory pale face, but not her eyes. Warmly glowing and heather purple, they rested on me with patient assessment.

"I hear I'm to advise you on how to win a woman's heart without annoying the love of her life, the captain of her heart and mate of her soul." Tiny fangs were revealed with the curve of her lips. "More precisely, her meal ticket."

If anyone would be qualified in the subject, it would be Promise. And I didn't mean that in a derogatory way. I had no idea what had gone on with her and her husbands—her many, many husbands—but I did know Promise well enough now to know that she would've been honest with them. Not honest about being a vampire, let's be realistic. But she would've been honest about her emotions, about what she offered and what she expected. Although I had the feeling Promise's expectations were high. Very high.

"Yeah, well . . ." I tried for a grin, but I could feel the humorless stretch of it. "I haven't had much experience with girls. You know, other than trying to kill them."

"The two aren't as different as you might think." She patted my hand again and picked up a menu. "Now, tell me, before we discuss the way to a succubus's heart, do they have anything here that is as delicious as your pancakes?"

There wasn't a hint of dimple in that smooth cheek, but the high arch of a delicate brow had me scowling suspiciously. "In your dreams," I muttered as I reached for my own laminated list of heart attack specials. "I am the pancake king."

There was no comment. A very tactful no comment.

After a careful study, Promise decided to go the safe route with a muffin and glass of orange juice. Coward. I ordered the bacon grease special. Bacon, eggs fried in bacon grease, and fried potatoes with bacon and onions. I took a runny yellow bite of egg and a forkful of potatoes, then ignored the rest for a cup of lethally strong and pathologically bitter coffee. Promise sipped orange juice from a squat, ugly glass, treating it as if it were the finest crystal. Blotting her lips delicately with a napkin, she encouraged, "Eat, Caliban. You're not doing anyone any favors by starving."

I shook my head and replied honestly, "I'm not hungry."

"Really? That's very interesting," she said lightly. "Now eat."

I couldn't describe the tone of that last command. It was no longer cajoling or encouraging and it damn sure wasn't a suggestion. On the other hand, I wouldn't call it threatening, not quite, but there was definitely steel under it. Whatever it was, it made me feel simultaneously sullen, weirdly appreciative, and about thirteen years old. Pulling the plate closer, I grumbled, "Damn it, you're pushy. Are you this pushy with Nik?"

"I thought that particular subject was one you didn't wish to discuss." Her eyes glittered with warm amusement.

Oh, man. I glared at her as I ate a piece of bacon. I hadn't been hungry—that had been the truth—but once I started shoveling it down, my appetite woke up fast. I buttered a biscuit and ate it in two bites before mumbling, "So, what about that crown?"

"So, how about those Yankees?" She shook her head and smiled. "Master of the conversational segue,

I bow before you." She didn't wait on a response. It was a good thing because other than an egg-choked snarl, I didn't have one. "There wasn't much that I could discover. Apparently the crown is so ancient that it has been mostly forgotten. I was able to match the description we received from Caleb, although I was unable to discover its origin. The crown is actually one of a paired set and they were called, I believe, the Calabassa. At one time both were highly sought after. But that was thousands upon thousands of years ago. They've apparently been long separated, and in this time, few have heard of them, no one knows what they do, and no one particularly wants them, together or apart."

"Except Caleb." My lips thinned and I stabbed a chunk of ketchup-covered potato with unnecessary force and malevolence.

"Yes, except for him." Copper-colored nails passed over the muffin she held in her hand. "And Cerberus. He has it, does he not? If it has a function, he may know what it is. Then again, the onyx and rose gold it's made of, while not overly valuable, might make an interesting bauble. He may have it as a plaything for his mistress with no idea it could be more."

And we knew it had to be more. All this for some cheap trinket? No. Caleb was a ruthless and amoral son of a bitch, but he wasn't stupid. After all, he'd gotten the better of us . . . for the moment. This time, I really was finished with breakfast. I dropped my fork on top of the food, and Promise didn't try to push any further. I suppose she recognizes an angst-ridden snit when she sees one, I thought as I abruptly shoved away from the table. "I'll be right back."

In a diner, a nice bathroom wasn't precisely like winning the lottery, but it was close. As the door opened, I grimaced. Still a loser, all the way around.

It wasn't dirty, simply gray and bleak and smelling strongly of Lysol. It matched the rest of the eatery. I was surprised Promise had picked a place like this to meet. The entire joint wasn't as big as the living room of her apartment. And the bathroom? Hell, she probably had makeup cases bigger than this. It was a few steps down from a penthouse on the Upper East Side, no doubt about it. I closed the door behind me and took a cold, calculating look around. Something had to go. There was no way around it. Garbage can, empty paper-towel dispenser, the mirror . . . the goddamn gleefully, horrifically bright mirror. I automatically averted my eyes and stood with impotently clenched fists. I shook minutely as the rage inside struggled for release. It wanted out.

And it wanted out *now*.

When I finally returned to my chair nearly ten minutes later, Promise tilted her head and asked with resignation, "Can the damage be covered in cash or do I need to write a check?"

"Neither." I picked up the coffee mug and drained it. "I was a good boy." Not that it hadn't been close; it had been . . . right down to the wire. But just before my fist would've hit the mirror, I changed my mind. I wanted to save my rage, every molecule of it. It was all for Caleb. I wasn't going to deprive the bastard of that, and I wasn't going to deprive myself. Reaching into my pocket, I fished out a tie and pulled back my hair. "You know, I was wondering," I said, once again master of the segue, "why this place? Why'd you want to meet here? It's kind of . . ." I let the words trail off as I took another look around. There were overweight waitresses with straggling hair and spider vein legs, and a cook with a shaved head and homemade tattoos who slouched behind the counter with a toothpick between his thick lips and a floor so coated by grease fumes that it was as slick as an ice rink.

"Dingy, unsanitary, cheap?" she filled in archly.

"Not you," I temporized with a tact I didn't know I had in me.

"I think you might be surprised." She popped a cranberry from the muffin into her mouth and crushed it between white, white teeth. "This is a palace in comparison."

"In comparison to what?" I asked with genuine curiosity. All I knew about Promise was the here and now. Her history, her past . . . it was a mystery.

Her hands began to pink in the spill of sun reflecting on our table, and she quickly tucked them back under her cloak. "To where I was born." Her face was as smooth as always, but beneath that, I thought I saw an almost imperceptible tightening.

I couldn't remember precisely when I found out vampires were born and not made, how old I was. I thought it was our first year on the run. Maybe. Part of that time was a little fuzzy. Two years in the tender loving care of the Auphe will do that to a person. I hadn't remembered any of those two years when I'd returned, still didn't, not consciously anyway. But it was clear that in the muck and slime beneath the conscious, something had lingered. For months after I'd reappeared, I'd slept *under* the bed, a tightly wedged fetal ball with a knife in hand and nightmares that were never remembered in the light of day.

Sixteen then. I would've been sixteen when we ran across the vampire children in the park. They were playing beneath a midnight sky. Running, jumping, laughing, they were just like human kids, except they were faster. And they could jump higher. Flat-footed they would leap into the branches of a tree, swing, and giggle. They were cute . . . bows, barrettes, and tiny baby fangs. It could've been a scene from one of those creepy horror novels with all the velvet, homoerotic vampire nooky, and tormented vampire children who could never grow any older. And for a second I'd actually bought into that. Sickened, I'd stood beside Niko and waited for them to drop out of the tree and drain some night jogger dry.

Then we saw their mother.

Or maybe it was their nanny, babysitter . . . Who knew? There were quite a few kids, and as long as vampires lived, I couldn't believe they'd breed that fast. Whoever it was, she was pregnant. A pregnant vampire, elegant in white maternity wear—no black velvet for her. With glossy blond hair coiled on her head and large, dark eyes, she was the picture of contentment and impending motherhood. That is, until she saw us. Hormones—it was the same for pregnant humans and pregnant vampires. Cranky, cranky, cranky. She must've sensed we were different from the average park goer, whether it was the Auphe in me or the hunter in Niko. We ran. What else were we going to do? Stake a mom-to-be? As options went, it wasn't so hot. To sum it all up, vampires reproduce, not recruit, and pregnant vampires can still run pretty damn fast.

Live and learn.

"Where were you born?" The waitress refilled my cup with more coffee-flavored sludge. I dumped three sugar packets in it and waited for it to cool. Caffeine and sugar, they were my new best friends.

"Seven hundred years from here," she said obliquely before giving me the shadow of a smile. "I'm an older woman. Don't tell your brother."

I was sure he already knew. I was sure he knew

more about Promise than I would ever know. "You know Nik," I offered, curling up one side of my mouth. "He's mature for his age. A geezer on the inside." I rolled the mug between my palms. "Seven hundred years, huh? That means you used to . . . you know. . . ." Lifting my upper lip, I bared nonexistent fangs.

"Yes," she replied simply. "I once did."

From the nineteen hundreds on, most vampires discovered a different way to live. That was a story I'd already heard from Promise. They had discovered what drove the vampire thirst for blood, and it wasn't that different from a human condition known as porphyria, which caused a sensitivity to light and a less proved craving for blood. Some vampires even thought they and humans might share a common primitive ancestor. A genetic mutation had occurred, a species had split, and voilà: Humans clubbed their prey by day to eat the flesh, and vampires clubbed their prey by night to eat the flesh *and* drink its blood. After some time that blood didn't satisfy the physiological need. It was too different from their own. Who did that leave? Yep, you bet. That's when the humans became the prey. Hey, no hard feelings. It's just biology. The mammoth in his boneyard no doubt laughed his woolly ass off. After all, turnabout is fair play.

But science does march on. For the better part of the last hundred years, the majority of vampires depended on massive doses of iron and other chemical supplements to fill the need for blood. That wasn't to say some didn't still indulge. Blood became like alcohol, not needed for survival, but a pleasurable vice nonetheless. Of course, there are always psychos . . . in every species, in every walk of life. The vampire ones needed the kill more than they needed the blood.

But that was the psychos. Still, you couldn't escape the fact that any vampire over a hundred years old had once drunk blood. Human blood.

But that had been a hundred years ago for Promise, and I was all out of stones in my roomy glass condo.

"Seven hundred years, huh?" I drawled. "No wonder you're so short." It was an exaggeration. The top of her head reached Niko's chin, which put her at about five six. It wasn't tall by any means, but it wasn't short either . . . quite.

"I'll have you know I was an amazon in the old days, a veritable giant," she said with mock outrage. Then she rested her fingers lightly on the back of my wrist and went on to say softly, "Thank you." She didn't have to elaborate. I knew why she was thanking me.

"I'm a lot of things, Princess." A lot of nasty, nasty things. "But a hypocrite is not one of them."

An emotion, so fleeting that it was impossible to identify, shimmered behind her eyes and then was gone. "No, never that," she responded sadly. Straightening in her chair, she moved on briskly. "Now, let us plan a little romantic strategy for seducing your succubus."

"Flowers and candy?" I said with a grimace.

"Oh, Caliban." Eyes bright with humor, she shook her head. "The only use a succubus would have for flowers is to lay them on your grave."

Sounded about par for the course.

It was hours later when I realized Promise hadn't gotten around to telling me where she was born, the place that made that diner look like a palace. Unintentional oversight? Doubtful. Promise wasn't the type for unintentional anything. Always careful, always discreet, every action analyzed before it was performed . . . every word considered before it was said.

It was too bad that this time her carefully considered words hadn't done me a damn bit of good.

Goodfellow's weight settled next to me on the park bench as his long legs stretched out to bask in the nonexistent sun. "You rang?"

Oh, I'd rung all right. Pride, dignity . . . I'd flushed it all down the toilet and sent out a big fat SOS. I wasn't big on asking for help, yet here I was. For the first nineteen years of my life, Niko had been the only one I'd turned to. Then we had met Robin, a stranger, who oddly enough *wanted* to help us. That was a first. It had only taken him risking his life a few times before I actually believed it. And even when I'd believed it, I'd remained reluctant to accept it. A year later it was still difficult for me . . . admitting I needed someone besides my brother. Lifelong habits, they die hard, don't they? Shifting my weight, I tapped irritable fingers on the wrought-iron armrest before admitting reluctantly, "I need some help."

"I gathered that." With hands locked behind his head and eyes hidden behind sunglasses, he clucked a smug tongue. "My expertise in all matters is legendary. Many worship at the altar of my brilliance and who can blame them?"

Yeah, this was improving my headache. I closed my eyes and knuckled my forehead for a few seconds. "Brilliance. Worship. Gotcha. Now how about we get down to business?"

"Aren't we especially cranky today? And after I took a bolt in the leg for you too." Sighing, he sat up and waved an imperious hand. "What do you need, ungrateful supplicant?"

I ignored that little rewriting of history and focused on the matter at hand. The humiliating matter at hand. "It's the succubus."

That perked him up. "Today was the day, then?

Niko mentioned this morning that you were going to pump her for information." Eyebrows rose suggestively. "So very unselfish of you, throwing yourself on the grenade like that. What nobility, what fortitude." He gave a lecherous smirk. "Tell me all the filthy, filthy details."

Details. He wanted details. I looked up at the sky. It had been clear earlier; now it was a morose gray. I wondered if the sun was disappearing along with George. Gunmetal gray and heavy with heat, the clouds hung low . . . almost as low as I was hanging right then. Finally, I turned back to Goodfellow with a scowl. "I taste bad," I gritted between clenched teeth. "There's your detail. I taste bad. Happy?"

Mobile lips twitched with surprise and something less flattering. Slipping off the sunglasses, he looked at me with suspicious blandness. "You taste . . . bad." He rolled the statement over his tongue and repeated, "Taste bad."

I was glad he was so fucking entertained by this. "Yeah, taste bad," I snapped. "But, hey, that's okay because the snake sex is not me." I suppressed the shudder before it made it to the surface. The tongue had been bad enough, forked and slick and *cold*. Icecold. Bad enough all right, so much so that I had absolutely no desire to know what lurked under her clothes . . . what little of them there were. I'd gone in with no idea how far I would go. I did know how far I *couldn't* go. I wasn't willing to risk birthing another Auphe/human mix, and I damn sure didn't think an Auphe/succubus/human mix would be any better. I didn't know if it could happen or not, but it was one lottery I wasn't going to play. But thanks to my genes, push hadn't come to shove on the carpet of the warehouse office. For George's sake, I shouldn't have been relieved, but, goddamn it . . . I was. This time the shudder did surface as a twitch in my shoulders. "Very much not me."

"Not embracing the serpent intimacies, then. That's probably better for you in the long run." He tilted his head curiously. "Taste bad as in you actually, physically, taste bad, or was it your energy that was too much for her delicate palate?"

It had been the energy. Apparently mine was too Auphe for comfort. What does that say when even a succubus would sooner send out for General Tso's than suck you dry? What the hell does it say? "Moving on," I said grimly, "I need you to talk to her. See what you can find out."

"I see." He replaced the glasses. "You want to use me. You want me to be a gigolo . . . to whore myself for your convenience."

"Pretty much," I admitted without compunction.

He laid an arm along the back of the bench and gave a grin birthed in vice. "Who could say no to that?"

The warehouse was as deserted as it had been that morning. Most of the crew were keeping as low a profile as possible after yesterday's failure. They would trickle in around dark, heads down and tails tucked. Cerberus was gone. High-level Kin meeting, stress-relieving massacre up north—I didn't know and I didn't care. I simply seized the opportunity. And after said opportunity spit me out I was back with reinforcements. "She's in the office," I muttered, scanning the gloomy interior for any unexpected visitors. "She's bound to be suspicious, though, a strange puck just showing up out of the blue. How are you going to get around that?"

Managing to swagger and limp at the same time, Goodfellow shot the cuffs of his shirt. "Succubi don't think like that. They're interested in eating and sex and they never have to work very hard at either. She won't think twice about me walking through the doors. She'll just light a few candles and put on a bib." He ran a smoothing hand over his hair. "Snakes don't wonder where their food comes from. They simply accept it. It's all about the ego."

"Too bad they're not humble like you," I said dryly, stopping in front of the door. "You want an introduction?"

"No." Linking his fingers, he extended his hands to pop knuckles. "It would only slow me down." He opened the door, then closed it behind him, disappearing into the office. Exhaling, I leaned against the wall and did my best to not picture what might be going on behind that door. I doubted I'd ever look at a snake again without feeling the phantom sensation of cool scales under my fingers and a slithering tongue twisted into a noose around my own. And the taste. Wet sulfur, it had tingled in my mouth like venom. Still did.

I'd bent over to spit when the sounds started from behind the wall. A rattle filled the air, buzz saw sharp and spine twisting in its intensity. A hundred pissed-off rattlers or a hundred orgasmic ones—I didn't even want to guess. Moving several feet away, I fervently hoped that was a good sound and not an indication that Robin was being swallowed whole by a supernaturally horny boa constrictor. Covering my ears would've been the cowardly thing to do; instead I folded my arms and tried to keep my head down . . . mentally speaking. I counted floor tiles, roaches, whatever I could lay my eyes on . . . anything to keep my mind occupied and out of the office.

When the door opened, I automatically checked my watch. Twenty minutes. Only twenty. I would've sworn it'd been an hour at the very least. Hair still immaculate, Goodfellow stepped out into the hall and shut the door quietly behind him. Unfolding my arms, I straightened out of my slouch. "You find out anything?" That's when I noticed the stains on his shirt. Deep blue, they were splashed liberally over a sleeve and half the chest. Not Robin's blood. I'd seen that and it was ordinary crimson. Ah, shit. "What happened?" I demanded.

The hand that had been hidden behind his back appeared holding a knife. It was a match for the shirt, dripping cobalt. Ignoring my question, he countered with one of his own, "Who here deserves to go down the most?"

"What the hell happened?" I repeated as I stepped closer. Now I could see the claw marks on his neck. They bled sluggishly. "Jesus, Robin."

"She wasn't in the mood," he replied with grim savagery. "Now, who deserves to go down? Aside from Cerberus, who is the most evil son of a bitch here?"

It was a question that didn't require much thought. Flay or the revenant, and we still needed Flay. "The revenant," I said automatically. "You killed her? You couldn't just . . . damn. Haven't you ever heard of no means no?"

"She was in the mood for sex," he snapped, heading past me. "She wasn't, however, in the mood to talk. She was more afraid of Cerberus than she was stupid, and that's saying something. This revenant keep any personal things here?"

We clattered down the stairs with Robin using his free hand on the banister to keep his leg from giving out beneath him. "How the hell should I know?" I shot back. "I've been here a grand total of two days. If the Kin passes out employee lockers, I haven't got my combination yet."

"Think." He hit the bottom and whirled to face me.

"If we don't pin it on someone else, you'll go down for it. You're the new one and all suspicion will fall on you. I did get some information, but we'll need you in at least one more day to verify it. So *think*."

"Son of a bitch," I hissed under my breath, more at the situation than at Robin himself. Scanning the warehouse, I tried to replay yesterday. Where had the revenant stood? Where had he come from when he'd slunk over? I focused on one area hidden behind a row of dusty, empty crates. "Over here."

Behind the crates was a messy conglomeration of blankets, empty bottles, spilled cards, and other mounds of discarded garbage. The employee lounge. One blanket was off a little from the others. In the midst of the wool nest was half of a desiccated human leg. Bite marks were evident in the long dead limb, and graveyard dirt was a litter beneath it. "There." I indicated the blanket with a grimace of distaste.

Goodfellow ignored the leg and shoved the blade under a fold of cloth. "All right. Let's go."

"Won't they smell you? On the blade or upstairs?"

"Do you smell me?" he challenged, wiping his hand on his pants without a single wince for the ruination of fine fashion.

As a matter of fact, I didn't. There was only the sharp smell of musk and spice. Cologne, and a strong cologne at that, to cover up any hint of puck scent. "Neat trick," I admitted reluctantly.

"It's a special mixture. I've been wearing it since this whole debacle started. I prefer to stay nameless and scentless until all of this passes. I'm a survivor." He moved toward the door at the quickest pace his limp allowed.

I studied the blood on his shirt as he passed me. "Yeah, I noticed."

That stopped him in his tracks. Green eyes hit me,

harsh and uncompromising. "Do you want George back?" He leaned closer. "Well? Do you?"

It struck me that I might not know Robin as well as I thought I did. Complacent in his loyal but breezy friendship, I'd forgotten who he was. Who he'd been. Who he would always be. Pucks were good at most things, but they were absolutely exceptional at one. No matter what they had to do, they got their own way. Luckily, Robin's way was fairly benign. Comfort, luxury, a wildly varied sexual life, all of that came easily to him with little effort expended. But now . . . now he wanted George back.

Guess what. So did I.

"I want her back," I replied levelly. "I want her back and I don't give a shit how we do it."

When she'd first been taken I'd worried how she might feel if bad things were done to get her back. As the days went on and she remained lost, I decided I just wanted her back. Period. Bring on the bad things. Bring them the hell on.

The dark gaze lightened, then ran clear. "And we'll get her back." We moved on to pass from the warehouse into the light. "Don't waste any tears on the succubus. She'd killed more humans in her long life than you could begin to count. A predator falls. It's the way of the world."

"Law of the jungle?" I snorted with dark skepticism.

"If you want to be clichéd about it." He gave a weary sigh, rubbing at the weeping claw marks on his neck. "Let's get something to drink, several somethings in fact, and I'll tell you what I learned."

Goodfellow usually chose bars that reflected his personality, upscale and pretentious. This time he threw image to the wind and picked the first one we came across. We lucked out. It was dark, as all good bars are, but it was clean—from what I could tell. Plants were everywhere . . . hanging in baskets, creeping over the tables, casting branches toward the ceiling. And I'd have sworn there was a bird on every one of those branches. Parrots, finches, parakeets . . . and a shitload of others I couldn't identify. I wasn't much on our fine-feathered, jet-force-crapping friends. These seemed well behaved enough, chirping or squawking only occasionally, but I still shot a wary eye upward when I grabbed a spot at the bar. "Weird place," I commented, checking the pretzel bowl suspiciously for white streaks.

"Bacchus be damned," Robin groaned. "It's a peri bar. Just my luck. My catastrophic, bowel-churning luck."

Before I could ask what the hell a peri was, the bartender came over . . . wings and all. Dove gray barred with silver, they were tucked neatly against his back. In a black T-shirt and jeans with short wavy black hair, he looked like your typical Mario from Queens. The wings could be a gimmick of the bar and stuffed in a locker before he headed home. Could be, but apparently weren't. Stopping opposite us, his round black eyes fixed on Goodfellow and he said without preamble, "Ishiah wants to talk to you."

"I don't remember asking you what Ishiah wanted," Robin responded in a bored tone. "Two beers with a whiskey back."

The peri's wings rustled in annoyance, and without further comment he moved down the bar to fill the order. "What's a peri?" I asked. Wings, feathers. Nah, it couldn't be. It had been a long time since I'd been as naive as that. Pre-third-trimester was about where I'd place it. It didn't stop me from yanking Goodfellow's chain. He needed it. We both needed it.

"They're not . . ." I looped a finger over the top of my head. "Are they?"

Robin rolled his eyes in disgust and said, "You truly are an uneducated delinquent, aren't you?" The alcohol arrived. As the peri slid the glasses in front of us, he opened his mouth to speak again. Goodfellow beat him to the punch. Holding up a finger, he said coldly, "Don't." Then he pointed the same finger down the bar. "Go."

Shedding a few disgruntled feathers, the peri hesitated, then obeyed with a scowl. There were other customers waiting to be served, oblivious humans and creatures as odd as any peri. "Overgrown cockatoo," Robin muttered. Not wasting any time, he did his shot, my shot, then chugged half his beer. Setting the mug back down, he said with reproof, "You have mythology books in your apartment, absolute reams of pertinent information. Pages and pages. Do you use them to blow your nose or to wipe your ass?"

I snorted into my beer, then took a swallow. "They're Nik's books. Hell, you already *know* they're Nik's books. Besides, out in the wild, he points and I shoot. It's a good arrangement."

"Gods. And you embrace your ignorance. That's what so astounds me." Goodfellow shook his head and finished his beer.

I examined a pretzel carefully and popped it into my mouth. I wasn't hungry. I didn't want it, but it was there. So often in life that's what it comes down to. It was there. "Yeah, yeah. Not angels, then?"

He cast a disgusted look at me over the top of his empty glass. "Yes, that's exactly what they are. And on Fridays they have a potluck with St. Nick, the Easter Bunny, and the tooth fairy." Resting his forehead in his hand, he mumbled, "You exhaust me, I swear it."

I had another pretzel. "So," I repeated offhand, "not angels, then?"

"Hermes, blow me." Reaching over the bar, he snagged a bottle of whiskey and poured it with a liberal hand before starting the lecture. "The peris, as a race, have been around as long as I have. Perhaps longer. They've been thought to be angels, fallen angels, the offspring of demons and angels. Always colored with the brush of the holier-than-thou. Messengers. Creatures of light. Creatures of power." He laced the labels with all the mockery in him, which was a helluva lot.

"And what are they really?"

"Publicity hogs." He slammed another shot. "Nosy, pushy publicity hogs. Nothing more. Trust me, Caliban, I've seen nothing of the divine in them." His eyes went distant and dark. "Nothing of the divine in this world."

There he was wrong. Maybe I couldn't touch it or be a part of it. . . . Maybe it wasn't for me, but there was something special to be found. In George. I pushed the pretzel bowl away. We'd needed a breather from what had happened at the warehouse, needed a moment of the mundane. Now that moment had passed. "What did the snake tell you?"

Amber glowed in his shot glass as he turned it this way, then that, in his fingers. "The crown." He drained the glass. "She'd seen it. She'd worn it. And she was not particularly impressed by it. It didn't complement her coloring." He looked down at the blue that had dried on his shirt. "Obviously."

Jewels for the mistress, as Promise had conjectured. Close. My hand tightened around the mug. We were so close. "Where is it?"

"Normally, in Cerberus's penthouse."

"Penthouse?"

"Where did you think he lived? A doghouse?" he commented cynically. "He's a Kin boss. That tends to keep you in kibble and wall-to-wall carpet. But that is neither here nor there. The crown is now in Cerberus's car, luckily for you. At least, I think it is."

"What do you mean, you think?" I demanded.

"Snakes are liars. With their last breath they'll tell you a lie." He raised a hand for another beer and finished with savage bite, "We have that in common."

It was unusual to see Robin be hard on himself. He typically embraced with a vengeance his more colorful qualities. "You're not lying to me right now," I pointed out as I slid my beer in his direction.

He accepted it and lowered the level steadily. "It's more entertaining by far to tell you the truth. Watching you ignore it and fall ass over heels into the worst kind of trouble . . . it's better than cable."

On that note I took my beer back. "Cerberus has three cars that I know of. A limo and two town cars." None of which had been at the warehouse today. Flay had used one the previous night to dispose of Fenrik's body, what was left of it. He would probably have taken the car somewhere to clean it up today. Can't dump a corpse without detailing the car the next day. Now that was the law of the jungle right there. As for the other ones, Cerberus had no doubt taken the limo this morning with some of the wolves following in the other town car.

"You up for staying under long enough to search them? Another day perhaps?"

And if the succubus had been lying, I could be under much longer than another day, assuming Caleb allowed me that much time. "A man's gotta do what a man's gotta do." All the old movies said so, and I guessed the same was true for someone who was only half-man.

Robin grimaced. "Heroism can be so banal." He finished the new beer deposited before him. Up, down, bang against the bar. "Let's quit this place before we come down with a raging case of histoplasmosis."

As we stood, the bartender said sharply, "That's thirty bucks."

"Put it on Ishiah's tab," Goodfellow replied derisively. He started to walk toward the door before reconsidering. Turning back, he picked up the bottle of whiskey and carried it away with him. "This too. It's the least of what that bastard owes me."

"Who's Ishiah?" I asked as we climbed the stairs up to the street.

"Someone almost as annoying as you."

Goodfellow did have a way of ending a subject. Outside the sun was still missing in action, the claustrophobic clouds thicker and darker. It made the bloodstains on the puck's shirt an even deeper blue. On the last stair, his leg nearly gave way and I pretended not to notice as he braced himself against me momentarily to regain his balance. When Robin wanted attention, he'd let you know . . . very clearly and very verbally. This wasn't one of those times. Steadied, he took a swig from the bottle. "I'm going home to take a hot shower and mourn my favorite shirt. Hold my calls."

I moved my gaze from the choking sky to Goodfellow's still face and said quietly, "Thanks, Robin. For what you did." I almost said, "For what I couldn't do," but that would've been a lie. If I'd known as the puck had that it was the only way, I would've done it. Not as well, not as efficiently, but I would've done it and lived with the consequences. It hadn't happened that way, though. The consequences weren't mine to claim.

Robin didn't acknowledge the thanks. After tipping

the bottle again, he said without emotion, "Find the crown." He started down the sidewalk. "Find George." Unspoken was the message: That will make it worthwhile.

Hell, it might even make it bearable.

12

I was a hawk. Soaring high. Streetlights swung beneath me, bold as fireflies. The wind was a rushing current around me, gloating in my ear, plucking at my clothes. The sliver of a moon swam pumpkin orange off to my left, magnified in the warm air. I could've stretched out a hand to touch it.

Flying.

Only I wasn't.

A hand as big as my head held me by the throat and dangled me over the edge of the warehouse roof. Eyes the same pumpkin orange as the moon studied me with the clinical interest of a vivisectionist.

The day hadn't started out quite this crappy. I'd spent it in the warehouse, keeping my head down. It was a good idea, especially with the flying body parts. Robin had been right. Cerberus, arriving in his limo, had pinned the succubus' death on the revenant quickly enough. The rest of the day had been spent mopping up the mess and staying out of Cerberus's way. His mood, needless to say, wasn't good. Not that there was undying love between the succubus and him. She'd been convenient sex to him, nothing more. But that didn't matter. He *owned* her, and someone had dared pick his pocket. No Alpha was going to appreciate that. The sounds that had come from his office at various intervals had most of the wolves lurking by the door for a quick getaway. Roars of rage and the sound of furniture shattering against the walls didn't make for ideal working conditions. And then there had been the silence. No one knew whether to be relieved or even more panicked than they already were.

Finally, the day passed. We survived, although poor damn Mishka probably had serious doubts as to whether he wanted to. There were no jobs lined up for the coming hours and eventually the place had emptied. Cerberus remained in his office, but had calmed down enough to engage in a little cleanup of his own. I couldn't believe revenants tasted that great, but each to his own, right? He would eat; I would search. Simple. And it had really seemed that way up until the point where he caught me midsearch and pulled me from the car and tossed me bodily over it.

"Bastard thief." The words had followed me over. Apparently it was all right to steal for Cerberus, but not from him. It was when he attempted to show me just how not all right it was that I got up off my ass and ran. I left the crown. It had been in the limo after all. Under a seat. What was valuable enough to cost George her life had been discarded like trash. I could picture the succubus tossing it on the floor in a fit of spoiled pique. The jewels weren't large enough, not precious enough, weren't the right color. It wasn't flashy at all. I'd held it in my hand for nearly a full second before I'd been yanked out of the car. A simple circle of reddish gold set with the occasional onyx, it wasn't especially feminine or attractive. In fact, it looked almost . . . utilitarian. For one brief second I thought I felt it pulse under my hand, a single, warm heartbeat. But then it was gone—flying from my hand as I did the same from Cerberus's.

It was still down there, lying on the warehouse floor. I was counting on Niko to grab it on his way up. Not that up had been the best decision I'd ever made, but I hadn't had much choice. Cerberus had been on me fast and furious. I hadn't had time to draw my gun in the face of his unnerving speed, much less pelt across the warehouse to the front door. The stairs up had been my closest choice. Now that choice had me dangling off a building.

Not so long ago while climbing a Ferris wheel, I'd thought that I didn't have a fear of heights. As my feet kicked in empty space, I decided I might just change my mind.

"An Auphe." "I would've been better off hiring a piranha." The heads weren't speaking the distorted words to me. No, they spoke to themselves—muzzles nearly touching, fangs half again as long as my hand dripping dark brown saliva that fell like rain. Cerberus was easily twice as large as any wolf I'd seen, maybe three times. He'd retained just enough control of his human form to remain upright. His shoulders hulked, mountain wide, under fur so black that it was nearly lost in the night. He towered almost eight feet tall; the chest was broad and made to store oxygen to feed that massive body. Legs as thick as my waist were banded with the breadth of muscle that could propel their owner unbelievable lengths. The fingers that curled around my neck were rough with callous pads thickened from years of running. The claws were jetty, curved like fishhooks, and every bit as long as the fingers. Oh yeah, and they were piercing my flesh. Fun, fun. I could feel the warmth of blood on my neck. It wasn't much blood, probably not even a teaspoon. It didn't raise my hopes. What Cerberus had in store for me was much worse than a torn-out throat.

Abruptly, the hand dangling me over the edge shook me hard enough that I felt the vertebrae in my neck howl in protest and spots spilled across my sight. They were orange too, the spots. But through them I could still make out Cerberus. As looming as a god and inescapable as the inevitability of mortal death, he blocked out the sky, blocked out the world. Breath, hot and rank with the stench of raw flesh, passed over my face and neck . . . He was a predator searching for the softest and most tasty portion. My skin tightened in instinctive withdrawal. I tried to hang on to the thought that behind me, on the roof, was Niko's knife, its glass shattered. Not that I could see it, but I knew it was there.

Hoped it was there.

I'd dropped the dagger full of ingenious electronics that Niko had given me . . . the "My ass is in deep shit" device. I hadn't heard it hit the asphalt of the flat warehouse roof. The sound had been lost in the bass roar that had literally vibrated the framework of my chest, my ribs resonating under my flesh. The hunting cry of Cerberus, it was intended to paralyze your legs, freeze your bowels, and loose your bladder. And it might have worked—it *would* have worked—on someone who hadn't lived through the Auphe. Me? I just ran faster. But as fast as I could run, Cerberus could run a hundred times faster. One leap and then another and he was on me. I'd zigzagged to one side, sliding in the tar crumble beneath my feet, only to be snatched up . . . a child in the grip of a grizzly bear. Of course, not many toddlers pack a gun that could easily be strapped on a tank and used as a cannon.

Still half-blind, I scrabbled desperate fingers for the

.50 Magnum under my jacket. "A toy." Twin maws pulled back from my throat to stretch in silently mocking laughter. "You threaten me with a toy. Shall I make you eat your toy, Auphe? Ram it down your traitorous throat inch by inch?" I was shaken again as the change-defiled voice ground on. "Or shall I put it elsewhere? Not inch by inch, but all at once."

I didn't need any encouragement to get to my gun faster. I'd seen what he'd done to Fenrik, a fierce opponent. I'd both seen *and* smelled what he'd done to the revenant earlier today. Less fierce, but the damn things were nearly impossible to kill. Revenants could regrow nearly any part, including their head. Their brains, assuming they had any, were obviously kept elsewhere. To kill a revenant you practically needed a tree shredder. Cerberus had done the job with teeth and claws, and he'd done it in under fifteen seconds. A wolf of some serious talent, my former boss, and now he was turning that talent to me. And when he said he was going to take my gun, shove it up my ass, and pull the trigger, I tended to believe him.

But first he had to get it.

He was quick, but I was quick too. I couldn't run as fast, or leap as high, but I could pull a trigger with the best of them. I yanked the Magnum free of the holster and fired. I'd picked the gun with a goal in mind. Supposedly, it could bring down a bear. A bear didn't have shit on Cerberus, but maybe I could slow him down. Slow him down, run like hell, and pray for reinforcements. Niko was just outside the warehouse; he'd be here any minute. Any second. No goddamn time at all.

Round one ripped a hole five inches across in that black chest. Round two tore flesh from his ribs. There was no round three. Cerberus staggered a step back . . . Jesus Christ, *one* lousy step . . . then he dropped me. I could carry my weapon with me all the way down or I could let it go and try to save my life. I let it go. Four stories down. In retrospect, I should've held on to it and said the hell with the whole gravity–sudden death issue, because after the momentarily sickening sensation of free fall, I caught the edge of the roof. My shoulders creaked in protest as they worked to halt my fall.

The metal under my fingers was as cool as the metal of the Calabassa had been. There was the rip and pull of the stitches in my arm popping free as I kicked my feet, trying to find purchase on the brick shell of the warehouse. I managed to snag one foot on something, a cracked brick maybe, and pushed up. Cerberus kindly helped me the rest of the way. One giant misshapen hand on each of my arms, he lifted me up high. Then, like an evil-minded child with a struggling fly, he started to pull. The pressure increased instantly to an unbearable scream of muscles and tendons pushed far past their limits. He was going to rip me apart as he'd done to the revenant, and there wasn't a damn thing I could do about it.

But someone else could.

A pale blur hit Cerberus from the side, bowling us both over. Teeth flashed yellow in the moonlight and buried themselves in the black throat closest to it. Blood surged free, turning Flay's white coat to wine. Landing on my side, I watched as an unlikely ally fought a creature even more monstrous than himself. Just as he couldn't turn fully human, neither could Flay become completely wolf. Instead, he became a rangy man-wolf, upright but crouched, covered with fur yet retaining vaguely human hands and feet. The shoulder-length hair had changed to a bristling mane, but the eyes were the same. As murder red as the hatred he was visiting upon Cerberus.

"Not stupid." The white head rose, then fell again, fangs ripping. "*Not* stupid."

It seemed Flay's Alpha had underestimated him once too often. I wasn't going to make the same mistake. But I also wasn't going to assume Snowball could take Cerberus. He wasn't a match for the two-headed wolf. Not alone.

Good thing he wasn't alone.

The familiar grip of my knife pulled from my calf sheath grounded me as I pushed up and ran across the roof. Unlike Flay, Cerberus had gone all wolf. Pure in form, infinite in rage, immense, implacable, and scary as fucking shit. Rolling on top of Flay, the black wolf planted all four paws on the ground and dived at the white throat with one pair of snapping jaws. The other head turned to gaze at me over the slope of its shoulder. Dilated pupils turned orange to ebon. Black holes sucked me in for an endless moment in time, found me wanting, then spit me back out. The head turned back and joined in the attempt to rip Flay's head from his shoulders. Part Auphe I might be, but Cerberus still considered me too human to be any threat. With soft flesh, fragile bones, no claws or fangs, and useless human weapons, what could I possibly do to him?

He was about to find out.

Throwing myself onto the broad back, I held on to the black fur with a one-handed death grip. The other hand had designs of its own. The serrated blade lodged in Cerberus's spine just above the bunch and swell of his back legs. Wolves were durable as hell, but a parted spinal cord would still give one second thoughts. Speaking of second, that was hardly my only knife. I planted the next one midway up the back. With no idea where the spinal column split off, I was more than willing to work my way up. And with more time I would have, but the split second of surprise that had frozen Cerberus passed and I was tossed off in an explosion of muscle, fur, and madness.

My plan hadn't worked; at least not completely. I hadn't sliced the cord, only nicked it, and I had my doubts that was going to do the job. Now, with one back leg hanging uselessly, Cerberus turned his attention from Flay to me. I barely saw the motion that took me down. I wasn't stupid enough to shove my arm in either mouth of this wolf. With Boaz, I'd ended up with a mauling bite and a possibly cracked bone. With Cerberus I'd end up armless. Instead, I put my faith, such as it was, in my last blade. Cerberus landed on me, his weight driving that blade into one neck. Blood immediately frothed forth in a pulsing arc. I'd hit a carotid artery. From one bubbling throat to another, I yanked the knife free and sliced again. I couldn't tell if I hit the artery that time. Already awash in blood and crushed beneath five hundred pounds of lycanthrope, I continued to slash blindly. Abruptly, the weight increased and what little air I had in my lungs was forced out. I fought against the choking bands of suffocation, tasting Cerberus's blood as it fell onto my face and lips. Slashing again with the knife, I heard through ringing ears what sounded like an entire pack of wolves snarling over me. Flay was still in the game. Subtract the added suffocation and that could've been a good thing. Then weight on me suddenly vanished and I could breathe again. I could see the sky again. I could also see the familiar face that moved into my field of vision.

"I believe you dropped this." Niko held out the Magnum and clucked a disapproving tongue against the roof of his mouth. "Very careless of you."

I let the knife fall beside me and closed a slippery hand around the butt of the gun. Dragging air back into my lungs, I coughed a few times, then sat up. "Better down there . . . ," I said hoarsely, standing, "than where it almost ended up." But I was speaking to empty air. Niko had joined the rolling pile of bestial violence. Sure feet balanced on the slope of a shaggy back, he swung his sword high and Cerberus became as singular as he'd always considered himself to be. One heavy head was impaled, the metal length punching through skull, brain, and jaw and into the roof below. Flay used the opportunity to wriggle from beneath Cerberus. This time the blood on him was his own. Staggering several feet away, the white wolf fell, then curled into an unmoving ball. Snowball was down for the count. Cerberus . . . Cerberus was not.

The Alpha reared up, ripping the sword that pinned the head of his deceased twin free from the tar. The glitter of silver piercing the dangling head was brighter than the rapidly dulling eyes. Blood and brain matter dripped from the loll of dead tongue. Cerberus was dead. Long live Cerberus . . . but how exactly long *was* long? Not only was his back leg still useless, but the front one on the same side had stopped moving as well. What I'd started with my knife, Niko had added to with his sword. Each head controlled its side of the body, and now half that body was dead.

The solitary howl of pain and loss was followed by one of unadulterated murderous fury. What remained of the wolf might not have much time left to him, but he was going to make the most of it. He spun on one back leg and propelled his mass toward us. It was an unbalanced rush, but powerful as a freight train just the same. Nik, who had landed lightly beside me after being bucked free of Cerberus, murmured matter-of-factly, "Do him the mercy."

It would be an act of mercy. Did he deserve mercy?

Doubtful, very goddamn doubtful. It didn't matter; I gave it to him anyway.

I emptied the remaining four rounds into his skull. It was amazing what you could accomplish with the luxury of aim and a handheld cannon sturdy enough to survive a four-story fall. Bone disintegrated, flesh peeled away in chunks, and a giant fell. A look of incomprehension flickered in swirls of black and copper and then died along with Cerberus. He changed back. That part of the legend was true. A nude heap sprawled in a tangle of muscular limbs and cold metal. He was still larger than life, but the misdirection of size didn't change the fact that now he looked human. Odd, yeah, but human. An unsettling quirk of chance had caused the two ruined heads to roll toward each other, and rest forehead to shattered forehead. Brothers. I tightened my jaw and slid my gaze away, focusing on Niko. "You want your sword back?"

"A given. I'll retrieve it." He looked me up and down, then zeroed in on my gore-covered face with a concerned frown. "Is any of that yours?"

"No, believe it or not." Putting the gun away, I swiped a sleeve across my face. "Miracles do happen."

"Yes, they do." He dipped a hand into his snug black jacket, then extended it toward me. "Here. Something else you misplaced."

It was the crown. I'd known he would find it below, but I couldn't deny the relief that thumped behind my ribs, liquid and warm. I accepted it, turning it in my hands, one way, then the other. The metal was cool to the touch, the stones even colder. That flash of heat I'd thought I felt before was nowhere to be found. "Hard to believe," I said softly. The unsaid conclusion echoed my earlier thought. Hard to believe this was worth George's life. Nik's hand gave my shoulder a

brief squeeze of agreement before he moved over to
Cerberus to work his sword loose. I moved as well,
toward the far edge of the roof. There the illumination
from the streetlight was brighter as it drifted up from
below. The dark gold appeared brighter, but things
weren't any more clear. It was just a . . . thing. A
piece of crap. *Nothing.*

And then it was. Literally nothing. In my
hand . . . nothing.

He came out of nowhere . . . like all bad dreams do.
He must've been perched on the side of the building,
waiting. They were good at that—waiting. One moment I stood alone and the next he flowed up over
the edge to stand before me, a horrifically distorted
reflection.

I froze. I'm not proud of it, but it's a fact—one of
those cold, hard ones you're always hearing about. He
stood there before me, simply stood . . . as if he wasn't
a ghost. Wasn't a figment from a life now led only in
nightmare. Wasn't Auphe.

Transparently white skin, narrow face, sullenly
burning molten eyes. Flaxen hair lifted on a nonexistent wind, and a thousand needle teeth bared and
washed with a foaming saliva. It was a sight I'd
thought I'd never see again. "Traitor." The voice was
flat and harsh, the dry rasp of scales across a stone
floor. "I've been searching for you." He crowned himself with the gold circlet that had been so easily
snatched from my paralyzed fingers before he flashed
a taloned hand toward my throat. "High and low."
The claws punctured skin without the restraint Cerberus had shown. "Far and wide." The face leaned
close to mine until its fetid breath soured the air in
my lungs. "Here and now."

My eyes closed involuntarily. They believed wholeheartedly what my mind wanted to. It wasn't true. It

was an illusion. It was a dream. I'd open my eyes and it would be gone. Just like that . . . gone. Only it didn't happen that way.

"I am the way, tainted cousin." The grip on my airway tightened. "I am righteous vengeance. You cannot close your eyes to that."

Transfixed, immobile . . . fucking *useless*. I should've shoved the fear and terror down. I should've concentrated on the loathing . . . the hate. Submit to an Auphe? Lie down for this pasty-ass shithead? No. *No.* I could snap the heel of my hand under his pointed chin and shove him away. I could plant a foot in his gut and throw him over the edge. The motions were so clear in my mind. I could see them, but I couldn't move. He was half the size of the Cerberus wolf, and still I couldn't move. Everyone has something in their life, in their world, that can break them. You might not be able to imagine it or to even fathom it exists . . . but it's there. For every single person, it's there. Mine, however, couldn't break me. It was far too late for that.

Couldn't break what had already been broken.

"Get away from him." Niko's taut voice was behind me. It couldn't have been far; the roof wasn't that large. There was no reason he should sound a world away. "Get away from him *now*."

The warning claws sank deeper in my flesh, a catchall deterrent. "Betrayed your kind," the Auphe hissed. A strand of colorless hair touched my cheek. It was slippery and it burned, a track of cold fire. "Betrayed your own."

He wasn't wrong. I had betrayed the Auphe. Biggest and best accomplishment of my life to date. I'd participated, although not as much as I'd have liked, in the wholesale destruction of what remained of their race. Niko, Robin, and I had kept them from turning this world into what it had once been before humans had ruled. We'd stopped them from taking us back to when the supernatural was natural, the water and air were perfume sweet, and humans were at best toys and at worst a mild nuisance. While a world run by the Auphe might be more ecologically sound, the murder and mutilation ratio would be a definite downside.

"Did you think we were all gone, traitor child?" I could taste blood in my mouth as the elongated fingers continued to tighten around my throat. "Did you think there would not be consequences for one such as you?"

No. I'd never thought that. I'd been living with the consequences of the Auphe all my life. Only recently had I been dealing with the consequences of their death. I would take the second over the first any damn day. Or I would have done that until now. Of course, none of my thoughts were quite that coherent. Rapidly disintegrating, bits and pieces of them would roll and surface briefly, silvered fish in a storm-driven sea, before vanishing under an ever-rising swell of sickened disbelief. It was a disbelief that refused to die despite the evidence before me. It couldn't be a live Auphe. Couldn't be.

"Did you think you would be safe?"

Could.

"Did you think you would escape your beloved family?"

Not.

"You shall not."

Be.

Nails were ripped free from my neck with callous efficiency. Bloodstained, they were held up for my examination. "But it will not be this simple. For you, never this simple. Never this painless.

"Every moment." Lipless teeth touched my forehead in a hideous parody of a paternal kiss. "Of every day." He took a step back, graceful as a striking snake. "We will watch you. We will take all from you. All and everyone." A red-tinted claw traced the circlet on his head. "As I took this."

I tried then. I really did. It was as if I'd forgotten how to make my body work. Nerves were sluggish . . . joints fixed and rusty, but in a pathetic, drunken fumble, I was able to reach out with a numb hand.

Slow, too slow.

"This, betrayer, is only the beginning. We have such games planned for this world." The grin was as bright and cold as a slice of winter sky. "What a pity your sanity shall not survive to see them." One more step and he balanced on the edge of the roof, then plummeted off.

Niko's sword, still wet with wolf blood, struck the edge a fraction of a second after the Auphe's plunge. *"Fuck,"* came the viciously spit curse. That sounded like me, not my calm, cool, collected brother. At any other time I would've been amazed and amused that Niko would admit to knowing the word, much less using it. At this particular time, however, I didn't feel amazement. I damn sure didn't feel amusement. In fact, I suddenly felt nothing at all. My legs gave way and I fell to my knees.

"Cal."

I didn't feel the rough surface beneath me, or the way it scored my flesh raw as I methodically beat my fists against it.

"Cal."

I didn't feel the pressure of hands on my shoulders or the hard motion that shook me. I could see it all, distant and hazy, but I felt absolutely nothing and that was fine with me. Hands stopped my fists from their pounding, then wound around fistfuls of my shirt to pull me effortlessly to my feet. The keen of a siren floated over Nik's voice, giving the words peculiar halos of red light. "The police are coming, Cal. We have to go."

Go? Where could we possibly go? In a world where the Auphe still lived, where could we go? We'd already learned the hard way that we couldn't hide forever. Not from the Auphe, and not from what I had done. George's best chance of coming home, George's only chance . . .

And I'd just lost it.

13

Numbness can't last, as much as you might like it to. Too bad.

I sat on the edge of the tub and focused on the tiled floor as Niko finished mopping the blood from my skin. He'd removed the torn stitches from my arm and cleaned the half-healed bite, but otherwise left it alone. The copper that had filled my mouth when facing the Auphe had been from a savagely bitten tongue; I kept that less-than-heroic gem to myself. The only real damage had been done to my neck, and that wasn't nearly as bad as it could've been. The Auphe had made it clear my death would be the least of my punishment. They didn't want to try to use me again to bring an end to this world. They knew I was a less-than-reliable tool, and from the sounds of it, they had other ways in mind. No, they didn't want to use me anymore; what they wanted from me was far more simple than that: pain.

The bite of antiseptic stung under my jaw and I hissed. It was the first thing I'd felt since the rooftop and my first real reaction. "Welcome back," Niko said with quiet relief, opening a package of small butterfly bandages.

Not exactly happy to be back, I shifted my shoulders and remained silent. Turning over my hands, I gazed at the skinned knuckles. Niko had saved them from worse. Time and again, he'd saved me from all kinds of worse . . . including the Auphe. This wasn't any easier for him than it was for my worthless ass— to say the least. And he didn't have the luxury of going catatonic. Raising my eyes to his, I asked diffidently, "Are you okay?" The question came out stiff and uncertain as if I'd spent days mute instead of only hours.

"I've had better days." He applied several of the bandages. "Many, many better." Sliding the flat of his hand around to the nape of my neck, he squeezed lightly. "How are you?"

How was I? Now, there was a question. "Me?" I flipped my hands back over to see callused but undamaged palms. Our psychic was gone; there was no one left to read the lines and creases. "I'm fine. Just fine. Couldn't be fucking finer."

"Well, goody for you, because I am anything but," Goodfellow said, appearing in the doorway with his mobile face pale and set. Robin had the distinct displeasure of having been around nearly as long as the Auphe. He knew them as well as my brother and I did and hated them almost as much. "Niko, you may want to look at Flay. He's out here bleeding like the proverbial stuck pig, and he's doing it all over your carpet. I personally don't care if he lives or dies, but you may have some things to discuss with him."

"Flay?" Nik's face darkened. His hand gripped my neck tighter, then dropped away. "This promises to be interesting." As Robin turned and walked away, my brother watched me carefully as I stood. I wasn't sure if it was physical or mental balance that he was worried about. "We'll survive this, Cal," he offered with absolute certainty. "I swear it. We defeated the Auphe once. We'll do it again."

And George? How are we going to get George back now? I wanted to ask, but didn't. I didn't know that I was ready to hear the answer.

I didn't remember Niko phoning Goodfellow or Promise, but he must have, as both were in the living room. Flay was as well, looking like extra-large road-kill. "How did he get here?" I asked impassively, leaning against the wall with folded arms and watching as Promise and Niko knelt beside him. Yeah, Snowball may have saved my life—emphasis on *may*—but I didn't delude myself into thinking that was his goal. He'd wanted Cerberus dead. Helping me had been an accidental by-product at best.

"From the looks of the hallway, dragging himself on his stomach while vomiting blood the entire way," Robin answered grimly. He'd retrieved our mop and bucket from the kitchen. "By the way, I do not do windows." He exited to dispose of the evidence, slamming the door behind him to underline his displeasure at the bout of manual labor.

Promise pressed another folded sheet to Flay's chest and turned to Niko. "I didn't know if you wanted him alive. If not, I apologize for your ruined linen." Her normally temperate voice was briskly businesslike. She wasn't wasting any Florence Nightingale sympathies on the half-dead wolf. Her hair hung in a tail down her back, tightly disciplined and smooth, but her clothes were a set of delicate lounging pajamas. Spiderweb fine, the white material wasn't snug, but it definitely molded her petite form. The long cloak she'd worn over it had been discarded on the couch in a jumbled hurry. She clearly hadn't wasted a moment rushing over upon receiving Niko's call. Her eyes when they lifted to mine were as soft as the silk she was wrapped in and full of an empathy I wasn't prepared to deal with. I dropped my eyes toward Flay instantly.

"I'm not precisely sure myself," Niko returned acidly as he used a thumb to pry open one of Flay's closed lids. Flay was still in his quasi-wolf form, his best chance of healing himself, and his fur-covered face was fixed in a rictus of pain. He was hanging on, but only just. At Niko's prodding the glassy red eyes opened. Surrounded by a line of nude baby-pink skin, they looked oddly vulnerable. "What are you doing here, Omega?"

Omega, the lowest-ranking wolf. Flay had been Beta, second-in-command, under Cerberus, but in our pack he was pulling up last all the way. When you were as intelligent as Niko, you could tailor an insult to even the most obscure of monsters. "No . . . where." Pink froth stained the white fur around his mouth. "Else . . . go."

True enough. He'd helped take Cerberus down, normally a good career move for a wolf. Upward mobility and killing your boss were one and the same in the Kin. But Flay hadn't fought one-on-one. He'd joined in with a human and a half Auphe to destroy his Alpha. When the first wolf caught a whiff of Niko's and my presence on the roof, Flay would hit number one on the Kin's most wanted list. As for Caleb, Snowball hadn't lived up to the expectations of that master either. I didn't know what Caleb's reaction would be, but judging from Flay's appearance in our apartment, I guessed it wouldn't be pleasant. Poor Snowball, he was a fur ball without a country.

My heart wept for him. Truly.

"Kill him," I said coldly. "He didn't know shit before. I doubt he knows anything now."

Niko gave a fractional lift of his eyebrows at the remark, but his only comment was, "Perhaps Robin could use some help in the hall."

He thought I might not be thinking precisely straight. He was right, and guess what? I was actually smart enough to know it. I left the three of them and walked out into the hall, closing the door with exquisite care. I thought that if I'd slammed it as Goodfellow had, I might not have stopped until it was nothing more than splinters.

"Good. A sour and sulky helper. Who says dreams don't come true?" The puck tossed me the mop and leaned gratefully against the wall, shifting the weight off his healing leg. The cheap tile floor was as much of a mess as he'd said. Exhaling harshly, I dunked the mop and got to it. The work went quickly. Luckily, it was late enough that none of our neighbors were up and about to make things dicey. As a matter of fact . . . I checked my watch and blinked. Four a.m. Shit. I'd been mentally AWOL a little longer than I'd thought.

"I was thinking Angistri."

I didn't bother to stop the rhythmic slap and swirl of the mop. "What?" I said, incurious.

"Angistri. It's a Greek island. Fairly secluded, utterly beautiful." He massaged the top of his leg and smirked. "Nude beaches." The leer faded as quickly as it had come. "It will be a long time before any Auphe finds us there. We'll find George and off we'll go."

The mop continued to move of its own accord. Back and forth. I followed along with it, silent. I'd finished half the hall before I finally spoke. "I'm sorry."

Having given up on the hopes of getting any sparkling conversation out of me, Goodfellow tilted his head. "Pardon?"

I watched as red-tinted water dripped into the bucket for several seconds before I submerged the mop again. "I'm sorry. Nik and I got you into this mess with the Auphe." The Auphe had made it clear that he'd take what was important to me before he actually took me. The means to save George would be only the first. What would be next? My brother, my friends . . . I swallowed and clenched the wood handle with a tight fist. Even if Robin hadn't been my friend, he'd still be on the Auphe's shit list. He'd been just as instrumental in bringing them down, if not more, than I had been.

"Caliban." Robin's mouth lengthened, then turned up slightly at the corners. "No one held a gun to my head." His eyes gleamed in reminiscence. "A knife to the throat, yes, but not a gun." He straightened and limped over to take the mop from my hands. "I made my choice, and believe it or not, I have no regrets." He swabbed. "Well, other than my constant exposure to what you imagine to be humor."

"What?" I rubbed a hand over suddenly weary eyes. "No swipe at my fashion sense?"

He took in my jeans and bloodstained T-shirt and gave an exaggerated sigh. "I know defeat when it rears its ugly poly-blend head."

As he started to clean, I pulled the tie from my hair to let the ponytail fall free. I ducked my head and strands of hair swung over my face, a curtain between me and the world. "Robin . . . thanks."

"For what?" he asked promptly. "For allowing you the privilege of basking in my charm? Gifting you with my wit and wisdom? Of course, it *could* be that I've saved your melancholy ass on more than one occasion."

I gave an involuntary snort, then looked up to say quietly, "I meant, thanks for sticking around."

"I'm good at many, many things. Excellent really."
He finished mopping up the last bit of the blood trail
and curled his lips in self-deprecation. "But sticking
around hasn't always been one of those things. So . . .
gold star for me." He opened the exit door to peer
down the stairs and cursed. "All the way down. All
the thrice-damned way down." Threading fingers
through his hair, he flashed me a humorless grin.
"Fetch the bucket, Cinderella. We have a long night
ahead of us."

It was two hours, tops, but it felt longer. Sore and
bone tired, I carried the mop and bucket back into
the apartment, stepped over the bloodstain on the carpet, and fell onto the couch. No Flay on the floor
meant he either was recuperating in the tub, or on
one of our beds, or had been tossed out a window.
The way my luck had been running it was probably
one of the first two options. Damn it. Too tired to
reach out and turn off the lamp, I crooked my arm
over my eyes and waited for the darkness to come.
Promise came first.

"He's scared."

I opened my eyes as her weight settled on a cushion's edge. Her hair lay across her breast in a sleek
tail; her face was pale and grave. "Flay?" I grunted.
"He should be. Where is the shithead? He better not
be bleeding all over my bed."

"Flay is in Niko's bed." Her hand was small, but
her grip was strong as she curled her fingers around
mine. "But it wasn't Flay I was speaking of."

"I know," I murmured. No, not Flay, but I'd wanted
to hang on to the pretense for a moment or so. Niko,
who feared nothing on his own behalf, took on the
weight of the world when it came to me. I sat up and
gently extricated my hand from hers. I'd always
thought Niko would've been better off without me.

Now I had to face up to the fact that everyone who knew me was in the same boat, including Promise. "It's the Auphe." An unnecessary statement if ever there was one. "They . . . shit." I rested my head in my hands. She had seen the worst of it last year; she knew about the Auphe. But there was something I wasn't sure that she did know. I wasn't sure it was something that anyone but Niko and I could know. Straightening, I said frankly, "Last year was bad, but it was just the icing on the cake. The Auphe have been with us our entire lives." My mouth twisted and I corrected, "My entire life. Nik's first four years were monster free." I wondered if he thought that had been long enough.

"And you thought it was over."

"We thought it was over," I confirmed heavily. "If we hadn't, I'm not sure . . ." I shook my head. Stupid, pointless thoughts. "You and Nik can have my bed." If she stayed, and for Niko's sake I hoped that she did. "I'm too tired to get off the couch anyway."

"Caliban." There was a touch on my hair. Sympathy, understanding, solace . . . and I wanted none of it.

Pulling away with care, I lay back down. "Good night, Promise. Take care of him."

She sighed and stood, bending to brush a kiss over my hair. "You already do that, the same as he does for you."

The Auphe, George, none of it could stand against the exhaustion. I didn't need a pillow or blanket. Sprawling on the couch in the dim light of the lamp, I slept hard with no dreams. When a nightmare comes true in your waking hours, it doesn't need to follow you into sleep. At least not this time. As tired as I was, I didn't sleep long. The sun, bright and hot, was streaming full force through the blinds when I levered sticky eyelids open, and I put the time around ten.

Four hours' sleep. All things considered, it was more than I'd hoped for. As I pushed off the tenacious remains of sleep, I saw something else as constant as the sun. A dark blond head rested against the arm of the couch, breaths even and deep.

I groaned. "Jesus, Nik. You turn down a bed and a beautiful woman to sleep on the floor. I wonder about your priorities, Cyrano. I do."

"Who's to say I didn't split my time equally?" He'd awakened immediately, probably before I managed to get the first syllable out of my mouth. Instantly alert, he sat up from the boneless slouching position he'd slept in and sheathed the knife that had been cradled in his hand. My own was still tucked under the cushion.

"Trust me. Time spent with Promise and time spent babysitting me don't work out quite the same." I rolled over onto my back and rubbed the sleep from my eyes. "You worry about me too much, Nik." My hand made an automatic grab for a braid that was no longer there. I missed Niko's hair, if only for the annoyance it gave him when I tugged on it. Letting my empty hand dangle toward the floor, I went on, "You should worry more about yourself. So should Promise and Goodfellow."

"Don't," he said firmly.

I turned my head back toward him. "Nik, you heard what—"

"I said *don't*," he overrode me. "It doesn't matter what it said, Cal. Not to me, and not to Promise or Robin. A few may have survived the warehouse explosion, but they won't survive for long. They . . ." He stopped, lips pressed tight. Closing his eyes, he massaged his forehead with the heel of his hand. "I'm an idiot. They're back, aren't they? They're truly back. Bastards."

I extended an arm and hooked it around his neck for a rough squeeze. "Goodfellow says there's a Greek nudie island he could take us to."

His eyes opened, and he snorted through his long nose. "And how is that better than the Auphe? Or less dangerous, for that matter?"

I stretched my lips into the closest thing to a grin I could manage. "Good point." I released him and sat up. "Do you think . . . ?" I hesitated, but then pushed on. "Do you think the Auphe took George?"

"No," he said with the certainty that let me know he'd already carefully weighed the possibility before dismissing it. "The Auphe are straightforward in their maliciousness. If they had wanted George, they would've taken her. Simply, and without the distraction of Caleb and the crown."

I felt something inside me unclench a little. George in Caleb's hands was gut-wrenching; George in the hands of the Auphe . . . it was a connection in my brain that I couldn't even make. "Okay." I blew out a heavy breath and repeated, "Okay." I retrieved my blade from under the cushion and watched the sunlight ripple on its surface. "Now tell me, why the hell is that mangy Flay in your bed and not headfirst down the incinerator where he belongs?"

"He wouldn't fit?" he offered with a raised eyebrow. At my unappreciative growl, Nik stood, stretched, and relented. "He doesn't know anything useful that he's aware of. But now that he is persona non grata with the Kin and Caleb, he may be able to advise us on what Caleb's next step would be. It would only be a guess, but a guess is more than we have now."

It was smart thinking and good strategy, but in the end, it came to nothing. In seven hours Flay didn't wake once. Oh, sure, he'd shared his bodily fluids, *all* of them, with us . . . all over Nik's bed. But consciousness? Words? No. Promise said she'd seen it before, a self-induced coma that concentrated all a wolf's resources on healing. Nothing could wake the son of a bitch and don't think I didn't try. I did. And with an enthusiasm I didn't like to think about. Finally, Niko dragged me out to the kitchen and pushed me into a chair. "Drink," he commanded, depositing a glass in front of me.

Looking at the container of brown liquid dubiously, I said, "Yeah, thanks anyway. What ails me I don't think your wheatgrass can cure."

"And torturing an unconscious wolf will?" he retorted.

I felt the burn behind my skin spread to tingle in my mouth. Shame. What had seemed completely justified only minutes ago now seemed far less so under my brother's gaze. So I did the very least I could do. Taking the glass, I drank. Expecting the usual healthy concoction, I nearly choked on the scorch of whiskey. Considering our mother, it was the last thing I'd expected Niko to slip me, but oddly enough it was just what I needed. One swallow was enough. Hot as my rage, the alcohol burned a path down to my stomach and woke me up. That was the best way to put it. It woke me up, jarring the cycle of fear and hate and letting me step free of it for a moment.

"Let me make myself perfectly clear, Cal." He put his hands on the table and bent down to fix me with an unwavering look. "I don't give a damn what you do to Flay. I do, however, give a damn what you do to yourself. All right?" He didn't give me time to respond. "Now . . ." After removing the still half-full glass to the sink, he sat down opposite me. "Goodfellow called. He's had an idea."

Justifiably suspicious of any patented Goodfellow scheme, I asked, "What kind of idea?"

"Abbagor."

That had been the original Goodfellow extrava-
ganza that had birthed my suspicious nature to begin
with. To hear it repeated was the nastiest sort of déjà
vu. "You've got to be shitting me." I jerked back in
the chair so abruptly I nearly tipped it over. "Jesus.
Tell me you're shitting me."

"Would that I could," he said impassively.

"He tried to kill us last time, Nik. You do remember that, right?" I said caustically. I sure as hell did
and as memories went, it wasn't among Christmas Day
and the smell of puppy breath for warm and fuzzy.
Abbagor was . . . Shit, Abbagor was Abbagor. A mass
of living flesh, buried victims, and an appetite for violence and blood that was legendary. He was also a
troll, but not like any fairy-tale troll I'd seen in any
book. He was not like anything I'd seen ever . . .
anywhere. And what he had nearly done to Niko . . .
Christ. "He tried to kill us, and he tried pretty
damn hard."

"As Goodfellow reminded me, with considerable
condescension, he'll most likely try to kill us this time
as well. But apparently Abbagor knows everything
about anything," he said with distaste. "He is our best
chance at tracking down the other crown."

"The other crown?" I frowned. "You think it still
exists?"

"It's possible. The first survived. Why not the second? I think it at least bears looking into. And the
best place to look into it happens to be with Abbagor.
He, as he's proven before, knows something about
everything."

I closed my eyes. Unfortunately it was true. The
troll was an information miser. If there was something
worth knowing, he knew it. Hell, even if it wasn't worth
knowing, he knew it. "Great. Just . . . great. I don't

suppose you'd do me a favor and hang around topside when we go visit the son of a bitch?''

"Considering the three of us barely walked away last time, I would have to say no," he said dryly.

What went unsaid was that the previous year we'd been at top form. No wounded arm for me, no Goodfellow limping around like a lame horse. "Wonder where I can get a bazooka on short notice," I said, grimacing.

"Sufficient unto the day the ass kicking therein." Nik's hand landed on my shoulder, then urged me up. "We'll worry about it later. Facing Abbagor without sleep isn't wise."

Facing Abbagor at all wasn't wise. As a matter of fact, it wasn't anything less than suicidal. And it didn't matter a damn. We were backed in a corner; we were drowning. If Abbagor was the only straw within reach, then . . .

We'd just have to grasp it.

14

Abbagor dwelled in a labyrinth of tunnels under the Brooklyn Bridge. Where else would a troll live? How long he'd been there, I didn't know, but it didn't really matter. From the housewarming on, he'd made the place his own. It was his hunting ground and playground all in one—think about that the next time you haul your butt over to Brooklyn. Night was the worst. It was the time Abbagor ranged the length of the bridge, looking for food . . . looking for pets. Better to be food. If your car stalled there some night late, you'd better keep your ass inside with doors locked and pray. Pray hard.

Not that anyone seemed to be listening.

Behind a shielding abutment rested the door to Abby's summer, winter, and forever home. Last year when we'd come seeking information about the Auphe, there had been a heavy layer of mud over concrete around the entrance. And the smell . . . I hadn't hurled, but it'd been a close one. It was better this time, the ground hard and dry at our feet. The grate we had dropped through was back in place and secured with a shiny padlock. I looked down at it and kicked the lock, saying fatalistically, "Maybe it's a sign."

"If only." Robin pulled his wallet out and teased

out a small piece of metal. In less than three seconds the lock was history. Goodfellow with a lockpick was faster than I was with a key. "There," he offered with a healthy dose of self-conceit. "It's the least I can do."

I cut him some slack; he wasn't nearly as smug as he normally would've been. Niko and I were going below, but Robin was staying behind. My arm and sore ribs were bad enough, but Goodfellow couldn't run. That crossbow bolt had torn up a good chunk of his leg muscle when we were attacked in that alley. I still wasn't sure who was behind that, although I had some ideas. It was either another one of Caleb's happy little tests to prove we were tough enough to take on the Kin or a dark and twisted game of the Auphe. There was no real way of knowing one way or the other, but from the rambling of our attacker, I was betting Caleb. "He said and you came," the guy had said. "*He* said . . ." Caleb appeared almost human. He was a "he." Faced with an Auphe, I doubted two things: that the man would've been at all coherent about what the Auphe said, and that he would've called an Auphe "he." Your average human with both feet in the mundane and normal world would've gone with "it," combined with a few throat-tearing screams for punctuation. Besides, when the Auphe subcontracted, they did a whole lot better than a nut job with a crossbow.

Since Robin couldn't run, a high priority when in Abbagor's lair, he was sitting this one out up top. Moral support in five-hundred-dollar sunglasses. The lawn chair he had carried from his car had cost considerably less. I watched as he unfolded it and took a seat. Lacing fingers across his stomach, he leaned back and turned his face to the sun. "Comfy?" I inquired caustically.

"Nearly." He yawned. "Have Abby send up a margarita, would you? Frozen with salt."

"Yeah, sure," I snorted. "No problem." As Niko bent, hooked his fingers in the grate, and tossed it aside, I rubbed at weary eyes. Through my own dark glasses the sun seared my retinas with the pain and brilliance of a laser. I'd slept another night, despite my dismal expectations, but it had left me feeling hungover and a headache throbbed steadily at the base of my skull.

"Ready?" Niko prodded.

I pulled off my glasses, tossed them in Goodfellow's lap, and grunted, "So where's that bazooka?"

"You've one good arm left, little brother." Niko crouched on the lip of the opening and scanned the darkness below. "I'm quite sure you can arm-wrestle Abbagor to his death if it comes to that." With that, he slipped over the edge and disappeared from sight.

I sighed and trudged to the reeking black square. "Have a good nap, Loman."

He waved me off. "Scream if you need anything." Unfortunately, if it came to that, there wasn't a single, solitary thing Robin could do to help us. He knew that as well as we did, and if he wanted to pretend this was going to be a walk in the park, who was I to screw up his sun-worshipping, margarita-chugging psychological defense mechanism? Facing Abbagor was going to suck, no two ways about it, but the helpless waiting, that was no picnic either. We all knew, from past and current experience, that waiting was a special hell all its own.

"Screaming I can do," I said with grim cheer as I sat on the opening's edge. "See you later, Goodfellow. Don't forget the sunblock." I jumped down, the midcalf-deep muck softening the landing just as it had done the last time. No matter how dry it was above, here it was always wet, always a swamp. And it always stunk to the unseen heavens. The stench of rotting flesh and old blood, the smell of a slave master wallowing in his own filth—it didn't exactly qualify as aromatherapy. But this time I came prepared. Pulling a small tube from my pocket, I deposited a minute amount of astringent muscle-ache ointment on my upper lip. That opened the sinuses like a fire hose, but it was a much more acceptable smell, one I could deal with.

Niko was waiting on me with folded arms and a curious, tilted head. "Clever."

"Hey, I watch TV, same as anyone else." And if ever there was a crime scene, this made the cut. Finishing up, I reached back and retrieved the gun hung on my back. No bazooka, but a Browning semiautomatic shotgun. It probably wouldn't kill the troll. Could be nothing would. I'd emptied a clip in his skull the last time without much effect. Regardless, investing in a little more stopping power was never a bad thing, and this had more field of fire than the Magnum. I would've priced grenade launchers if we hadn't been headed underground.

I wrapped the leather strap around my arm and set the stock against my hip bone. "Well, fearless leader? Are we ready?"

"And what makes me the leader?" Forgoing the flashlight we'd brought, Niko began to walk, smoothly and unhindered by the mud. The faint glow of luminescent lichen on the walls shed enough light to just see his outline. It was more than we'd had last time. Someone was being awfully welcoming.

"You kicking my ass every time I say different ring any bells?" I slogged. Niko skated across the sticky surface like a water bug on a glassy pond, and I slogged. Preternatural genes didn't help worth a damn when it came to swimming through slop. Didn't it figure?

"I'm forced to do it so often I can't be expected to remember every occasion." Holding up a hand, he added softly, "Now, quiet."

"Why? He already knows we're here." Before us was a doorway I recognized. Carved through the concrete wall with diamond-sharp talons, it was a gaping eye socket to the troll's labyrinth. Beyond, maintenance tunnels had been expanded far into the earth and God help the potbellied city worker that stuck his nose through that door. A union card didn't carry much weight with Abbagor.

"I'm sure he does, but since we want his assistance, try for a minimum of manners." His sword already in hand, Miss Manners stepped through the doorway.

"You want us to show respect for the evil bastard? Jesus, Nik," I complained, but my heart wasn't in it. We'd do what we had to do, for George. If that meant playing nice with this malicious shithead, then that's what we would do. And if that didn't work, we could try chopping off pieces of him until he felt a shade more cooperative. Hey, I was flexible.

Subsiding into silence, I followed behind my brother as we retraced our path from last year . . . mentally and physically. I had better memories and not many worse. Niko had very nearly died in this place. No, that wasn't true. What had almost happened to him was worse than death, far worse. Abbagor killed, true, but he also liked his "pets." How he made them I couldn't begin to guess. I wasn't even sure of the end result; I hadn't caught more than a glimpse of them, but Niko said they were—God help them—aware. Reduced to bits and pieces, but conscious. And Niko would know. He'd been halfway to becoming one, swallowed whole by the roiling mass of tendrils that

formed Abbagor's massive body. Every time that
memory hit me, so did another. An anonymous
hand . . . male, with a rose tattoo. It appeared between
tentacles to stroke the gray pallid flesh with a reveren-
tial motion. Living . . . *existing* in the prison that was
Abbagor, was a horror that was hard to grasp. I didn't
want to and Niko didn't have to. And here we were,
walking right back into his reach. Desperation . . . it
could make you do some crazy shit.

Crazy.

Picking up the pace, I shouldered past Niko right
as we entered the cavern hollowed out in a masonry
tower. Maybe he could all but walk on mud like some
sort of bargain-basement messiah, but it hadn't helped
him last time. Abbagor had his own issues with me.
If I could keep his attention focused on me, it would
give my more mobile brother a better chance. A better
chance to fight; if worse came to worst, a better chance
to run. I'd take whatever I could get. I would die for
George, but give up my brother? It wasn't a choice I
could live with. Wasn't a choice I would make.

Of course, Niko would tell me it wasn't mine *to*
make.

"Cal," he hissed under his breath with annoyance
as I passed him, but before he could attempt to snare
my arm Abbagor's voice came through the gloom.

"Auphelingggg." It was a wet burble, a last breath
forced through a mouthful of blood.

I looked up automatically. Last year Abbagor had
descended from the three-story-tall ceiling like a
bloated spider. Although at our level there was a dim
light emanating from the glowing-slime-covered walls,
above there was only infinite darkness. I strained my
eyes but saw nothing. "I'm flattered as hell, Abby," I
said laconically. "You remember me."

"I remember all," came the clotted gurgle. "And

always shall I remember you." He appeared in the mud at our feet, the slow rise of a methane bubble rising through a fetid swamp. There had to be a drop-off, a pit dug to accommodate his mass. That was new. The muck covering him wouldn't have hidden us from him. He had no eyes, Abbagor, only shallow indentations in the knotted flesh, but he didn't need eyes to see better than we could. His back, a twisted terrain of tangled tendrils, surfaced last, preceded by floating arms and a misshapen head. The back of his skull was a mass of shattered bone forming jagged peaks covered by thick skin. I might not have killed him, but I'd messed up his pretty looks. Yippee.

"Where is the little goat?" Freed of the mud, the python mouth formed words mellow and clear as the ringing of the purest crystal. His voice was completely at odds with his hideous appearance and peculiar enough to send an atavistic shiver down my spine.

"Goodfellow had a previous engagement," Niko said, stepping up to my side. "He sends his apologies."

"Destined to forever be forsaken," was the doleful reply. It was accompanied by a sigh as mournful as the sound of crying angels. "That is my fate. My ever-lasting sorrow."

He'd said that before . . . that he was forsaken. But then he'd said it about the Auphe. Nearly as ancient as they were, Abbagor had the original love/hate relationship with the Auphe. He loved to hate them. Loved to mutilate . . . to rip limb from limb, whatever he could manage. And to his pleasure, the Auphe were a good match for him. Apparently, Abby had a problem with boredom, and he'd do anything to relieve it. That his own blood was often spilled in the battles didn't bother him at all. When we'd come to him for information before, he'd attacked in the hopes of provoking the Auphe. He'd known they wanted me badly and would come to retrieve me. But he'd been denied that festive little party and had ended up with a head only a mother could love.

"That's a different look for you, Abby." My finger was taut on the shotgun's trigger. "New hairdresser?"

For once Niko didn't bury a pointed elbow in my ribs. He knew that manners alone wouldn't bring us Abbagor's cooperation. The monster had to be entertained. A bored Abbagor would no doubt try to kill us, but an amused one might play with us first. Give us what we wanted to know. It would make our despair sharper when he took us . . . more enjoyable.

"A memento, Aupheling, keeping your memory forever warm in my heart." He continued to float with all the grace and charm of a corpse bobbing in the river.

"I don't know what pumps your blood, Abby," I gritted with disgust, "but it's not a heart."

Niko jumped into the conversation before I could "entertain" the troll further. "We're looking for something, Abbagor. A crown. Goodfellow says there is very little that passes in this world that you are unaware of."

After a long stretch of silent contemplation, Abbagor commented with melodious complacency, "True. All falls under my benevolent eye." He stood upright, in all his self-proclaimed benevolence. Nine feet tall and nearly as broad, he might have been vaguely man-shaped, but he towered over us like a tree. Granted, it was a flesh-eating tree from hell, but I stand by the analogy. The liquid earth cascaded off him, showing more of the twining slate-colored flesh than I wanted to see. The shifting and the rustling of the tendrils made my stomach do a slow nauseated turn. With every unnatural, sinuous movement, I expected to see a flash of pale skin . . . human skin. Slave skin. "You may describe it to me."

Okay, it couldn't be that easy; nothing in this life was. And neither was this. We'd come here expecting the troll to put us through our paces, and the game was already under way. Abby wasn't wasting any time in screwing with our heads. "I have a picture." Niko held up the sketch with his free hand.

"Ahhh, the Calabassa," Abbagor said with instant recognition. "Barely ten thousand years old. Modern trash," he added scornfully, "from a refuse race."

And now we had a confirmed name for it. That was just peachy. "And that would be?" I asked impatiently.

"The Bassa." The head, equally as massive as the rest of him, with the upswept ears of a bat, fixed me with its unnervingly unblind gaze. "Your kind, uneducated Aupheling, wiped them out not long after that crown was made. Every male and female, every child, every egg. And then, if I remember correctly, you ate them." His jaw unhinged into a gaping grin. "Quite tasty the Bassa were, once the poison sacs were removed. The most tender of meat, sweet and mild."

I ignored the yank of my chain. It wasn't news to me that in their day the Auphe had maimed, tortured, and killed anyone or anything that had crossed their path. *They* had; I hadn't. I didn't. I wouldn't.

Whether Flay agreed with me or not was a different story.

"I'm sure it was a hell of an all-you-can-eat buffet, but that's not what we want to know. If the Bassa are gone, where is the crown now?" Niko and I had decided it was best not to bring up the fact I'd already lost one. If there were two, we might luck out and Abbagor would know the location of the other. If we told him what had happened, he would no doubt lie out of pure capricious spite.

"Its purpose, if it has one, would be helpful as well," Niko added.

"Both hands out begging." The troll expelled a huge sigh, the scent of which nearly dropped me. The ointment on my lip didn't have a prayer of blocking that out. I smelled . . . God, so many things. Vomit and bile, blood and the adrenaline of hearts terrorized to their physical limits. Ripe decay and the sloughing of rotting skin. I smelled a graveyard of the half-dead, I smelled Abbagor's victims. Viciously, I bit my lower lip until I reached a precarious truce with my own bile.

He was looking at me. I don't know how I knew that, but he was. "You want and want, greedy little half-breed, but what do you give?" Tendrils began to loosen from Abbagor's torso with their questing tips twitching in parody of a sniffing motion as they hung in the air.

"I don't know, Abby. You have my charming company. What else do you want?" I demanded, baring teeth in a humorless rictus of a grin. He wanted to play all right. But for every minute he amused himself, George spent that same minute with Caleb. And that put a serious crimp in my Abbagor fun-and-games tolerance level.

"I want . . . I want . . . ," he mused as the tentacles crept closer to us slowly and cautiously, showing none of the speed of before. "I want to touch. I want to taste. I want to know what I knew before. I want to know the part of me that is gone." The tendrils began to drift toward Niko and it hit me in an explosion of fear and rage.

Nik. He wanted Nik.

"No way," I snarled, immediately putting a pound of pressure on a two-pound trigger. "No fucking way."

"Be calm, Aupheling." Soothing, so soothing . . . not. "I only wish to touch. I've missed my fair-haired thrall."

I didn't need any college to know that "thrall" was a fancy word for slave. I'd have to remember to tell Niko that the next time he nagged me about higher education. "Then touch yourself, you piece of shit. Just wait until we're gone to do it." The shotgun was already cocked and I raised the muzzle to point directly at Abbagor's face.

Suddenly disinterested, the troll turned his head away. "That is my price. A touch for what only I know. Pay or no, I care not."

"I could make you care, you son of a bitch." The pound of pressure had gone to one and a half when Niko's hand closed on my shoulder.

"Wait," he ordered calmly.

"No, Nik. Absolutely not." I didn't have to hear the words to know what my brother was going to say. And I didn't have to hear them to say no.

"It's only a touch, Cal," he pointed out in his most practical tone. Reasonable, logical, and a complete and utter lie. The lightest of brushes from Abbagor's tendrils could and *had* resulted in less-than-innocent things. On our first meeting, he had dragged me at a breakneck speed by my ensnared arms and had co-cooned Niko so quickly that my brother had disappeared right before my eyes. He had been lost inside Abbagor. He had been *gone*. A touch wasn't simply a touch with Abbagor, creepy PSAs aside. And no matter how composed Niko might appear on the outside, he had to be screaming on the inside. I know I would've been. Shit, I *was*, and I'd only seen what had happened to Niko. I hadn't lived through it as he had.

"No, Cyrano." I shook my head stubbornly. "It's not going to happen. So shut up and start chopping."

I had doubts, serious doubts, that there was anything we could do to Abbagor that would force him to talk, but I would rather give it a homicidal whirl than let him touch Niko.

The hand on my shoulder tightened. "It's a game, Cal. Only a game." Resolute and serene, but so what? Niko would've been resolute and serene at his own execution. "Besides, isn't it better to know that it's coming?"

He had me there. It was coming, one way or the other. I had no delusions that the troll was going to let us walk out of here with a smile and a slimy handshake. Then again, feeling that cold ribbon of muscle loop around you in the heat of battle was different from waiting for it, quiet and accepting. Considerably, horrifically different. I shook my head again. "No. Just . . . no."

"It's for Georgina." His eyes held mine, gray to gray. "She would do it for me, Cal. Allow me to do it for her."

Dirty pool. Honest and true, but dirty nonetheless. "Jesus." I lowered the shotgun muzzle fractionally and did my best to swallow the apprehension that was a noose around my neck threatening to choke me. "Fine. Do what you want, Nik. You will anyway. Play footsie with the monster all you goddamn please."

The corner of his mouth quirked at my ill-tempered surrender. "Love you too, little brother." Not a hint of sarcasm, not a whisper of irony—there was only tolerant affection. Not only had he gotten all the human genes in the family, but all the emotional stability too. How fair was that? "Very well, Abbagor," he continued, voice hardening to the unwavering blue of steel. "You have your taste. Ten seconds. Longer than that and you and your tentacle part ways."

"So bold. So audacious . . . for a human." Abby

was entertained but good now. The mud sloshed around his waist as more tentacles shot into sight. The pit had to be five feet deep. If we tumbled into that . . . if Niko was pulled in, there would be no getting out of it. I hooked the fingers of my free hand onto the waistband of his black pants. It was probably futile as hell, but I did it anyway.

"Bold, audacious, and highly annoyed," Niko said flatly. "Get on with it, troll."

"Such an impatient race. Comes from being barely evolved, I suppose." As the words flowed, so did the tentacles, but they weren't alone. In his trench, Abbagor moved. Ripples of mud spread sluggishly from his path, releasing a smell of decay so strong that it rivaled the stench that already saturated the place. It wasn't the by-product of corpses, although I was positive there were plenty of those to be found below the bubbling brown surface. It was the smell of sickness, the putrescence of *living* flesh, not dead. Abbagor was sick. Maybe I'd done more damage last year than I'd thought. Or maybe Abby had picked up a really bad fungus down here in the swamp. Who knew? But from what I was getting a whiff of, he was rotting from the inside out.

I tensed as the troll approached, but stood my ground. He was moving slowly, cautiously . . . so careful not to scare the kiddies. He didn't want to ruin his good time, now, did he? "That's close enough," I warned with lips twisted in disgust.

"A true Auphe, king of all you survey." Abbagor had teeth. Fangs actually. I hadn't noticed that last time. Curving and black as the talons on his hands, they were full of poison, if the yellow dripping from the top two were any indication. "You are the word made law, and I obey."

That'd be the day . . . the day Abbagor was a particularly pungent fertilizer. Abbagor bowed to no one, not even the bygone Auphe. And a sick Abbagor was only that much more dangerous. I'd seen those nature specials when Niko had refused to turn over the remote. Predators tend to get cranky when wounded. When he'd previously tried to kill us, the troll had actually been in a good mood. I really didn't want to see a bitchy, disgruntled Abby in action.

Attention back on Nik, Abbagor murmured again, "A touch. Only a touch." But it wasn't a tentacle he extended toward my brother; it was his hand. Four or five times the size of a man's hand, it was held out palm up. And in the center of that palm was a mouth, a human mouth. Pale lips, soft and full. Not just human, but a woman's mouth. One of his prisoners. How they were dissolved within Abbagor, how they continued to live, I didn't know. I didn't *want* to know. If I did know, I had doubts that I would ever sleep again. Then again, the sight of a rosy pink tongue tip peeking between those lips might have just sealed that deal for me anyway.

It also happened to be the trigger to Niko's losing it.

Of course, a loss of composure and temper came off a lot better on my brother than it would have on me. Lips thinned to nothing and eyes dark with a cold fury, Niko said in a tone that would've been conversational if not for the razor edges lining every word, "Remove it from my sight or I'll remove it from you." His sword was already in motion, stopping to hover bare millimeters above the clay-colored wrist. The blade hung perfectly motionless, still and sure.

Personally, I was all for the chop. Yeah, big fan of the chop. But Abby gave in, the son of a bitch. "Very well," the troll sighed dolefully, pulling the hand back. "I bow to your prejudices, human." *Right*. "Prejudices," it would've almost been funny if not for the revulsion and horror that saturated the air like a dank humidity.

An especially plump tendril took the place of the hand. Deftly avoiding the naked blade, it rested gently on the back of Nik's hand. "Ahhhh, I remember. That piquant flavor, so unique. You taste of metal and blood, of green grass and blue sky. And, after all this long, long time, you still taste of . . . me." The tentacle didn't curl or grip; it didn't threaten in any way. At least, not physically. It simply . . . petted. A light caress, a soft stroking, harmless, right? Wrong. Niko's olive skin faded slightly as old memories came to a boil. It was the faintest of differences, nearly undetectable, but it was enough for me. And by God it was more than enough for Nik. "Okay, that's it," I snapped, knocking the writhing cord aside with the shotgun. "You've had your jollies. Now tell us about the Calabassa."

"That was hardly the agreed-upon ten seconds." As one, all the tendrils retreated with an unnatural speed to wrap themselves back into the whole of Abbagor. "Seven at best."

"Close enough, you bastard," my brother said with a deadly calm.

There was going to be a fight—we'd known that going in—but as it stood now Niko just might beat Abbagor to the first blow. And if he didn't, I was more than happy to move up in line. But at the last moment it looked as if the battle might be postponed for a minute or two. Abbagor was going to speak and there was nothing Abbagor liked more than showing off his knowledge. Funny, you never think of killing machines as being proud or full of an almost human conceit, but sometimes they can be.

A heavy, pregnant silence surrounded the troll like a poisonous fog. Finally, he pronounced with a rip-

pling displeasure, "Disguised cheaters, prating mounte-
banks." I recognized that it was a quote, but I couldn't
identify it. Not much of a surprise, considering what
I read in my spare time. Didn't you just hate it when
monsters were more literate than you?

"Seek out your kind," he continued. "They have
the Calabassa. They're quite enamored of baubles."

My kind. He knew. How could he know already? It
was impossible. It had only been a little over a day.
"My kind," I said between stiff lips. "What do you
mean, my kind?"

"Not *your* kind." The venomous grin gaped wider
and the large head tilted in Niko's direction. "His
kind. Gypsies." Both of us, Niko and I, were half-
Gypsy through Sophia, but my human half was easily
washed away, it seemed.

"Gypsies? Which clan? And what is so important
about the crown?" Niko asked, sword still in hand.
"Does it perform some function? Is it especially valuable in any way?"

"One taste, one question." The mud sloshed as Abbagor took another step in our direction. It looked as
if playtime was over. "But here is a question for you.
I see all. I know all. I *am* all. Did you think the passing
of the Auphe at your hand would escape me?" Another step, slow and ponderous. "Did you think I
wouldn't know what you've taken from me?"

Ah, shit. I knew. We'd destroyed what he considered his only real rivals and, in an odd way, his only
real love. At least, we'd thought we had. We'd taken
away the battles, the blood, the happy-go-lucky massa-
cres. Yeah, we'd ruined his good time. And now, after
playing with us, he was about to ruin ours. Never mind
that it turned out the Auphe weren't completely gone,
although they'd apparently kept a low enough profile
that even the troll who knew everything hadn't known

about their survival. We could tell Abbagor his information was thirty-six hours out of date, but I sincerely doubted he would buy it. And why would he want to try when it was so much more fun to kill us? As much as Abbagor liked to talk, he liked to kill more. And killing us would be the best part of his day.

But first he had to catch us.

We ran, but not before I fired the shotgun. I didn't hope to kill Abbagor; I already knew the futility of that. I just hoped to slow him down long enough for us to make our escape. As hopes went, it wasn't a big one, but you took what you could get. I had time for only two successive shots before the troll was out of the mud and on us. The first shot shredded his neck in a spray of meat and viscous purple blood. The second tore away half of his face, revealing the bone beneath. It only made his grin wider as the flesh peeled away. "Aupheling, don't go," bubbled playfully through the blood. "You are all that is left to me now. The last of my nemesis. My companion in pain and pleasure."

Uh-huh. If only that were true. My shoulder ached from bearing the brunt of the shotgun's recoil, but I didn't let that hold me back . . . especially once I saw what the troll had been hiding under the mud. His once-mighty muscled legs were now green mottled bone wreathed in ligaments, tendons, and bands of naked muscle. They also were hosting the occasional chunk of putrefying flesh that stubbornly refused to release its grip. The legs of a corpse, yet they moved— and moved damn fast. It was like seeing long-flattened roadkill come to life and chase you.

With our feet churning up the filth, Niko and I headed for a tunnel opening. It wasn't the one we came through, but any port in a troll-made storm. We were nearly there when the crude doorway crumbled instantly, collapsing in on itself. For a split second of confusion, I thought I actually *had* brought that grenade I'd been wishing for earlier. But no . . . a crumpled half of a steel beam was buried in the dirt above where the opening had been. Great. The troll was actually throwing pieces of the bridge at us now, as if the Brooklyn Bridge could spare any. God knew what else he had squirreled away in that pit of mud . . . a small Volkswagen maybe? I'd been accused more than once of having a hard head, but that much of a test I didn't want to put it to.

Both Niko and I whirled around and split hastily into opposite directions as Abbagor hit the now-solid wall where we had just stood. The blow shook the entire cavern, and more earth and rock showered down. The place was falling apart; a sick troll apparently wasn't much in the home-improvement-and-repair field. Swiveling, I backpedaled as I fired the shotgun again, this time hitting the monster in the back. If he'd been a man, he would've gone down as limply as cooked spaghetti. Of course he wasn't a man. He was a killing machine whose time had finally come. It was too bad that the extroverted son of a bitch wanted company on that ride.

Back twitching from the shot, he turned and literally exploded into a mass of weaving tentacles, several of which flashed across the expanse between us and wrapped around my legs with astonishing speed. Or it would've been astonishing if I hadn't seen it the last time Abbagor had tried to kill us. Dropping the gun, I scrambled for the knife that had saved my ass with the bodachs. We'd see if it stepped up a second time. I was aiming a quick slice to free myself when I was jerked bodily in the air and tossed. I landed squarely in Abby's keepsake box.

Drowning in mud is not something I recommend.

Drowning in mud that reeks of a thousand and one slaughterhouses, not surprisingly, is even worse. The force of my fall took me completely under the cloying liquid, and I struggled desperately to find the surface. I'd thought the mud was five feet deep, but I'd thought wrong. It was deeper. The mud was thin, but it wasn't water and swimming was pretty much out of the question. It pressed against my nose, mouth, and blind eyes with the cool touch of the grave. Lungs burning, I continued to thrash frantically only to feel myself sinking deeper. Then the hard grip came on the back of my neck, and I was pulled upward, and yanked onto firm ground. As thanks to my rescuer, I rose to my hands and knees and promptly puked on Nik's shoes. That I'd made it this far without tossing my cookies was something of a miracle, but to be swallowed whole by the stench . . . there was nothing left to do but turn my stomach inside out. There were a lot of things to curse the Auphe over, but I never guessed their acute sense of smell might be the one that did me in. The filth on me, the air around me, it was all so noxious that I actually felt my nervous system began to short-circuit. It beat anything the government whipped up in their poison gas labs, hands down.

I could feel my brother's presence hovering above me, hear the hiss of his blade cutting through the air. Pieces of gray tendrils began to fall like rain around and onto me. Sliced, diced, and still moving with sluggish life. I did my best to ignore them and focused on trying to clear my darkening vision. Breathing would've been nice too. Instead I vomited again.

"Cal."

That reached me. Through fading vision and hearing that went in and out like a bad cable connection, it still reached me. Swallowing convulsively, I looked up just in time to see Niko disappear upward. I struggled up to a kneeling position to bring him back into sight. Dangled by the neck from a twisted tendril noose, he swung a deadly accurate sword only to be snagged anew before he dropped more than a few inches. The troll could've broken a comparatively frail human neck in less than a heartbeat, but where would be the fun in that? Now, watching my brother's face slowly shift from olive to lavender, then deep purple . . . that was entertainment. Or it would've been if it had gotten that far. I wasn't about to let it. I was halfway around the mud pit before I even realized I'd managed to struggle to my feet. It was more a drunken stagger than a run, but it took me where I needed to go and that was all that mattered at the moment. Spots were swimming across my vision, but I sucked in air fiercely and managed to clear the majority of them. When I reached Abbagor I could see well enough to pick out my target. My knife, although coated with mud, was still in my hand and I wasted no time in putting it to use. Diving under flying tentacles, I chopped at what was left of the troll's legs. The bone, as big around as my waist, was far too thick to make a dent in. Instead I focused on what I *could* damage. The tendons, the ligaments, the gray-green muscle—I tore at it all with steel and sheer rage. Bare seconds passed before I was snared again, but it was long enough. Decaying flesh disintegrated under my knife, and suddenly hamstrung, Abbagor fell.

But not before he threw Niko.

My brother flew through the air in a hurtling rush and hit the edge of the tunnel where we had entered. The packed earth gave way and he tumbled on through. He hit hard, hard enough that he lost his sword. It pinwheeled lazily through the air, silver and bright.

And then it was over, all of it. Abbagor hit the

ground, bringing everything, including me, down with him. The impact was like a bomb going off, and the cavern began to fall apart. Dirt and concrete fell in massive chunks and the glowing fungus that lit the place began to flicker and die. I saw the doorway Niko had disappeared through cave in as the other one had. At least he was out. The tunnel was smaller, more stable. It would hold. It would. It had to.

"Aupheling."

Shit. When was enough enough? When the *hell* was it enough?

"Aupheling." The voice was still thick with blood, but now it was heavy with gloating as well. "Now we both pass this world, as it should be. Old rivals cannot exist without one another." The chuckle was fat with superior satisfaction. "And why would we want to?"

He had fallen close enough to me that I was covered in a blanket of tentacles, cool and heavy. They rippled over me, petting . . . soothing. Almost hypnotic. "Almost" being the key word. I tore at them with hands and blade, fighting my way free. It could be I was going to die, but if that was the case, it was going to be at the opposite end of this death trap from Abbagor. My bones weren't spending eternity intermingled with his. That was no kind of heaven and every kind of hell.

"There's no place to run, little Auphe. No place at all." The eyeless face watched me with an indulgent bare-bone smile.

I gave it a shot anyway. I ran, and Abbagor let me. Because, in his mind, where would I go? All the tunnels had vanished in an avalanche of earth. Okay, fine. I'd dig my way out. I had a few seconds, right? How hard could it be? A chunk of stone hit my shoulder and knocked me sprawling. Good answer. Yeah, good answer. More of the ceiling fell with a rumble that

grew until it was the deafening scream of a jet engine.
I pushed up and ran again. This time I didn't make it
three feet before I fell again. It was a knot of metal
rebar and it hurt like hell. Lying on my stomach, I
could see what Abbagor saw. The dirt had been like
rain. Now it was a thundering waterfall. I couldn't
even see the walls, much less where the tunnels had
been. My legs were already half-buried and I was beginning to choke trying to breathe through the falling debris.

Abbagor was right. It was over.

Try telling that to my spasming heart, my fingers
digging into the ground beneath me. The fight-or-flight
response didn't know anything about an inescapable
fate. It didn't know resignation. And it didn't know
shit about giving up. Move, it screamed. *Move.* But
there wasn't anyplace to move to. No place to go.
None. *Fuck.*

And then it happened.

I felt something twist inside as if two hands were
clawing their way through my internal organs. My seiz-
ing heart turned over, then did its damnedest to burst.
A blazing heat rolled through my body, frying every
nerve ending. It was like being electrocuted; it was
like dying. Dying before dying.

That's when the gateway opened.

It opened before me, ripping a hole of hellish light
into space itself. It was a talent peculiar to the Auphe.
It was how they traveled—within this world, out of
this world, in worlds that couldn't be imagined. I
should know. I'd been dragged kicking and screaming
through a few myself. But this one . . . this one *I* had
made. I'd felt its birth, felt it form in and of me. This
door, ugly and raw, was mine. If I'd had the time or
anything left in my stomach I might have been
tempted to throw up again. Didn't I have enough

monster in me already? Did I need more evidence that I wasn't human? There'd been a time I'd been sure that was all behind me. When the Auphe had all died . . . but that hadn't happened, had it? They were still here. . . . I was still here, and more like them than I'd ever wanted to admit.

I all but felt the hard swat to the back of my head and heard an invisible Niko order at my ear, Whine later. Escape now. Even in my imagination, he was right. I had no idea where that unholy rip led to, but it didn't matter. Midair, underwater, New Jersey—it couldn't be worse than here. Taking a deep breath, I dived through headfirst. As I hit the light, I heard Abbagor scream. Maybe he sensed the gate or maybe he just smelled my sudden sliver of hope. Whichever it was, his incoherent fury and rage might be the last thing I ever heard.

"Swing Low, Sweet Chariot," it was not.

15

I destroyed our coffee table.

I came out the other side of the gate four feet in the air and landed in a classic belly flop on top of a wood and faux-marble table, heavy emphasis on the "faux." The piece of furniture folded like cheap cardboard and I wound up with carpet burn on my chin. Disoriented, I rolled over hastily and tried to scramble to my feet. I failed dismally, listing dramatically sideways until I grabbed a handful of couch cushion to hold myself up in a sitting position. That's when it struck me that everything looked familiar, more than familiar. Home. I'd opened a passage home.

It made sense. Desperately striving for survival, instinct kicked in and did what I had no idea I could do. Darkling had done it while in my body; I knew the potential was there. But alone I'd never been able . . . had never *wanted* to do it. And I wouldn't have had the first idea as to how to do it. We had been one, Darkling and I, but I had a serious block on even attempting to initiate that churning twist in your brain and gut that opened a door. But what I wouldn't attempt, my subconscious had. It was logical that whatever tangled bit of blackened genes was responsible would fashion a destination of the most familiar place I knew. I didn't like it. In fact I hated it, but I understood it. And right now that was the best I could hope for. I didn't have time for anything else.

Shaking off the dizziness, I pulled myself up onto the couch and grabbed hurriedly for the phone. I punched in the number as quickly as I could get my fingers to move. No answer, just voice mail. I tried again, then cursed myself through gritted teeth. Of course Niko had turned off his phone before we'd gone underground. Having "Kung Fu Fighting" ring in funky cheer while we were approaching Abbagor wasn't the best of game plans. I dialed again, this time trying Robin's number. It rang twice and then Robin was breathing fast into the phone, "I'm busy. Go away." Click.

Shitshitshit.

I tried again. This time the answer was in Greek, but I had a pretty good guess at what four-letter suggestion it translated into. I didn't get out a word, hell, not even a consonant. Son of a *bitch*. Look at the number, Loman. Look at the goddamn number. What the hell was he doing anyway? Breathing fast . . . unless he'd picked up a passing fancy, sunbathing wasn't exactly that strenuous. Unless . . . crap. He was running . . . as best he could with an injured leg. He must have felt the cave-in rumbling under his feet and gone down to help us. Of course, Niko was the only one left to help at the moment, but Robin didn't know that. *Niko* didn't know it, which was precisely why I felt like beating the phone against the wall.

Third time was the charm. Goodfellow's voice came through, suspiciously questioning. "Who is this? Promise?"

It was a good guess, if wrong. Who was left to be calling from our apartment? George was gone, and Snowball was out for the count. "Put Nik on," I snapped. I didn't bother to identify myself. Good-fellow knew my voice. As he'd once said, it was a unique combination of peat whiskey and sullen snarki-ness. The whiskey was courtesy of my ever lovin' mother who had a voice made for lullabies although she had never sang a single one. The snarkiness, to give credit where credit was due, was all my own.

"What? Cal? How in the name of Nero's syphilitic dick did you—"

"Nik. *Now*," I overrode ruthlessly.

There was a confused and aggrieved snort and then a relenting, "I don't see him y . . . oh." The soft exhalation was all I needed to hear to know Robin had finally spotted my brother. "All right," came the grim follow-up. "Hold on."

He was still running. I could hear the accelerated rasp of his breath and then he rapped out my brother's name. "Niko. *Niko*." There were more mumbled in-comprehensible curses, this time more empathetic than sincere. "Niko, stop. *Stop*. I have Caliban on the phone. He's all right. He's home. Safe. Here, talk to him."

My hearing was good old human, ordinary and not especially keen, so I couldn't hear what Niko was doing, but I didn't need to. He was trying to dig me out. Niko, who was practical to the nth degree, showed logic the door when it came to his only family. Sur-rounded by dirt and concrete that could collapse at any time, and he wouldn't give up. Wouldn't abandon me. He could only claw at the dirt and ignore the grim truth staring him in the face.

I heard the fumbling of the phone passed from one hand to another and then, "Cal?" There was a rigid self-control and an inescapable disbelief. I didn't blame him. He'd seen me buried before his eyes. Un-seeing that would be difficult to do. Believing I was alive under tons of earth was difficult to pull off. Believing I was alive, whole, and in air-conditioned comfort miles away was an absolute bitch of mental acrobatics.

"It's me, Cyrano," I assured quietly. "I'm okay. I'm back in the apartment."

He didn't say anything for the next few seconds. His breathing, as uneven from exertion as Robin's had been, slowly smoothed. When he spoke again, the control was still there but the skepticism was gone. "How?"

To the point as always. "Like father, like son," I said with weary bite.

"Ah. Unexpected." There was the sound of his hand running over his face. "Stay there. We'll be back as soon as possible." There was an uncharacteristic hesitation. "You're not hurt?"

"Not a scratch," I said immediately. It wasn't entirely true, but it was what he needed to hear. And in reality, the coffee table had done more actual damage to me than Abbagor. It wasn't much of an epitaph for a near-eternal evil. Served the son of a bitch right.

"Good." There was a long exhalation and then a brisk echo. "Good. Then you can have lunch ready for our return. We'll discuss what we've learned then." Click.

I snorted and leaned back. Snatched from the jaws of death cut you exactly five seconds of slack around here, and repression was the only name brand my brother wore. I dropped the phone on the end table and realized something. The glossy black plastic was coated with pale brown, and so was I. I was still covered in rancid mud . . . as was the couch, the remains of the coffee table, and part of the floor. Luckily, my sense of smell had finally cut out, packed its bags, and headed for the hills. I hoped it stayed there. It was definitely more trouble than it was worth. Giving an internal groan, I rose stiffly to my feet and headed for the shower.

"It didn't go well, then?"

Promise stood still as a statue by the hall. I imagine she'd been there the entire time. Her hands were clasped formally before her. So calm. On the surface. Hard to believe my stealthy furniture destroying and loud cursing had caught her attention at Flay's side.

I rubbed a sleeve across my face and gave her the best reassuring smile I could dredge up. "Nik is fine. He's on his way back with Goodfellow."

The set of her shoulders relaxed, but all she said was, "How did you get here, Caliban?"

I had the feeling that she already knew. And truthfully I was in no mood to talk about it. "I have to grab a shower," I said evasively. "Mind ordering some takeout? Pizza maybe?" I moved past her and disappeared into the bathroom before she could comment.

The pizza arrived twenty minutes later, followed shortly by Niko and Goodfellow. I gave them a throwaway salute when the latter walked through the door, and kept working on my piece of pepperoni and mushroom. I couldn't taste much of it with my blunted ability to smell, but I ate it anyway. Robin gave the ruined couch and table a fastidious sniff. "Fragrant and fashionable. What more could one want?"

Niko took it in, gave a minute shake of his head, and let it go. As far as he was concerned I spent too much time lounging there anyway. Moving over to me, he gave my wet ponytail a tug. The yank was hard enough to let him know I was real . . . alive, but not enough to hurt. Much. "Hey," I protested with a wince. "How is this my fault?"

"I haven't quite figured that out yet." He frowned.
"When I do, trust me, you'll be the very first to
know."

Yep, repression, thy name is Niko. Or maybe it was
Ninja-with-Panties-in-Twist. Whichever it was, I didn't
take it personally. My temper tantrums tended to be
much louder and more destructive. I could suffer
through the Niko version with ease. "Your veggie special is warming in the oven." I swatted his hand away
from my hair. "And Promise is waiting for you in
the bedroom."

His eyes narrowed. "Excuse me?"

My eyebrows rose. "I saw you hit, Nik. Abby tossed
you like a Frisbee. If you're not bruised from neck to
tailbone, then you're not human." I pulled a piece of
pepperoni off the top of my slice and toyed with it.
"And that's my gig, not yours. I've laid out the ice
packs, the muscle ointment, the whole nine yards.
Promise said she'd like to help, but if you'd rather get
half-naked in front of someone else"—my lips quirked—
"that's your prerogative." The eyes narrowed further,
but he disappeared silently into the back. He knew
as well as I did that Robin might have a limp, but
he was still a predator, through and through. And if
the Puck had a weakness, it was for half-naked *anything*.

"You don't play fair, do you, Cal?" Goodfellow sat
at the kitchen table and eyed the pizza without enthusiasm. "A man after my own shriveled little heart."

"I play to win." I popped the pepperoni into my
mouth and chewed without much enthusiasm of my
own. "It doesn't get more fair than that. You've
taught me well, Obi-Wan."

"That can't be taught, kid." He helped himself to a
piece with a mournful sigh at my poor choice of cui-
sine. "You're either born with it or you're born with

a conscience." The brilliant grin flashed on and off as quickly as a neon sign. "You can't have both."

That didn't explain his flight into the depths to try to save us, but that was Goodfellow, a contradiction in terms and not half as heartless as he imagined himself to be. Changing the subject, he reached for a napkin and said lightly, "Niko said you were able to get some information from Abbagor. That's excellent news. We're that much closer to getting George back."

"Yeah, excellent," I parroted colorlessly, losing what little appetite I had. "If we knew which tribe had it. How many could there be in the world anyway?"

"O ye of little faith." He gave a superior smirk. "I might not know everything, but I *do* know everyone. Give me time and I'll find out which tribe it is and where they are. Things will come together, Caliban. We'll have George home soon. Safe and well. Try to believe it." He fixed me with eyes as green and fathomless as the primeval forest "You were the one who once told me that life is a fairy tale and everyone lives happily ever after."

Yeah, but it had been a lie then and it was a lie now. "You were shit-faced then, Loman." I gave up on the pizza. "I'm surprised you remember anything I said. Besides you were too busy sniffing Nik's hair." I tilted my head back and offered innocently over my shoulder, "Oh, hey, big brother, fixed up already?"

The utterly blank face was better than any scowl. "Amazing how well you hear when you want to." Niko retrieved his pizza from the oven, sat in the seat next to mine, and pushed my discarded plate back toward me. "Eat. I'm not dragging about your malnourished form from here to there. I've better things to do with my time."

I turned to Promise. "An ice pack is okay for a sore

back, but it isn't much help with the cranky SOB part, is it?"

She brushed a hand over my hair and gave me an absent smile, but there was a sliver of unease behind her eyes. I think that she'd forgotten Niko was human . . . vulnerable. Well, relatively vulnerable. This was Niko we were talking about after all. "You two." She touched a cool fingertip to the bruise forming on my jaw. It was courtesy of the coffee table, not the troll, but that was between me and the furniture. "Always falling in with a naughty crowd."

"Abby's nothing if not a bad influence." I slumped down in the chair, a combination of aches and exhaustion making an upright position not too desirable. "Pretty much a shithead too, if you were wondering."

Niko gave a reproving snort, then commented, "I believe all that he is has become all that he was. He was ill to begin with. He couldn't have survived the cave-in."

I wouldn't have thought he could've survived an entire clip to the brain either, but he'd proved me wrong. This time, however, the troll had wanted to die. When he'd thought the Auphe's time had passed, he was ready to follow. They must've been lying extremely low for him to have believed they were truly gone. Either that, or the sickness had affected his mind. "Here's hoping," I muttered, resting my chin on my chest and rubbing the back of my neck. The movement felt clumsy, as if my hand were moving through a thick fluid instead of air. "Loman says he can find the Gypsies." I closed my eyes against the eye-searing brightness of the kitchen light.

"How long will it take to locate them?" That was Nik . . . who suddenly sounded far, far away. I didn't hear Robin's reply. I didn't hear anything at all. When I woke up, the light was off, and I was covered with

that comforter from my bed. There was also the taste
of fermented garlic in my mouth and a god-awful crick
in my neck. I straightened my head and was rewarded
with the howling protest of abused muscles. Hissing
at the discomfort, I checked my watch. Five hours. I'd
slept five hours. Goddamn it. I threw the blanket off,
put my hands against the table, and pushed up. I staggered for a moment, as stiff as a ninety-year-old man.
It'd been a long day. Long week.

Long, Georgie. So damn long.

I made my way through the darkened apartment
back to my room to ask Niko what had happened
after I'd fallen asleep. Pushing open the door, I took
in the spill of sable and silver on the pillows and the
curve of a naked shoulder. I smiled to myself. About
damn time.

"You feel better?" I turned at my brother's low
voice at my ear.

"The question is," I countered with a knowing grin,
pulling the door shut between Promise and us, "do
you?"

He'd come out of the bathroom and now motioned
me back toward the living room. "You nearly died
once today. Are you so anxious for a repeat showing?"

I didn't bother with the overhead light, instead relying on the light coming through the window from the
street. Sitting on the couch, I took in the blanket and
pillow piled with hospital neatness at one end. The
cushions had been scrubbed with ruthless efficiency
and smelled of nothing but soap and water. No mud,
no Abbagor . . . nothing of that remained. Nik. He
couldn't fix George, couldn't fix me, so he concentrated on the little things. Until he could get his hands
on Caleb, he'd impose order on the chaos available
to him. "I'll pass on the beatdown, thanks." I watched

as he leaned against the wall, still as a statue, but something was different. He wasn't completely happy. He couldn't be, not under the circumstances, but he was relaxed. And my brother was never relaxed. He might appear at ease on the surface, but underneath he was always taut, always ready. Always walking the edge of constant vigilance. But now . . . who would've thought?

"That's probably wise."

When I'd woken up I'd been panicked at the time lost. Five hours sleeping was five hours waiting for Caleb to find out what had happened. It was five hours that I wasn't trying to find George. Worse yet, it was five hours that I wasn't thinking of her, wasn't imagining what she might be going through. It felt like a betrayal, but . . . I exhaled and fell backward onto the couch. There was more involved here than just George and me. Above, the ceiling was striped gray and milky white. It was never dark in the city. Never. You think that'd be a comfort to someone who knows the things that giggle insanely in the dark. It's not. At least, not always. Sometimes a blanket of swaddling black velvet would be . . . nice. Sometimes not seeing is better than seeing. Then again, sometimes seeing isn't so bad. I turned my head toward Niko and smiled at the recollection of striped hair and long lashes resting on pale cheeks. "She's beautiful."

"Inside and out." He bowed his head, a strand of hair falling across his eyes. Rumpled and disheveled, completely unnatural for my brother.

I grinned again. "It took a vampire to make you human, Cyrano. What are the odds?" Then the grin melted and I went back to watching shadows crawl sluggishly across the ceiling. So, George, who's going to make me human?

The cushion dipped under Niko's weight as he settled on the edge. He sat quietly for a few moments before asking, "Can you do it again?"

I had no trouble following the change of subject. "I don't know. I don't know how I did it to begin with." Didn't know . . . didn't *want* to know. All I did know was that being able to rip a hole in reality was no kind of inheritance. Where was the gold watch? The hefty life insurance payout? Monsters, they never thought ahead. "Could be that the next time the world falls in on my head, it might kick in again."

"And then again it may not."

"Mystery." I shifted my shoulders. "That's what life is all about, right?"

"I know you'd rather not hear it." The dim light gleamed on his bare back and was in turn swallowed by the inky blackness of his sweatpants. "But I wouldn't mind you having the equivalent of a parachute."

"A get-out-of-jail-free card?" I snorted and rolled over onto my side. "I'd rather do without."

"Stubborn." The cuff on the back of my head that I'd imagined in Abbagor's cavern materialized. "Get some more sleep, Cal. There's nothing we can do until Goodfellow gets back to us, and we need you rested and sharp. Georgina would tell you the same."

Ever read those books? See those movies? Someone will be missing or presumed dead, yet their loved one will "feel" them. They'll know, without a doubt, that they're out there . . . alive. Sense the unbreakable glowing bond between them. Feel the touch of their invisible hand. How nice for them. As for me . . . I didn't feel shit. Okay, the big black hole where George had once been, that I felt. Emptiness and the ground falling away beneath my feet. Yeah, that was pretty goddamn palpable. But George? A honey-colored hand on my shoulder? The softness of her hair against my face? Those were nowhere to be found.

Nowhere.

The present came the next day.

Wrapped in expensive paper of muted blues and greens and tied with a thin silver cord, it waited in the hall outside the door. I'd been on my way outside to grab some breakfast for Niko and Promise, who were still warming the sheets at six a.m. That was serious sleeping in for my brother, but, damn, who could blame him?

Nudging the package with my toe, I eyed it suspiciously. It was about the size of a shoe box, and I knew instantly who had sent it. Pricey wrapping paper, innocent exterior—it had to be Goodfellow. I couldn't begin to guess how he'd known this night had been the night for Niko and Promise. Maybe he'd picked up on some subtle verbal cue between them that I'd missed when I'd dozed off. Hell, maybe he'd smelled it on them.

If Robin had a sixth sense, it was focused solely on sex . . . a radar for arousal so powerful that it could pick up a horny Martian across the vast emptiness of space itself.

However he knew, it would be just like him to send them a little "gift." Probably one picked up in the type of store that used to grace Times Square. Or could be it came from his own personal collection. Gah. I picked it up gingerly with the tips of my fingers and carried it back to the kitchen table. I didn't have much choice. The coffee table had gone to an early grave. It didn't change the fact I was having serious doubts about ever eating in the kitchen again. The box wasn't addressed to anyone, so, braver than any hero of legend, I threw myself on the grenade. Oils, things that buzzed and vibrated, tiny scraps of leopard-spotted cloth—I was expecting pretty much anything.

Except George.

When Niko found me it was not quite an hour later. I'd left the apartment without my phone. It was just me and my present. And it was mine, no one else's. I had left a note, though. With the Auphe out there, I couldn't just walk out. I hadn't said where I was going or why, but I should've known Niko would track me down sooner rather than later.

I didn't look up when the bell tinkled rustily as the front door opened. I didn't have to; I knew who it was. The soda shop was empty except for the two of us. Mr. Geever had closed it up while George was gone. People kept coming in to see her, leaving flowers and colored paper stars, creating a memorial for a girl who wasn't even dead yet. Geever couldn't handle it. The street outside smelled overwhelmingly of roses and lilies, funeral flowers. I'd swum through them to use the key I still had from opening the place for him two weeks ago. Only two weeks. Jesus.

"So." Niko slid into the booth opposite me. "When did the overwhelming craving for ice cream hit you?" When I didn't answer, he asked quietly, "What's in the box, Cal?"

It sat in front of me, stripped of paper and ribbon . . . just a plain white box now. No cheerful paper, no shiny silver ribbon. Nothing left to distract from what lay inside. "George," I said tonelessly, looking up at him. "It's George."

He reached over and pulled the box out from beneath my hand. Lifting the lid, he stared down at the contents. The fury behind his eyes was swiftly squelched, but his lips remained a knife's edge as he dipped a careful hand in to lift out a mass of copper curls. It could've been worse. I knew that. It didn't change the fact that when I'd opened the box for the first time and saw George's hair I felt something break inside.

"Encouragement from our friend Caleb. He knows, then, about the crown." He rubbed a thumb along a length of red silk and gently returned the tumbled coils to the box. "We're almost there, little brother. A few days at best and we'll have another one to put in his damned hand and your George will be free."

Not mine. If I ever had doubts about that before, I didn't now. George wasn't for me, not if she wanted to live to see the ripe old age of twenty. Caleb had admired our work. He had wanted something from us and chose the most vulnerable person in our circle to use as leverage. Why he'd gone to such lengths we still didn't know, but did that matter? The result spoke for itself.

"Flay wake up yet?" I asked, reaching over to put the lid back on the box. I couldn't look at it anymore.

"Actually, yes." He stood. "Why don't we go discuss things with him? It'll be much more entertaining to hurt him while he's awake."

"You're trying to cheer me up, aren't you?" I said suspiciously.

"Perhaps. Is it working?"

"A little," I admitted. Picking up the box carefully, I slid out of the booth. "Let's go chat with the furry prick."

Promise had been relieved of guard duty and was gone. Goodfellow had taken over—if you could call watching porn on cable guarding. He was also on our phone, speaking some Slavic-sounding language. A helluva long-distance call, but if it found George, he could run it into the millions for all I cared. Niko took the box from my hand and placed it carefully on Robin's lap. It was a combination of incentive and a simple right to know. Goodfellow had a great deal of affection for George too.

We didn't wait to see his response. Our own had been enough. We entered Niko's bedroom and closed the door behind us. "Snowball." I bared teeth in the nastiest sort of grin. "I hear you're feeling better."

Better, maybe, but he wasn't completely healed, not yet. The slashes that had run from chest to navel were brutally ugly and red, but they had mostly closed. A few more days and they'd be shiny pink scar tissue. The glassiness had faded from his eyes, leaving them alert if not precisely sharp. There was still a wheeze to his breathing from a damaged lung. That might take more than a few days to heal, maybe a week, but it would. Wolves were tough bastards. You let one crawl away from a fight and chances were it would keep crawling.

Flay's red pink eyes glared at us and the muzzle wrinkled to show a few teeth of his own. Still in wolf form, he yanked at the sheet with shredding claws. "Hungry." The throat spasmed with effort. "Hungry."

"Really?" I sat on the edge of the bed and patted my stomach in consideration. "Whatta ya know? Me too. And you know what they say about Auphe." I leaned close until my nose was a bare inch from his neck and inhaled. "We'll eat anything." I hated the Auphe, loathed that they were a part of me. That didn't mean I was above using them when I had to. Why not? They'd done their level, hellish best to use me.

A hand landed on my shoulder and pulled me back. "You'll get indigestion," Niko said with reproof. "If not a hair ball." The blade of his sword flashed past me to land edge first on Flay's stomach. It balanced with the utmost serenity, needing but one really deep breath from the wolf to slice open his abdomen. "We talked earlier, you and I," my brother noted almost idly. "But I wonder if perhaps you didn't put your all into that conversation. Now, with Caleb less than pleased with your efforts, you might be able to search your mind." Several split white hairs floated upward. "Truly *rack* it. It certainly wouldn't hurt you to get on our good side."

"And it might even keep you alive," I added darkly. I didn't mean it, of course, but I could lie with the best of them. A lifetime of being on the run is good training in deceit.

"Begin with why you led Caleb to believe the crown would be so difficult to locate in Cerberus's organization. It took us barely days." Niko made a good point. It hadn't been exactly a Herculean endeavor.

Flay looked down at the line of silver crossing his stomach before letting loose with a resigned growl. "I knew. I . . . saw it . . . was for her. Vain whore. But knew . . . couldn't—" The jaws worked painfully. "Could steal, but . . . couldn't get away. Also wanted . . ." This time the jaws worked in a different way, into a hateful grin. "Cerberus dead. Wanted him *dead*. Couldn't do. Not by self."

I felt a grudging respect for the wolf. He'd pretended to Caleb to be less than he was. Less intelligent. Less cunning. In actuality, he was pretty damn smart. After all, who had ended up taking the upfront risk? Not Flay. He had made his move only when Cerberus had been distracted trying to kill me. First in his puppy class after all.

"Clever." The curl of Niko's upper lip lent a different flavor to the word. He said it in the way you might compliment a cannibal on his willingness to experiment outside a burgers-and-fries diet. We may have lived in deceit, but not once had my brother ever embraced it. He did what he had to do, but I didn't doubt that it chafed at his sense of honor. "Tell us how you met Caleb."

"At Moonshine." Ears flattened to his skull. "Never seen him . . . there before. He talked. Wanted me on inside. Wanted spy. Offered money." There was drool on his muzzle. It was the kind you saw on a dog when it stumbled onto something that tasted bad. Apparently Caleb's offer hadn't gone too well. "Wanted to. Hated Cerberus. Stick it to him—what not good? But . . . afraid. Hated him, but afraid. Know my limits. Know my *worth*." From the way he spit the word, obviously he found it lacking in himself. "Turned him down."

"And what changed your mind, asshole?" I asked with disdain. "Figure out your little plan of having someone else do the dirty work for you? Or did he up the price?"

His eyes bored into mine, so foreign, yet they held an emotion so common to every living, thinking creature that it floored me. "You." He coughed and it wasn't from the tattered lung. His hands tore the sheet over him, ripping it to forlorn streamers. The next sentence he said with the utmost care. It was the first nearly complete and whole one I'd heard from him even as he struggling to produce every word with all the clarity he could muster. "You aren't only one with a George."

Slow, odd sounding, and it clearly hurt his non-human mouth, but it resounded with truth. I didn't bother to ask how he knew about what George was to me. He would've smelled her on me at our first meeting. What I did bother with was what he had said . . . and what it meant.

"Oh, shit." The room seemed to shrink in size, the air becoming thick and stifling. I'm not sure what I would've said if I'd had the opportunity, but at that moment the phone rang. Robin must have finished his call, and five seconds later he appeared with the receiver in his hand. "It's Caleb," he announced with white-lipped anger. "He wants to talk to you."

Why me over Niko I wasn't sure, but I accepted the phone with all the enthusiasm I would've shown if he'd handed me a piranha who'd just scented blood. "Motherfucker," I said flatly in greeting. Not precisely phone etiquette 101, but it was the most I could manage.

"And a pleasant morning to you as well, Caliban." Caleb's smooth, placid voice hit my ear. "Are you enjoying a relaxing break after your abject failure?"

I wondered if Flay had filled him in, but then dismissed the thought immediately. Flay had been on the verge of dying as he'd dragged himself after us. It was highly unlikely he'd been capable of stopping to make a report—even with a life depending on him just as George's depended on us. Making a split-second decision I was probably going to regret, I covered for the fur ball, saying harshly, "Did that son of a bitch Flay fill you in? I could've swore we left his ass dead on the roof."

"Ah, that would be telling." The mocking lilt deserted his voice abruptly. "You lost it, you miserable Auphe. You lost the crown and now I'm betting you're quite curious to know what else you're going to lose."

"We'll get it back." I could barely hear myself through the sudden ringing in my ears. "Give us a week and we'll get it back. Seven days, that's all."

"You sound so sincere," he said with a hideous parody of reluctant doubt. "But I have to question your work ethic. Now, how can we provide an incentive you can't close your eyes to?"

"Don't." One word, just one, but it was all I could get out.

"Come, now, you can't tell me you don't want proof that that precious girl is still alive. My little present didn't prove that, did it? It only proved I have a pair of scissors." It was said with a patient tone—a long-suffering accountant explaining for the tenth time why a deduction was so questionable. "How would you like your proof? I pride myself on being an accommodating business partner."

"We'll get it, you son of a bitch. We'll get it. Don't hurt her." Me . . . who'd never begged. Not to an Auphe, not to any monster. But I was begging now. Raw, rage filled, but begging.

"You have your week," Caleb said with the brisk efficiency of a true businessman. "I would say good-bye, but I believe I'll let someone do it for me."

Seconds later, the phone fell from my hand to thud onto the carpet. I watched it tumble with a distant gaze. "We have seven days," I said remotely.

"What happened?" Goodfellow demanded. "Did you speak with Georgina?" Niko said nothing at all; neither did Flay, whose exceptionally sharp ears had flattened to his head. They knew . . . both of them.

"Seven days," I repeated, and then I turned and walked away.

"Not your fault."

He hadn't made her cry. Couldn't make her cry. It would've gone easier for her if she had just given him what he wanted.

"Not your fault."

An exoneration . . . absolution. And yet it didn't make hearing the sound of the thudding blow and the switchblade snicking to life any more bearable. Funny how that worked.

I walked through the apartment and on out. No mirrors to be found. We'd made sure of that. But the lobby had one. It hung over a cheap table with an even cheaper vase host to plastic flowers. Small and oval—a silver window that had once nearly ended my soul and *had* ended my life. Briefly. Since then mirrors had been a phobia that ruled by mundane details. Looking away from my reflection in plate-glass windows. Averting my eyes from every mirror in every public place. But now I was ready to look. I *needed* to look . . . needed to see. With my back to it, I took a breath that filled my chest to the aching point. And then I turned. You'd think I'd expect to see a monster, a long-dead one or maybe a brand-new one with an intimately familiar face. I didn't, though, and I hadn't expected to at all. In the end, I saw exactly what I'd suspected I would.

There was nothing there . . .

Nothing at all.

Not even me.

16

She was just a girl, Georgina King.

Granted, she was a girl in trouble, but that didn't change who she was. A girl who was nothing special to me. Yeah, I'd do my best to help her, like the others would. Give my life to save hers—because it was the right thing to do. She was an innocent. . . . I was not. It was a fair trade. But George? George herself?

George was only a girl I knew.

Too bad I hadn't figured that out sooner. It would've saved me a lot of melodramatic brooding. And Goodfellow would be the first to say I didn't need any extra encouragement there.

Just a girl . . . it was the only way I could survive.

"You're cleaning your gun."

I rolled my eyes upward to see Niko gazing down at me with an overly bland expression. I recognized the look. He was perturbed by something. "You made it clear that my ass was lazing in that department."

"I did," he admitted, brow furrowing lightly. "But since when do you actually listen to me?"

I turned back to the task at hand. Cleaning the barrel with the rod and a solvent-soaked patch, I said seriously, "I always listen, Cyrano. I'd be damn stupid not to."

He considered that for a moment and sat at the table with me. "It worries me to no end that you're actually admitting that." When I responded with only an absent nod, he moved on. "Where did you go earlier? After the call?" He paused. "Can you tell me?"

"Sure." I finished with the barrel and began to oil the disassembled parts. "I went downstairs to the lobby."

He picked up on the implications of that with lightning speed. "The mirror."

"We can get another one for our bathroom, if you want," I said, putting the weapon back together with several movements more practiced than they had the right to be. "I'm over that now. Pretty stupid shit to begin with, wasn't it?"

"Hell." He stared at me, lines bracketing his mouth. "You've . . . hell."

I completed the thought for him. "Gone off the deep end?" The corner of my mouth quirked up. "Wasn't a long trip for me, was it?" I started on the next gun. It was a new Glock that I'd gotten to replace the one lost at Moonshine. "Seriously, Nik, I'm okay. Actually, I'm better than okay—I'm functional. And right now, that's what we need."

He was far from convinced, I could tell. I pushed the Magnum in his direction. Something to keep his mind off his worries. "Clean it?" When his eyes darkened dangerously, I said reasonably, "You know you'll do a better job of it."

His disquiet didn't fade, but he took the gun in hand. "That's a given."

"Did Flay say who Caleb took?" I squirted more cleaning solution on another swab. "You know, to keep him in line."

"His son." Niko shook his head grimly and went to work on the Magnum. "He's three."

"Caleb, he's making friends right and left." I shook my head and clucked a tongue. I absolutely did not think of a small child. A little fuzzy no doubt, but as afraid and lost as any human child.

"Flay had no choice. That hardly means he's on our side or even a decent creature, but we have to recognize he was powerless in this situation."

"Well, he's not powerless now," I pointed out. "He can help us and help his cub all in one. Bonus points all around."

"Yes, and I'm sure that's a great comfort to him right now," he said impassively.

Yeah, probably not. "Goodfellow come up with any leads?"

"He's close, he says. Very close."

Very close turned out to be three days and over a thousand miles away. Lady Lucia, Florida. I'd thought it was sweltering at home; these people breathed lava masquerading as oxygen and somehow managed to keep from spontaneously combusting as they walked in the noontime sun. Promise, who trusted her cloaks and sunblock only so far, stayed in the RV. With the nonvampires of our group practically bursting into flames, I didn't blame her.

"It's hot." I averted my eyes from the unholy white fire shimmering in the midst of a hard blue sky.

"Yes, you said that." From behind opaque black glasses, Niko scanned the shimmering stretch of dead yellow grass that covered the field before us.

"It bears repeating." I wiped at the sweat on my forehead that had formed the nanosecond after I'd wiped the previous moisture away.

"It's closer than the inside of Hephaestus's jockstrap." Goodfellow shaded his eyes, then hissed in outrage when he caught sight of the darkening of his shirt around his neck and underarms. "I'm *perspiring*." He pulled his shirt away from his chest with fastidious fingers. "Sweat, *actual* sweat, and there's not even sex involved. It's an abomination." He turned and started back toward the RV he'd provided for the trip. "I'll wait inside with Promise."

Niko snared him by the arm and pulled him to a stop. "We may need you, Goodfellow."

"Suck it up, Loman," I grunted. "You don't hear Snowball bitching."

"He's panting too hard to breathe, much less complain," Robin grumbled.

Unfortunate, but true. Flay, while back in what passed as his human form, was panting with gusto. It was an odd look—a well-dressed albino man with a mane of hair and a continuously moving red tongue. He was wearing a pair of black jeans that belonged to Niko and one of Goodfellow's silk shirts. He'd given a derogatory sniff at the offer of one of my shirts. I loved that. The pound reject thought my stuff wasn't fashionable enough for him. Or more likely, he'd been yanking my chain. There wasn't a whole lot of love lost between the two of us, and while Flay was cooperating with us, it didn't stop him from taking a swipe here and there. I didn't hold any grudges. I tried to torture him while he was comatose; he scorned my clothes. If that's all I had coming to me, I was ahead of the game.

Flay's tongue was dotting his shirt with saliva as he growled with frustration. "Wait."

He disappeared back into our home away from home. Goodfellow had gotten the RV on loan from one of his fellow sales sharks. It slept six, had a bathroom and a kitchen, and all in all was about the size of our apartment. At least it had seemed that way the first few hours. As time wore on, it began to rapidly shrink. Ten hours into the trip it was approximately the size of a shoe box. Even a clean Flay had a pungent musky dog smell that followed him wherever he went, and to add insult to injury, it turned out that one of the most dangerous men alive, Niko, was allergic to dander.

Less than three minutes later, Flay was back . . . wearing orange-and-black plaid shorts and a T-shirt that read FLORIDA, THE SUNSHINE STATE.

Goodfellow winced. "I don't want to live anymore. I honestly don't."

Well-muscled but transparently pale legs were covered liberally with a dense mat of curly white hair, but it was the frighteningly long, horrifically furry toes revealed by thong sandals that were the crowning touch. Flay scowled at Robin and offered smugly, "Promise said look good. Promise *likes* way I look."

Promise had picked up a new admirer during the trip, or at least it had seemed that way at first. It wouldn't have been a big surprise, Promise being Promise, but it did give new meaning to the phrase "puppy love." Every inch that she moved in the RV, soulful ruby eyes would follow her. During meals, the best and biggest portion of the fast-food fare would be snatched up and placed before her. A definite, raving doggy-style crush, I'd thought, until I caught the wicked grin Flay flashed at Niko's back. It was all about revenge . . . annoying, evil, but basically harmless revenge. It should've been funny, but truthfully, nothing was funny much anymore. The world was all gray now. But, hey, you know what they say. You take the bad with the good. Balance. I was all about the balance now.

"Yeah, you're styling," I muttered, grabbing his arm to push him into motion. "Let's go."

We headed across the field toward a gathering of RVs, some similar to ours and some barely mobile, from the looks of them. They all squeaked under that bizarrely blue sky with nothing but swamp as far as the eye could see. After living in New York for a few years, I felt small and exposed in the midst of all this open space. It made me want to pull my knife on the off chance that an alligator or a rabid monkey jumped out of the scraggly brush. They had monkeys down here, didn't they?

Lady Lucia was in southern Florida, land of gators and pissed-off monkeys, and no one could tell me differently. A near ghost town, it was nowhere near the ocean or a pretty, pristine lake. It sat on the edge of the Everglades and the local industry seemed to be mosquito ranching. I slapped the one on my neck and kept moving. We'd been phenomenally lucky. Of course, George would've said it wasn't luck, that it was the way things were meant to be. Meant . . . to . . . be. I slapped my neck again, thought gray thoughts, and kept trudging.

Goodfellow, purveyor of this fabulous luck, had connections with a few Gypsy tribes—like we didn't see that coming. After a few hundred calls he'd finally pinned a rumor on one particular tribe. The Sarzo tribe had emigrated from Eastern Europe nearly seventy years ago. They tended to follow a route all over the country, but Lady Lucia was their home base, as much as Gypsies had a stationary home. The Sarzo also boasted of the oldest lineage among Gypsies. Once upon a very long time ago, they'd been a tribe of half-naked nomads when the wheel was still five thousand years away from being the latest and greatest. They'd also known the Bassa. The Bassa had been nomads too . . . following the sun. Cold-blooded and reptilian, the Bassa weren't huge fans of winter

weather. They'd been allies, those who would become
the Sarzo and a species who'd slithered rather than
walked. If the Bassa had left anything behind, the
Sarzo would know about it.

Or so went the theory.

Theories were great, but I was never one to under-
estimate the invariably piss-poor mood of reality. As
we walked on, a few people began to venture out into
the heat. Not many, only a few sharp-eyed men and
an even sharper-eyed old woman. "Is it like coming
home?" Robin asked as we walked.

He knew something about our lives, Goodfellow,
but he didn't know everything. This happened to be
one of the things he didn't know. He knew Niko and
I were Gypsy. I was half, and we really didn't know
what Niko was. He could be half, could be whole.
Sophia, not one to answer what she considered boring
questions, had actually answered that one. She didn't
know. Couldn't narrow it down if she was sober and
had a week to think it over. It could've been a Gypsy
from her tribe. The blond hair meant nothing. Sophia's clan had traveled much of Europe, dwelling in
Greece for a time. They'd intermarried there on occasion, although it was frowned on by both sides. A
blond northern Greek had slipped in there somewhere. We'd seen evidence of that in the few pictures
Sophia had taken with her; they were scattered care-
lessly in the bottom of a small trunk that held her
fortune-teller costumes. Groups of close-faced, dark-
skinned Gypsies with one or two bright heads spotted
throughout like patches of sun. With his olive skin,
Niko could be one of them, but there was no way to
be sure. Sophia had left her people before Niko was
born. Half or whole, neither of us had been nourished
in the welcoming arms of Sophia's kin. It made it difficult to consider them ours.

Not quite like coming home at all.

I didn't say that, though. Niko would put it in a more diplomatic fashion than I ever could. I was right. "We've not met our mother's clan," he said from behind.

Goodfellow seemed surprised. "Didn't you try to track them down?"

"We were a little preoccupied," Niko replied dryly, "what with the Auphe situation and fleeing for our lives."

That was two—count them—two blatant lies from my brother. Of course we'd tried to trace them. Sophia had been murdered, I'd been kidnapped, and we were being hounded day and night. We knew that we needed all the help we could get. We'd searched for Sophia's tribe, and we'd found them. Her relatives, her family . . . what should've been ours.

They had spit on me. Literally. Forking the evil eye with thrusts of their hands, they'd hissed in fear and hatred, and spit. As homecomings go, it doesn't get much more festive than that. How did they know what I was? It seemed while Sophia might have left them, they hadn't left her . . . not completely. They'd kept tabs on her. She was Gypsy. She might not have cared about that, but they did. They probably would've contacted Niko once he was old enough to understand, but then I came along. Sophia's own knew what she'd done. They knew of the bargain and saw the result born. They'd written her off then, her and anyone with her. And when I'd shown up with my pale, pale skin, they'd known exactly what I was, and Niko was tarred with the same brush. They didn't spit on him, he was an abomination by association only, but they turned away from him. He was invisible to them. Nonexistent. Dead.

That was the beginning and end of our family reunion.

Goodfellow didn't question the lies, although there was a good chance he recognized them for what they were. Niko didn't lie often, but he did it exceptionally well. That didn't stop me from suspecting that the puck still knew. He'd had tens of thousands of years' experience in the field. "Preoccupied, yes, I can see that. And family? Who needs it? Take the Borgia family for example. When I was staying with them for an extended holiday . . ."

I tuned out as beside me, Flay grunted and reached into the pocket of his shorts to pull out a baseball hat. He smacked it on his head, walked faster, and muttered, "Talk. Always talk, talk. Make ears hurt." It was nice to know that the Goodfellow charm transcended the chasm between species.

By the time we crossed the field Niko had smoothly pulled ahead of us. It didn't take any discussion to know that it would be best if the token human among us did the talking at first. Robin and I might look human, but you never knew when someone was going to have a quirky ability to sniff you out. With Flay . . . hell, even your average human living in blinders was going to do a double take. And Gypsies weren't average in any way, shape, or form. They'd know a wolf when they saw one. We'd thought about leaving Flay in the RV with Promise, but decided at the last minute it might not hurt to flex our muscle. Gypsies weren't known for their cooperative ways, not unless there was something in it for them. They had a lot in common with Goodfellow in that. Whether wearing a thousand-dollar suit or a five-dollar wife beater, businessmen were all the same. If you wanted them to play, you had to pay.

And the one in said wife beater looked like a helluva negotiator.

His skin was dusky, a shade darker than Niko's. Wavy black hair was paired with a thick, drooping mustache and impenetrable dark eyes. Impressive muscles bulged as he folded his arms over his chest. As he eyed us with suspicious disfavor, the old woman whispered in his ear. Two other men flanked them, each casually swinging a baseball bat.

"What do you want here?" the obvious leader demanded harshly when we stopped about ten feet away. "We're not running a boarding kennel." The slow sneer was flashed at Flay. Flay yawned, unimpressed, yet showing some rather impressive teeth. He'd heard it all before, most of it from me.

Niko ignored the posturing. "We're in search of something. To buy."

That perked the Rom's ears up although he refused to show it. Looking Niko up and down, he curled his lip. "Vayash, eh?"

He was right. Our mother had been of the Vayash clan. That in and of itself wouldn't have been too amazing of a guess; the Vayash were the only clan to spawn blonds. How he knew Niko was of Gypsy stock was another matter.

"Yes," Niko confirmed. "Our mother was Vayash."

There were worlds of meaning behind that statement. We were Gypsy, but we'd not been raised Gypsy. The man nodded and frowned. "That hair, those eyes, that nose. Vayash." His eyes traveled past Niko to take me in. It couldn't be more clear that Flay wasn't Rom, and neither was Goodfellow with his coloring. "You." He shook his head. "The Vayash, always polluting themselves with the Gadje." Gadje . . . outsiders, non-Gypsy. "We thought they'd finally seen the error of that particular way."

It was a free pass if ever we'd been given one. They didn't know I was Auphe. Sure, I was half-Vayash at best. Polluted, second-class, not *true* Rom, but it was a definite step up from abomination. It was also a helluva lucky break and Niko didn't waste any time in taking advantage of it.

"Our acquaintance"—he indicated Goodfellow with a jut of his chin—"has a good deal of money. Perhaps you can help him spend it . . . if you have what we're seeking."

Robin's groan was nearly inaudible, but considering his money-grubbing ways, that was the equivalent of a ringing endorsement. Four sets of dark eyes focused on him, brightening with a look I'd seen more than once in Goodfellow's own. Baseball bats hung at rest and white teeth flashed expansively under a thick black mustache. "We have many, many things. Surely one will be what you seek. I am Branje." He swept an arm toward an RV to the right. "We'll sit, we'll talk, we'll drink. We'll take very good care of our new friends." Bullshit, every word of it. We knew it, and Branje most likely knew that we knew it, but it was the game, and the game had to be played.

Although not by me. Flay didn't seem much interested in the dark and gloomy interior either. Instead he wrinkled his nose, shook his head adamantly, and sat his furry ass on the ground. I kept him company under the broiling sun, leaning against the hot metal. Drinking and conniving, watching the highest levels of tricksters, the Rom and a Puck, going mano a mano, none of it much interested me. I'd sooner sweat and bake.

"Smell weird."

The clack of the door closing above our heads had been several minutes ago, and I'd been sitting with eyes shut as I listened to the sound of a million enraged bugs. At least it seemed like a million. Swatting yet another mosquito on my forearm, I asked incuriously, "What smells weird?"

"You."

I opened my eyes and slanted a glance at Flay's moist face. I'd have thought the panting would mean he wouldn't have to sweat, but it seemed Snowball had gotten the worst of both worlds there. "Yeah, yeah, I smell like Auphe. Monster. Stinky. The subject's been covered."

Eyes rolled in annoyance under the brim of the baseball cap. "No. Smell weird. Not just Auphe stink. More. *Human* weird."

"So you're saying, now I'm stinky *and* I smell weird?" I summed up as I wiped the sweat from my face. "Great. My self-esteem says thanks for playing."

The T-shirt-covered shoulders shrugged. "Tell what I smell."

At any other time that would've been funny. The casual toss off by a tourist-gear-wearing wolf. I almost wished I could appreciate it, but if I did, there would be other things waiting to push in . . . things I would appreciate a lot less. I closed my eyes again. "Promise likes calla lilies. Her apartment is always full of them, all colors."

Seconds later I heard Flay get to his feet and start moving from RV to RV, knocking on the doors. I seriously doubted he would find any out here, but then again you never knew. It was nearly twenty minutes later when I was interrupted again. The sun had started to fall and the temperature had dropped nearly an entire degree when the door flew open and Goodfellow came storming out. He was cursing at the top of his lungs; I didn't have to recognize the words to know just how filthy they were. It was Romany he was speaking, the original language of the Gypsy clans. The dialect tended to vary from clan to clan, tribe to tribe, but as a rule every Rom knew it. Niko and I, however, didn't. Sophia hadn't let more than an occasional Romany word slip and those hadn't been exactly educational. Apparently, Robin's grasp of Rom foul language far exceeded Sophia's own, because I'd yet to hear anything that I knew.

Pointing a finger back at the RV, Goodfellow swore again, then switched to English. He'd once remarked to me that no language was quite as good as English for spitting disgust and disdain. French was close, but English won out in the end for sheer crudeness. "Soul-sucking harridan. Shriveled, toothless old crone. Put your malicious, grasping fingers away. You won't get a single penny from me."

There was the gentle thud of boots in the dirt beside me and Niko sighed, "Negotiations have begun. This may take some time."

"They have it?" I almost slipped. I almost felt the desperation. Yeah . . . almost. But you know what they say about almost. Hand grenades and horseshoes. Nothing but hand grenades and horseshoes.

"It's a possibility." He sat beside me to watch the show. It turned out that the old woman, not the man with the mustache, was the leader—at least in the field of negotiations. "Abelia-Roo is a cagey opponent."

She came rocketing out of the RV shaking a wrinkled fist and swinging an elaborately carved cane. Not sharing Goodfellow's belief about English, she howled out a string of consonants and vowels in Romany that had even the perpetually jaded Robin's eyes widening. "My hair? My *hair*? You prune-teated old goat, you'd best take that back. Take it back or I'll rain fire on this miserable campsite until it's wiped from the face of the earth."

"Can he actually do that?" I asked skeptically.

Niko snorted. There was the tart smell of blackberry brandy on his breath. He had swallowed the traditional thimbleful to start the business at hand. "Hardly. If he could, every two-star restaurant in the city would be smoking ruins."

That was true enough. I watched as two gnarled fingers went up behind the white head like horns and Abelia-Roo made a sneering comment. "A leash?" Goodfellow shot back. "I think you're sadly mistaken, witch from hell. You've never kept one of my kind on a leash. Oh, I think perhaps you *worshipped* us as lowly cave apes should, and if anyone wore the leash, it was you." He spit onto the dirt at her feet. "Lying, thieving human."

This time she did switch to English. "Lying, thieving puck." Her spit actually hit Goodfellow's shoe.

Ah, it was like old times. I stretched my legs out into the dirt. "We're on a schedule, Nik. This is going to take forever."

"Have faith." His shoulder butted against mine. "Our shark against theirs? How can we not prevail?"

"I don't know. We've done a pretty good job of it so far." I drummed fingers on my leg and said pragmatically, "We could hurt someone. That would speed things along nicely, I'll bet."

There was an uncustomary hesitation on Niko's part before he said smoothly, "True." His finger thumped my knee before pointing. "How about her? She doesn't look precisely fleet of foot. We could run her to the ground in seconds." A pregnant Rom girl peeked at us from a doorway across the camp. Seeing our eyes on her, she quickly disappeared and slammed the door behind her. "We could break her wrist. It wouldn't take more than a minute at the most."

As brotherly lessons went, it was a little less subtle

than usual. "I was thinking more of Branje," I drawled, "but you've made your point."

"Have I?" He was poised to say something more, but Flay moved past us carrying a handful of plum-colored lilies. Niko watched his progress as the wolf loped back toward our home away from home. A less-than-amused look was then turned on me. "I'm curious, little brother. How long have you had these suicidal impulses?"

"You're not afraid of a little competition, are you, Cyrano?" I elbowed him in a move so automatic that it worked entirely independently of my brain. "Besides," I added, "it gives him something to think about other than his kid." I closed my eyes again. "Wake me up when Goodfellow stops talking."

There was a swat on the side of my head, not hard enough to hurt, although it definitely stung. The words were more gentle. "Hang in there, Cal. We're halfway home."

Hours later, we were still only halfway there and Niko was giving new consideration to my idea. Eyeing Branje across the leaping campfire, he said thoughtfully, "We could rip off his mustache and feed it to him. That is sure to inspire a little spirit of cooperation."

The fire, less for heat and more for driving away the bugs, billowed with a peculiar green smoke. It worked. The air was thick with the acrid smell of sage and eucalyptus, but the mosquitoes were gone, though the night had brought out another kind of predator. Promise stood at Niko's side, a single lily tucked in her hair. I'd seen the look exchanged between the two of them when she'd first appeared wearing the flower. Pure affectionate humor.

"It is an exceptionally unfortunate mustache,"

Promise agreed. "You'd be doing him a favor. I'm sure he'd be much more attractive without it."

Goodfellow chose that moment to stomp over with an expression of outraged frustration on his face. "I give up. I do. That maniacal old crone cannot be reasoned with. Not now. Not ever." His hand moved up to nervously smooth his wavy hair. "She cursed me, said my hair would fall out before the next full moon." He pulled his hand away and peered at the palm carefully for any deserters. "My *hair*," he murmured, still shocked over the audacity.

"You don't actually believe in Gypsy curses, do you?" I asked with a faint overlay of scorn.

Green eyes narrowed on me with impatience. "Of course not. I, an immortal creature, am only standing here with a vampire, a half Auphe, and a walking talking wolf. Why would I possibly believe in something as ludicrous as a Gypsy curse?" He rubbed the heel of both hands over tired eyes and went on to snap, "And then there's that entire year I spent impotent thanks to one."

Niko skipped straight over that information as more than any of us wanted to know and said, "They won't sell it, then?"

"Sell it?" he repeated with disgust. "They won't even admit to having the Calabassa. They have, however, tried to sell me everything else under Zeus's infinite regard."

"After all that time?" Promise touched a shimmering nail to her lower lip. "Abelia-Roo must be a formidable opponent indeed."

"She would eat every one of my salesmen for breakfast and have room for a champagne chaser," he said glumly.

Goodfellow went on to say something else, but by

then I had drifted off. It was a casual stroll with what looked like no particular destination in mind, yet I ended up past the fire and closing in on Branje. I didn't pull my Glock. The Rom were skilled knife fighters; they didn't respect the gun. And I wanted their respect. I wanted their fear more, but a little additional respect wouldn't hurt matters any. Branje, drinking from an unlabeled brown bottle, didn't see me coming until he was on the ground and the knife at his throat. I wasn't quite as practiced in the art of silence as Niko, but I was close. After all, I'd been taught by the best. Branje was tough, though—I had to give him that. With my knee buried in his stomach and my blade in the softness under his chin, he cursed and grabbed at his own knife on his belt.

I cut him.

The wound was two inches long and shallow, but it was enough to still Branje's hand. "My men will kill you," he hissed.

"I think they have their own problems," I said serenely. I didn't look up to verify that. I didn't need to. I could hear the whip of Niko's sword through the air and his cold command of "Back away. *Now.*" I'd heard his low curse as he'd spotted me right before I reached my goal, and I'd known he wouldn't be far behind me.

The Rom's eyes flickered from one side to the other, then back to me. "Then Abelia-Roo will curse the pecker right off your body."

I moved the knife from his throat to insert the tip in his nose. "Probably, but how much comfort will that be to you after I cut your nose from your face? Or maybe your ears." I considered for a few seconds as I idly twisted my wrist. A tiny trickle of blood began to creep from his nostril over his lip. "Or maybe—just maybe—I'll take it all. Nose, ears, eyes, tongue." I gave him a consoling smile. "I'll leave the mustache. You seem very proud of it."

I felt him twitch beneath me, but his face remained unmoving and stoic. Like I said, he was tough. But were his people gathered around us as tough? Some might be, but there were bound to be others with slightly weaker stomachs or softer hearts. Someone would break . . . sooner or later. I pulled the knife back and said truthfully, "It's nothing personal, Branje. Try and keep that in mind." This time the blade found his ear. He had large, fleshy lobes. I could take half off and he'd still have enough to spare. The first drop of blood had appeared when a voice stopped me.

"Now, here is one who knows how to negotiate." There was the approving smack of Abelia-Roo's toothless gums. "Now, here is a *man*."

If you only knew, I thought with dark amusement before my emotion shifted to cautious surprise. This wasn't the surrender I'd been shooting for. This was Grandma having balls to put all ours to shame and a shriveled soul to match mine. I looked up to see her duck under Niko's blade as if it were a garland of flowers. Arthritic knees popping like gunshots, she crouched beside Branje and me. "You want the Calabassa, do you?" Brown eyes flecked with gold and black nestled in the midst of tissue-paper skin folded into hundreds of wrinkles.

"I'm sure as hell not here to spread around my plastic surgery skills." I kept Branje pinned to the ground as I wiped the scant amount of blood from the metal onto my jeans and then sheathed the knife.

"Do you have any idea of the crown's purpose?" From the avidly gleeful flush in her face, I had a feeling it was nothing good.

"Granny," I said, "I couldn't give a shit if I tried."

17

I should've given a shit, and Abelia-Roo was more than happy to gloat over every detail that told me why I should. I'd thought the crown had looked too drab and plain to be your typical bauble. I was right. The Bassa had made that innocuous bit of metal for a reason—a very dark and infinitely practical reason. They'd created a thief . . . or a tool for a thief. Wear the crown and take from a person anything you wished. Their life, their knowledge . . . their power. I doubted Caleb needed any help taking lives or was interested in any extra smarts. He thought he was as clever as they fucking came.

But power . . . that was a different matter entirely. Take away the first two and it's the only option left. He wanted the ability to take someone's power . . . their gift. Although it couldn't be as easy as all that. Not many creatures in the world had talents he might envy. What could he want? What did he covet so profoundly that would be worth this much trouble—oh. God, I was stupid. So damn stupid.

There had been more unpleasant information dancing on the tip of the old Rom's tongue, I could tell as I'd cursed my idiocy, but at the last second she decided to keep it to herself. For fun or profit, and since she wasn't haggling for even more money, I was guessing it was pure, malicious fun. Granny had a way about her; she damn sure did.

"So he wants Georgina's gift." Niko held the circlet up to the dimly flickering firelight after I shared my grim thought. "He could see whatever he wanted. Know the future, the past, and all that lay between. It makes sense; what Georgina has is invaluable." He exhaled and shook his head. "But it also complicates things to no end."

"How?" I demanded. "It's not as if we planned on letting Caleb walk away in the first place. The second we have him in our sights, we give him the crown." I watched the fire reflect sinuously in the curve of the metal. "Promptly followed by a bullet to the brain."

"I have a feeling it won't be quite that simple."

Through the drifting smoke I saw that across the campsite Goodfellow was handing over two duffel bags of cash to Branje. Abelia-Roo didn't waste any time muscling him aside to unzip them and count their contents with flashing fingers. Both Promise and Robin had contributed to the Calabassa fund, since Niko and I barely had two nickels to rub together. The price wasn't that of a small country . . . quite, but it was damn close. "No?" I looked back at the crown and frowned. Ugly goddamn thing. "Then I guess we'll just have to make it that simple."

"Easier said than done." Between one breath and the next Niko had crossed the six feet between us. He was closer than close and as angry as I'd seen him. Scratch that. He was furious . . . with me, and that I had never seen. "Nothing is simple at the moment, not with your recent moronic behavior. What the hell were you doing with Branje?"

"Is that why you're pissed?" My frown deepened. "Hell, Cyrano, it was your idea. Rip off his mustache and feed it to him, you said. I just picked different things to slice and dice is all."

"Cal, you cannot go off without thought, without reason. . . ." He tilted his head down until his eyes were level with mine, utterly pissed off and completely inescapable. "Without *backup*."

"You watched my back," I pointed out with what I thought to be fairly evident logic. "You were right there, same as always." *Same as always* . . . you always remember the words that come back to bite you in the ass, no matter how much you'd like to forget them.

"I could've been there more quickly if you'd bothered to let me know what was going through your head." His free hand fisted in the collar of my shirt. "Branje isn't much of a threat; you could've handled him before you could crawl, but if you try that imbecilic recklessness on someone else, someone along the lines of Abbagor or Cerberus or worse yet the Auphe, they will put you in your grave. Is that what you want?" He shook me, hard enough that I felt the snap of it in my neck. "Is it?"

It was a fair question, and denying that would be a lie. George was gone, the Auphe were back, and things had long spiraled out of control. But as selfish as I was, even I had my limits. I couldn't do that to my brother, no more than he could've done it to me. "No, Nik," I answered soberly. "It's not what I want."

The fury, a masquerade for something much starker, drained away as quickly as it had come. "All right, then." He exhaled and released my shirt. "Let's not have this conversation again."

I looked down at my shirt, then stuck my finger through the new Niko-fashioned rip and said wryly, "I'll try and keep that in mind."

He gave one abrupt nod and ordered, "Do that." Then, letting the issue go, he went on, "Let's eat.

We've been invited to dinner by Abelia-Roo. I think . . ." Reluctant amusement tweaked his lips upward. "I think she may have her eye on Goodfellow. She might find him less than a man when it comes to haggling, but apparently that isn't the only standard of measurement she uses."

She should be grateful she wasn't around when Robin had "haggled" with a succubus. That may have changed her mind about his manhood damn quick. "Sounds entertaining." And a few weeks ago, I would've paid good money for that kind of entertainment, but now . . . I looked up at the sky. It was moonless and clear; I could see hundreds, thousands of stars and every fiery blink was a second lost. "But we need to go. We don't have much time."

"We have time to eat, to relax—even if only for an hour." His hand reached for mine and folded my fingers around the Calabassa. "Besides, it will maintain a little goodwill with the Sarzo. We might need their help again someday."

"We couldn't *afford* their help again," I groused, but relented. "An hour, okay? Then we go."

"An hour," he agreed. "I'm sure Goodfellow will be indebted to you for that. He's even more anxious than you to get on the road."

With a toothless Roo on his tail, I didn't blame him. I turned the metal under my hands, my skin crawling at the feel of it. There was one last thing I needed to do before we sat down to a heaping helping of Goodfellow humiliation. "Here," I said gruffly, pushing the crown back into his hands. "You hang on to it."

"Cal." The amusement reflected in the quirk of his mouth faded.

"I've already lost one." I folded my arms and tucked my hands out of sight. "That's my limit, thanks."

I'd half expected an Auphe to appear the instant

the Gypsy Calabassa had been unveiled. I *fully* expected to wake up every night with Auphe claws in my throat and a doorway to hell before me. I'd slept with my knife for so long that it'd finally become a comfort to me. But knowing what I knew now, I could sleep with a thousand knives and it wouldn't make one bit of difference.

I walked away before Niko could try to convince me that I hadn't frozen in the face of the enemy. I had. It had cost us the first crown, and I wasn't about to risk losing another. Frankly, guarding George's last chance wasn't a responsibility I was up for.

An hour and a half later we were back on the road, flush with success . . . and something else. "Jesus." I grimaced as the alcohol fumes wafted my way. "Goodfellow, it's actually coming out of your pores."

A haunted look sought me out over a rapidly emptying bottle of fruit brandy. I'd long lost track of how many such bottles he'd sucked down during the previous hour. "I've lived through the fall of Rome, the Hundred Years' War, even that sleazy Troy debacle, but I've never faced anything such as that." He took another hurried pull on the bottle before repeating in a shell-shocked whisper, "Never."

Dinner had not gone well for our puck. Abelia-Roo's hands had been anywhere but on her fork. For once, Robin had been the hunted, not the hunter, prey of a wizened, bare-gummed predator. Niko, behind the wheel, was not surprisingly unsympathetic to his plight and offered little comfort. "Be grateful we didn't leave you there. She seemed quite serious about the leash threat." He arched an eyebrow in consideration. "Then again, it may have been more of a promise than a threat."

Goodfellow had a response to that. By now, I knew that he had a response to anything. I managed to turn on the radio just in time to drown it out. After tuning in to the first station I came across, I pulled on the lever on the bottom of the passenger seat to ease it back. Toeing off my shoes, I put my feet up on the dashboard, shifted onto my side, and dozed off. Stomach heavy with food, mind dull with heat, there wasn't much else to do. There was a long stretch of blissfully empty darkness that was broken what must have been hours later by a hand on my shoulder. I squinted at the orange and pink sky outside the window and revised my estimate. *Many* hours later—it was morning. I sat up and ran fingers through sleep-rumpled hair. Beside me, the owner of the hand that had pulled me from sleep growled, "Trouble."

Trouble all right, and it was reflected in the rearview mirror as flashing red and blue lights. Fan-fucking-tastic. I glared at Flay, who seemed to have replaced Niko at the steering wheel, and asked with typical morning ill humor, "Do you even have a license, Snowball?"

"Do *you*?" came his impatient gargle.

He had a point. Mine hadn't come as a prize in a box of cereal, but neither had it come from the DMV. While it was good enough to pass a casual glance, it couldn't fool the computers, which was why we were driving instead of flying. Good fake ID was easy enough to come by; excellent fake ID was increasingly rare in this hyper-security-sensitive world.

"Shit." I looked over my shoulder. Niko, Promise, Robin—they were all already awake. I immediately pegged Goodfellow as our best bet. He'd been running under the radar longer than the rest of us by far. If anyone had passable paper, it would be him. It was a good thought, in theory, until I took in the bloodshot eyes and white-knuckled fists pressed to his head, and

breath that could embalm a corpse. I went immediately to our next best hope. "Promise?"

She could've pulled it off, I think. If not by convincing the cop that she'd been driving, then by the simple
fact of being Promise. I'd never know, because it
didn't come to that.

The Auphe came first.

I didn't see the rip in the air he plummeted through,
but I doubted that it was more than ten feet up. He
came down fast—too damn fast.

Walking toward us, the cop was freshly stamped
from the hero cookie cutter. Square jaw, wide shoulders, impenetrable sunglasses paired with an impenetrable expression. Disciplined, stalwart, a noble
defender of order—it took less than five seconds for
him to die. The Auphe landed on top of him, knocking
him to his hands and knees. An infinity of teeth found
the bare strip of skin over the starched collar and
passed through it as if it were no more substantial than
a flesh-colored mist. Then there was another mist, this
one red and viscous. I didn't remember moving, yet
somehow I'd traveled from my seat to the back of the
RV. Hands pressed against the glass, I saw the cop
try to struggle upward. With one hand supporting his
weight, he used the other to claw at the nightmare on
his back. It was futile. His strength had disappeared
with the blood pouring from his mutilated throat.

I wouldn't have recognized the growl that filled the
air as my own if it hadn't been for the searing sensation of barbwire in my throat. I did recognize the gun
in my hand, and better than that, I recognized that I
could shoot through the window glass as if it were air.
But as my finger tightened on the trigger, someone
beat me to the punch.

Niko was a dark shadow in the sun's morning glow.

He was on the Auphe as quickly as the Auphe had been on the cop. Unfortunately, the Auphe had preternaturally fast reflexes, something his victim lacked. Or rather, had lacked. The dark glasses had fallen from the cop's face to reveal eyes that passed from stunned to empty. Arms and legs spasmed, then gave way and the cookie-cutter hero fell. He didn't get up again. He never would.

The Auphe rode him all the way down. Lean and sleek, the bundle of sinew and claws showed the new day a dripping crimson smile. It was the same grin he turned on my brother as Niko's sword swung to separate head from body. Overconfidence—it wasn't a failing exclusive to humans. The Auphe knew how fast he was—what he didn't know was how fast Niko was. It was a mistake, a big one, and it lost him the bottom half of that charming smile. The narrow mandible disappeared in an explosion of black blood and bone as the Auphe flipped backward, saving the rest of his head. Niko followed so closely that it was impossible the Auphe could escape. Unless . . .

Shit. *Shit*.

I tore through the RV, tumbled through the door, and ran. A car, the first to pass since our stop, nearly hit me. It had slowed to gawk at the fallen cop. When I rocketed into its path with a gun and a matching metallic snarl, the driver swerved, gave up on the looky-lou, and sped off with squealing tires. I ignored the breeze of a bumper kiss and kept running. I passed the dead man lying in the emergency lane, vaulted the dry ditch, hit sand and scrubby grass, and kept moving. I was still fifty feet away when I felt it. It was only a shadow of the eviscerating sensation I'd felt when I'd unwittingly opened my own, but it was still a first. I'd never been able to sense an Auphe doorway before it opened—not until now. A ghostly hand pulled my intestines into a knot just before the air began to bleed gray.

The Auphe couldn't speak, not without a jaw, but he made sounds nonetheless. They were horribly triumphant gobbles that sprayed blood in an arc as he threw himself on Niko's sword with enough force to impale himself right up to the hilt. Arms wound with ropy muscle wrapped around Niko's shoulders and with what was either a laugh or a death rattle, the Auphe fell backward with him toward the gate. I hit them both in an impossibly long tackle, taking us away from that hungry silver light. As we hit the ground, I screwed the Glock into one pointed ear and pulled the trigger. Repeatedly. The pointed skull deflated into a misshapen mass and turned the surrounding soil into a rancid blot. Repugnant, but not as much as the door that hung before us—still open, still ravenous.

"You don't want to go there."

Niko's hand was on my arm gripping hard. "Where does it go? Cal, where does it go?"

"You don't want to go there," I said again dully, my eyes locked on the doorway. It was bad, what lay behind it. There wasn't a word for the bad of it.

Then it closed, like the popping of a soap bubble. And with it, the awful blackness in my head receded. Blinking, I levered myself up off Niko and the dead Auphe. "Cops." I cleared the hoarseness from my throat and tried again as I swiftly patched over the cracks in my artificial calm. "The cops will be coming. We need to get out of here."

"Damn it, would you change your antifreeze and have an emotion already?" came an irritated snipe from behind. A rumpled, snarling Goodfellow stood there. One hand held a sword and one had a death grip on his aching head. "It was Tumulus, wasn't it, Caliban? He tried to take Niko to Tumulus."

Tumulus, we'd learned, was Auphe hell, a dimension of bare rock and endless desolation. Their home away from home. I'd spent two years there when the Auphe had taken me at the age of fourteen. I didn't remember any of it, at least not consciously, but it was clear that some part of me was aware enough to recognize a gate to the Abyss when I saw it. I'd survived that place, but only because the Auphe had wanted me to. I didn't think they'd be so inclined with Niko.

It was a conversation for another time; I was nowhere near ready for it now. Looking away from Goodfellow, I focused in on the body of the Auphe. Colorless hair mixed with coarse soil and dark blood. The pale skin was now tinged with a creeping gray that spread like fungus. "I wonder what CSI will think about him," I muttered and closed my eyes tightly.

Not a whole lot, as it turned out. We stuffed him in the trunk of the police car and then we blew it up. Auphe and car . . . sky-high. Robin had suggested we put him in the RV with us and dispose of him later. Niko flatly refused, and he did it so that I didn't have to. Be in close proximity to an Auphe, even a dead one, for more than a few minutes? I couldn't have done it. I would've either thrown him out onto the road or jumped out myself.

Luckily, Flay had casually tossed off the inferno suggestion. Working for the Kin had provided him with the flexibility of mind and soul to assess a problem and immediately decide to blow it to kingdom come. Despite myself, I was beginning to have a reluctant—very reluctant—appreciation for the wolf. And when he jury-rigged a fuse for the gas tank out of one of the RV's ugly plaid curtains and detonated the car, all in the space of two minutes, I had to give credit where credit was due.

After that, we hauled ass. The poor damn dead cop was beyond help and we left him where he'd fallen. Flay had suggested we put his body in the car, but the rest of us couldn't go along with that. Bad enough he was dead; we could at least leave his family something to grieve over. He would've called in our license plate number, but there was nothing we could do about that. The first rest stop we came to we would swap our plates out with another vehicle. Goodfellow said that the Auphe would burn almost entirely. Their bones were softer and more flexible than a human's; there wouldn't be much left for the crime lab to work with. And what was found would be considered a hopelessly contaminated sample. A hoax, a fluke . . . a mirage. It would be explained away. It'd been done before, and it would be done again. As long as humans didn't want to see, they wouldn't. Hell, I envied them. I wished I were that blind.

"Is it as Robin said? Did it try to take Niko to that place?" a voice asked softly.

I was curled up in the back with my head against the curtain-shrouded window and my knees pulled up against my chest. I had flexible bones too. Was it youth or something else? Didn't know, didn't care. As Promise sat down in the seat opposite mine, voices floated back from the front. There were soft, undecipherable murmurs that made the space seem much larger. Niko, Goodfellow, Flay . . . they could've been miles away. If I concentrated, I could've brought them closer, but I was content enough in my self-imposed exile. Rather—I gave Promise a stony glance through strands of unbrushed hair—I *had* been.

"I don't want to talk about it."

"Caliban." My name was said with patience and empathy, but also with determination. She was worried about me, but she was also worried about Niko, and if she had to push me, then she would.

"I said, I don't want to talk about it!" This time I snapped and bit.

When it came to pushing, Promise was among the very best. From gentle persuasion to an icy will, she had her ways of bringing you around. But her ways didn't compare to the ways of what was burning on the road far behind us. She could push all she wanted, but I'd been pushed all my life. I'd been watched from my first breath, and hounded to what should have been my last.

In other words, if I didn't want to talk, no one on this side of that gray doorway could make me. Recapturing a balance that was getting more precarious by the hour, I leaned my head back against the wall. "Go away, Promise."

Now I was the one pushing, and with a lot less finesse than Promise would have used. I didn't have to see the flash of temper that initiated; I could feel it on my skin, as intense as that noontime Florida sun. "I know you're afraid, perhaps even terrified." The typical Promise serenity was sounding taxed to the limit, and I had a feeling that if I bothered to look at her, I would see teeth revealed with those words, the kind of teeth you didn't want to see from a vampire. "But closing your eyes to the situation like a child isn't going to change things."

She was half-right. Behaving like a scared kid wasn't going to make this shit go away. The only problem was, nothing was going to do that. Not a goddamn thing. The sole reason we'd been able to defeat the Auphe previously was that they'd all been gathered in one location. I sincerely doubted that was going to

happen again. We were screwed. Front, back, and all
ways in between. We could talk until we were blue in
the face, but that fun fact wasn't going to change. So
why talk at all?

Instead, I did what she told me not to do. I closed
my eyes. Literally, metaphorically, figuratively . . .
choose your poison because I meant them all. Velvet
darkness loomed behind my eyelids, but it didn't stop
me from feeling the very quality of the air itself
change as Promise decided I didn't deserve her patience anymore. "Not even for your *brother* would you
try to face what is before you?" Cool and merciless.
"Not even for the one who has thrown his life away
for you?"

Strong words . . . I'd thought them to myself long
before Promise had ever entered the picture. They
didn't sound any different aloud than they had the
thousands of times I'd heard them in my head.

"Promise, don't."

Different words, but in a way they were the same.
Exactly the goddamn same. I opened my eyes to see
Niko's forbiddingly impassive face tilted down toward
the only person in his life he had loved aside from
me. There he was, my big brother, doing what he invariably did . . . throwing his life away. Same as
always.

Thanks to me.

"No," I said quickly, straightening. "No, she's right.
I should tell you what I can, even if it's only
guesses . . . impressions." And with that admission
they came, whether I was ready for them or not. Trig-
gered by the doorway to Tumulus, they'd been waiting
in the wings poised for the faintest hint of an invitation. Stupid me, I gave it to them.

I swallowed convulsively as I tasted air not of this
world. It was cold and acidic, and it tasted of slow,

lingering suffering. Not death. Death was easy. What I tasted made you long for the pillow over the face, the cleansing shot of potassium chloride to stop your heart. My fingers dug into the cushion beneath me, but I felt the grit of an alien soil that was more cutting than ground glass. I heard hundreds of voices whispering words I couldn't understand. Consonants that cut the throat, vowels that made your ears want to bleed. It was when I began to repeat the words over and over, strangling on their unnatural shape, that the hard slap rocked my head back.

The world came back. The good world—bright and warm. Plaid curtains, the hum of an engine, the smell of musky wolf. Good. Even the blood on my lip was welcome. In comparison with what I had tasted, it was wine . . . chocolate. Wholesome and so *normal*, salty but clean. I touched a tongue to it and reveled in the tang of it.

"Cal, can you hear me? Stay with me, all right? Stay with me." Niko didn't look too happy as his hand gripped my shoulder, and as I saw the tiny wisp of winter fog roiling in the air before me, I could see why. It was small, the size of an orange. It wasn't a door, not yet . . . a keyhole at best, but it was the last one you wanted to peer through.

"You don't want to go there," I said in a low and shaky echo, my eyes locked on the eddy and swirl of it. "But I guess maybe it wants to come here."

"Can you close it?"

I felt it inside of me, the way it turned . . . how it fed off of my energy, how it grew strength from my concentration and focus. It was in control, not me. "Knock me out," I said sharply as it doubled in size, gobbling up air and space. *"Now."*

Niko didn't hesitate. He knew a little temporary pain was nothing compared with what would come crawling out of that rip once it grew large enough. It didn't hurt much. He didn't have the time to painlessly choke me out, but I barely saw the fist that flashed at my jaw with surgical precision, and I scarcely had time to register the crunch of knuckle against bone before I was gone where pain couldn't follow. I could only hope I took the door to hell with me.

18

The pain hadn't followed me into unconsciousness, but it was waiting for me when I woke up. My jaw ached, but less than I would've imagined. It was no worse than the throbbing of a sore tooth, and the stillness within me was more than worth it. The doorway was gone. The passageway to Tumulus was shut. We were safe. Of course, it took a few minutes to corral a confused brain into making that conclusion, but I got there.

Just as I did, there was a freezing touch on my jaw. "Hey," I mumbled, and slitted eyes in annoyance. "Cold."

"Ice packs most often are," Niko said levelly. He tapped a finger on the back of my hand. "Take it."

I obeyed, holding it in place as I slowly sat up. The inside of the RV spun once, then settled into place. We were alone—as alone as you could be in a hotel room on wheels. I could see the chiaroscuro of Promise's hair up front, and I had a feeling she hadn't moved of her own accord. Damn. Cautiously, I worked my jaw back and forth, then moved the ice pack a little higher. "You did a good job, Cyrano. Everything's where it should be."

"Considerably different from the last time, then."

He pinched the bridge of his long nose as the briefest of grimaces crossed his face.

You could say that. The closing of that particular doorway hadn't been brought about by a simple punch. Instead, it had involved Niko's sword burying itself in my abdomen. As Niko had saved the world with that move, I didn't hold any grudges. It had been the right thing to do. Even if it hadn't spared the world, with the shape I'd been in, it still would've been the right thing. I wished, not for the first time, that he could see that as clearly as I did.

"Sorry about the door," I said, kicking his ankle with a foot covered by a dirty sock. I hadn't been too concerned about putting on shoes when I'd made my mad dash out into the clear Florida morning.

"It wasn't your fault." He stopped my antics with an unrelenting heel that pinned my foot to the floor.

"Wasn't hers either." I pointed my chin toward the front and immediately regretted it as a sliver of pain branched through my face.

"She knows what happened when Goodfellow hypnotized you to access your lost memories." His voice was low, but I knew it was easily audible to a vampire if she cared to listen. "I told her."

"Hearing about it and seeing it are two different things, Nik," I pointed out, feeling the tingling stretch of swelling skin as I talked. "And, hell, it wasn't that bad this time. Robin didn't toss his cookies and I didn't try to gouge your face off." There'd been no screaming, no clawing through walls, no huddling in a corner unseeing and unknowing. A quick and easy pop to the jaw was nothing in comparison with that. Certainly nothing to lose Promise over. Niko wanted her, he deserved her, and if things went as badly in the future as I thought they might, then he was going to need her.

"We need better memories, little brother, if you're making this one out to be less than absolutely shitty," he said somberly.

He sounded like me and that was never a positive sign. Time to give a little push of my own. I let the ice pack fall and passed it back and forth between my hands. "Then go make some."

Releasing my foot, he looked away with an uncustomary avoidance, then shifted his shoulders. "She wanted you to know that she was sorry."

"I am, Caliban. I cannot tell you how much." Promise had drifted over to us, so silently that I didn't know she was there until I felt the touch of her fingers on my shoulder, her lips brushing over my bruised jaw. "I let my concern for Niko get the better of me—the better of you. The blame for what happened lies with me, no one else."

The apology was as gracious as Promise herself, and she meant it wholeheartedly. A few hundred years would give anyone more than a few chances to learn how to lie. I knew Promise was no different there, but I'd lived with a woman who lied for a living for the first fourteen years of my life. I'd also spent a lot of time in Goodfellow's company in the past year. If you listened to him, he'd all but invented the lie. The bottom line was I knew bullshit when I heard it, whether it came from a talented amateur or a ranking pro. Promise meant what she said. And even if she hadn't, I still would've been tempted to swallow it for Niko's sake . . . although his bullshit detector was as honed as mine.

"You thought it was for Nik," I said matter-of-factly. And in my book, that trumped any transgression known to man. I gave an awkward pat to her hand, then gently removed it from my shoulder as I stood. For the first time I noticed it was dark outside the windows. I narrowed my eyes in disbelief. No wonder the pain was muted. "Jesus, how long have I been out?"

"Thirteen hours. We're about five hours from home." As Niko filled me in, I became aware of another sign of the passing time. A bursting bladder. "I didn't hit you with that much force. Robin said that opening that door must have drained you and to let you sleep."

It made sense. Tumulus had to be more than a hop, skip, and jump from our world. Opening a doorway from the Brooklyn Bridge to our apartment . . . no big deal. Opening one to a place that existed outside our own was markedly different. It was an issue worth exploring, if exploring just that type of thing hadn't been what had gotten us here to begin with. Besides, my bladder was a damn sight more insistent than any curiosity.

"Trouble is, there are some parts it didn't drain." I dumped the ice pack in Niko's lap and headed for the small bathroom. "Take my seat, Promise. I might take a shower while I'm in there." The warm water might unknot muscles that were suddenly protesting thirteen hours of inactivity. It did, a little too well. The second time I woke up it was to the sound of a shower knob being turned off and the distinct smell of wet dog.

I blinked and swiped at the cool water washing over my eyes. I was sitting on the shower floor, propped in the corner. I'd been sound asleep, although it couldn't have been for too long. The water wasn't cold, only cool. "Unh," I said with a not-so-amazing lack of coherence. Opening that door really had taken it out of me. What a relief to know if I ever did shape another one and go through, I'd sleep through the following torture and mutilation.

"Out." Flay shook the water from his arm and then threw me a towel. "Out."

Flay didn't strike me as the shy type. I had no doubt I'd see more than I wanted to if I lingered. I didn't. As the door closed behind me, I kept one hand holding up the towel around my hips and the other juggling my clothes.

"Summarily evicted, eh?"

Goodfellow was sprawled on the couch adjacent to the kitchen booth, the same couch where I'd recently spent so many unconscious hours. He looked as tired as I still felt. "Yeah." I yawned with only a twinge of my jaw. Niko, undisputed master of the surgical-strike fist. "You too?"

"It's Promise's turn. Flay drove eight. I drove five." He waved a hand at his leg and schooled his face into a saintly expression of noble suffering. "In deference to my hideously painful wound."

"Is that thing healing on an installment plan or what?" I dressed quickly and flopped down beside him.

"Unsympathetic brat." He yawned as well and regarded me with eyes that while sleepy were still wary. "Quite the trick you've developed."

"Sure, if you want to spend your summer vacation in Tumulus." I considered my dirty socks and discarded them, leaving my feet bare. "That's not for me, but, hey, whatever floats your boat."

"Aren't you the cool one?" he mused, wariness transmuting to something close to reproof. "You're walking a precarious road, Caliban, and it's one that is going to end in a very messy explosion or a nice, padded room at the local loony bin."

"Uh-huh," I remarked with disinterest, and nodded toward the front. "They make up yet?"

The green eyes darkened. "I'm serious. I know something of this; I'm not an amateur."

"Yeah, yeah, you taught Freud everything he knew. I remember." I leaned over and snagged a box of cereal sitting on the booth table. My stomach felt as neglected as my bladder and I poured a generous quantity of dry cereal onto my hand. Studying it, I recognized his effort, then dismissed it. "You can't help me, Robin. Not right now. Maybe later . . . after all this shit is over." I filled my mouth and chewed methodically.

He didn't comment for a moment; then he folded his arms and sniffed disparagingly, "You assume I wanted to help. I'm simply giving advice. Whether you take it is up to you." I was getting better at pushing people away, but Goodfellow could give me some serious competition. Too bad for the both of us that trying seemed to be the best that we could accomplish.

"And, yes, they seem to be working through their differences," he continued. "Curse my luck."

I offered him a handful of cereal in sympathy. When he sneered at the culinary effort, I ate it myself. "You and Flay bond while I was out?"

The sneer faded. "He talked about his boy."

"Oh." That couldn't have been a happy conversation. "What was his name again?"

"Slay." Despite his somber expression, that brought a subtle quirk to his mouth. "I suppose it's better than Flay Junior." As I gave a noncommittal crunch, he sighed, "Anyway, we talked or rather, he did. It's a curse, this face. Understanding, compassion, it radiates from every perfect pore."

He would've gone on—with Goodfellow that was a given—but Flay came out of the bathroom and he was looking marginally more wolfish. "Hungry." He slammed the bathroom door. "Food. Now." He scowled at the box in my hands. "Meat. No sawdust. No chicken. Red meat." We'd had a chicken dish with the Rom, spicy and filling, but not filling enough for a wolf apparently.

"We're almost to the city," Robin pointed out. "Perhaps you could wait until—"

"Now." Fangs and claws lengthened, and the mane of hair bristled.

Okay, those were some severe hunger pangs. "Nik, Promise," I called. "I think we need a burger stop, like, pronto."

Three hours and about forty rare burgers later we were home.

It was night and what I once thought to be a hot summer had a much less vicious bite than the heat that we'd faced at the Rom camp. I'd missed the concrete, the lights . . . the ability to hide in the midst of millions. You had to be practical even in the grip of a homesickness you would never have guessed you could experience. Niko and I had learned a long time ago not to get attached to any place, any person. It wasn't only being on the run from the Auphe. Before that, Sophia had moved us from place to place at the drop of a hat. She'd been on the run too. The police, angry clients, unpaid rent, responsibility—you name it and Sophia had shown her heels to it.

The apartment was as we left it. There were no new presents waiting at the doorstep, and I felt something inside me unclench as I opened the door. We had dropped Goodfellow and then Promise off at their respective apartments. Niko had escorted the vampire to the front of the building with a grave and correct courtesy that let me know that while things were improved between them they still weren't right. Flay drove off with the RV, saying he would return in the morning. Where he thought he would park that borrowed leviathan in the city, I didn't have a clue.

Inside the apartment there was the faintly stale smell that spoke of abandonment. We'd been gone only two and a half days; I would've sworn it was much longer. My bed was also as I left it . . . wrinkled and unkempt. That didn't stop me from eyeing it wistfully. I was still wiped. Finishing the sweep of our small space, I rejoined Niko in the kitchen. "Okay, we have the crown. Now what?"

"We wait for Caleb to contact us. He's obviously keeping a close eye on our activities." He looked toward the window in the apartment. Too large for blinds, it had been covered days ago by an obscuring sheet. "He'll know we're back. By tomorrow evening this could all be over."

"Except for the Auphe."

"Let's focus on one life-threatening disaster at a time. Multitasking at this level of catastrophe isn't quite feasible." He stretched, working out the kinks of the long trip. "I'm going to take a quick run to loosen up."

"Hold on." Mentally groaning at the thought, I went to retrieve the sneakers I'd discarded in my bedroom and tried not to look at the bed.

Eyebrows lifted as I reappeared. "You're running? Voluntarily?"

"Have to keep an eye on you," I explained, bending over to tie laces with quick jerks. "This isn't like the good old days, Cyrano, when they only wanted me. Now they want you." To hurt me, and to punish us both. "This time around I get to be the babysitter."

"You don't believe I can take care of myself?" The eyebrows came down, but there was an affectionately mocking flavor to the question.

"You didn't think I could handle myself these past couple of years?" I countered.

"I said so often enough, didn't I?" He pulled me

upright by the scruff of my shirt. "But point taken. I'll try to be as graceful about it as you were." As he let that jewel of a threat sink in, he went on, "You're tired, I know. For you, I'll cut it back to a quick five miles."

"You're one generous son of a bitch," I gritted as I followed him out the door.

By the time we got back, I was as stiff-legged as the Frankenstein monster. It wasn't the length of the run—for a Niko one it was short. But the exhaustion that hadn't been much relieved by my long sleep was making itself known with a vengeance. I barely made it to my bed and fell across it. You've heard people say they fell asleep the instant their head touched the pillow? I think I fell asleep midair. On our run Niko had said he would stay up and keep watch. I'd told him it wasn't necessary. If an Auphe opened a door, I would know it . . . now. But, as he'd brought up, if it opened one down the block and scuttled to our place, that would kill our advance notice. It was good thinking, and I hoped it kept him company on his watch, because I was down for the count.

I woke up to the smell of doughnuts and fresh coffee. Someone else had to be in the apartment. Refined sugar and caffeine? Niko would sooner chop off a hand. I thought about taking a shower before investigating, but decided that for all of us who'd spent days shut up with Flay, I was smelling like a rose in comparison.

Returned as promised, our musky companion himself sat at the kitchen table proving that wolf did not live by red meat alone. He had a gallon-sized cup in one hand and a bear claw nearly as big as his head in the other. Niko, nursing a steaming tea and dry toast, was watching with critical eye as sticky pecans rained onto the floor. I sat down and helped myself to one of the gooey pastries from the box resting on the table. My body welcomed the sugar rush with gratitude. "All quiet last night?" I asked Niko around the mouthful.

"All quiet," he confirmed.

Swallowing, I moved on to Flay. "You actually parked Goodfellow's bachelor pad on wheels downstairs?"

"No." He drained about half the coffee in one long gulp. "Decide keep it. For Slay and me. New home. Travel . . . leave this place."

"Lone wolf and cub, eh?" I took another bite and said thickly, "You know that's not Goodfellow's to give, right? He borrowed it."

Flay shrugged, showing little interest in Robin's business affairs. He was still wearing the baseball hat he'd picked up in Florida. It didn't make him look any less deadly. "Mine now."

And who was I to argue with that? My body was craving more carb- and sugar-induced energy and I was reaching for a second bun when the phone rang. Niko had it in hand before I managed to drop the bear claw. I couldn't deny a sliver of craven relief that he reached it before me. George was only a girl I knew, no more and no less, but I didn't want to hear her pain. Not again. My sticky fingers clutched the edge of the table until the metal bit into my flesh. No, not again.

Niko placed the receiver to his ear and his face hardened instantly. He listened for several minutes before saying remotely, "I understand." He then hung up the phone with a violence that was so carefully restrained, it said volumes.

"Caleb." I didn't bother to phrase it as a question.

"Caleb," he verified tightly. "We meet tonight."

"Did you talk to . . . ?" I didn't finish, instead prying my fingers from the table and wiping the syrup on my sweats with studious attention.

"No. I didn't think it wise to push."

"You're probably right." He would have to keep her alive, wouldn't he? He wouldn't be able to transfer her psychic abilities if she were . . . if she weren't alive. I wiped harder. The goddamn syrup wouldn't come off—as hard as I scrubbed. I stood jerkily with an anger far out of proportion to the situation and moved to the sink. Squirting dish detergent into my skin, I scoured my hands. "Where's the meet?" I asked deliberately.

"At that werewolf club, the one he pointed us toward for Boaz. I suppose he thinks he'll have a better chance if we're surrounded by those who don't precisely love us."

He was right. The clientele there didn't care for humans, Auphe hybrids, or Kin traitors. We'd have to be on our guard against not only Caleb but every other living creature in the building as well. "Gee, a challenge," I commented with a darkly false cheer, watching the water wash over my skin. "I hope I have enough hardware to make it interesting for them. You have any more of those explosive rounds like you gave me for the bodach?"

"I was saving it for your birthday," he responded wryly, "but, yes, I have a few boxes."

"You're better than Santa Claus." I dried my hands and held on to the subject with something close to desperation. "What are you bringing to the party, Snowball?"

Both arms and hands grew larger, bunching with muscle, hair lengthening to a pelt, as Flay raised a fist and punched four-inch talons through the wood of the table. The piece of furniture shivered and threatened to fold up like wet cardboard. "Elegant in its simplicity." Niko nodded as we both looked under the table to play peekaboo with at least three inches of claw. "Inexpensive and you can take it through a metal detector."

I leaned on one end, stabilizing it as Flay pulled free. He took a large chunk of the wood with him. "And this is why we buy the cheap stuff." I shook my head. It was all a good attempt at distraction and naturally it didn't work worth shit. Giving it up, I asked somberly, "You'll make the calls?"

"I'll notify Promise and Goodfellow," Niko verified. "Go ahead and start gathering your weapons. Tonight will come sooner than you think."

I wasn't sure which to hope for: that he was right and it would fly by or that he was wrong and it would creep. Either way, we were headed toward an uncertain ending and I didn't know if I wanted to race toward it or drag my feet every step of the way. If only I could know what would happen—if only I could *see* . . . but I couldn't.

I wasn't the psychic one.

19

It flew.

The day was a blur, running on feet that scarcely touched the ground. I should've taken it as a sign. Good things take forever to come. Bad ones chase you down with a speed that leaves cheetahs in the dust.

I was pulling on a black T-shirt when Promise came to the door of my bedroom. It stood ajar, but she gave a discreetly soft knock regardless. I grunted and she chose to translate that as "Come in." Anyone else, I think, would've interpreted it along the lines of "Stay the hell out and mind your own damn business." But, as I'd noticed many times before, Promise wasn't just anyone.

"Caliban, I have something for you."

"Really?" I slipped on the holster and filled it with an Eagle loaded with explosive rounds and the bodach knife, as it was now permanently labeled in my brain. "A happy ending maybe? I'd pay some big bucks to see one of those."

She wilted my sarcasm instantly with what she had coiled on her palm. Coming up beside me, she held out her cupped hand. In it was copper hair, woven into a tiny plait.

I took a step back in silent denial.

She snagged my arm with her other hand and held me still without mercy. "I know you're quite good at running, little brother, but before you do so again I want you to think on something." Her grip tightened. "Georgina wasn't chosen because of you. It's far more likely that you were chosen because of *her*. Caleb needed a psychic, and Georgina is the sun among the lesser stars when it comes to talent. That you and Niko have a different talent of your own, one that would help you find one of the crowns, was but a fortunate bonus to him." Her hand traveled down my arm to my wrist. "You didn't get her into this, Caliban. Try to remember that."

My wrist was then tugged toward her and she deftly tied the delicate twist of red hair around it. She said in a voice true and firm, "To keep close to your heart what you're fighting for."

I touched it with a hesitant finger, then exhaled and dropped my hand. Grabbing a long-sleeved gray shirt off my bed, I shrugged into it, leaving it unbuttoned over the T-shirt. I'd chosen it to cover the shoulder holster, but it would cover something else as well. I pulled the sleeve down over my wrist. I didn't have to see the bracelet, but I couldn't do anything about the feel of it against my skin. As hard as I was working to keep her far, George kept creeping back. Stubborn for a girl who wasn't even here.

"Thanks," I said woodenly. I didn't even know myself if I meant it or not. Bracing a foot on the edge of my bed, I strapped on an ankle holster. "Want a gun? I have some extras."

"No, thank you. I'm happy with the weapons I already have."

I thought she meant her natural ones, fangs and uncanny agility, but when I looked up it was to see her holding a small but wicked-looking crossbow that had materialized from behind her. The weapon had been slung on her back with a tooled leather strap. It was an odd choice and I said so. "I thought that's what people used on vamps, not vice versa."

"True." She hefted it and sighted a distant spot on the wall. "But back in the day there tended to be so many lying about. Free. No self-respecting woman could pass up a bargain like that." Unsaid was that there were the same number of dead vampire hunters lying about as well. "Of course no one believes in us in this enlightened age and I now have to purchase them, but it's difficult to give up the familiar."

"Just don't puncture Goodfellow's ego with it," I said as I jerked the leg of my jeans down over the holster.

"I heard that," snapped Robin's voice from the living room. He then said in disbelief, "You did *what*?"

I assumed he wasn't talking to me with that last bit and I was right. When I entered the room, he was standing by the couch with his face shoved inches from Flay's. The wolf was sprawled on the cushions and seemed unimpressed. "Over two hundred thousand dollars, you mangy cur. That tacky conglomeration of metal and plaid costs over two hundred thousand dollars, and I am *not* eating that wad of cash."

Flay gave an exaggerated yawn. "For Slay."

"Yes, I heard you the first time, and while I appreciate your desire for a playpen on wheels, I'm not footing the bill. Now where is the *hrithia* RV?" Goodfellow might have believed English among the best languages to curse in, but he made Greek sound nasty enough in its own right.

About equally as nasty as the growl spilling from Flay. "For Slay. For *son*."

I had thought all along that Flay was showing a remarkable equanimity regarding his son's kidnapping, and Caleb had had the kid for weeks longer than George. But it seemed that the wolf was simply good at hiding his pain. He was leaking emotion now, though. There were serious contents under pressure and they were about to explode all over Goodfellow.

"Children, let us save our violence for someone more deserving." Niko's hand fastened on Robin's shoulder and steered him firmly away.

"I always have more than enough violence to share," the puck informed us haughtily, but he allowed himself to be ushered off. He was still limping, but his leg had improved enough that he was going with us. Not that he didn't bitch and moan and profess undying cowardice. He did . . . at great length. We paid no attention. It was just the Goodfellow way. In a fashion, it was calming. I wouldn't say it compared to a lullaby or anything, but it was dependable. And in the knife-edged world we lived in, the dependable could be reassuring, soothing.

It didn't last. The bitching did—there was an infinite supply of that. But by the time we pulled up blocks away from Moonshine, I wasn't in the mood to be soothed by anything or anyone. We'd driven past the werewolf club once and it was dark. We'd thought that there would be a crowd for Caleb to use against us, but the place appeared to be closed. Not surprisingly, I wasn't reassured. I tightened my grip on my knife. I'd unsheathed it the second we'd gotten in the van and hadn't turned loose of it yet. The van itself was the same one Robin had obtained for us previously, wolf dents and all. From behind the wheel, he'd given Flay a glare that burned with the searing power of a green-tinted laser. "In case you get any ideas, you leg-humping thief," he'd offered between clenched teeth, "there's a LoJack on this one. Drive all you want. I'll find you." I was beginning to think

Goodfellow was more annoyed that someone dared steal from him, he who considered himself the ultimate thief, than at the actual loss of goods.

After we parked, I was the last one out of the van. From the curious quirk of white eyebrows, I could tell that Flay had thought I would be the first . . . or, at the very least, fighting him for the honor. Sorry, Snowball, think again. In my mind, good things didn't come to those who waited. No, I was more of the opinion that bad things couldn't find you if you didn't show up. Stupid and impractical, but for a second I embraced the theory. Maybe, deep down, you wanted them over, those things couched in bad expectations, but what would happen when expectations became reality? Caleb needed George alive, but who was to say what he might do if his back was to the wall? I had hundreds of guesses and not one of them was pleasant.

I didn't want to face the way this might go. I wasn't too sure how long my little trip to denial land would last then. All that great, fun-time counterfeit calm that surrounded me might give up the ghost. No one wanted to be around when that happened—most especially me.

Taking a deep breath, I stepped out onto the asphalt. One step and it felt like jumping from a plane with only the spit-handshake promise of a parachute. "Let's go."

On the phone to Niko, Caleb hadn't bothered to tell him to come alone. He was too wily for that, knew it wasn't going to happen no matter what lies we told him. That combined with the closed club didn't bode well. Caleb was a confident son of a bitch behind that literal shark grin, but he had the right to be. He'd turned Flay into a lapdog and had manipulated us from the beginning. Neither of those were particularly easy tasks, but he sure as hell made them look that way. Just because the club looked empty didn't mean it was. Even if he didn't know we'd found out what the crown could do, he would know we weren't leaving without George and Flay's kid.

It was too bad he was somehow watching us so closely. It would've been nice to have Flay held in reserve. . . . As it was now, we had to hope Flay didn't find his kid in the first two seconds and leave us in the lurch. And he'd probably take the van with him, LoJack or no.

Promise took out the streetlights ahead of us as we moved. There would be the subdued twang of the crossbow, followed immediately by an explosive pop and the bell song of falling glass. It didn't make it dark. In the city, nothing could do that, not a true darkness. But it did spread the shadows and we disappeared into them. By the time we reached the club no one could've seen us coming. Smelled us, yeah, if that's the way you were built. Heard us? Possible, but not as likely. Seen us? No. Not even pale Flay, who was dressed in all black including a jacket with a hood pulled down low over his face. We were all good at hiding. Training, genetics, the skills of a hunter, the habits of a thief—whatever the reason, we knew our way around the night.

Niko was going in the front carrying the crown. Flay and Promise were in the alley and Goodfellow and I were taking the back. Before I slithered off, my brother barred my path with his sword. Designed for night combat, the blade was coated black and I felt it rather than saw it. The flat of it rapped my shins smartly, halting me in my tracks. I had only the shine of his eyes to zero in on. The olive skin didn't show and the lighter hair was covered by his own hood.

"Do *not* do anything stupid," came the warning, so faint it could only hope to grow up to be a whisper.

Easier said than done, but I nodded and reached over his shoulder to tap him on the shoulder blade. He got the message instantly. Watch your back. I felt the familiar tug on my ponytail as his agreement and then he melted away. If anyone needed to watch his back, it was Caleb. Given the faintest of opportunities, Niko would cut him down like wheat. I only hoped I got to see it.

In the back Goodfellow had already jimmied a window. There was no alarm system that I could see, but if there were one, Robin would have handled it and probably without breaking stride. He disappeared inside and I followed on his heels. I slid through and carefully placed feet on what felt like the surface of a desk. It was darker in here than outside and I relied on my sense of touch to find my way to the floor. I didn't bother to try to catch the scent of anything. The place was so soaked with alcohol and the imprint of thousands of different creatures over time that there was no way to pick out one. Maybe Flay could—a wolf's nose was more discerning than mine—but if Caleb was here, I couldn't tell.

I pulled a penlight from my pocket and shielded it with my palm. The trickle of red light that seeped past my flesh was just enough to tell we were in a storage room. The desk was actually an unopened crate. The space was full of boxes, some empty, some not. They were mostly containers of food or different types of alcohol. Goodfellow bent over one already-opened crate and reverently lifted out a bottle. In the gloom all I could see was that it was dusty, squat, and, to me, a complete waste of time.

Moving toward the closed door, I elbowed him in the ribs. "Put it down," I hissed.

He gave a pained grimace but put it down with the same utmost care and pried reluctant fingers from its neck. "Do you know what that's worth?" he whispered wistfully.

"Not George's life," I answered with rigid control. I started to put my hand on the doorknob, then hesitated. Looking up, I considered the cheap tile ceiling and said slowly, "You think?"

Goodfellow followed my gaze. "I do." He grinned. "I do so think."

Alone I walked out into the tiny hall that was off the storage room. The floor was brown industrial carpet, the walls a dingy cream. Floating in the midst of the stale lanolin-colored paint was a single pristine handprint. Dark red, it hung about the height of my shoulder. Fresh enough that I could see its still-liquid shimmer, it was a grim halt signal frozen in time.

It was too large; I knew it. That didn't stop me from putting my hand beside it in measurement. It was the same size as mine, not small or delicate like George's. My fingers pressed against the plaster, then fell away. No matter what the size, the blood could belong to anyone. It didn't have to belong to the finger painter who had left it.

I moved on, leaving the lonely print behind. The carpet, stained beyond repair, kept my solitary footfalls silent. The hilt of the knife was fast in my hand with the blade lying flat against the underpart of my forearm. Appearing unarmed, if only for a moment, could lead attackers into believing you were vulnerable. It made them arrogant, and it made them careless. Arrogant I could do without, but careless I liked.

As I slid up to another door off the hallway, I got my wish. My first opponent was careless, left himself wide open, and either didn't notice or didn't care that I had a knife. Despite all that, he put his all into taking me down. And I let him; I didn't have much choice. The door was pushed open and something

flashed through. Immediately following, searing pain
tore though my calf and I fell on my hip. As I landed,
I flipped the knife in my hand and sent it flying downward in one swift, continuous movement. I only managed to stop by millimeters the point from impaling
the furry head. Feeling the cold steel ruffle across the
top of his head didn't faze Slay in the slightest. He
continued to gnaw at my leg was if it were the choicest
of soupbones.

He wasn't white like his father, but a shade of apri-
cots and cream, with large liquid eyes that were rich
as chocolate and twice as sugary sweet. That is, they
were until you noticed your blood on his muzzle and
the tatters of your pants tangled in needle-sharp baby
fangs. Hands down, he was the cutest little flesh eater
I'd seen, but I still needed my leg. Grabbing him by
the scruff of his neck, I tried to pry him off. It didn't
work. He snapped again, and more nerve endings
howled in pain. Swearing, I shook my leg hard and
pulled harder. The small fangs sliced flesh as they
went, but I finally managed to get him off. He snarled
in pure disappointment and twisted in my grip. He
weighed only forty or so pounds, but he was as slippery as a weasel and I nearly dropped him from my
one-handed grip. Tucking the barrel of his body under
my arm, I held him as still as possible and whispered
firmly, "Hold still, you little fur ball. Your father sent
me. He's here. Flay's here."

From the flying foam and outraged growls, I was
guessing he didn't buy that. His paws paddled frantically and he kept snapping at air. His mother must
have been of classic breeding; he was all wolf. If and
when he wanted, he would be all human as well. Too
bad that wasn't now; it would make it easier to haul
his homicidal little butt along.

Around his neck was a braided rope fastened with

a metal clamp. The straggling end had been chewed through. As thick as it was, it must've taken the pup a while. Baby fangs were better for shredding legs than well-made rope. I took a quick look in the room where he'd been imprisoned. There was a bowl of water, scattered newspapers, and empty cans of dog food piled in a corner. Dog food. Jesus. There was also the reek of old urine and shit, but the room was fairly clean. It didn't make it any better. He was a kid, no matter how he looked. He'd been there a while and treated like an unlucky street mutt, given the minimum of care to keep him healthy. Caleb had to keep him that way if he wanted to continue to manipulate his father. However, I imagined, once Flay was no longer in the picture, his son wouldn't be long behind him. Poor damn kid.

That poor damn kid managed to whip his head around and snare my shirt. With a jerk of his muzzle, he tore a grapefruit-sized piece free and promptly ate it. While his jaws were occupied, I seized the opportunity to switch him under my other arm to keep my knife hand unencumbered. I gave serious thought to ripping a strip of shirt and tying it around his muzzle to keep him quiet. There were only two problems with that plan. First, I'd probably lose an appendage doing it. Second, Flay would take the ones I had left once he saw what I'd done.

I gave it one last shot. "Seriously, kid. Be quiet. Your dad's here and we're going to find him right now, I swear. But if you keep making noise, the bad guy might find us first." "Bad guy" is a relative term, but hopefully to a three-year-old it might still hold some meaning.

It did. The eyes remained wild and wary as ever, but the growls gradually died down. They continued to vibrate his rib cage, but none escaped the teeth that remained fiercely bared. It was the best I could hope for and I took it.

The door at the end of the hall wasn't locked; like the one to Slay's room it didn't even *have* a lock. Sounded like good news, but it wasn't. Caleb wasn't expending the slightest effort to make things difficult for intruders, and that didn't make me want to jump for joy at what might lie beyond. For a second I considered taking Slay back to his room and tying him back up. Fighting one-handed was hazardous as hell, for both him and me. I hesitated, then shook my head. In the end, he was marginally safer with me than left alone at the mercy of whatever might pass by. Caleb wasn't alone here. Couldn't be. He was too goddamn smart for that.

I retrieved the penlight I'd dropped when taken down by Flay's ankle biter and shut it off before shoving it in my pocket. The darkness was nearly complete as I shifted my knife over to my right hand. There was only the dimmest of gray illumination seeping from beneath the door. Turning the knob with the heel of my hand, I set my shoulder against the wood and nudged lightly. There was the creak of rusty hinges, but it was faint and couldn't be heard more than a few feet. The air was heavy with the same smells I'd noted when I entered the building—alcohol, the olfactory remnants of those who had drunk it, and apparently something else. There was an eager snuffling at my hip as Slay pulled air into his nose and then, before I could guess it was coming, a ringing howl that split the air like a siren.

I didn't speak wolf, but I didn't have to. I knew a scream for Daddy when I heard it. I also recognized the vanishing element of surprise. At least, thanks to the pup, I knew that one of us was definitely inside.

Flay's return howl wasn't necessary. I got it anyway. Wolves. Ruled by emotion, unfettered by brain cells.

"Goddamnit," I muttered as I automatically dodged to one side and sought cover. It kept the machete from taking off a good chunk of my skull. The metal thudded into the frame of the door and a bubbling hiss of disappointment followed. Sloppy. I instantly homed in on the sound and slashed. The light was still all but nonexistent, but my eyes were adjusting. As the jolt of blade impacting meat traveled up my arm, I saw the vaguest outline of my attacker. Curved lines, flesh that was cold and clammy, blood that smelled of rank river water—it was a vodyanoi. I'd seen one only once before. They rarely left the water, although they were happy enough to eat anyone who might be unlucky enough to fall in. Picture a humanoid leech the size of a man. They were as quick as sharks in the water, but on land they were slower, hence the machete. If I had to choose, I'd rather be chopped to bite-sized pieces than have my internal organs liquefied and sucked out. Personal preferences, there's no accounting for them.

My knife had sliced through where a man's neck would be. A vodyanoi didn't have one. Below the rough and wet charcoal sketch of a human face, nature's trickery, there was only thick, rubbery flesh. Unless you were armed with a chain saw, you could whack at it for hours without accomplishing a damn thing. I jerked my hand back, dropped my blade, and went for the Eagle. A regular bullet wouldn't do much either, but my early birthday present might.

As I pulled the gun, the vodyanoi flowed closer and raised a pulpy three-fingered hand to swing the machete again. The hiss came again from the pulsating mouth sucker, but this time it was edged with pain.

Slay, an annoying but feisty little shit, was making a meal of one of the fluttering tendrils that lined the ventral lower portion of the vodyanoi. Hell, I couldn't let the pup have all the fun. I aimed midtorso and fired.

The explosion was muffled, but the moist splat of destroyed tissue hitting the walls was less so. There was an unnatural ripple and flex of the vodyanoi's head as it peered into the massive crater in its middle. The crater must have in actuality been more of a tunnel because the leech then swayed and fell flat. As I evaded its descent, I felt the fast beat of a small tail against my back and arm. Apparently the fuzzbutt had liked that. Like father, like son.

Retrieving my knife, I moved on. There were noises now—the sounds of battle, the sing of metal, and a distant enraged growling that I recognized instantly. Flay was trying to make his way to us and, from the sounds of it, not having much luck. My eyes had become as used to the gloom as they were going to, and I could tell we were in the club proper now. The wolf wasn't there with us yet, but that didn't mean Slay and I were alone.

Caleb was here.

The monster who had taken George. The creature who had pulled our strings time and time again. The piece of shit who kidnapped children and ruined lives. Finally, here was my chance to pin his hands to the floor with Spanish poniards, rip his heart from his chest, and then cram it between those pointed teeth. As images went, it was a very specific one, wasn't it? Detailed as hell. So how, you might ask, did I come up with it so fast? I didn't.

Someone beat me to it.

The amiable piranha from our first meeting lay spread-eagled on the floor. His blue eyes were glassy and blank, empty marbles. The peculiar pointed teeth were buried in the meat of his own heart. Blood coated his hands and the palms were torn viciously where he'd struggled against the pinning metal as his chest had been cut open. The predator was now the victim.

I'd invested so much hate, so much rage, before I'd come to my frozen peace. Now I could feel it stirring far down in the murk, uncomprehending and fighting for release. My emotions might not have understood the situation, but my mind did. We'd asked Flay when he'd first told us about his son why he didn't simply force Caleb to tell him where Slay was being kept. The two of them had been together when we'd first been in Caleb's office. Why hadn't the wolf started stripping skin and flesh until that smug bastard gave up the cub between screams?

He had *associates,* the aforementioned piece of shit. One missed phone call and his son would die, Flay had said; Caleb's associates would take care of that. What we hadn't known was that Caleb was one of the associates. He wasn't the one behind the scheme. He was a pawn, same as us. And like all good pawns, he'd been sacrificed—not in the chess sense, but in the literal, bloodletting one.

"I really do need to put the *no freaks* sign in the window. My property values are plummeting."

I recognized the jaded contempt that came from behind as quickly as I'd recognized the poniards. A master of machination, someone who was as hungry for power as he was tricky and ruthless . . . a piranha could never be as qualified in those areas as a puck. Son of a bitch. I'd stared at him over the bar, *talked* to the bastard, and not once had a glimmering that he was anything but a lethally bored immortal. How lethal I was about to find out.

Before my brain's desperate command to turn could travel down nerve impulses and trigger muscles, he stabbed me. In a burst of fiery hot pain the metal entered midway down my back on the right. I more felt than heard the crunch of the blade hitting bone. Waves of nausea accompanied the ripping of flesh as I pulled free and stumbled to my knees. Slay tucked, rolled, and disappeared on fast-churning paws into the deeper darkness behind the bar. Gritting my teeth, I flipped over, crouched, and raised the Eagle. It was kicked out of my hand in a motion so swift it was a blur in the gloom. The same heel impacted under my chin, knocking me onto my back.

"Educational." Shadowed green eyes brooded from the bloody blade to me. "That's a mortal wound for an Auphe. Freaks seem to be more resilient. Keep your heart in the human location, do you?" Another poniard was in his hand; he must've bought them by the gross. He tossed it in the air, and caught it in a throwing position. "Let's test that theory."

He was Goodfellow, every inch of him. I'd half forgotten how uncanny the physical duplication was. The only thing missing was the grin. Whether it was smug, lascivious, cajoling, breezy, arrogant, salesman voracious, Robin usually had one version or another on his face. This puck never smiled. Not even with the psychotic glee of a killer. He was empty, a vessel of ice filled with the lung-suck of nothing. The pride, though, he had to have that. Any member of the race would crumple up and die without that overweening ego. It was the only weak spot I could hope for and I went for it.

"Why didn't you do it yourself?" I gritted between hard-clamped teeth. The blood was soaking the back of my shirt, but he was right. It wasn't mortal. Hell, if I was given the chance, it wouldn't slow me down that much either. "Take the crown from Cerberus? For that matter, why didn't you let Caleb do it?" My backup piece was at my ankle. I could easily reach it, if I could just distract him. It was a damn big if. Robin would've been too smart to fall for it. If the same went for his evil twin, I was well and truly fucked.

"Is it too difficult for your half-breed brain to determine, freak?" he asked mockingly. "Then let me clarify for the low functioning among us. Caleb didn't have the intestinal fortitude, which is more obvious than ever now." The eyes seemed to take on a bloody cast, a reflection of what remained of Caleb. "And Flay," he snorted disparagingly, "breeding will tell. He's barely house-trained. As for me, I wouldn't have been welcome. Unjustly labeled thief, amoral turncoat . . ." The grin I'd thought he didn't have in him blossomed, chilling and dead. Whatever emotion had lived in him had curdled and died long ago. "Who am I kidding? I'm the original reason there is no honor among thieves. Cerberus wouldn't accept me. No member of the Kin would."

"That's one good thing you can say about them." I inched fingers farther down my leg and kept my eyes unwavering on his. I couldn't deceive like a puck—no one could—but I wasn't an open book either. If I could fool him long enough . . .

But of course I couldn't.

"As much as I enjoy playing this tedious game with you"—his gaze flicked to my ankle and back—"I have things to do." He cocked his head, gauging the sounds around us. Flay in some other part of the building. Screaming and howling out front, meaning Niko had yet to make it through the door. "Psychics to drain. Blood sacrifices to make. Freaks to kill." His foot slammed down on the gun at my ankle, pressing the flesh and bone beneath it to the breaking point. Before I could make a suicidal lunge at him an identical voice stopped us both.

"Hobgoblin."

It came from above and then from next to us as Goodfellow plunged down through flimsy ceiling tile. He landed neatly, doing what had to be everything in his power to conceal his weakened leg. His own blade, not as elegant as the poniard, but as deadly, came to rest along the neck of his carbon copy. "Long time no see," he finished silkily. "I thought you dead. Justly dead."

My attacker's head turned easily and the smile came back, that god-awful, ghastly grin. "I go by 'the Hob' now, a title for my inferiors."

"Which would be everyone, yes?" Robin's face was a mask, the skin stretched inhumanly tight.

"No one would know that better than you, Good-fellow." His foot ground harder and I felt my ankle-bone creak under his heel.

I didn't wait for Goodfellow to give him a warning. I yanked my leg free and rolled to one side only to discover Robin hadn't given one at all. Instead he'd done his best to decapitate Hob—be damned if I'd call him *the* Hob. I looked up in time to see the end of the backswing and the whole of the follow-through. It was a beautiful blow, if anything so inherently violent and fatal can be called beautiful. Economy of motion, grace, and a stunning speed . . . yeah, it was beautiful. It was also an utter failure.

Hob was as agile as Goodfellow, if not more so, and he was unwounded. One moment he stood at Robin's side; the next he was gone. Robin's sword cut nothing but air. He almost stumbled on his injured leg, caught himself, and then turned just in time to catch the poniard blade on the hilt of his sword. I didn't stand on ceremony. Grabbing the small .38 at

my ankle, I fired. I thought I hit Hob, but I couldn't
be sure. As my shot rang out, he threw off Goodfellow's attack, crouched, and then propelled himself
upward, disappearing through the same opening
Robin had appeared through. A flat-footed jump of
nearly ten feet and he performed it with ridiculous
ease. "Son of a bitch." I aimed upward and sent five
more shots after him. "You can't do that, can you?"

"No." Lips a bloodless line, Goodfellow shook his
head. "He's older than I. He's grown stronger, faster."

I measured the jump again with my eyes as my hand
impotently squeezed the butt of the .38. Ancient or
not, he still had one helluva leap. "How much goddamn older?"

"The oldest. Perhaps even the first. The original
Mad Hatter," he said darkly, "without the sense of
humor. He's insane, Cal. Utterly. He wants what he
wants and no price is too high, no consequence worth
considering. He's been the power behind a hundred
thrones. Alexander himself bowed to him."

"Yeah, that's all very fascinating." I reloaded, then
shoved the gun in the back of my pants. "Boost me.
Then go find the others and tell them what's going
on."

"He'll kill you," Goodfellow said instantly. "I'll go."

Now, that was a total lack of faith if ever I'd heard
one, but I didn't have the time or the luxury to be
offended. "Fine. Get your ass in gear. I found Slay,
but not George. If your evil twin gets away, we're
screwed." I cupped my hands and sent him flying up.

There was the grunt of effort as he caught the edge
of the hole and heaved himself in. "Without the crown
he won't go far."

"How about we don't let him go a fucking inch.
Now *go* already." But I was talking to myself. He was
already gone. But that didn't mean that I was alone.

I heard a scuttle and scrape before four revenants flowed into view, climbing over one another in the fashion of hungry rats competing for the same meal. I hadn't liked the revenant I'd butted heads with in Cerberus's organization, and I wasn't looking to like these any better. What little light there was gleamed off the moist flesh and curdled in milky eyes. Curved incisors were bared with appetite, not anger. No, these were *happy* little pseudocorpses—right up until I put a bullet in each squirming brain. Sometimes the movies are right. They went down, tumbling and twitching. It slowed their five friends waiting in the wings not in the slightest.

I had two bullets left and no time to reload. Firing twice, I dropped the .38 and scrambled to find the Glock Hob had kicked from my hand. It had gone to the right; I'd heard it skitter and slide as it hit the floor, but I didn't see any sign of it. One of the revenants was faster than the others and made its leap. Strangely jointed arms reached out for me with grasping hands, hooked fingers, and talons like fishhooks. I ducked beneath the charge, but the revenant wasn't as easily avoided as that. It twisted in midair with the agility of a cat and snared my shirt in its claws. I dived to the floor and rolled, dislodging it with the ripping of cloth. I still had my knife and I used the blade to slice it along the length of its torso when it threw itself on me again. The warm blood soaked me, and I kicked the revenant off as its teeth snapped at my neck. It hit one of the others, knocking it flat, but two more were still coming and coming fast.

Scrambling to my feet, I grabbed a chair from one of the tables and swung with enough force to put one over the fence. The flimsy bundle of plastic and metal disintegrated in my hands and didn't do a damn thing to my attacker. Swearing viciously, I hooked an arm around its neck as it landed on me. Swiveling, I threw it down to the floor and planted my knife in its chest. The effort allowed the last one the opportunity it needed. It landed on my back and rode me down. I landed hard on the wounded revenant beneath me as the one on my back buried teeth in the meat of my shoulder. The one below me wasn't about to sit this one out either, knife in chest or no. It snarled soundlessly, brown blood frothing from its mouth, and wrapped moist, spidery fingers around my throat.

Growling, I twisted the knife in the revenant's chest, eliciting a bubbling scream, then threw myself backward. I was trying to simultaneously break the hold on my throat and throw off the one on my back. I was only partially successful. The fingers fell from my neck, but the son of a bitch on my back was hanging on for all it was worth. Its teeth ground in my flesh and its arm snaked around my chest to clamp me closer to it. It was strong as hell. They might look like skinny corpses fresh from the grave, but they had a grip like steel and bundles of muscles as strong as metal wire. As I tried for a grip behind its head to flip it over my shoulder, its legs wound around mine, anchoring itself to me. Jesus, if I let myself get taken out by a fucking revenant, it would be better to be dead. Niko would ride my ass until the end of time.

The fangs in my shoulder began to withdraw and I knew the next target would be my throat. If it took out my carotid artery, I would be unconscious in minutes and bleed to death in five. I needed a move, no matter how desperate, and I needed it now. However, when it was made, it wasn't mine. There were two consecutive twangs and the revenant jerked on my back . . . once, twice, then fell. The other revenant I'd knocked from its feet was starting to rise only to be bowled over with a quarrel through an eye. Staggering with the loss of weight from my back, I regained my balance and then bent over to rest hands on my legs until my breathing evened out. "Thanks," I said hoarsely, and in the same breath, "Don't tell anyone."

Promise materialized beside me, her eyes tranquil and her unpainted mouth a gentle curve. "We all have our bad days." Extending her crossbow to indicate Caleb's mutilated body, she added, "He would no doubt agree with me."

Stripping off what remained of my outer shirt, I twisted it rapidly and tied the makeshift bandage tightly around my waist. It would stanch the blood trickling from the Hob-inflicted slash in my back until I could get Niko to stitch it up. "It wasn't Caleb," I said with a poisonous quiet as I bent down and ruthlessly yanked free the two poniards that pinned his dead hands. I offered them to Promise. "It's the puck. That slimy piece of shit that runs this place. You know, Hob, the one I talked to without a fucking clue he was even involved?"

"Hob?" she repeated in disbelief. "That was *Hob*? Hob of legend? Hob of old?" It was a Promise I hadn't seen before, one well and truly shocked.

"Yeah, and apparently that's not a good thing." Hurriedly, I scanned the floor. I found only the Eagle. The .38 was missing in action and I didn't have time for an in-depth search. I also retrieved my knife from the chest of the revenant. "Slay, you little fuzzbutt, get out here now," I snapped off toward the bar. "We're going." Where, I wasn't sure. Up after Good-fellow or out front to where Niko was still fighting the good fight. Maybe Promise and I would split up and do both.

"You found." It wasn't a question; it was a heartfelt prayer of thanksgiving. "You found boy."

Flay hovered in a doorway behind us. Blood stained

his white fur liberally and although he stood upright, more or less, he was in his wolf form. His clothes were gone and his back legs were the graceful curve of a greyhound's. His ears perked slowly from their flat position against the wedge of his skull as he sniffed the air and then he crooned. As difficult as it was to picture a gore-stained predator crooning, that's what it was, and it received an immediate answer.

Slay came rocketing into view. He ran so fast he was little more than a pale orange blur, and then he jumped. When he landed in Flay's arms, he was a boy—a small, naked boy with vodyanoi blood smeared around his mouth and coating his tiny white teeth. But he was also a boy with freckles, a thick shock of apricot hair, and a grin that wouldn't quit. Small arms were wrapped around his father's throat and he put his round face close to the pricked white ear to whisper.

No matter what you thought of Kin wolves or of cubs that might grow to raging carnivores, it was a bright moment. And there was no damn time left to appreciate it. Making a fast decision, I told Promise to take the back while I took the front. Flay could stay here with his cub. Whether Hob and the trailing Robin ended up outside or back here, we would be there. We would be ready. What a lie. I wasn't ready for what I found. I wasn't ready at all.

Niko was gone.

20

Bodies littered the cracked sidewalk in front of the building. Vodyanoi, revenants—there were at least twelve of them. It wouldn't have been enough to overcome my brother. But in the midst of the bodies there was the spore of something that had been. Slim and silver, another poniard lay. By the gross, I thought numbly. He bought them by the gross. It didn't lie there alone; Niko's sword was beside it. Both were bloodied. And both were what it took to split me in half.

I'd held it together, mostly, this past week. I'd found a place within me to hide, carved out a craven sanctuary. I was stunned at how quickly that sanctuary crumbled, and I was almost immolated by what swelled free of it. Fear, red and raw. Hatred, black and suffocating. And over it all, fury—white-hot and blinding.

Blood sacrifice.

That's what Hob had said when I'd been more concerned with trying to kill him than paying attention to his cryptically poisonous words. And now Niko was gone. He wasn't lying wounded or dead by his sword. Hob, who wouldn't lift a finger himself to do anything that he didn't absolutely have to, had taken him. Hob, who needed a sacrifice. I'd tried to guard Niko from

the Auphe when something else wanted him as badly.
This was what Abelia-Roo had kept from us, out of
pure, malicious spite. We'd sensed the crone was holding back something about the Calabassa. We should've
guessed. We should've goddamn *known*. The world is
about sacrifice, our world even more so. For the crown
to take, someone would have to give. It would grant
George's gift to Hob, and it would take Niko's life in
return. The Rom and the Bassa had been allies, ac-
cording to Abbagor . . . their lives intertwined. It took
the blood of one to make the device of the other
work. Elegant, logical . . .

And not going to happen.

I couldn't hear anymore, or perhaps there was nothing to hear. Velvety silence surrounded me as I bent
down and reverently cradled Niko's sword. It was his
katana, modern but with the heart of the ancient im-
plicit in its spare form. He would've said he didn't
favor one weapon over the other, that they were tools
to be respected and admired . . . nothing more. That's
what he would've said, but I knew better. He did play
favorites with his edged family and this one was his
pride and joy. It wasn't made in the old way—no one
did that these days—but it was as close as you could
come. He loved that damn sword, and guess what?
He was getting it back.

At the hesitant touch on my shoulder, the hilt found
its way into my hand and I whirled, surrounded by a
halo of silver steel. There were flashes, disjointed and
vague. Brown, green. Fox face and mobile mouth. To
carve all that from the face of the earth wasn't a decision I made. It simply happened. The sword flew and
I followed.

"Cal, don't!"

The words beat at the layer of pulsing rage that
cocooned me. Sound had come back. It faded in and

out, but it was there. Real. The sight that was before me was real too—as little as my anger wanted it to be. Robin, not Hob, was on his knees in front of me. He was panting with exertion as his white-knuckled fists gripped his own sword and kept Niko's blade from his neck by bare millimeters.

"Don't," he repeated between clenched teeth. "Don't make me hurt you. Please, don't make me."

I didn't delude myself into thinking it was only talk. Goodfellow very probably could hurt me. He predated swords; he'd had a lot longer to practice with them than I had. Not that it mattered. I didn't want to hurt him any more than he wanted to hurt me. I saw what my rage was slow to recognize; it was Robin. It was my friend. Not the monster who'd taken Niko.

Not Hob.

I let the tip of the katana fall toward the ground. My hands shook and cramped from the anger that had no outlet. "Nik's gone." If I hadn't felt my mouth move, I wouldn't have recognized the thick, choked words as mine.

"I know." Robin let gravity take his own blade and sat back to rest on his heels. Head down, he passed a hand over his face. "I know."

"Where would he take him?" The twitch of one of the downed revenants was visible from the corner of my eye. I swiveled, gave a vicious swing of the sword, and turned back before the brown blood had time to drip from the blade. *"Where?"*

"I don't know. I haven't a goddamn inkling." In a sudden explosion of frustration, he threw his sword against the asphalt. "He was supposed to be dead. Why couldn't he stay dead?" he said savagely before looking up at me. "And why Niko? Why not take just the crown? He already has a hostage. What would he need with another?"

"For the Rom blood." My mouth twisted. "For the damn Bassa, who made sure there was a price to be paid for what you took." I had the key in me as well, so why hadn't Hob taken me instead? He might know who was dogging my steps lately and not want the added distraction of vengeance-crazed Auphe dropping in on the ceremony. Or maybe the Auphe gene in me was so strong it tainted all the rest, made the Rom half of me unrecognizable to the Calabassa. It would be a chance that a scheming son of a bitch like the puck wouldn't want to take.

"Niko?"

Promise had moved up silently behind us. "Hob took Niko? No." She shook her head in denial. "He couldn't overcome Niko. No one could." Then her gaze touched the katana in my hand and pansy-colored eyes turned velvety black, even the whites swallowed whole by the dark cloud. "The first of your kind, Robin, but he will not live long enough to be the last. I'll kill him myself."

"Get in line." I started back toward the club. I didn't expect to find clues or hints to Hob's location, no bullshit like that. Hob wouldn't be anywhere close to that stupid. But there was something in the building that would help. *Had* to help, because it was our only shot. I quickly grabbed what I needed and hauled it back outside.

Stopping by the pile of Niko's attackers, I gave Flay's fur-covered arm a hard shake. "Niko," I snapped. "Find him."

When his cub had been taken, Flay had come home to discover shattered furniture, blood, and Slay's dead grandmother broken on the floor. The kidnapper's scent turned out to be that of Caleb, but the wolf wasn't able to determine that at first. Too many changes of cars were made; too many hours had passed. He lost the trail. He hadn't been able to find his son. But while the trail had been old then, and degraded, it was fresh now.

"*Find* him." I shook him again.

Slay, resting against his father's shoulder, growled. It was a wholly lupine sound emitting from wholly human lips. With clawed hand cupping the ginger head tenderly, Flay made a wordless soothing sound before wrinkling his upper lip at me to reveal red-stained teeth. "You find mine." He put his blunt muzzle up and drew in great draughs of air. "I find yours." There was one more sampling, and then he ran. Slinging the boy to sit up on his neck, he went down on all fours and became the wind.

Goodfellow ran for our transportation while Promise and I followed Flay on foot. Three blocks away the van caught up with us. It slowed and we both climbed in while it was still moving. Robin then careened us around a corner and up onto the curb to take out a newspaper box, and kept going. He wasn't the only one scorning the streets. Flay and his passenger didn't stick to them either. Alleys, vacant lots—it was all fair game. We managed to keep him in view, flickerings of phantom white our guide.

There were other flickerings . . . red and yellow ones ringing my vision. The rage wouldn't die, wouldn't subside. The fear was side by side with it. It wouldn't let me take a breath without squeezing my lungs with acid-coated fingers. Without Nik, *I* was nothing. Living life to prove your genes wrong wasn't worth doing. Living life to be the reflection of who your brother thought you were, thought you could be, that was worth it. That made the price of existence not quite so steep.

"Won't Hob suspect we'll use Flay to follow him?"

Robin addressed Promise's question with a logic

that proved familiarity breeds contempt. "I strongly doubt it. He'll assume Flay has what he's come for and will move on. Hob doesn't understand the concept of loyalty. He especially wouldn't apply it to one who runs with the Kin. Arrogance, it's the downfall for my race. For every last thrice-damned one of us."

I had something else planned for Hob's downfall. The metal glimmered across my lap with the coldest of comforts. Goodfellow went on. "He wants George's ability so he can rise to power again. With it, he could blackmail anyone, manipulate *everyone* . . . be what he once was. It's not as it was in the old days. The brightest, the most respected, even the most cunning, they don't always win anymore. He needs an edge if he wants to play in these politically unenlightened times." If it had been any other situation, he would've waxed poetic about the time when all you needed was a toga and an in with the Roman army. But it wasn't any other situation. It was this one.

This one.

"Drive faster," I ordered gutturally. It whirled in me, the rage, bright and furious. An emotion so intense that it was nearly an entity all its own. Aware . . . plotting. When your subconscious has a mind of its own, things happen. They fucking do indeed.

"I can't. This is as fast . . ." The words trailed away as Goodfellow checked my reflection in the rearview mirror. His shoulders twitched and he hissed, "Not the time. So very not the time."

The shadows swirled out of Promise's eyes as she turned and looked behind me. "No. Not now. Not now." As I gazed back at her implacably, she said with a worry strained to near desperation, "You're doing it again, Caliban."

Like I didn't know. As if I didn't feel the turn and suck of the gateway behind me. It was small, no larger

than the size of my hand. I didn't have to see it to
know that either. It was mine and I knew it, inside
and out. The shifts and eddies of it, the ferocious bite.
It was an attack dog, only mildly loyal and completely
untrained. I had a choke chain on it for now, but the
leash was slipping through my fingers so fast I could
feel the burn.

"Where does it go?" Robin asked with a desperation that mirrored that of Promise.

I smiled.

"Ah, gods," he breathed, "what are we going to
do?"

The smile grew and I bared my teeth in a death's-
head grin that would've done any Auphe proud.
"Drive faster."

He did. At one point he nearly ran down our wolf.
I heard the yip and snarl of surprise through the metal
walls of the van. It didn't restrain Goodfellow's driving. The gate was traveling with us . . . with me . . .
and that concerned him more than a close call with
Flay's hairy ass. Fifteen more minutes passed and I
wondered in the back of my mind, the only portion
that still had the smallest grip on rational thought,
how long the wolf could keep up the brutal pace. He
was lupine, but even a wolf couldn't run forever. Fortunately, he didn't have to. We stopped at a church,
old but lovingly maintained.

"A house of God. Appropriate," Goodfellow murmured. "He always considered himself one of the
first."

He'd killed the lights a block down when he'd seen
Flay begin to slow. The van rolled quietly to a stop
and the panting wolf flowed inside to deposit a grinning three-year-old into a seat. "Again!" Slay demanded, bouncing on the cushion. "Again!" Someone,
at least, had enjoyed the headlong rush.

Flay's eyes widened to show the whites as he saw
the now cantaloupe-sized whirlpool of gray light behind me and he put himself between it and his son.
"Inside church. Puck, brother, girl. Others."

"What others?" Promise had discarded her cloak
and stepped out as a singular figure of black silk and
cold steel.

"Same. Revenant. Vodyanoi. Many." He shifted uneasily on splayed feet as I passed him on my way to
the street. The gateway followed me, a luminous
shadow. "I not go."

I hadn't expected him to. He had his family to protect now. He had his life back, and I hadn't anticipated
his risking it again. I nodded in acknowledgment.
"Keep the engine running. Just in case."

Unease and impatience twisted his face as his features slid into something closer to human, but he nodded. "Fifteen minutes. Then we go."

It was a fair offer and I took it. I turned and headed
toward the church, making no effort to hide. How the
hell could you begin to hide a rip in reality itself as it
trailed behind you? And it was still there. Hungry,
impatient, and growing inch by slow inch no matter
how I tried to rein in the process. It was pulling at me
harder now, every minute. I didn't have much longer.
"Heel," I murmured under my breath. "That's a
good boy."

Robin came up beside me, giving me a little more
personal space than usual. "I say we forget splitting
up," he suggested. "It didn't precisely net us many
gains last time. Let's go in the front, the three of us,
and take whatever comes. It would be the last thing
Hob expects. Brute force over cunning."

"I don't have a problem with that." I'd taken out
the Eagle as we walked. Reaching the bottom of the
church stairs, I aimed at the front set of double doors

and fired . . . all ten rounds. It was impressive, to say the least. Sheer destruction, how can that not do a vengeful heart good? Running up the stairs through the sharply acrid smell and smoke, I kicked aside what remained of the doors and entered the church. I didn't wait to see if Goodfellow and Promise were behind me. Truthfully, it wouldn't have mattered either way.

I holstered the gun and concentrated on the weapon in my other hand, Niko's katana. It knew me. Inanimate object or not, it knew me. I swung it double-handed and sliced through the neck of the first revenant with quicksilver ease. Another loathsome jumble of spidery arms and legs began to leap for me only to reverse and tumble away at the sight of the gateway at my back. "Auphe," it hissed, crouching on its haunches.

"Yeah," I snarled. "Auphe. Tell all your little friends."

It recoiled and scuttled away. Too bad I hadn't been hauling my badge of dishonor around at the club. It could've saved me some work. Several more revenants plunged from between the pews and followed the first. The only illumination was candlelight and it dappled the wet flesh as they rippled out of sight. The vodyanoi weren't so easily impressed. They dealt very little with the dry world, rarely creeping from their rivers. They had knowledge of the Auphe, but to them it was mostly rumors. Legends. It wasn't an intimate acquaintance.

Not yet.

They didn't have the spidery motion of the revenants. The vodyanoi flowed like the water that had whelped them. They weren't fast, but there were enough of them that it didn't matter. And like their lost and unlamented cousin, they were armed. Some

with identical machetes, some swords . . . anything
with an edge. Their crudely formed fingers were too
large to fit in the trigger guard of a gun.

"What a shame you wasted all your explosive
rounds knocking on the door," Goodfellow gritted at
my elbow.

"I didn't." I pulled out the gun and shoved it into
his hand, and then followed it with a box of ammunition. "It's sighted for me. Aim a few inches high."
Whirling, I sheathed Niko's sword in a tiny black eye.
The vodyanoi bubbled a cry of agony, a thin, mucous
scream. I withdrew the blade and hit the heavy rubber
of its chest with my shoulder. It fell onto its back,
where it thrashed wildly. Promise followed my example and sent the one behind it down with a quarrel
through an inky orb. And then the one to the left and
the one to the right. Her face a tight ivory mask, she
was a cold wind of destruction sweeping through the
place. And when she ran out of quarrels, she used her
hands to pierce their eyes, and her teeth to peel their
thick flesh down to bone. An enraged vampire isn't
something anyone would want to face, not even a
vodyanoi.

I didn't stick around to see how the rest of the
battle went. I didn't have the time, and Niko and
George didn't have it either. There was no up in the
church other than a vaulted ceiling and the jigsaw puz-
zle of darkened stained-glass windows. That left down.
I ran through the milling vodyanoi, dodging and par-
rying blades. I heard another of the shrill screams in
my wake and turned to see one seal-blubber arm
sliced off cleanly at the elbow. The stump was pumping blood, but the amputated section was gone. The
gateway, it had passed *through* the vodyanoi and gob-
bled the creature's arm as it went.

It was bigger. Almost big enough for what I heard whispering on the other side. Yeah, running out of time—on all fronts.

I found the stairs to the basement and was forced to sacrifice speed for stealth. If he heard me coming, Hob would be sure to rush through whatever twisted ceremony he was conducting. Or he might escape as he had done before. Couldn't have that, the rage murmured in the back of my thoughts. Couldn't have that at all. My quiet care was successful. He didn't hear me.

I spotted George first. Her hands and feet tied, she was propped up against the wall. Her beautiful hair was gone, leaving a close cap of tight red waves. It made her eyes look impossibly large, like those of a child. There was a cut on her upper arm, six inches long and scabbed over. It was where he had cut her. Him or Caleb—they might as well have been the same. While I'd been on the phone, they had cut her to give me a dose of encouragement. God.

She saw me before Hob did. Not because she heard me or glimpsed me in the shadows. She saw me because she knew I would be there. Her eyes were trained on the spot before I appeared. Luminous and calm, waiting and knowing.

Then I saw Niko. I should've seen him first. I think . . . I think I didn't want to. He was in chains, suspended from an overhead beam, half-nude. His skin was more red than olive. The bastard had sliced him up like a Christmas goose. A circle nearly eight inches in diameter had been cut into his chest. A representation of the Calabassa, it ran with blood. My brother ran with blood.

The whispering behind me was louder now. I could feel a numbing cold flowing from behind like an arctic tide. I had minutes, maybe less.

My teeth bit savagely at my lower lip until I could

taste the salt. He was bloody, but he wasn't d—wasn't gone. The wound, although gory, wasn't fatal. But from the contemplative expression on Hob's face, it was only the beginning. He stood before Niko, tapping the point of one of those goddamn poniards against his chin.

"This is the only symbol required by the Calabassa before sacrifice," he said mockingly, "but I've always said going the extra mile never hurts." He leaned closer and touched a finger to the blood winding its way down Niko's abdomen. "I misspoke. It doesn't hurt me. You, my filthy, inbred Rom trash, are a different story."

If he was standing that close to Niko, there had to be . . . yes, I saw it. My brother's feet were chained as well, with the chain fastened securely to the floor. It was the only reason the puck's head was still attached to his shoulders. Nik lifted his head and said flatly, "You breed with yourself, goat. I believe you have the corner on inbreeding."

"Who else would be worthy?" Hob had plainly learned to keep his temper over the innumerable years. He rubbed the blood between his thumb and forefinger, then touched the circlet of metal resting on his head. The Calabassa pulsed with light, white and hot, once, then subsided. The illumination had passed through Hob as well. He had glowed, as if he were glass and lit from within. "Ah, apparently it likes the way you taste. How fortuitous." He flipped the blade in his other hand up into the air. "And when it's had its fill of you, I'll be ready for the sighted one." His gaze slid toward George and her eyes were already on his in anticipation. Satisfied, he turned back and flipped the poniard one last time.

I cut him in midspin.

He saw me. Too late for him and too early for me.

He slithered to one side and my blade penetrated flesh only to bounce off a collarbone. Hob melted away with a speed that fooled the eye. But I followed with a desperate speed of my own. I couldn't protect both Niko and George unless I stayed with Hob, *on* Hob. He ignored the blood that stained an unbuttoned white linen shirt as fine as anything Goodfellow owned, and spread his hands in welcome. The poniard was a glittering punctuation. "Ah, the freak show can commence. The star performer is here. And he's learned a shiny new trick."

The gateway was now centered in the room. It no longer trailed after me, but I could feel it turn with my every movement—a sunflower to the sun. Or more aptly a flytrap to meat. "Not so new," I said with a false stretch of smile. "Not anymore."

"You won't swing it wide, that gate," he countered scornfully. "I hear them, you know, your true family." He tilted his head as if listening. "They're waiting and not very patiently. They would destroy everyone in this room. Everyone."

Like Robin, he was a talker. Talk. Talk. The fury in me didn't want to talk. It wanted to kill. Luckily enough, that's what I wanted as well. I lunged at him as he was explaining what I would or wouldn't do. He was better than I was; I knew that. He'd taken Niko. That made him just about better than anyone on the planet. But there are things that can give you an edge in a fight, things that can at least get you into the game. One of those—the best one, in fact—was no fear of death.

I didn't want to die, but if I couldn't save Niko and George, I was dead anyway. If I saved them, I could go without complaint. And pure, unadulterated rage helps in that, blurring the survival instinct. It can make you sloppy, but it can also help in certain situations.

The ones where you don't care if you walk away top the list.

Hob caught the katana on his Spanish blade, twisted his wrist so that I would hit the point of the poniard if I didn't pull back. I didn't. The punch of metal tore through my hip, lodging in bone. I think it hurt. It must've hurt. I didn't feel a thing. I did a half turn, ripping the dagger from his hand. I then sliced him across the chest with Niko's sword. He was still too quick for it to be fatal, but it staggered him enough that he retreated several feet. I used my left hand to yank the poniard from my flesh and bone. "Lose something?" I said with false sympathy.

"I have more, freak," he hissed, his hand disappearing in his shirt to appear with another. "I always have more."

The primeval-forest eyes, the tangled brown curls, the pale olive skin—he was a force of nature . . . deadly but stunning. You could see in him that he might well be the first. You could sense the age and the cold-blooded apathy that comes from knowing all things pass. All things but you.

This time he brought the fight to me. I blocked the one aimed at my heart, barely, and the one at my neck, although I felt the tug of a nasty slice. Still no pain . . . liquid adrenaline had taken the place of blood in my veins and it blocked everything but the burn of single-minded purpose. I pressed in close to him as I blocked the return slash. This close the sword was no good, but I had the dagger in my other hand and I rammed it into his thigh. I received something in return. I knew I would. He was too skilled. . . . It was too bad for him that he valued his life so much. It was really holding him back.

This time I felt the pain as a blade sliced through my side, opening a gaping gash. "I can do this as long as it takes," he murmured with infinite boredom by my ear. "Piece by piece, strip by strip, I'll have you down to dripping bones, and when I'm done draining your gifted girl, I'll beat her to death with what's left of you."

Under his detachment, I heard something. A sliver of agony, the smallest taste of fear, it was there. "Before that, I'll throw it open." I twisted the knife in his thigh and watched the cords in his neck stand out in pain. "If we're going to die anyway, I'm taking you with us, you son of a bitch. I'll even tell them you're Goodfellow. They really have a hard-on for him."

Abruptly, he pushed me away hard and I stumbled backward. He followed me and took me to the ground. Pressing the poniard against my neck until my head was hyperextended back, he wiped the blood from my neck and raised his crimson hand high. Nothing happened. The Calabassa remained dull. "See, freak? Do you see? The crown turns away from your polluted blood. How does it feel to have proof you are the monster you always thought you were?"

He'd known Freud too, I guessed. And maybe at any other time it would've hit me hard. Right now, it was just more meaningless blather from an asshole that was making himself too damn hard to kill. Fortunately for me, I wasn't going to do the killing. Not personally. "I lied." As I grinned with teeth tasting of my own blood, he leaned harder with the blade and I could feel more warmth well across my skin. "You're right. I wouldn't let them through." A faint shimmer of uncertainty crossed a face that had known nothing but triumph its entire long life. "But we can go to them."

The blade pressed deeper for one brief moment before George's blow nearly took his head off. He'd underestimated us, *the* Hob. Underestimated us all. I saw the six-foot-tall candlestick in her hands as she swung. Her wrists were raw and weeping where she'd torn free of the ropes. She must've worked for hours upon hours, but why not? She knew we were coming.

The knife had flown from my throat and I was up and moving. Hob was on his knees, already recovering from the shocking wound that soaked his brown hair scarlet. But recovering wasn't recovered and I took my chance. I hit him, wrapping my arms around him, just as he staggered to his feet. Face-to-face. Old monster to new. Off-balance for that split second, he wavered under me, then fell.

Through the door to hell.

Taking me with him.

I expected it. It was a price, a high one, but it was one I was willing to pay. I imagined they called after me, Niko and George, but I didn't hear them. It was just as well. I didn't want them to hear me either. Niko had heard me scream one too many times in his life.

Hob screamed too. In that place of tomb stench, frozen air, and a sky that pulsed like a cancer. Where the whispers punctured eardrums and the molten eyes swallowed you whole. Where talons touched and caressed as intimately as murder. He screamed and screamed. On and on, it seemed like forever, but it couldn't have been. It couldn't have been more than one scream really or a small part of one. Because then he was there and I was here and the gateway was gone. I was on the floor of the church basement with Promise's hands locked in my hair and Robin's clutching my clothes. They'd pulled me back. As I was closing the rip, they yanked me back through.

"You did it on purpose." Goodfellow's voice was both awed and horrified. "You opened the door to Tumulus for the sole intention of pushing him through." He held me up in a sitting position, but his eyes were locked on the empty air where the gateway had hung.

The air here was thicker and it took me a moment to reply. "I'm learning," I finally said with bone-deep weariness. And I was learning. Fast. Motivation was one hell of a teacher. "Nik?"

"I have him." Promise's hands disappeared.

George's took their place. She tackled me every bit as wildly as I had Hob, but with much kinder intentions. Her hands threaded into my hair, then clasped behind my back as she squeezed me with a strength you would never suspect her small frame held. Robin, who had been supporting me, melted away and she rocked with me. "He was wrong," she said fiercely, smudged and dirty face determined as I'd ever seen it. And then she kissed me. There were no words for what it was like, the living poetry of it. Time changed with it too, as it had with the gate to Tumulus. But this change was far for the better. When it was done, her hands framed my face and her voice, while soft, was every bit as determined as before. "You're not a freak, Caliban. You're a light, do you hear me? A light in the darkness."

Over two weeks she'd been his prisoner. Over two weeks gone from her family, gone from those who loved her, and this was what she had to say. It was beyond humbling. I buried my face in the silk of her neck and struggled to breathe air suddenly heavy and choking. And for the first time I held her. Arms tight around a warmth I'd thought impossible for me. For the first time . . .

And the last.

21

The cops came.

Considering all the noise we'd made . . . *I'd* made . . . destroying the church doors, I wasn't much surprised. They pulled up as we rounded the far corner in the van. Flay had genuinely been prepared to wait his fifteen minutes, but we made it out in just under ten. It had seemed longer . . . hours, weeks, decades. The mind plays strange tricks under that kind of pressure. This time there was no opportunity to burn the building as we had torched the cop car. The revenants had fled, but what the police would make of heaps of dead vodyanoi was anyone's guess. I had the feeling we wouldn't see anything about it in the *Times*. Goodfellow had suggested as we'd run out that we sprinkle them with salt and melt them like garden slugs. If Hob had been the evil twin, Robin definitely didn't occupy position of the good one in that dynamic. The annoying one would be his highest achievement.

We made it back to the apartment and watched from the curb as Flay and company took off in the van. It was two blocks down and cornering when Robin remembered that it was *his* van and he'd been screwed yet one more time. LoJacked or not, he was never going to see that van again. He swallowed his cursing, though, and helped us upstairs. By the time we passed through our door, Niko was wavering and I was down. We'd both lost the kind of blood that would have even your most sedate iron-popping vampire weeping at the waste. Unless that vampire was Promise. She hovered over Niko like a moon-drenched guardian angel of the night. Her halo would be the mist-shrouded moon and instead of harps there would be sobbing violins.

Moon-drenched? Yeah, I was out of it all right. Loopy as hell. Sobbing violins . . . Jesus.

As she supported him to his room, George and Robin carried me to mine. It was safe to say that unless you were into the Capone look, our carpet was history, my mattress as well. I still bled, but it was the doorway that had truly sapped me. The one that I had opened in the RV had lasted only seconds and it had knocked me flat. The one I'd tailored for Hob I'd kept open for nearly a half hour. If I'd been alone, I would've bled to death. Coma might've been too strong a word, but only just barely. There were hazy images of George helping Goodfellow roll me from side to side to tightly wrap my numerous slashes. Her hands were scratched and her nails broken from her captivity, but her touch was soft. Her eyes, warm and wise, held mine as long as I was conscious.

"I knew you'd come," she'd whispered at my ear. "I didn't need to look. I *knew*."

I only wished I'd been so certain.

She was gone after that, replaced with a dreamless black night that cradled me for what seemed like an eternity. Three days . . . an eternity . . . is there any real difference there? When I woke up, I was lying on my side as someone stuffed something behind my back. I blinked in a sleepy daze, but before I could move I was rolled with expert efficiency to my other side. I heard the familiar sound of snapping sheets and I raised heavy lids to find myself in the middle of a bed change. Niko stuffed the bottom sheet under the mattress, then pulled the top one along with a blanket over me. I turned over onto my back with the creak and howl of protesting joints and muttered, "You're so domestic."

"When your roommate's sole hobby is cultivating bathroom fungus, you don't have much choice." He sat on the edge of the bed with a stiffness an ordinary eye wouldn't have picked up on. My thoughts were still slow from sleep, but I snagged at a handful of his shirt and tugged. "Okay?"

His eyebrows lifted. "I'll have an interesting scar, to say the least, but I'm healing. I do think you edged ahead of me in number of stitches. That's quite the new fighting technique you demonstrated. What do you call it again? Suicide?"

"Nah." I shook my head. "Not catchy enough. I'll think of something." I ached all over, especially my side and the hip Hob had imbedded with steel. The clock on the bedside table as well as the bright light streaming through the blinds told me only that it was early afternoon, not what day it was. "How long this time?"

"Three days."

Hell. That explained the sheet change. I felt the flush of heat in my face. "Damn, sorry."

The corners of his mouth lifted fleetingly. "I wiped the infamous Cal ass when you were an infant. I can survive a repeat performance. Just, please, don't make a habit of it."

The heat increased and I scowled. "I'll try and restrain myself."

"You always were a good brother." And then he smiled. Niko wasn't much for smiles. They happened—

don't get me wrong—but they were subtle. The faint
curve of a lip, the sly twitch of an eyebrow. Sometimes
it was reflected only in the amused turn of a dry word.
They were smiles all the same and you did have to
watch for them more carefully, but they were there.

This one was different. This one anyone could have
seen. It was small, but plainly visible. Grave but content. And it was his way of saying the things that
honestly didn't really need to be said. I was still me,
gateway to hell and all. He was still my brother and
that was never going to change. My hand tightened on
the cloth of his shirt still clenched in my grip. Never.

"I'll get you some soup." He waited patiently until
I released him. "Georgina has been by several times
a day to sit with you." As I tensed, he shook his head.
"She's fine. Truly. Whatever Hob's tastes, they didn't
run in her direction. She was mainly dirty and tired.
He kept her fed and in good physical condition for the
Calabassa. And apparently she and Slay were together
much of the time. Such a babysitting detail is good
for occupying the mind. She is whole and as she was."
It was a long speech for Niko and I appreciated it.

"Good." I coughed against the dryness of un-
breachable sleep, then cleared my throat. "Good to
know."

It was. I couldn't see George as anything other than
what she'd always been. People change . . . sometimes,
but it's usually not for the better. George was already
perfect within herself. I didn't want to see her altered,
withdrawn, suspicious, or uncertain. Shadowed. I
didn't want her time with Hob to have changed her.
I didn't want anything to change her.

Not even me. Especially not me.

"She'll be back soon." As I started to sit, he put a
hand behind my shoulder and assisted me. "I'm not
sure she would leave our apartment if her mother

wasn't so insistent. Considering what her family's been through, I can't blame them."

"Promise?"

"Left this morning." He cupped the back of my neck before pressing a ponytail holder into my hand. "Chicken broth or potato barley?"

I grimaced and chose the lesser of two evils. "Potato." Twenty minutes later and minty of breath, I was in the kitchen, wobbly but upright, and spooning down steaming soup. After half of it and a piece of dry toast, I felt steadier. And when there was a knock on the door I was recuperated enough to stand and answer it myself. I opened it, knowing who was waiting on the other side. Not knowing in the way that George knew, but it was a knowing all the same.

"Caliban." She smiled brilliantly as she saw me. Feature by feature she wasn't perfect. Her eyes were too large; her mouth was too wide. Her hair now so short made her appear childlike. It didn't matter. "You're awake." Her hand rested on my cheek in a move so familiar I knew she must've done it countless times as I slept. It was a hand still scratched, with nails short and cracked from her ordeal.

It hadn't been my fault that she'd been taken; I knew that now. Hob had been after her from the beginning. We'd been swept up in that net with her. She wouldn't have blamed me if the situation had been reversed, and I didn't blame her. How could I? It wasn't her intention that a tidal wave carry us away. After all, she hadn't looked . . . not at herself. That was George; that was her way. She was an innocent who accepted the world with all its wonder and all its flaws.

I wasn't.

It hadn't been her fault we'd been pulled in over our heads. It would be mine if the same happened to her. George had had one enemy . . . one who coveted her. I didn't know the number of mine, but it was far in excess of one.

Curious as I continued to block the door in silence, she tipped her head back to study me more clearly. "Caliban?"

"Do you ever look, George?" I asked quietly, although I knew she didn't. "Do you ever look at what happens to us? To you and me?"

"No, that would be cheating." There was an impishly gamine turn to her smile. That was George's philosophy. You took what life gave you and you loved it or you learned from it. Small things could be gotten around—could be changed, but never the big ones. As she said, that would be cheating, and George wasn't a cheater.

I leaned toward her and kissed her softly. It was a suspended moment. It was the only moment. Then I pulled back and touched her face as gently as she had touched mine. "I think you should look."

And I closed the door between us.

Read on for a taster of the next
instalment in the Cal Leandros series:

Madhouse

Coming in August 2012

1

I hated kidnapping cases. Hated them with an unholy passion.

And trust me, unholy was something I knew about—hell, I wore it like a faded old T-shirt. One I'd had since birth. There were those who said I couldn't let go of that, and that it was long past time I did. But hey, if you can't bitch about your monster half, what can you bitch about?

As for kidnappings, no surprise there on how I felt about them. Several months before, someone I knew had been kidnapped—two someones, actually. Although the second taking had lasted less than an hour, the first had lasted two weeks. Despite the difference in time, they had both left their mark, physically and mentally. My shirt and jacket hid the first. I wasn't sure anything hid the second, but I gave it my best shot with caustic sarcasm, brittle bravado, and good old-fashioned denial. That was a triple threat that had done well by me for a long damn time, and I had no plans to give it up now.

I was briskly swatted on the back of my head. "I'm curious, Cal. Do you plan on paying attention any time soon or would you like to have the kidnappers reschedule? I'm sure they'll be amenable. Kidnappers so often are."

Niko Leandros. He had been one of those who had

disappeared on me, even if only temporarily. As brothers went, he was a good one, despite a horrifying obsession with health food, meditation, and things generally not revolving around pizza and beer. But we all have our crosses to bear . . . Mine was to be smacked when I wasn't with the program, and his was to be overeducated, as self-aware as the Dalai Lama, and to keep my ass alive. Poor bastard.

"I'm paying attention," I lied instantly, rubbing the back of my head and giving him a wounded glare.

He snorted, but didn't call me on it as sharply as I deserved. Apparently the swat was punishment enough. "Then let's move on before you pay so much attention that you fall asleep where you stand."

Like I said, a good brother, and good brothers, besides keeping your ass alive, also don't let it get away with much. But there was no denying he was letting me slide a little. Why? Because he knew me, and he knew a case like this wasn't going to trigger any good memories. Grunting in reply, I moved along at his side. "So they kidnapped the mistress of a vampire," I grumbled. "She's a lamia. I've seen lamias and I don't know why the hell anyone would want one back." Like vampires, lamias fed on blood. These days most vampires had found a better way, but lamias weren't looking to improve themselves. And although they fed on blood, there the similarity to vampires ended. A lamia's bite, usually on the chest—or if they were really into you, other, more sensitive parts— had a chemical in its saliva that paralyzed its victim. Like a leech they would stay fastened to you and drain your blood . . . very, very slowly. It could take days—days in which you couldn't move, couldn't scream, couldn't beg for a faster death.

Sure, that's *my* dream girl. Bring her on.

But obviously a vamp felt different and here we were. "I think it matters less about his taste in bed partners and more about us getting paid." I didn't see his dark blond head move, but I knew Niko was scanning the area unceasingly.

"I keep telling you, if you'd go with the whole trophy boyfriend thing, life would be a lot easier," I pointed out helpfully.

From the narrow-eyed look shot my way, apparently I wasn't as helpful as I'd thought. Niko was tight with a vampire of his own, Promise. Promise was, to say the least, loaded. Five excessively rich, as well as excessively elderly, husbands in the past ten years had her set up for . . . well, not life—after all, she was a vampire. But it would keep her comfortable for a long, long time. And Niko absolutely refused to take advantage of it, not that he had some sort of macho hang-up. He simply would make his own way as we had all of our lives. Right now, making our way revolved around an agency we'd set up with Promise. Kidnappings, bodyguard work, cleaning some killer clowns out of a carnival . . . we were up for all of it. The fact that it didn't quite cover our expenses yet had us working second jobs. Niko was a teacher's assistant at NYU (pity the kid who walked late into one of his classes—decapitation is a big deterrent for tardiness). As for me? I tended to move around a lot. Mainly bars. It wasn't good to get attached. I'd learned that from a lifetime of running from my relatives . . . the ones with claws and hundreds of teeth. And although the running had stopped, habits were hard to break. Which, I guess, is why we'd made monster hunting a career instead of an occasional necessity.

And Central Park was full of them.

They liked the park. It was big, and it was full of snacks. No one notices if a mugger, murderer, or rapist goes missing. It was a good place to hit the human buffet and not be noticed. We'd once had an informant here of the very same opinion. He was gone now, dead by Niko's sword.

Somewhere to the north lay a mud pit empty of a boggle with the worst New Yawk accent I'd ever heard. I kind of missed him sometimes. If nothing else, he'd been entertaining. Bloodthirsty and homicidal, but amusing—up to a point. Trying to kill Niko had been that point.

"Are we there yet?" I checked my watch. We had about five minutes until the meet.

"Did you look at the map that was sent with the instructions?" Niko looked down his long nose to ask in a forbidding tone that said he already knew the answer.

"That's what I have you for." I grinned. "I'm just here to carry the heavy stuff. The union says thinking rolls me into overtime."

Niko pulled his katana from beneath his gray duster, looked at the moonlight glimmer of it, and then looked at me with an eyebrow raised.

"Yeah, right," I dismissed, unfazed.

"You're assuming I wouldn't paddle you with it like the child you are."

Okay, that threat I bought. He could do it all right, and he actually might during one of our sparrings just for his own personal amusement.

"And yes," he added, "we are almost there." He took another three steps. "And now we are."

I looked around, but didn't see anything even in the bright moonlight. Shoving my hands in the pockets of my black leather jacket, I took a whiff of the cool November air. Instantly, I grimaced. I might not have seen anything, but I damn sure smelled it. The scent was dank—stagnant water with the ripe and rancid taint of day-old fish beneath it. "They're coming." I freed a hand and rubbed at my nose. "And they stink like you wouldn't believe. Something from the water." A fish of the day you definitely didn't want to order.

"Aquatic," Niko murmured. "That narrows it down to a few hundred in the nonhuman pantheon. Very helpful."

"Hey, I tried." Getting accustomed to the smell, I shifted impatiently on the grass and checked my watch again. "Crooks, monster or human, they're all the same. No damn consideration."

I suppose that's how my gun found its way into my hand as the first figure appeared out of the trees.

"Bishop-fish," Niko murmured. "Nothing extraordinary. Easy to kill."

If I was a little disappointed at that, I kept it to myself. As creatures went, it wasn't that impressive. I'd seen someone more grimly unnerving in a mirror. Sometimes I wasn't sure who I meant by that. It could've been the creature known as Darkling, who a year ago had crawled out of a mirror to put my body on like a snazzy suit and take it cruising on the road to hell, or it could've been my own mundane reflection. Either way, there was no denying the both of us had our moments and either of us could eat fish boy for lunch. Although dead Darkling, every molecule the monster to my half, might've enjoyed it a little more.

Maybe.

Dappled here and there with the ghost of scales over nearly transparent pale skin, the bishop-fish had the form of a human. Sort of. The shape of his head was a little off. Hairless and only lightly scaled, it was oddly flattened and the mouth had thick, rubbery lips and tiny triangular teeth. No kelp eater, this one. He wasn't wearing a stitch— not a damn thing, which told me he didn't rub shoulders with the local New Yorkers much. I looked down. Even they would give that a glance. Yeah, *that*.

Now I knew where fish sticks came from.

I decided keeping my gaze on his eyes was the lesser of two evils despite their unblinking bulge. Guess you can't blink if you don't have eyelids. Round pupils took us in and the mouth opened to gurgle, "These are the demands. First—"

That's when I shot him.

My patience with kidnappers was long gone before I had even taken a step into the park. I put a bullet in his chest, which exploded like an overripe tomato and splattered fluid in a wide arc. With his impossibly wide mouth gaping, he teetered and began to fall. I stepped forward and slipped the paper from the fleshy claw as Mr. Fish Stick crumpled to the ground with a disturbingly wet slapping sound. "I can read, asshole," I muttered.

Niko said from behind me, "Really? When did you learn?" Raising his voice, he asked mildly, "Is there anyone here we could negotiate with that my brother would find less annoying?" Like me, he knew there was someone else in the trees. I smelled them and he heard them. Rustle one leaf, step on one frost-brittle piece of grass, and he would hear it. He was all human, Niko, like our mother, Sophia Leandros, but when he did things like that you had to wonder.

The smell I was picking up from a distance wasn't as bad as that of the fish. It was the scent of old things and attic must and hundreds of abandoned spiderwebs. In other words, it smelled like Niko's library of books. Knowing Niko would be watching its approach, I squinted at the paper in my hand, ignoring the damp slime on it. If the moon hadn't been so bright and plump in the sky, I wouldn't have been able to see anything. I might have monster smelling—whoopee . . . what a superpower—but I had human vision. As it was, I could make out only a few words. Money wasn't mentioned. I wasn't that surprised. Very few monsters were into the material world. Vampires, pucks, and werewolves liked to live high on the hog, but most of the nonhuman world was more interested in eating. Lots and lots of eating.

The ransom mentioned people. Nice, plump people. Nice, juicy children. The kids. Why was it always the kids?

Some kidnappers don't want to earn their money, and

some don't want to catch their own dinner. Trade one lamia for a truckload of humans—what a deal. In the end they were all lazy psychotics and the one that finally came to Niko's call was no different. You could all but see the waves of craziness coming from her, shimmering like heat off a summer road.

"Black Annis." Niko sounded almost pleased. "I thought she was a myth."

She scuttled with the back and forth motion of a poisonous centipede. Part of the time she was on two feet, the rest on all fours. She looked like an old woman, but not a sad wraith in a nursing home or cheerful crocheting grandma—unless it was one who'd have no problem picking her teeth with a sliver of Hansel's gnawed leg bone.

Now, this was a little more disturbing than the fish. And it became more disturbing when six more of her appeared to race across the grass.

"You thought *she* was a myth. She. Singular. Is that what you were saying?" I dropped the paper to the ground. I still had my gun in my right hand and I drew my knife with the left from the double holster under my jacket. Ugly and serrated, the blade had been a constant and faithful companion for a while now. Niko did give damn fine Christmas presents.

"Apparently the myth is incorrect. It only makes things more interesting," he said blandly. "Surely a few old women don't concern you?"

Old women, my ass. The seven of them were covering the ground with freakish speed. Long, thick fingernails scored the ground, sending dirt and grass flying, and their teeth . . . let's just say they weren't the kind that got put in a glass on the bedside table. The Annises, Anni, Black Annies . . . whatever—they weren't identical, but they were so similar they may as well have been. They all wore the same ragged black shifts too. Torn to streamers in places, the cloth fluttered and tangled as they ran. I saw flesh through the holes, flesh I suspected was cyanotic blue although it appeared gray in the glow of the moon. Whatever color it was, I didn't want to see it.

"Fine. You play shuffleboard with the grannies and I'll cheer you on from the sidelines," I retorted. Not that I would have, but one of them made sure I didn't have the option. She went from scuttling to leaping. From nearly thirty feet away, she launched off the ground and propelled herself onto my chest with a force I didn't expect from her spidery frame. I hit the ground hard. Unable to get the gun between us, I buried the knife in her back. I was hoping to sever the spine or at least put a serious dent in it, but the blade practically bounced off the bony structure. "Goddamn it," I gritted, and went for another target instead. With her teeth snapping at my throat, I plunged the knife in the side of hers.

"Leave one alive, Cal, to lead us to the lamia."

Thick and bitter fluid flooded out of the Annis's throat and across my face. Trying not to retch as it worked its way into my mouth, I spat with revulsion and shot back, "I'll try and show some self-control." Then I stopped tasting the blood and caught the scent of it . . . or rather what was in it. "Oh, hell. We are so not getting paid."

I tossed the thing off me, its teeth still feebly gnashing, and saw Niko, who had moved a distance away to get a little elbow room. He was surrounded by four of them. "Forget the restraint," I called. "They ate her." I smelled it in the one twitching beside me . . . in the blood, on her last breath . . . hell, leaking out of her damn pores.

Niko shook his head. "Annoying." He swung at the nearest Annis to decapitate it, only to have his sword repelled by that unbreakable spine. I heard the grating clash of metal and impervious bone. He frowned. "Even more annoying." Stepping back with a deceptive speed of his own, he sheathed about nine inches of his sword through the Annis's single eye. Niko turned to present his side to her and lashed out with a foot to propel her off the blade and into another Annis.

He had things, as always, under control, and I decided to take care of my own business. Two more of them were circling me, wary of the knife. What they weren't concerned with was the gun I had hidden behind my leg. One snarled, I swear, just like the cranky old woman we'd lived next to in one of the trailer parks where our mother had set up her fortune-telling scam. That old biddy had sicced her yappy, ankle-biting dog on us more times than I could count. The Annis didn't need a dog, yappy or otherwise.

"Shouldn't you be baking cookies or playing bingo, Granny?" I gave her a black grin, tapping the muzzle of my gun on the back of my thigh. She crabbed closer, her hands bent into claws in front of her.

"You are no little boy." Her grin was so broad I could see the black gums gleaming slickly. "Your flesh will not be soft." It was gloating, the words rolling around her tongue as though she were already savoring the meat in her mouth. "We will eat it anyway."

I'd heard it all before.

I shot the mouthy one. I nailed her in mid maniacal, choking laugh. She saw the gun as I whipped it from behind me, and she'd already started to move. It didn't do her a damn bit of good. Despite the one second it took, the other one was already on me. Like I said . . . quick.

It hit me from the side. I'd already been turning to prevent it from getting behind me. This time the teeth did reach me, fastening on the junction of neck and shoulder. Like the ragged edge of a saw, they ground in and locked. And there went the chunk I'd been so sure that I wouldn't lose tonight.

As with the first one, I used my knife, but this time opened the belly. Whatever spilled free slithered down my hip and leg. Slithered . . . not fell. That was some serious motivation to get granny off my neck, and to hell with the mouthful of flesh she might take with her. Ripping her and her death grip off of me, I spun her and threw her as far as I could, and then I took a look at what was twining its way around my leg.

Holy shit. I mean, really . . . holy *shit*.

The bright pain and blood flowing steadily under the collar of my jacket to stain my T-shirt took a backseat just like that—because what felt like snakes wasn't. Not that that wouldn't have been bad enough, snakes falling out of someone's gut. But I couldn't get that lucky, could I? Nope. What I got was a crawling combination of worms and intestines with a little barracuda tossed in. They undulated slow and sure like the worm, were ropy and dripping intestinal fluids, and had the bear trap mouth of a barracuda. Did I shake my leg like I was having an epileptic seizure? Yes, I did. Did I scream like a B-movie bimbo? No . . . but it was a close thing. Niko never would've let me live that down.

I stepped back from the seething mass. "Jeeesus."

"Problems?" Niko was already peeling my jacket off one shoulder to examine the wound.

I swiped it with my hand. The pain was subsiding to a sharp ache and I decided the Annis had gotten away with less than the mouthful I'd thought she had. It had been an appetizer at best.

Past Nik I could see one Annis still alive. Her wrists and ankles were handcuffed, and she was writhing, hissing, and biting the ground like a rabid dog.

A monster wearing handcuffs—it was a little reality-jarring at first. We'd started carrying them months ago when we needed to restrain a werewolf, one who really didn't care to be restrained. He normally might've shattered them—I wasn't sure how strong Flay was—but he'd been injured and was barely alive. He'd been incapable of lifting his head, much less ripping apart steel. Still, it was a useful learning experience, and we'd carried them with us ever since.

Niko was still frowning at my neck. "It's more messy than fatal. They have the teeth of an adolescent crocodile."

"Didn't feel like a baby one to me," I grumbled as I felt the punctures and slashes. The blood was slowing and I dug in my pocket for something to hold pressure with. Of course there was nothing but a flyer for a Chinese restaurant.

Exhaling in resignation at my lack of preparation, Niko pulled a package of gauze and a roll of tape from inside his coat. With quick, efficient moves he had the wound covered and taped up in seconds. "It's amazing how hard I work to keep you from bleeding to death on so many occasions, and for so little reward." He finished and stepped over to the tortuous twining of the bile-dripping creatures on the ground. "Do you want a pet? One would fit nicely in a terrarium."

"Yeah, and I'm just one giant nummy num on the other side of the glass. Thanks, but no, thanks." I pulled a repulsed face.

"'All things bright and beautiful, all creatures great and small,'" he quoted.

"Right," I said drily. "God"—making the huge assumption there was one— "did not make those."

"Perhaps you're right." He pulled yet two more things out of his duster—a small container of lighter fluid and a pack of matches. Once the barbecue was started and the air stank of roasted barracuda, Niko made a call and we went, picked up the surviving Annis, and moved on. A vampire met us near the edge of the park. He stood among the trees; could've been one of them as he blended into the darkness. Black hair, black eyes, and an equally dark Armani suit. At least I assumed it was Armani. It was the only expensive brand I knew. To me, all fancy suits were Armani.

We dumped the snarling, spitting Annis at his feet, and I considered but decided not to stick my hand out for the money. I had a feeling I might draw back less than I put out—a few fingers less. Vampires mourn too, apparently even over lamias. Niko had already delivered the bad news over his cell phone. Now all he said was, "She is the only one left. The others are no more."

"And they suffered?" His voice was cool and empty. It didn't bode well for the Annis. At least with rage you would go quickly. It would be messy, but it would be quick. Icy retribution could go on for . . . shit, it didn't bear thinking about. My appetite for dinner had already been ruined by the smell of cooking intestines; I didn't need to kill it altogether.

"Yeah, they suffered," I confirmed. "And the god-awful things in them suffered too." The Annis hadn't really suffered, not the way he meant, but it was going to have to do. A job was a job and torture wasn't on our menu. Not for pay anyway. But there was no point in disappointing him. Cranky vampires are a pain, and I'd had enough ass-kicking for the night.

Despite what I'd said earlier, we did get paid. An envelope thick with cash was passed to Nik. Living off the radar, we didn't exactly have the ID to set up a bank account. We could've gotten the fake stuff and Promise had offered to keep our share of the payments for us, but once again, we fell back on the ways we'd always known. We'd bought a safe and stuffed what we made in there. Unfortunately, it was still pretty damn empty.

As we left, we heard one sharp scream after another. It seemed like torture was on someone's menu. I wondered if it sounded like the screams of the people that the Black Annis had killed over the years, because you know they'd screamed too.

Karma, she is a bitch. But in this particular incident, not my karma, not my problem.

We moved on. We were nearly to the edge of the park and for a few moments the night was perfect. Cool and crisp with the rustle of falling leaves. Perfect. Right up until we saw what was hanging in the last line of trees. Heavy and ripe like fruit, the color of a nectarine . . . pale salmon blooming with red. Lots and lots of red.

In the trees.

Bodies.

ROB THURMAN

NIGHTLIFE

'There are monsters among us. There always have been and there always will be. I've known that since I can remember, just like I've always known that I was one ... Well, half of one anyway.'

Cal Leandros is nineteen. He eats junk food, he doesn't clean up after himself and he fights with his half brother Niko. It's a fairly normal life, but for the fact that Cal and Niko are constantly on the run. Cal's father has been after him for the last four years. And given that he's a monster whose dark lineage is the stuff of nightmares they really don't want him and his entire otherworldly race catching up with them. But Cal is about to learn why they want him, why they've always wanted him - he is the key to unleashing their hell on earth.

Meanwhile the bright lights of the Big Apple shine on, oblivious to the fact that the fate of the human world will be decided in the fight of Cal and Niko's lives ...

He just wanted a decent book to read ...

Not too much to ask, is it? It was in 1935 when Allen Lane, Managing Director of Bodley Head Publishers, stood on a platform at Exeter railway station looking for something good to read on his journey back to London. His choice was limited to popular magazines and poor-quality paperbacks – the same choice faced every day by the vast majority of readers, few of whom could afford hardbacks. Lane's disappointment and subsequent anger at the range of books generally available led him to found a company – and change the world.

'We believed in the existence in this country of a vast reading public for intelligent books at a low price, and staked everything on it'
Sir Allen Lane, 1902–1970, founder of Penguin Books

The quality paperback had arrived – and not just in bookshops. Lane was adamant that his Penguins should appear in chain stores and tobacconists, and should cost no more than a packet of cigarettes.

Reading habits (and cigarette prices) have changed since 1935, but Penguin still believes in publishing the best books for everybody to enjoy. We still believe that good design costs no more than bad design, and we still believe that quality books published passionately and responsibly make the world a better place.

So wherever you see the little bird – whether it's on a piece of prize-winning literary fiction or a celebrity autobiography, political tour de force or historical masterpiece, a serial-killer thriller, reference book, world classic or a piece of pure escapism – you can bet that it represents the very best that the genre has to offer.

Whatever you like to read – trust Penguin.